River of Iron

By David Lee

To order additional copies of this book, contact:
Xlibris LLC
1-888-795-4274
www.Xlibris.com
Orders@Xlibris.com
622956

Dedication

This book is dedicated to the memory of
Bernard and Elsie Nelson and to their descendants.

Frontispiece—Oldest known photograph of Ishpeming, Michigan—1860.
Photograph courtesy of Superior View Studios, Marquette, Michigan—TO-Ish-10.

ACKNOWLEDGMENTS

ALTHOUGH THE AUTHOR created this manuscript through the lens of his own experience, many contributed ideas, editing, and encouragement. Most of all, the author thanks his parents, Ben and Elsie Nelson, for inspiring their children—and indeed this story. Having spent hours assembling and publishing Elsie's poems and family photographs in *Wandering Verse*[1], the children of Ben and Elsie believe their parents story should be told and remembered. This most assuredly is Ben and Elsie's story.

~~~

The author is indebted to his brothers and sisters and their children who encouraged him to preserve a unique story of immigrants and their offspring engulfed in a savage struggle to overcome the Great Depression—as so many families were.

Frederick J. Nelson contributed maps and diagrams of Marquette County, Ishpeming, Frenchtown, Negaunee, Tilden Township, and the Nelson farm, along with editing and substantive changes that have been incorporated into the manuscript. Fred contributed, among numerous other changes, the two paragraphs that close Chapter 5. Fred's daughter, Rebecca Nelson, also contributed editing and made valuable style suggestions.

Marian A. Sutton read the manuscript, and was the sounding board for details of the early years, the foibles of family members and of events that played out before her in real time. Marian helped to bring some of us into the world, to raise us, and was, and is, a treasure trove of memories. Her husband, John Sutton, who contributed maps and diagrams to *Wandering Verse*, also read and encouraged the manuscript.

Many photographs and details were furnished by the author's late sister, Ruth A. Merrill, and his late brother, William S. Nelson, both of whom lived this story and toiled mightily to support the family during the Great Depression—although they did not remain among us long enough to see this manuscript in its final form.

Kenneth B. Nelson and his wife, Loraine Bath Nelson, read the manuscript and contributed documents, photographs, *Red Dust*[2] booklets, news articles, and recollections that rounded out the history of the Nelson family. Ken's son, Michael S. Nelson, read the manuscript, supplied photographs, and offered the perspective of one who spent his career in the iron ore industry. Ken's son, Jeffrey J. Nelson, who commissioned the bas-relief depicted at the end of Chapter 23, supplied background information and photographs. Ken's son Gary Nelson also supplied photographs.

Dorothy A. Sarasin and her husband Robert Sarasin read the manuscript. Both were greatly supportive, contributed family photographs and tape recordings of conversations with Ben and Elsie, added color, and embellished and corrected many references to the Nelson family history. Bob's dad lived two miles from the site of the stump in Negaunee where iron was discovered. Bob later worked at the Mather B.

Joanne E. Montague read the manuscript and offered recollections and suggestions that extended the story to the younger Nelson children.

The author's wife, Judith, contributed—along with enormous understanding—numerous suggestions, corrections, and details concerning the Copper County, the city of Marquette, and the Olson family. Her sister, Wendy Olson Cornish, edited the manuscript, helped to fill in the history of the Copper Country, and restrained the author from going, "over the top," as he is otherwise prone to do where family is involved. Wendy also contributed the photograph of a sunset on Presque Isle.

Handwritten notes that Judy's mother, Lois Olson, and her aunt, Ethel Rowe, furnished several years back to the author's daughter, Julie R. Nelson, supplied many details on the history of the Copper Country and made its history come to life. The author also thanks Julie for encouraging him to complete this story, and his sons, David W. Nelson and Daniel E. Nelson, for tutoring him on how to do so on a home computer.

A big thank you goes to Roger M. Junak, Kathrine Savu (formerly Waters), and Richard "Tommy" Carne, all of Ishpeming, Michigan, for creating artwork, and authorizing its use, that revealed life on the Mountain of Iron.

The Cleveland-Cliffs Iron Company of Ishpeming, Michigan, consented to the use of photographs and diagrams. The Cliffs Shaft Mining Museum in Ishpeming and Leo Lafond, its president, furnished numerous records and historic sources that chronicle the history of iron mining on the Marquette Range. The Marquette Regional History Center and Superior View Studios, both of Marquette, Michigan, contributed and authorized the use of maps and photographs that provided context. Trinity Lutheran in Ishpeming and Alf George Kjesta of Evje, Norway, provided photographs.

The author also salutes Maxine Honkala, her collaborators, and all of the writers, editors, and teachers who annually compiled the *Red Dust* series of booklets that tell in graphic detail—in stories penned by grandchildren and great-grandchildren of the immigrants—what life was like on the Marquette Iron Mining Range during the Great Depression, World War II, and the years that followed.

Kenneth "Rudy" Larson, Maurice Hansen, Mary Aho Johnson, and Marie Flack Keto furnished photographs and articles describing National Mine, the National Mine School, and its basketball team.

Kudos to June Rydholm of Marquette, Michigan, for providing photographs, articles, and information on the glacial float copper specimen that her late husband, C. Fred Rydholm, helped to place at Presque Isle in Marquette.

The librarian at the author's law firm, Mary Margaret Serpento, edited the manuscript and made numerous substantive and structural suggestions that greatly improved the writing. Kimberly Kortes, the author's legal secretary, taught him the rudiments of Microsoft Word, and she formatted the manuscript.

A tip of the hat also goes to the Mountain of Iron itself, without whose existence and challenges none of it would have happened.

We have no other mandate
But to do the things we must.
Go with the tide at its lowest ebb,
Hang on tight and trust.

Elsie Carne Nelson

CONTENTS

TABLE OF PHOTOGRAPHS, PAINTINGS, SKETCHES, AND MAPS

FOREWORD

I T STARTED ONCE my kids were raised and I retired. That's what triggered it. Suddenly, I was hit with scads of time I wasn't using. Ma always warned that idle hands lead to mischief. But there I was—retired from the law business—sitting on the sidelines with idle hands—glancing back at a life that began in iron mining country in a Northern Michigan wilderness back in the thirties—and wondering what it all meant. Then the whole thing came rushing back. At first fanciful, my glance back swiftly morphed into a ghostly procession of ancestors, family, neighbors, teachers, and the kids I grew up with—all of them toiling, laughing, and frolicking on top of a hematite-encrusted, craggy mountain surrounded by primal forests. It was surreal.

I dug out some *Red Dust* booklets that my brother's wife Loraine had mailed to me over the years. They contained stories penned by children and grandchildren of the folks back home. I also dug into some cardboard boxes of stuff I'd saved at random, and pulled out some yellowing family photographs, magazine articles, newspaper clippings, tape recordings my sister Dort had made—and a battered cardboard box containing poems Ma had written. Had I been missing something? During the workaday period of my life details of my years growing up had drifted away. Suddenly, they were back. They started to occupy my day, accompany me when I walked, and interrupted my sleep. What to do? Looking for clues, I pored over Ma's poems. Most of them had been written while I was being raised, so reading them generated a lot of tears. That's okay—I expected that. A verse in one of them, "Neighbors," caught my eye. It concerned ants if you can imagine:

> Then, busy as their forebears,
> They commence with much aplomb,
> Heaping sand one grain at a time
> For the new little ants to come.

I loved Ma's poems, of course, but what in hell did an anthill have to do with iron mining—with anything? It didn't fit until I pondered the last two lines of Ma's poem:

> Just follow the hills near the walkway . . .
> They lead right up to my door.

All of the ant-people in my dreamlike procession were stained with hematite; they all wore bib overalls, hard hats with lights, and identical rubber boots. But their faces were all different. Why were they laughing? They were burrowing into a mountainside and carrying out baskets of broken rocks that they dumped onto a raft. A string of rafts manned by ants with human heads led away across a deep blue expanse. I shook my head. Was it Alzheimer's, dementia—was I a candidate for the funny farm? Who were these creatures? Why were they doing this?

I went to work, enlisted my brothers and sisters, and we published "Neighbors" along with all of Ma's poems as *Wandering Verse* while she was at the Mather Nursing Home. Even with that I couldn't get the anthill out of my head. In the end I sat in my study pondering the folks who created the iron mining country where I was born and raised. Exactly how did that great big anthill someone had called "a mountain of iron," come to be? What forces radiating from its granite cliffs had forged the people among whom I spent my childhood? The following is the result of my musings. It contains errors and omissions I'm sure, but it's not fiction. It's as true and accurate as the failing memory of a tired old man assisted by family, relatives and friends can make it.

CHAPTER 1

"Hillbilly Country"

MICHIGAN'S UPPER PENINSULA had been nothing but a rocky, isolated wilderness inhabited only by wild animals and Native Americans until the 1840s. Nobody else wanted to live there. A map of the "Settled Region of the United States of America 1840" doesn't show one single county, city or village in the Upper Peninsula and doesn't even bother to show the boundary line between Michigan and Wisconsin.[3] That's when copper boulders were found on the Keweenaw Peninsula off to the west and iron ore was discovered protruding from a rocky mountain range that ran through the middle of it.[4] That changed everything. Mines and mining camps suddenly appeared in the nameless wilderness, and boatloads of Europeans crossed the Atlantic to dig their fortunes out of solid rock. My ancestors came across with them. The immigrants clustered in frame houses around the iron mines and burrowed into the mountain to extract iron ore. They proceeded to create villages with fine schools, courthouses, churches, and stores. The villages grew into cities as deeper mines were dug. My old stamping grounds were dead center in the middle of it.

Once the mines were up and running, immigrant labor mingled with ore and speculators' capital in a relentless stream that began in open pits and in workings deep beneath the rocky terrain. It flowed out in tramcars. It was hoisted from deep underground in "skips," borne away by rail to docks that loaded ore boats, ferried across the Great Lakes, and emptied at the steel and copper mills in the Midwest and on the shores of Lake Erie. There it was smelted, forged and re-cast to build America's skyscrapers, railroads, freeways, electric grid, and the armament that sustained its military strength. Ore dug near where I was born joined a tumultuous river of iron that cascaded out of the wilderness, engulfed the immigrants and their children in brutal labor and poverty, and precipitated my family's struggle to eke out a living on a rocky ten-acre farm near where the iron lay.[5]

I was born on that ten-acre farm at the headwaters of the river of iron on October 23, 1931, smack in the middle of the Great Depression. On the day I arrived, our log house was still being spiked together in a "location" five miles south of Ishpeming called Green Creek—known to the locals as "Green Crick." It became my childhood home. My first cries would never have been heard anywhere in the universe, had not iron drawn my ancestors there from across the Atlantic.

I learned from books when I turned eighty that amateur archaeologists exploring the rocky hills of the Keweenaw Peninsula off to the west had discovered copper mines dug thousands of years before Columbus sailed—long before any Europeans arrived. Or so the books say. I've also read in newspapers that international conglomerates are currently buying up mineral rights and opening new mines in the Keweenaw and the nearby Huron Mountains in search of copper, gold, silver and rare earth metals. Now all that is impressive stuff to contemplate. But, as my dad used to say from as far back as I can remember, "There's daylight in the swamp, get your boots on—there's hay to make and wood to cut."

I hear from educated city people with a penchant to demean that the place where I was born is hillbilly country—rare earth metals or not. Even those that don't go that far refer to my home town as being, "up there."[6] I guess it makes them feel better about the place they come from. Over time stuff like that burned my cork—and would have ticked off those early copper miners. But my family and the neighbors of my youth didn't give a damn what they said. We loved wilderness and freedom. We laughed at city slickers and trolls[7] who didn't have brilliant stars studding their night sky, northern lights glinting off "Gitchee Gumee," homemade cream to pour over wild berries, or rapids full of speckled trout.

I'd picked a bad day to be born. The Tin Lizzy, Tea Pot Dome, Prohibition, The Charleston, and bath tub gin had had their fling. The "Roaring Twenties" were finished. Al Capone would be sentenced for evasion of income taxes about the time I got my own butt spanked. The river of iron had dried up. Two years before, on October 25, 1929, the New York Stock Exchange crashed, and the price of everything collapsed. City slickers whose stocks went to zero were jumping out of skyscrapers. On the day I was born local grocers offered a two-pound bag of flour free with a purchase of two pounds of Clover Farm butter at thirty-six cents a pound. Three grapefruits cost thirteen cents, two regular cans of pork and beans cost fifteen cents, and three pounds of coffee fifty cents. Fashionable ladies' coats could be purchased for as low as $14.75.

Not many living around where I was born could buy very much even at those prices. Most were scrambling to find part-time work so they could eat. The well-to-do—some of the locals called them "swells"—didn't have to scramble for food, raiment, and shelter. I'm not saying that. But they sure got glassy-eyed when their businesses tanked and went under. While it's tough to have a business you built or your stock account go up in smoke, it's different for the poor. For them the Great Depression was survival. Two cans of pork and beans for fifteen cents doesn't mean much if you don't have fifteen cents.

While the poor staggered about looking for work and the economy shrank almost to nothing, big-shot professors of economics, politicians, and pundits earned their keep by putting out papers and haggling over how it all happened and what the country ought to do to dig out of it. Looking back, none of them seemed to be doing much digging, and they never did agree on what caused it or what to do about it. They cared more about arguing in favor of their pet theories than they did about the plight of the poor. No matter what ingenious schemes spewed forth from Congress, editorial pages, scholarly papers, or over the radio, nothing was working. Unable to find work at the iron mines or anywhere else, the children of the immigrants descended into poverty.

The Great Depression I was born into became the signature economic issue of my time on earth. Finding its causes and solutions has proven to be more elusive than the identity of those ancient copper miners. Politicians and pundits tell you—even today—that they know what caused it and what you ought to do to cure one. They're not willing to admit that no sane businessman would do much investing in stocks, bonds, or iron mining after the stock market crashed, or that it took World War II to wipe out the Great Depression in a tsunami of debt, wreckage, and blood.

Ma and Dad didn't have time to waste on fancy talk. After the economy collapsed, they found themselves in an iron-mining encampment out in the wilderness, with four kids and without a job, bank account, or house. They couldn't use credit—no bank would loan them a dime. They'd have to build a place to live with their bare hands. They decided to build it on ten acres of Green Crick land they bought for about seventy-five dollars five miles south of Ishpeming. My sister Marian says it was a hundred dollars. Okay, but the deed registered with the Register of Deeds says "$75.00." Just between us kids, I think Grandpa Ole helped them build it—although he had been crippled at the mine—and may have furnished some of the tools, spikes, and seed money. I'm not clear on all of it, but I do know that Grandpa Ole had picked up some carpentry skills in Norway, that while the new home was being spiked together Ma was carrying me, and that I now have the carpenter's ripsaw Grandpa Ole gave to my dad. It has the log house they built painted on it, and it has a fine wooden handle—things were well made in those days. I treasure it. My nephew, Jeffrey Nelson, has the carpenter's crosscut saw Dad used to build the farmhouse. It has Dad and the farmhouse painted on it.

The cool, cloudy October day that I joined the family without the aid of a doctor or a midwife must have been one god-awful day for them. It was Thursday, but for sure Ma and Dad were not thanking goodness the next day was Friday. They had no car. There was no hospital within five miles, the cracks between the logs hadn't been chinked, and a bitter winter that might produce thirty degrees below zero and four feet of snow was coming on. Of their four kids the oldest, Marian, was seven, and they did not need another mouth to feed. They were using washed-out flour bags and cattle feed bags for diapers. Somehow I got fed and baptized into the Christian faith, but they didn't have a crib to put me in and didn't notify the county clerk until the following January that I'd been born. It's a good thing God heard about me. I found out later that most of the families living around us were in the same fix.

In addition to being an iron miner, my dad was a farmer, carpenter, butcher, and woodsman when he had to be. He actually enjoyed hard work—looked forward to it. Along the way he sired eight kids with my ma. My sister Dorothy (Dort) dubbed him the "iron man." He was not interested in recreational hunting, fishing, or sports—he made that clear many times—although eventually he did go in for horse-pulling contests and raising beagles that he ran in field trials. He believed everything he had was the best there ever was and bragged about everything he did including the animals he picked, the raises he helped blast through jasper and granite at the Lloyd and Mather A mines, the trophies his beagles won, and his kids. He bragged about his "farm" and said he only moved the family out there because he'd always wanted a farm. It is unlikely that anyone today would acknowledge that it was a farm. I'll discuss that later.

My ma's people had never been miners or farmers. She was housewife, poet, teacher, piano player, philosopher, and pure kindness all rolled into one. Ma never did brag a lot, but she and Dad agreed on a lot of things. They both loved discipline, hard work, and each other. They also loved to curse the Crash of Twenty-nine and all of the misery it left in its wake. But Great Depression or not, Ben and El, as they called each other, were at the core happy people who loved their kids—all eight of us. They told the same jokes over and over and burst out laughing each time they did. In spite of the Crash of Twenty-nine they imparted an indomitable spirit of work, thrift, honesty, survival, happiness, and humor to the kids they raised. All of us remember the wonderful days they gave us during those hard times, and we are very proud of them.

Ma and Dad explained that being poor didn't have to be a badge of shame—that you should make the most of it. Not that poverty was a blessing conferred upon us by the Almighty, you understand, but that there was nothing sinister or bad about it. "Look on the bright side." "Hold your head high." "Roll up your sleeves—get busy." "Make hay while the sun shines." "Don't cry over spilled milk." And my favorite, "Poverty is a stepping stone to happiness."

So we kids obeyed our elders. We told jokes and laughed along with them, did our chores and our school work, played hide-and-go-seek, worked hand-me-down jigsaw puzzles, read comic books and "Little Big Books" sent up from lower Michigan by our cousin Donna Mae, went ski riding, shot slingshots, bows and arrows, and rubber guns we'd made ourselves, and played basketball using an old leather ball that iced up in winter and a bushel basket with the bottom knocked out that my older brother Kenneth (Ken) nailed to the garage. Ma and Dad never did figure out how to beat the Great Depression, but they taught us how to survive one. I didn't record all they taught us at the time, of course, but I wish I had. I have always believed their story ought to be told and—by God—remembered. Cemetery headstones don't tell you much about a person's capacity for love, nor their dreams, their challenges, or their achievements.

Let me be clear. We were not tied up in knots over our predicament. We were as happy as hell—not like I see today. I suppose it's natural to wonder how that could be. Well let me tell you. Nothing, and I mean nothing, will ever beat that big gold moon that rose over the pine trees east of our little farm lighting ski trails we spent all afternoon packing in the snow on the hill west of our farmhouse, skiing down with homemade rubber inner tube binders, slewing to a stop at the bottom, fish-boning back up the hill, or the hot cocoa and Ma's bread with fresh butter that was on the kitchen table when we trooped in with wet mittens and rosy cheeks. You can't make that up. When you're eighty-two it's good to think about—it warms the soul.

But, yes, I am eighty-two. I've become a surgically scarred and balding old man seeking redemption. The family farm has been sold; my grandparents, aunts, and uncles, Ma and Dad, my sister Ruth, and my brother Bill and his wife Jean are gone, and I'd like to hear some straight answers to a few questions before I pass on to my reward. Who caused the Great Depression? If one strikes, what should poor people do to dig out? With vast mineral wealth lying all around the Upper Peninsula—how could it possibly be that immigrants committed to the work ethic were living in poverty?

To understand my family's quest for survival after the stock markets crashed, I guess you have to know something about poor people, about family people, and about those who earn a living with their hands and their backs. But to get your head around that, you have to stand back a bit, visualize the scenes these words describe, and consider the true meaning of human dignity and perseverance. So come along. Let's head north across the Mighty Mac Bridge and go back to where I was born. Let me take you through the iron country. You'll get a kick out of it.

But for the mines, the place would never have been settled at all. It wasn't really suited to farming or city life. To get to know the folks I grew up with, you have to understand iron mining. The whole place depended on it. At one time the ancient rocks in the Lake Superior region produced eighty to ninety percent of the iron manufactured in the United States.[8] The place where I was born was a big part of it. Millions of tons of iron ore were shipped from underground mines on the Marquette Range before the big open pits and pelletizing took over. My ancestors helped blast it loose.

Take a look at a map of the Marquette Iron Range. By 1968 ninety percent of Cleveland-Cliffs Iron Company's domestic ore shipments came from five pellet plants on the Marquette Range—Humbolt, Republic, Empire, Pioneer, and Eagle Mills.[9] The Republic, located in Republic, obviously, and the Empire, located near Palmer on the east end of the Marquette Range, were both open pit operations. Pellet shipments from the Tilden, an open pit named after the township where I was born, began in 1974.[10] In 2012 the Empire and the Tilden, combined, shipped over nine million long tons of iron-ore pellets. I'm told it takes more than twenty-five million tons of raw ore to produce that many pellets. The market for iron pellets is now worldwide. It wasn't always like that.

If you want to understand what happened you have to get up to speed on the history of iron mining—and in particular the "workings" of an underground iron mine. At first mining was mostly underground. When I was a kid, long trains of raw iron ore were a common sight. Back then mines bore names like the National, the Athens, and the Maas. Once I got out of high school, I helped build railroad tracks at some of them. I also worked underground at the Mather A shaft. Listen up; I know what I'm talking about.

Underground mines have personality. There's something about roughnecks in digging clothes, hard hats, and headlamps being dropped underground in cages while laughing and telling ribald jokes that gives a mine character. It's tied in to their casual dismissal of cave-ins, dynamite blasting, noxious gases, floods, and other dangers I suppose. In the early days the mines were referred to as "she" and talked about the way sailors talk about the ships they sail. Most of the old mines are plugged now. All that's left are stockpiles of low-grade ore, waste rock, old railroad beds, and a couple of museums.

There's no way I can take you underground to show you the stopes where the ore once was, but the stopes are still there. They're huge caverns filling with water. Even today though the sites where the head frames of those old shafts once stood bear a mine's name. I grew up among the iron miners who sank shafts into solid rock to create them. Let me take you back to the beginning and tell you about some of them and the iron-mining country where they spent their lives.

~~~

Figure 1

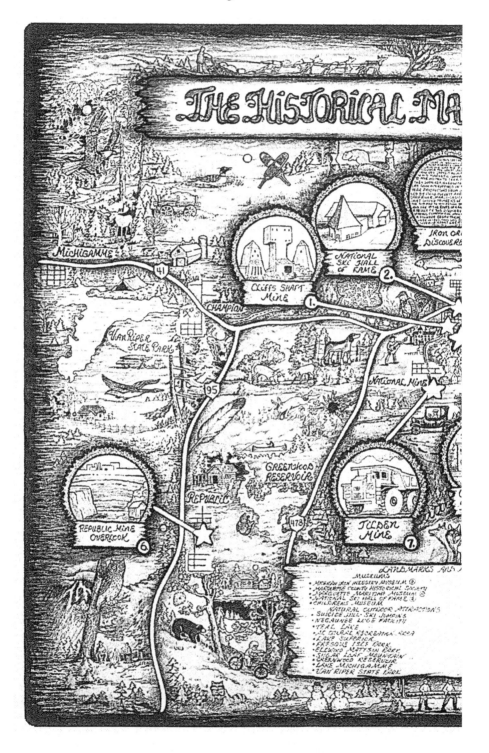

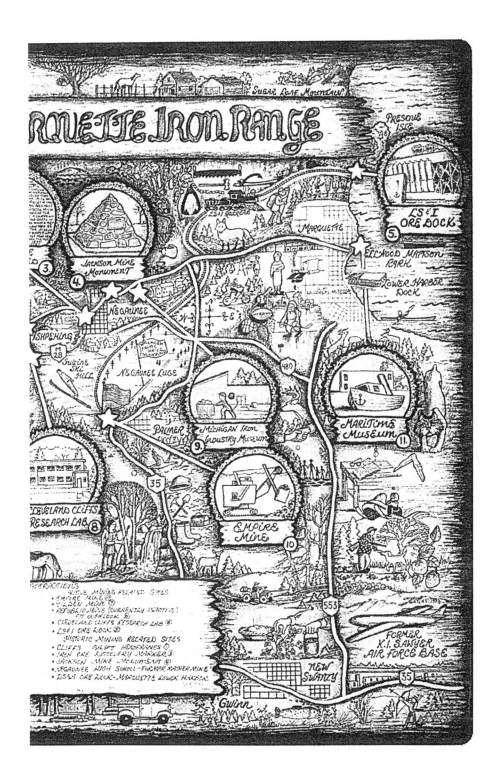

The chart on the previous page was drawn by Kathrine Savu, formerly Waters, of Ishpeming, Michigan, for the former Ishpeming Chamber of Commerce. It is printed here with the artist's permission.

CHAPTER 2

The Mountain of Iron

I LOOKED IT up in some old books, articles, and newspaper clippings I had stashed in my basement and in my study over the years. I'm not an expert on the subject by any means, but as far as I can tell about four billion years ago the whole earth coalesced into a radioactive molten mass. As it cooled, heavier metals like iron migrated to the core of the earth. Later, as the molten mass congealed, rock plates formed on the earth's surface, and iron, copper, silver, gold, and other precious metals precipitated and solidified in the crevices and fissures. After billions of years of turbulent plate collisions and upheavals, meteor strikes, volcanic action, erosion, and several ice ages (not to mention inland seas that once occupied the area), it came to be that the Upper Peninsula of Michigan and the bed of Lake Superior had been smelted, silted, and carved into the rugged crust of the Earth.

The colossal rock plates heaved up to create the Upper Peninsula contained pockets of copper and iron. As the last ice age receded, crystal-clear water filled the Great Lakes—including Lake Superior—the largest freshwater lake on earth. Sturdy maple and oak, pungent pines, and spruce, along with softer woods like cedar, birch, and poplars, spread across the rocky terrain. Black bears, whitetail deer, wolves, foxes, and beaver occupied the forests, birds took to the skies, brook trout filled the streams, and bass flourished in the inland lakes. The stage was set.

Then, about ten thousand years ago, humans from the Eurasian land mass migrated across the Bering Strait to North America. While little evidence of their passage remains, some of them settled in tribes along the breathtakingly beautiful south shore of Lake Superior. There is evidence that the tribes who lived along the shores of Lake Superior began to mine copper, which did not have to be separated from an ore, and hammer it into tools and jewelry thousands of years before the Europeans came to the Upper Peninsula. The Europeans at that time knew nothing of the valuable metals that impregnated the Upper Peninsula or of the native tribes that mined copper there. But that too would change.

The Northwest Territories became part of the United States as a result of the Revolutionary War. The land that became the Upper Peninsula of Michigan, originally claimed by the State of Virginia, was part of the Northwest Territories ceded to the United States. The Northwest Ordinance was adopted on July 13, 1787, to supply a system of limited self-government for the Northwest Territories until they obtained populations that qualified them for statehood.

On January 26, 1837, at the convention where Michigan became a state, Michigan ceded its claims to a four-hundred-sixty-eight-square-mile tract of land known as the Toledo strip to the state of Ohio in exchange for the Upper Peninsula. Many of those attending the convention "truly believed that it [the Upper Peninsula] was such a wasteland that only Indians would ever live there."[11] In fact, the only residents of the Upper Peninsula at that time were Native Americans.[12] Fifteen counties were later laid out across the Upper Peninsula. Each of them exceeded the entire area of the Toledo strip—the largest was Marquette County.

There had been several early explorations of the Upper Peninsula, among them that of Père Marquette in 1669, but no settlements were established.[13] The remoteness, weather, and difficult terrain of the Upper Peninsula kept everyone except the Native American tribes away. In 1832, Henry R. Schoolcraft set out from Sault Ste. Marie and led a canoe expedition along the south shore of Lake Superior to the famous "Ontonagon Boulder"—which had been discovered by Native Americans years before in the Ontonagon River at the far western end of the Peninsula near the pits allegedly dug by the ancients to extract copper.[14] Dr. Douglas Houghton—who was a botanist, geologist, physician, and surgeon—accompanied Schoolcraft on the expedition.

The boulder—about 3,500 pounds of almost pure copper—was later moved to Detroit and ultimately to the Smithsonian Institution where it rests today. When it came to light in the 1840s, the boulder created such a national sensation that the Upper Peninsula suddenly became Cinderella, and a horde of fortune seekers with glass slippers headed north to stake out claims. Many who rushed in to claim their fortunes found the rocky terrain, swamps, and rugged winters far too challenging, so they turned around and left. But the hearty ones stayed and gave birth to the Copper Country.

There had already been inklings that the Peninsula contained iron. Around 1830 a fur trader, Peter Barbeau, who hailed from Sault Ste. Marie, delivered specimens containing high-grade iron ore to Professor Charles T. Jackson, a mineralogist who had come to the Upper Peninsula to search for evidence of copper. Barbeau couldn't pinpoint the area that produced the samples, but claimed he received them from Indians while buying furs near the Carp River, in what later became Marquette County.[15]

The headwaters of the Carp River gathered immediately to the north of the ten acres where I was born—roughly twenty-five miles southwest of what later became the Lake Superior port city of Marquette. The land that became the cities of Ishpeming and Negaunee lay within the watershed of the Carp River on the hunting lands of the Ojibwa— sometimes called the Teal Lake Band. Those hunting lands were said to include a "Mountain of Iron" that the Ojibwa viewed with superstition. It has been reported that the Ojibwa "would circle the mountain and back toward it."[16] Whether because the surge to mine copper in the Keweenaw was building, or because of challenging terrain, unforgiving wilderness and fierce winters in what became Marquette County, these early hints of iron were not pursued.[17]

There were, of course, no settlements, amenities, or laborers on the Peninsula to sustain iron mining. The first known white settler was Abraham Williams. He moved to Grand Island off the shores of what is now the city of Munising on July 30, 1840.[18] Williams and his wife raised twelve children there. In 1845, after prospectors found silver and lead in a rocky cove at the north end of Presque Isle, Williams was hired to build two cottages out near the mouth of the Dead River in what became the city of Marquette.[19]

When the State of Michigan was formed in 1837, Douglas Houghton became its state geologist. As one of his first acts, Houghton organized a geological and land survey of the Upper Peninsula. The most popular theory of how iron was discovered near Teal Lake is derived from Houghton's choice of William Austin Burt to perform the land survey. Burt had invented a solar compass to correct deviations in the magnetic compasses he was using.

Figure 2

Stump where iron was discovered at Negaunee, Michigan, in 1844.
IM-JACK-13
Photograph courtesy of Superior View Studios

I'm not an expert on compasses either, so I can't discuss technicalities, but on September 19, 1844, Burt reported that his magnetic compasses began to wander while he was surveying land on the south shore of Teal Lake near what is now the city of Negaunee just east of what became the city of Ishpeming. Burt also reported that the deviations he was seeing could not be corrected by use of his solar compass. The Burt discovery theory claims that in the investigation that followed, iron ore was discovered in a pine stump just south of Teal Lake. It's a great story that C. Fred Rydholm included in his carefully researched book.[20] Today, a stone pyramid with a metal plaque marks the spot.

The discovery of iron in the Teal Lake area is reported somewhat differently in *Iron Will* by Terry S. Reynolds and Virginia P. Dawson. They write in their well-documented book that businessmen from Jackson, Michigan, sent an exploratory group to the Upper Peninsula in June of 1845 to locate copper deposits. While the businessmen were at Sault Ste. Marie, they were introduced to Louis Nolan, a French Canadian of Indian ancestry. Later, according to this theory, Nolan led the Jackson group to Teal Lake and to Marjijesick, an Ojibwa chief, who brought the Jackson group to a "mountain of solid iron ore, over 150 feet high," that looked "as bright as a bar of iron just broken."[21]

Whatever account is accurate, the explorations that followed revealed that the "worthless wilderness" was sitting on outcroppings of iron ore with pockets of iron ore deep beneath. To speculators and investors, the place reeked of money. The problem wasn't just that there were no miners—smelters would be needed to convert the ore to iron, and smelters need coal. There wasn't any coal anywhere near the Mountain of Iron. Small, conical, charcoal kilns were built to melt the ore down into pig iron, but the volume they could handle was pitiful. Remnants of the kilns can be found in Marquette near the mouth of the Carp River. Foundries were also tried, and blast furnaces were mentioned, but none of that worked out.

The reality was that most of the high-grade iron ore lay deep underground in a remote wilderness hemmed in by the Great Lakes and the rivers and waterfalls connecting them. Ore boats would be needed to deliver the ore to smelters hundreds of miles to the south, and locks would be necessary to lower the ore boats from Lake Superior to Lake Huron. It became painfully clear that a whole lot of investor capital would be needed, and that the task of digging the iron ore out of the mountain and transporting it to smelters would be as tough as the granite and jasper in which it was embedded.

Once word got out, though, that the Marquette Range was impregnated with iron, mineral claim permits were sought, United States land patents were obtained by investors and their corporations, and iron-mining operations exploded as immigrants flocked there. Within a few years Ishpeming, Negaunee and other mining camps sprang up on the Mountain of Iron, and Yoopers, as immigrants like my great grandparents and grandparents came to be called by the city slickers, were drawn from all over Europe like iron filings to a magnet. They clustered around the mines in settlements the mining companies helped to build with logs and lumber hewn from the neighboring forests. The settlements were frequently named after the mines they served, or else bore names derived from Ojibwa words.

The Marquette Iron Range lay northwest to southeast in an area roughly fifty miles long (from Michigamme to Gwinn) and about twenty-five miles wide (from Republic to Negaunee). At first, the mining companies used sailboats to carry the ore across the Great Lakes. Considering the remoteness of the region, its terrain, and the difficulty of transporting ore to market, this swift development of iron mines on the Marquette Range was a remarkable tribute to human ingenuity and tenacity.

By the time the new settlers arrived, most of the lands where iron was located, or the rights to the minerals they contained, had been purchased from the United States by the mining companies or otherwise acquired from the original patentees. The new immigrants would not own iron mines; their role would be to dig the ore out of the mountain. It was the era of the horse and buggy in a climate that produced winter snows four feet deep and muddy two-rut roads that ran "uphill both ways." Food and supplies had to be carried in by pack animal or by foot.

Open-pit mining at the Jackson Mine commenced near the stump where iron ore had been reportedly discovered circa 1846.[22] The first underground mine on the Marquette Range may have been Section 16 which opened in 1853 in what became Ishpeming and later became part of several Ishpeming shafts included in the Lake Superior Group, including Section 21 and the Holmes. My dad (Ben Nelson) later worked at Section 16. By the close of 1887, seventy-six open-pit or underground mines had been dug in Ishpeming and Negaunee and the seven other communities on the Marquette Range that sprang up around them.

Cleveland-Cliffs Iron Company (CCI) records, some of which are kept at the Cliffs Shaft Mining Museum in Ishpeming, disclose that of the seventy-six iron mines on the Marquette Range, at least nine open pit and fifteen underground mines had been opened in Ishpeming when my Nelson ancestors arrived there in 1887—forty-three years after the initial discovery of iron ore in the hunting lands of the Ojibwa.[23]

The disparate coincidences that converge to create one's life can be mind-boggling. Iron metallurgy had been introduced in Europe in the eighth century to produce pig iron and wrought iron. But hematite ore was not the ore of choice for the manufacture of these and other iron products. In addition, the bulk of the ore on the Marquette Iron Range lay deep below the surface embedded in solid rock and difficult to extract. As a consequence, hematite ore from the Marquette Iron Range did not command the price or produce the profits generated by other types of iron ore when mining began in Ishpeming and Negaunee in the 1840s. Although it was iron and there was a lot of it, as the frontispiece of this manuscript reveals, by the 1860s Ishpeming was still a mining camp of frame buildings hacked out of a remote wilderness.

By 1871 railroad tracks had been installed to carry iron ore away from Ishpeming and Negaunee. At that time Ishpeming consisted of four primary streets and five or six cross streets lined with cookie cutter residences, churches, and retail establishments.[24] The name "Ishpeming" is derived from Indian lore and is said by its citizens to mean "Heaven." Those same citizens erected a statue of an Indian chief they named "Old Ish" in the city square and claimed that, according to Indian lore, the name of neighboring "Negaunee" meant "Hell."

Figure 3

Hercules Powder Company, National Mine, Michigan.
IM-MISC-73
Photograph courtesy of Superior View Studios

Starting in the 1860s scientific discoveries greatly enhanced the value of hematite iron ore in the Marquette Iron Range. Alfred Bernhard Nobel, a Swedish chemist and engineer, invented dynamite in 1867.[25] His discovery enabled hematite ore embedded in jasper and granite to be blasted loose with greater explosive force than the blasting powders that had previously been used. The Hercules Powder Company built a factory to manufacture dynamite in Finn Town, a location in National Mine near where I was raised.

Then, in the late 1870s Henry Bessemer in Britain and William Kelly in the United States independently discovered that molten pig iron taken from a blast furnace could be directly converted into steel. That was a huge advance. Prior to the Bessemer process pig iron could only be converted into steel through an expensive process that took many days—steel was looked upon as a semiprecious metal. The Bessemer process made steel "the material of choice for plates and rails." [26] Hematite ores located in the Marquette Iron Range—though less stable than other ores, more difficult to mine, and a generator of red dust that pervaded everything—suddenly became a highly valuable ore. It was low in phosphorous and could be combined with other ores to produce steel through the Bessemer process.[27] Had Nobel not discovered dynamite—and Bessemer and Kelley not developed the Bessemer process—my ancestors would not have sailed to America when they did, and I and the kids I was raised with would never have seen the light of day.

Not only that. Steel has enormous tensile strength and can carry the weight of skyscrapers, bridges, and large industrial complexes. One can get a sense of that strength by visiting freeway overpasses, the bridges that connect the Burroughs of New York City and span the Golden Gate in California and the Straits of Mackinaw. The Bessemer process allowed the mass production of automobiles, farm equipment, locomotives, battle ships, and a multitude of manufacturing and consumer products. Without commercially affordable steel, the industrial revolution could not have blossomed as it did, and the modern urban society where the city slickers live would not exist. The scientific genius that led to the discovery of dynamite and the Bessemer process cannot be overstated. It unleashed an explosion of iron mining on the Marquette Iron Range and other venues, and created the place I call home.[28] It created my parents and me.

The major mines operating in Ishpeming in 1887 were the Barnum, Boston, Cambria-Jackson, Cliffs Shaft, Detroit, Dey, Excelsior, Goodrich, Lake Angeline, Lake Sally, Lake Superior Group, Lillie, Marquette, Mitchell, National, New England, New York, Saginaw, Salisbury, and Winthrop.[29] CCI's records disclose that the Lake Angeline mine alone, which was opened during the Civil War, had both underground and open pit operations that between 1864 and 1922 produced 9,319,679 tons of iron ore. Cliffs Shaft, which opened in 1881, produced 889,862 tons up to 1897 and operated until 1950. Considering that the technology available to the people who built these mines and transported the ore away was primitive at best, the only appropriate response is "WOW!"

Equally astounding, CCI records kept at the Cliffs Shaft Mining Museum in Ishpeming disclose that another twenty mines had been opened in Negaunee prior to the close of 1887 and at least fifteen of them were underground mines, although the Rolling Mill mine is reported to have been both open pit and underground. Between 1871 and 1935 the Rolling Mill produced 2,997,802 tons of iron ore. The Jackson mine, an open-pit operation, produced 4,375,256 tons of iron ore from 1846 to 1909. Diamond drilling operations by the Jackson mine located substantial iron deposits underground that led to the development of other shafts in that area, including the Maas in 1902.

CCI records kept at the Cliffs Shaft Mining Museum in Ishpeming also disclose that other open pits and iron mines were developed in the area surrounding Ishpeming and Negaunee, starting with the Washington, opened in 1860 in Humboldt, and the Champion, which opened in Champion in 1867. The Old Volunteer opened in Palmer in 1871, and the Princeton opened in Gwinn in 1872. The Republic opened in 1871 in Republic, the American opened in Humboldt in 1880, the Imperial opened in Michigamme in 1882, and the Chase opened in North Lake in 1884. All of these were underground mines with substantial production. Combined, the American and Washington in Humbolt produced approximately 3,000,000 tons of iron ore between 1860 and 1922. There were additional but smaller operations in these outlying localities prior to 1887.

To carry all that ore away, the Marquette, Houghton, and Ontonagon Railroad commenced its operations in 1857 and operated from the Cleveland mine in Ishpeming and the Jackson mine in Negaunee. The early railroads were plank railroads with iron straps where horses and mules supplied the power. Rails were installed and steam engines were introduced in the 1880s, and by the turn of the century three railroads carried the ore to wooden docks built at thriving Great Lakes ports—the Duluth South Shore and Atlantic (DSS&A), the Lake Superior and Ishpeming (LS&I), and the Chicago and Northwestern.[30]

Before the ore could be hauled away, it had to be blasted loose. To appreciate the difficulty of blasting through solid granite at the depths where the ore was located, you have to consider how it was done. I wasn't there in the 1800s, but mining techniques then were a whole lot more archaic than what I saw on my first day at the Mather A shaft in 1951. In some cases the mining companies lowered horses down the mine shafts to pull trains of ore out to the shaft. In the early days, in order to drill holes to be filled with blasting powder or dynamite, one miner would hold the steel bit and turn it by hand while two other miners hit it, one at a time, with steel mauls. To put it mildly, the miner selected to hold the bit was a trusting soul. I've seen pictures of miners doing that with candles (later carbide lamps) attached to their mining hats, and of ore tramcars being pushed down underground tracks by hand. The light bulb hadn't been invented, so there were no electric lights in the underground drifts, nor for the headlamps. I went underground with a battery-powered headlamp, but from what I saw underground it was easy to imagine what had gone before me.

Early iron miners wearing candle lamps.
Photograph courtesy of Superior View Studios
IM-Misc-41

Underground iron-ore mining is about as labor intensive, isolated, and dangerous as you can get. No one sat in the bleachers cheering them on when two contract miners working up at the breast of a new drift lifted a sixteen-inch maple cap (lintel) atop two maple legs by hand, "spragged" (braced) the three of them in place with spruce poles driven in place between the rock walls of the drift and the timbers, and then installed cedar lagging between the timbers to hold back the rock ceiling and the walls of the drift (overburden) so they could resume drilling into the front end of the drift (the "breast") to blast the next cut. Sometimes several miners were assembled from neighboring drifts to place an unusually heavy maple cap. Nor were there any spectators when two miners drilled and blasted a raise straight up to get to the ore body and cribbed it with spruce cribbing. The miners' reward was knowledge that the drift or the raise wouldn't collapse on them. Sometimes steel bolts had to be hammered into holes drilled into the rock ceiling (overburden) to hold it in place. My dad referred to it as "savage amusement," a phrase he and other iron miners often used.

Miners went to work every day knowing the potential for crippling injuries or death was always at hand, especially for the careless or the unlucky. The Barnes-Hecker disaster west of Ishpeming put the exclamation mark on that when the last blast of the morning on November 4, 1926, blew out the bottom of an underground lake which flooded the mine with water and sand, killing fifty-one miners. One miner, Rutherford Wills, climbed the shaft with the flood coming up behind him. Friends and relatives who gathered on the surface waited in vain. Wills was the only one who got out. He left town after that. I worked underground with one of his nephews at the Mather A mine some years later. One day while we were sitting in a top-timber job eating pasty lunches (more about pasties and top-timber jobs later), he told me about his uncle scrambling up the Barnes-Hecker shaft ahead of the flood. By then Barnes-Hecker had become a legend, but it didn't close the mines. Mining went on even as injury, silicosis, and death took their grim toll.

The investors who sought to exploit the iron ore realized that powerful bodies that didn't fear death or shy away from hard work would be needed to sink the mine shafts, drive the drifts, and work them. To get them, the mining companies sent recruiters back "across the pond" knowing it took a special breed to dig iron ore from granite and jasper in a wilderness that was frozen over for half of the year and "tough sledding" for the other half.

Whether advertisements or recruiters got to them, or they just heard about it, my grandparents on both sides shipped out for "God's Country" in the Upper Peninsula with as much baggage as they could carry and all their stories of the "Old Country," believing Ishpeming was a land of milk and honey where the streets were paved with gold. I wish I could have shipped out with them on their ocean steamers so I could tell you what their feelings were as they peered out at the storms that buffeted them on the North Atlantic. I'm sure it wasn't a pleasure cruise. Later, I searched the National Archives in Washington DC to determine my ancestors' port of entry. I was not able to locate it, nor did I determine how they traveled to the mining country in Michigan's Upper Peninsula. My family is living proof that they did.

The Upper Peninsula or "UP" as it came to be called, that my grandparents found was populated by native Indians and the Europeans who had already migrated there. An 1890 photograph revealed a still tiny Ishpeming to be sure, but also a well-built municipality with solid brick and stone structures on its streets. (See photograph at end of Chapter 4, *infra*.) By 1900 Ishpeming was a booming mining town with a population over 13,000.[31] In the surrounding wild country, black bears, whitetail deer, and timber wolves roamed, and brook trout and small mouth bass swam in rivers and lakes you could reach on two-rut roads and bush trails. There wasn't any gold on the streets of Ishpeming when my ancestors arrived. The streets weren't paved with anything but a clay and stone mixture called hardpan, red hematite dust from the mines, and—in the spring or when it rained—mud.

It wasn't only iron that immigrants like my grandparents were after. By then copper mining was lucrative, Calumet was booming, and big-city theatrical productions were appearing at the Calumet Opera House on the Keweenaw Peninsula, which was dubbed the "Copper Country." My wife Judy's great-uncle, Albert Niva, was an usher at the Calumet Opera House when it opened in 1900. A first-rate theater with an orchestra pit and fine musicians, it presented productions starring Maude Adams, Lillian Russell, Harry Houdini, Sara Bernhardt, Douglas Fairbanks, and many others who came by train directly from New York. A tunnel from a hotel across the street provided the celebrities and "swells" with access to the theater no matter how deep the snow. And it wasn't just theater. Moonshine and houses of prostitution were also flourishing in Calumet and its surrounding villages. According to population data for 1900, Calumet (including surrounding villages like Red Jacket, Yellow Jacket, and New Town) had a population of 25,991. Some even claimed that in its heyday the size and population of Calumet was greater than that of the city of Detroit. It's too bad conventioneers from the convention of January 26, 1837 (where it had been decided that the whole Upper Peninsula was "worthless wilderness") weren't around to see that.[32]

While chunks of copper had been found in the Keweenaw on the surface or close to it—including the one now at the Smithsonian—most of the copper, like iron, was thousands of feet straight down. The Red Jacket shaft on the Keweenaw Peninsula was over a mile deep, and was reputed to be the deepest vertical mine in the world at that time. My wife Judy's great-grandfather on her mother's side, John Rowe, who had migrated to the Keweenaw from the silver mining country on Isle Royale, was captain of the Red Jacket in its heyday around the turn of the century. Another of Judy's great-grandfathers, Isaac Niva, worked in the Keweenaw's copper mines for fifty years and received a gold medallion for his service.

Figure 5

Jeffrey Nelson operating a
diamond drill at Ropes goldmine—circa 1981.
Nelson Family Photograph

The iron in the Marquette Range and the copper in the Keweenaw Peninsula promised great riches, to be sure, but silver had also been found, some of it intermingled with the copper deposits, and it was rumored that the Marquette Range contained gold. There never was a gold rush around Ishpeming like the ones in California or the Klondike as far as I know, but some prospectors did dig for gold at the Ropes Mine a few miles north of Ishpeming. If they found any they didn't talk about it, and those that did smiled and looked the other way. Years later, though, interest in the Ropes Gold Mine reawakened and my brother Ken's youngest son, Jeffrey Nelson, worked for a company that mined gold at that spot.

Truth was that the beautiful but harsh wilderness where I was born was brimming with mineral wealth when my grandparents arrived in Ishpeming around the gay nineties. But most of the high grade ore lay undisturbed deep underground. The demand for iron ore created by World War I, World War II and the Cold War greatly expanded iron mining on the Marquette Iron Range. Today it is well known that Michigan's Upper Peninsula is loaded with valuable ores that are getting scarcer all over the world. The original underground iron and copper mines have been closed, but iron mining is still carried on in open pits, iron ore is crushed, separated and pelletized before it is shipped, and international conglomerates are digging new mines to extract copper, silver and gold from the UP.

~~~

Figure 6

Ojibwa Camp NA-73

Chief Charlie
Kawbawgam NA03

Ore ships at dock in Marquette—1860. TO-MARQ-32
Photographs Courtesy of Superior View Studios

Figure 7
Miners toiling underground on the Marquette Iron Range in the early days.
(Photographs courtesy of Cleveland-Cliffs Iron Company)

Figure 8
Bird's-eye view of Marquette, Michigan—1871.

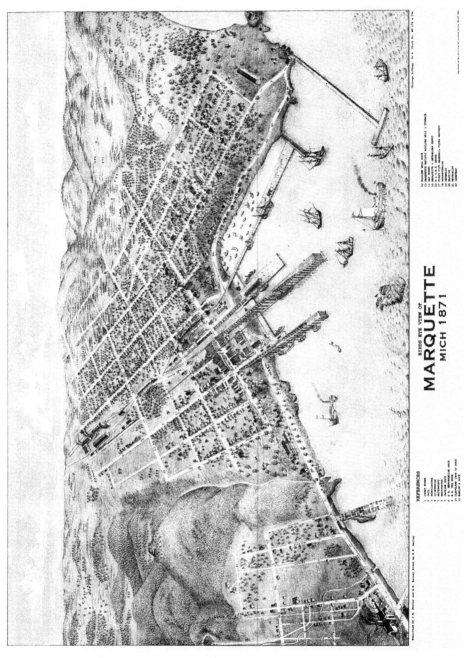

Courtesy of Marquette Regional History Center, Marquette, Michigan

CHAPTER 3

The Nelsons

MY DAD WAS Ben Nelson, and he was proud to be Ben Nelson. His confirmation photograph at Trinity Lutheran listed him as Bernhard, but he always signed his name Bernard. No one called him by either of those names anyway. At the mines he was "Benny Nelson." He didn't finish high school, read books, or write poems that I ever heard of. He came from a family of working people who had struggled to make a livelihood out of nothing since migrating to the "worthless wilderness." His folks came from silver-mining and hog-farming country in southern Norway, where people wrung their bread out of the earth or from the sea by working with their hands—and drew their faith from the Lutheran Church.

Dad was born in 1902, about the time Ma's people, Grandma and Grandpa Carne, were planning to sail from England. He was raised with one brother and five sisters three miles south of Ishpeming on leased land his family sometimes called "The Farm"—but mostly everybody called it "New Burt." His father, Grandpa Ole, and his mother, Aletta (Grandma Nelson), raised a family of proud Norwegians in a small farmhouse on Millimaki Road, now known as County Road 581, near where it intersects the road to National Mine.[33]

I recall Grandpa Ole as quiet, short, and somewhat stout. He sported a large mustache, walked with a cane, and most of the times I saw him wore a dark vested suit draped with a gold watch fob. There was nothing frivolous, comedic, or ostentatious about him. Pure and simple, he was a transplanted Norwegian who missed Norway greatly and seldom spoke his mind. Black-and-white photographs show that

Grandma Nelson posed the children in white frocks and suits when they were confirmed at Trinity Lutheran in Ishpeming.

Grandpa Ole worked in the iron mines, farmed at New Burt, and later helped Dad build our house and plant our potatoes. Being dressed for church was not his complete world. He may have even told ribald jokes out of earshot of his family, but I can't imagine him doing it. I probably remember Grandpa Ole suited up because he stopped at our house mostly on Sunday afternoons after church. Now my dad told ribald jokes, but I doubt he ever did in front of Grandpa Ole.

Dad's older brother, Uncle Nels, left New Burt in 1917 to serve in the United States Infantry and shipped out with the Doughboys. He helped lay down railroad tracks that carried supplies to the boys fighting on the front lines in France. My dad was only fifteen then, so he didn't go into the military.

Two of my dad's sisters, Ann and Bertha, married, left New Burt, and moved out of state before I was born, but his kid sister Adele (Dad called her Aidle) stayed at New Burt with Grandpa Ole, her husband George Corkin, and their two children Robert (Bob) and Gerald (Jerry) Corkin. My brothers and I used to fish with Bob. More on fishing later. Aunt Lily worked along with other wives and daughters of miners making ladies undergarments at the Gossard Company in Ishpeming, and later moved in with Dad's sister Ingeborg in Ishpeming. Ingeborg had married Leslie (Les) Kelly. Sometimes Aunt Lily also stayed at New Burt.

The folks at The Farm in New Burt were a big part of my childhood. I have fond memories of New Burt. Although I never ate meals or slept there, I came to look upon it as a second home. My brothers and sisters may remember things differently, but there was something about New Burt that made it mysterious and magical to me. I wondered where the name came from. It had to come from somewhere. My dad called my Aunt Bertha "Bert," but it didn't come from her. Growing up I thought there must be an "Old Burt" someplace and that if I ever found it I'd experience an even more magical place and establish the Nelson lineage.

The surveyor who discovered iron ore near Negaunee was named William A. Burt. The name could have derived from him. Mining records for the Marquette Iron Range indicate that a very early iron mine south of Ishpeming was named New Burt, and I believe the location was named after that mine. But that doesn't explain where Old Burt might have been. I couldn't find it in lists of mines on the

Marquette Range or on maps of Norway. I did find a town named Burt in the northwest corner of Iowa, in my *Atlas of the World*. Some of my dad's aunts moved to Sioux City, but it's fanciful to assume a town in Iowa was the namesake for the New Burt where my dad was raised.

There were only four or five homes located in New Burt when Dad grew up, and The Farm didn't have much land to farm. The land it did have was owned by the mining company. Grandpa Ole had a weather-beaten barn that housed a few cows, a hog pen, a pump that stood outside the kitchen, a crooked barbed wire fence sagging on wooden posts, and a big grindstone that I'll talk about later. There was nothing mysterious or magical about any of that. Grandpa Ole's farmhouse was clad in brown and green shingles which made it stand out. When I visited New Burt with my dad while I was growing up, I only picked up bits and pieces about Grandpa Ole's family. The folks at New Burt didn't bandy their heritage about with young whippersnappers or outsiders.

In a vainglorious belief that my family descended from heroic leaders, maybe royalty, I considered the possibility while studying world history in high school, that my Nelson ancestors had been Vikings crowned with horns who sailed the oceans in large boats with fire breathing dragons painted on their sails, fought their way across England and Ireland with battle-axes and broadswords, and discovered Greenland and America. But those notions didn't square with the quiet Lutherans at New Burt that I knew as a child. I never saw any of them wear horns or wield battle-axes or broadswords. I did learn that Grandpa Ole had been raised on a farm near Evje, Norway, and that his name had been Nielsen before he came to America.

Grandma Nelson died before I was born. She came from Mandal at the southern tip of Norway where it juts into the North Sea. My dad told me that all of Grandpa Ole's family, including my great-grandfather Nils Samuelsen, left Norway and migrated to America with Grandpa Ole. Nils Samuelsen later moved away to Tennessee and died there before I was born. Grandpa Ole and Grandma Nelson met at their confirmation class in Norway and married after she came to America. But without details on where they came from in Norway, what their lives there were like, and why they left, Grandpa Ole and Grandma Nelson came across as very proud Norwegians to be sure, but also as strangers. I wanted to know more about them and why they left Norway.

The way Dad and his family talked about it, which wasn't often, Evje, Mandal, and a location they called Syrtveit came off as faraway Nirvanas. I always hoped to see them. I'd like to think it was my thirst for knowledge of my heritage, but maybe it was a desire to understand why the Nelsons left the magical places they talked about and migrated to a remote iron-mining wilderness many looked down upon as hillbilly country. If living on a Norwegian farm at Syrtveit was Nirvana then why not migrate, if at all, to Wisconsin or Iowa and be dairy farmers? My dad would have liked that.

A few years back my son Dan won a trip for two to visit a china factory in Porsqrunn, Norway. I had laughed when my wife Judy entered all of my family's names in the contest. Judy laughed even harder when Dan won. Dan invited me to go with him because he knew I was burning to get there. It was manna from heaven. Judy wasn't about to let either of us go without her, so the three of us departed from Detroit, Michigan, on June 3, 1991, flew to Copenhagen, and on from there to Oslo, Norway.

I determined before we left Detroit that after we had visited Oslo and the china factory in Porsqrunn, I would find the Samuelsen farm near Evje so I could experience that magical place for myself and ferret out its mystery. When I phoned my cousin, Alden Graneggen (Aunt Ann's son), before I left and told him we were going to Norway, and that I would try to find the Samuelsen farm, he said it was near a waterfall. There are a lot of waterfalls in Norway, so that was not as helpful as I would have liked. My dad had gone to live with the Lord, so I couldn't ask him.

Although I don't speak or read Norwegian, I studied maps of southern Norway on the train from Oslo to Kristiansand and looked for a place called "Burt" or "Old Burt." I expected to find such a place near Evje, but if there ever was such a place I didn't find any names on the map that looked anything like "Burt." The group of English-speaking Norwegians who rode in our car on the train studied my map over my shoulder and told me none of them had ever heard of it. They had been on a soccer trip and were having a blast on their way back to Kristiansand from Lillehammer. As they laughed and told me to get an interpreter, I wondered if Grandpa Ole had ever been on a blast.

We spent the first night in a hotel in Kristiansand. The next morning we crowded into a rented Saab, left Kristiansand, and motored through beautiful rocky hills to Evje. Once there I was surprised to find that it looked very much like New Burt. I'd always envisioned it to be a whole lot more, but I was delighted to see that Evje was located at a waterfall on the Otra River. I assumed it was the one that cousin Alden described as the one where Grandpa Ole fished, and that the Samuelsen farm would be nearby. After shooting a slew of pictures of Judy, Dan, and me in happy poses and smiley faces at the waterfall, we decided it was time for dinner. We ate at a hotel named the Dronen where I enjoyed some excellent seafood and a glass or two of the local beer.

After dinner I got out my notebook and asked the barmaid, Unni Johansen, to tell us more about the waterfall we'd just photographed and the Samuelsen farm. Unni laughed and explained to my embarrassment that the farm was several kilometers farther up the road and that the waterfall I was seeking was there. While I studied my camera Unni gave me the general location, but told me I should get a guide. She gave me several names including that of Alf Georg Kjesta. I immediately phoned him. Alf came to the Dronen, and after I explained I was an American in search of my Norwegian roots, he offered to take Judy, Dan, and me to the farm the next day. Fluent in English, he was very friendly and knowledgeable. We had hit pay dirt.

At Evje I visited the churchyard of a Lutheran church. Alf told me it probably contained the remains of my ancestors. The church was painted white, had stained-glass windows and a tall tower, and, although larger, looked just like Trinity Lutheran in Ishpeming that had been Grandpa Ole's and Grandma Nelson's church. I didn't identify any relatives buried in the churchyard at Evje because researching names in Norway is tough, and there was no time for that. I decided I'd be better off tracing my genealogy at the archives back in Kristiansand than trying to decipher it from headstones.

Early the next morning I located the Norwegian archives in Kristiansand and found an interpreter. She helped me research the Nelson line. I didn't get back very far. I had always wondered exactly how the name Nielsen (which I had been told was the origin of my family name) morphed into Nelson. I quickly discovered from the archives that sometimes in Norway, but apparently not always, a father's given name becomes part of their children's surname.

According to the archives, Grandpa Ole's father was born Nils Samuelsen and his mother Ingeborg Olsdatter. Nils and Ingeborg were my great-grandparents. Nils Samuelsen's occupation was listed as "Gaard" (farmer). Grandpa Ole had been born "Real"—which meant inside wedlock—on May 15, 1868, and was baptized on June 21, 1868, as Ole Nilson. Ole's confirmation record, which we found in the archives, established that he had been confirmed at a school near Syrtveit as Ole Nilssen. Nelson, Nilson, Neilsen, Nilssen—what the hell was going on? How could I trace my lineage from generation to generation with all these names? While I was becoming increasingly concerned about all the names jumping around, and glancing at my watch, my interpreter confirmed Unni Johansen's description of Syrtveit as a small location north of Evje. At the very least I had found Nirvana.

Grandpa Ole's occupation was listed as "Gaardbruger" (farmer) and his knowledge level as "Smaa Evne." When I asked the interpreter what in the world that meant, hoping against hope that Grandpa Ole had been born a genius, she at first refused to interpret, and on being pressed assured me I wouldn't like it. When I persisted, she became embarrassed and shook her head, but ultimately did interpret the words in Grandpa Ole's school records to read "almost good" or of "small ability." After I finished laughing over the quaint but gentle manner in which Grandpa Ole's knowledge level had been described in his school records, I confirmed that Grandpa Ole's father's name was listed as Nils Samuelsen both on Grandpa Ole's birth record and on the record of his confirmation. But now Samuelsen became yet another surname to ponder. Okay, some guy named Samuel had a son, but who was Samuel? Where did he come from? What was his surname? There'd be no time to dig out answers to these questions if I wanted to visit the farm. While I was happy to find Syrtveit in the records, none of the records referred to Burt.

The archives disclosed that Grandma Nelson was born Aletta Pederson in Mandal, Norway, on April 14, 1872, "in wedlock." Her father's name was Bjorn Pederson. Her mother's maiden name had been Olene Birgitte Samuelsdatter. Bjorn Pederson's occupation was listed as "Arbeidsmand" (worker).[34] I didn't find a confirmation record for Grandma Nelson, or any record of when she left Mandal. Worse, the archives failed to disclose any facts to support my fantasies that I had descended from Vikings or royalty. My research was going nowhere.

Later that day Alf drove with us to the former Nils Samuelsen farm about five kilometers north of Evje. As we approached it, a road sign identified the location as "Syrtveit." I was thrilled to photograph that sign, but subdued when Alf explained that *syrt* referred to a sow or a pig, and that *veit* meant plain by the river. The bottom line was that Syrtveit was not magical at all. It was a pig farm by the river. The last vestiges of my fantasies were destroyed. My ancestors most certainly were not Vikings or of royal vintage. In fact, like New Burt, there were several small separate farms at Syrtveit. The plot described as 55b, Alf explained, was listed on the ancient record he had obtained in Evje as belonging to Nils Samuelsen.

The Samuelsen farm looked to be about five or so acres, but there were no fences to indicate the farm to which the acreage belonged. The two-story house, built high off the ground to accommodate winter snows, was white, and the barn was painted red. The farm reminded me of New Burt, except that a mountain stood behind it. We found a stone retaining wall near the barn that could have been built by Great-Grandfather Nils or Grandpa Ole. I had heard stories from Dad that in Norway hay was harvested high in the mountains in the summer and later carried down to the farms in the valley. I did not confirm that, nor did I see any fields on the mountain adjoining the Nils Samuelsen farm.

Figure 9

Nils Samuelsen Farm (foreground)
at Syrtveit near Evje, Norway (July 22, 1961).
Photograph courtesy of Alf George Kjesta

After we talked with the current occupants of the Samuelsen farmhouse, Alf took us to a waterfall about one and a half kilometers to the north. It was much larger and more picturesque than the waterfall we had seen at Evje. Dan laughed when I got out my camera and asked him and Judy to pose for more pictures. Alf explained that a large stone structure built out into the falls had been used in earlier days to guide logs into the river to float them to a hydraulic sawmill that at one time operated there. It reminded me of Flaa's sawmill just north of our ten-acre farm back in the United States—although Flaa's sawmill had been powered by a diesel engine.

Departure records I had located at the archives at Kristiansand the day before revealed that on June 10, 1887, the Nils Samuelsen family shipped out on the Allen Line when they migrated to America. My grandfather, Ole Nilsen, (No. 1937) was listed as an eighteen-year old *grubearbeder* (miner) from Evje. It isn't clear why Grandpa Ole listed himself as a miner since the silver mines near Evje, I was told by our guide Alf, didn't open until later. Grandpa Ole may have listed himself that way to gain passage to America. I found no other record of Grandpa Ole ever having been a miner in Norway. It also isn't clear why he was listed as eighteen years old since he turned eighteen on May 15, 1886. Grandpa Ole may have submitted his papers some months before he sailed.

Despite some inconsistencies I was satisfied by the names of the others who sailed with him that the person who sailed on June 10, 1887, on the Allen Line was indeed my Grandpa Ole.[35] Also listed with Grandpa Ole's family were Alfred Fredricksen (No. 1935) a twenty-year-old road worker from Sverge (Sweden), and Johan Fredricksen (1936) a twenty-four-year-old road worker also from Sverge. I mention this because, although spelled differently, a Fredrickson family lived in the farmhouse across the road from Grandpa Ole at New Burt, and Clarence Fredrickson of that family was a boyhood friend of my dad. It is a small world after all.

I was unable to find departure records for Salve Nilsen (Grandpa Ole's brother) or Aletta.[36] I don't know when my Great-uncle Salve came to America. He was not listed on the Allen Line record I saw at the archives. A family photograph of Grandpa Ole, Salve, Anne (Samuelsen) Rysta, and Ingeborg (Samuelsen) Peterson taken after the family moved to New Burt confirms that Salve did come to America at or about the time Grandpa Ole and his sisters came. My dad referred to Salve as Uncle Sam. He also told me that Salve died and was buried somewhere in Ishpeming, and that a building had been erected over Salve's burial plot.[37]

Following Norwegian tradition—observed by the Nils Samuelsen family until they came to America—my father's and his brother Nels' surname would have been Oleson, that of his sisters Olsdatter, and my surname would have been Bernardson or Benson. The records show that when he left for America, Ole's surname was Nilson. It somehow got changed to Ole Nelson when he went through customs in the United States. His name was recorded as Ole Nelson (Nilson) in Record Book 11 page 121—line 6 at the Trinity Church in Ishpeming when he arrived there. That is how I knew him, that is how my surname came into being, and that is how Trinity Lutheran became our family church. When I was baptized at Trinity Lutheran on April 24, 1932, I was listed as "David Lee." Aunt Ingeborg and her husband Leslie Kelley became my godparents.

Judy, Dan and I had to leave Evje abruptly because we had booked a flight to Bergen. After dropping off the Saab in Kristiansand, a harrowing ride in a taxicab to catch a small twenty-or-so seater, and a flight over spectacular vistas in the southern tip of Norway, we arrived in Bergen where we spent a raucous evening with a group of mathematicians celebrating post-graduate degrees at the Bryggloffet—a really fun place. They treated us as one of them, and we tried our best to be one of them and to sing along with them. The beer was flowing, but I did not test my knowledge of Norwegian words with this group of mathematicians, nor did I mention that my grandfather's knowledge level was "smaa evne."

The next day we set off on a tour we'd arranged called "Norway in a Nutshell." It was one of our happiest times there. It took us by bus to the fiords, then by boat through the fiords, and by rail over mountainous terrain in central Norway, where cross-country skiers were training in June, and finally back to Oslo. When we arrived back at the Stefan Hotellet on Rosenkrantz Gate, our hotel in Oslo, I wondered as we entered the lobby whether my great-grandparents, Nils and Ingeborg, or my grandparents, Ole and Aletta, had ever skied the mountains we'd just crossed or slept at our hotel.

Although Grandpa Ole's school records listed him as "almost good," and the archives unmasked my Norwegian ancestors as hog farmers and grubearbeders, the memories I carried home were those of farmers living along the banks of breathtaking fiords, a green-eyed blonde Norwegian jenta (girl) who greeted us on the dock at Flam on the Songenfiord fiord, meat cutters in white shirts and red ascots on holiday in Myrdal, cross-country skiers striding high in the mountains, trains curling into mountain tunnels, and of friendly, honest, and intelligent people living in a very beautiful country. As we flew back to Detroit, I studied pictures I'd picked up at Evje and wondered if Grandpa Ole had left Evje on the train pictured in one of them and what his thoughts were when he sailed for America. I wondered again, why did he leave?

Figure 10

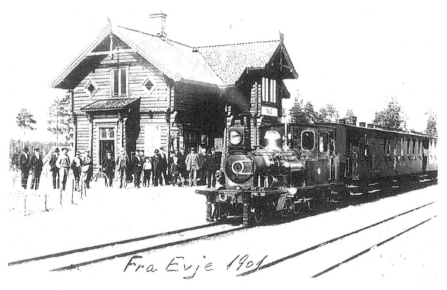

Train of the type Ole Nelson likely rode when he left Evje, Norway, in 1887.
Photograph courtesy of Alf George Kjesta

Figure 11

Front Street, Marquette, Michigan—1870. (TO-MARQ-41)

Front Street, Marquette, Michigan—1890s. (TO-MARQ-52)

Photographs Courtesy of Superior View Studios

Figure 12

Lutheran Church, Evje, Norway.   Trinity Lutheran, Ishpeming, Michigan.

A four-year-old Ben
with his sisters.

(L–R) Lily, Ann, Ben,
and Bertha—1906.

The family of Ole and Aletta Nelson—1918.

(L–R) Front: Adele; Aletta; Nels; Ole and Ingeborg;

(L– R) Back row: Ann; Bernard; Bertha; and Lily

Nelson Family Photographs

Figure 13

Trinity Lutheran Confirmation—1917
Ben is at the extreme right of the back row.
Nelson Family Photographs

Trinity Lutheran Confirmation—1918

This Stolen family photograph shows some of Ben's boyhood friends. In back: Henry Hansen (left), Joseph Flack (center), and Rudolph Larson (far right)*. In front: Harold Stolen (left), ** and Clifford Felt (right).

[*Kenneth (Rudy) Larson identified the young man listed as Ralph Larson on the church's copy of this photograph to be his father and Ben's barber Rudolph Larson. ** Harold Stolen became Ben's neighbor.]

Figure 14

1871 Bird's-eye view of Ishpeming, Michigan. Courtesy of
Marquette Regional History Center, Marquette, Michigan

Figure 15

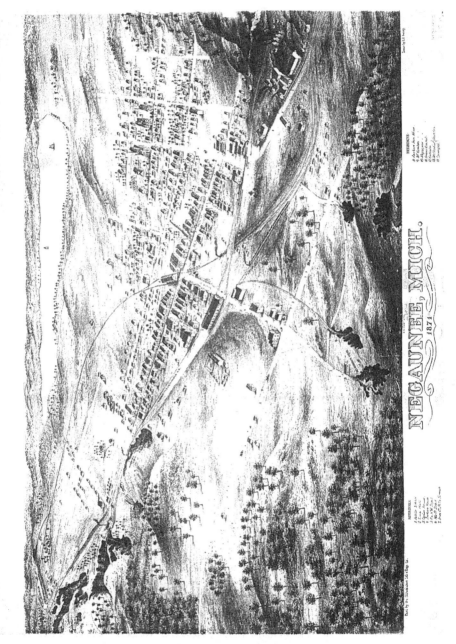

1871 Bird's-eye view of Negaunee, Michigan. Courtesy of
Marquette Regional History Center, Marquette, Michigan

CHAPTER 4

The Carnes

M Y NORWEGIAN HERITAGE encountered culture shock when Dad took us to visit Grandma and Grandpa Carne at their dingy brown, two-story clapboard duplex in Ishpeming that sat on the corner of North and Second Streets. I was six years old when I first visited Grandma Carne at her house—after the Depression hit Dad didn't have a car until he bought the 1937 Ford. The Carne residence is not shown in the lower left corner of an 1871 "Bird's Eye View of Ishpeming" map printed at the end of chapter 3—nor is North Street. They were added later. Ma's family was Cornish and English to the bone. None were Lutheran. Grandma Carne attended the Methodist church. Ma's brothers, Uncle John and Uncle Bill (everyone called him "Doc"), lived with them.

Grandpa Carne was a stocky, muscular Cornishman who sported bright red and royal blue tattoos on his forearms, always wore working clothes, and never went to church.[38] I never saw him in a suit. He came from the tin mining country in Cornwall, but it is unknown if he ever worked in the tin mines. My youngest brother Fred told me Grandpa Carne may have been a gardener when he lived in Cornwall. With his legs resting on his heels and outstretched before him, his powerful tattooed arms crossed over his chest, Grandpa Carne expressed views you better agree with—even when you didn't. But he didn't speak a lot, and sometimes rebuffed discussion with a look of total disdain. Ma was always good to Grandpa Carne when he came to visit, but in later years seldom mentioned him. When he passed, she said only that she wasn't feeling well and did not attend his funeral.

Ma's mother Laura (Grandma Carne) was different altogether. She was a petite English lady from Penzance who wore clean aprons, starched her curtains, and wore her silken white hair in combs. Like the English ladies she chummed with, she wore black veils on hats pinned with hat pins. Her ancestors were Cornish people who ran a store in Penzance and excursion boats to the isles of Scilly—and wore hats. She sure talked about that. It came to me later that Grandma Carne had traveled from one Land's End to one of a different type. Grandma Carne's English roots are what gave my ma her love of literature and her ability to blend thoughts into poetry.

When Dad drove us into town to visit, Grandma Carne would serve homemade bread with peanut butter, half a Cornish pasty, heavy cake, seedy buns, saffron buns, or blueberry pie. "It's good for you," she'd say as she set one of her creations before us on the oilcloth. Sometimes Uncle John would pull up the trapdoor in the linoleum that covered the kitchen floor and pull out a can of Eagle Brand milk for our coffee. I sure agreed with her then, and I do now. The stuff Grandma Carne put on the oilcloth was very, very good. Grandpa Carne—she called him Willy—and Uncle John used to take us fishing. More about that later.

Iron mining had continued apace between the time my Nelson ancestors arrived on the Mountain of Iron and when the Carnes did.[39] About 1907, Jackson Mine diamond drillers driving test holes hit pay dirt deep below. Cores from several sites revealed iron ore deposits lying deeper than one thousand feet. Because mining technology of that era did not support open-pit mining at those depths, miners would have to go underground to extract the ore. When the Mather A and Mather B shafts were opened in the 1940s, they were located near the site of the Jackson mine on top of the Mountain of Iron.

Grandpa Carne worked in one of the iron mines after he arrived in Ishpeming, but I have been unable to establish which one. My cousin Tommy Carne said to me recently that Grandpa Carne worked underground in an iron mine for only one day and quit as soon as the cage returned him to the surface. Tommy said he'd heard that Grandpa Carne remarked at the time that he did not intend to "make a living digging iron out of the bloody bowels of the earth." The aluminum lunch buckets Grandpa Carne used to carry live bait on fishing trips— "tins" he called them—were the type the miners used, so I don't know if Tommy's story is true.

After he left the iron mines, however long he was there, Grandpa Carne worked for the Pickands Coal Company in Ishpeming shoveling coal. I recall that in later years he worked for the City of Ishpeming doing gardening work at the cemetery where he and many of the Nelsons and Carnes who migrated to America are now buried. Grandpa Carne and his son John were fur trappers in their spare time. They captured and skinned silver foxes, red foxes, beaver, otter, mink, and weasel, and mailed their pelts to buyers like Sears and Roebuck. They did quite well doing this. Grandpa Carne used to laugh when he came out to our farm and talked about "city slickers" dressed in fancy suits. "If you took 'em by the ankles, held 'em up and shook 'em," he'd say, "You couldn't shake a dime out of 'em."

My ma (Elsie) was born in Ishpeming in 1906 a few years after my grandparents arrived from England. Never given a second name, she developed her love of literature and of the English language at the Ishpeming High School where she excelled. Dad called her "El." The Carnes at first lived on High Street in Ishpeming. When that house burned the family rented the clapboard duplex on Second Street that I remember as Grandma Carne's house. Ma was raised there with one sister and three brothers.

As the clock atop the grammar school across the street from the clapboard duplex bonged off one hour after the next, it reminded me of Big Ben in London. A wooden stairway climbed the bluff just north of the duplex. For a little kid off the farm, it was a wondrous place to play with my brothers and sisters when Ma visited Grandma Carne and "Big Ben" bonged. The stairs were like a jungle gym modern kids play on. When our cousin Donna Mae was visiting, she played with us.

Today, lawyers would see that stairway as an "attractive nuisance" and file lawsuits, I suppose. But not then. It was where we ran up and down the steps and slid down the banister, while Ma and Grandma gossiped with the Harveys, who lived in the other half of the duplex, and Mrs. Laver who lived down the street. In the summer they chatted on cane chairs in the backyard. Occasionally, Mrs. Shaeffer came by and joined in. All English ladies, they mostly talked quietly about the "Old Country." But they also gabbed about Ma's sister Aunt Mae who lived in Lansing, and her brother Uncle Dick (Donna Mae and Tommy's dad) who had moved away to Flint with his wife, the former Lucretia Laver, whom we knew as Aunt Cretia. Ma said Uncle Dick, who wore a mustache, reminded her of Clark Gable.

Figure 16

Donna Mae Carne Richardson—age 10—
shown in a dime-store photograph, circa 1940.
Carne Family Photographs

Yes, indeed. Uncle Dick was a tall, handsome, and powerful Englishman who worked for the electric power company in Flint, Michigan as a lineman. But I remember Uncle Dick and Aunt Cretia, not just because they had become handsome, glamorous big-city people from downstate, but because they let Donna Mae and Tommy stay with us out at the farm. Donna Mae taught us the big city method of selecting the kid who was it for our hide-and-go-seek games. She had us form a circle and hold out our fists while she struck them one at a time with her fist and recited, "one potato, two potato," etc. right up to "seven potato more." She used her chin for one of her fists. We removed one fist from the circle of fists each time she reached the last word of the litany. The kid with the last fist in the circle was it. Donna Mae never ended up being it. We found out later how to count fists in our heads in advance, depending on the number of players, and how to rig the outcome of that big city method. We just loved making an unsuspecting player it.

Grandma Carne had taught Ma how to make a house a home by starching curtains, aprons, and collars, scrubbing the floors and cooking wholesome tasty food. It wasn't until years later that my sisters discovered Ma liked to write poems and hide them in old sugar bowls. Ma's poems tell you a lot about her family. When the family later published them as *Wandering Verse*, my cousin Tommy Carne contributed some of the artwork. Ma should have been a teacher. She'd have been a good one, but she didn't graduate from high school or matriculate at college. Instead she married my dad and raised us kids. She was our teacher.

But I'm getting ahead of my story. Each time I eavesdropped on Ma's conversations with Grandma Carne or got to look at her photographs, it was, in the words of Yogi Berra, "dé jà vu all over again." I imagined how wonderful it would be to meet my relatives in Penzance, England—return to the lives Grandma and Grandpa Carne had left, walk the promenade, cross the footbridge of sand to St. Michael's Mount, stand at Land's End—and see boats lying on the sea bed when the tide went out at Penzance. Grandma Carne used to give me a few dimes to buy candy at the candy store up the street if I asked too many questions, but I picked up a lot by listening at the duplex, marveling at her photographs and asking my sisters. Just like with my dad's Norwegian family, I wanted to experience for myself the extravagant places in England Grandpa and Grandma Carne had left.

Grandma Carne was born Laura Hannah Jenkin and was raised in Penzance, England. Grandpa William Carne (Grandma Carne called him "Willy") came from the adjoining city of Newlyn. Both are located in Cornwall on the English Channel at the extreme southwest corner of England. They met on the Promenade at Penzance while in their teens and married in England. Aunt Mae was born there in 1902 before the family migrated to America.

Grandma Carne's father's name was Samuel Jenkin, and her mother's name was Elizabeth. We found old black-and-white photos Grandma Carne brought with her to the United States, but have been unable to locate any relatives, the "Mystery House," or the Jenkin Market shown in her photographs.[40] Whether from youthful exuberance or to seek freedom, adventure, or wealth, Grandma and Grandpa Carne and Aunt Mae sailed to the United States in 1903, and settled atop the Mountain of Iron in Ishpeming, Michigan.

My brother Fred and I visited England with our wives in 2011. Fred drove our rented SUV because he's younger than I and had experience driving in England, where they drive from the right side of the vehicle and on the left side of the road. Fred and his wife Lorraine did an excellent job navigating the roundabouts, except he drove so slowly on Cornwall's narrow, rock-fence-bordered roads we dubbed him "the

Cornwall Creeper." That aside, we confirmed that boats do rest on the sea bed in the harbor at Penzance when the tide goes out, just as Grandma described, and that the Promenade and St. Michael's Mount are as delightful as the photographs Grandma Carne brought to America and as she described on those many occasions in her kitchen.

We also drove to Land's End and stood on the rocky coast where Grandma and Grandpa Carne had undoubtedly stood and perhaps picnicked on Cornish pasties. We would have bought our pasties in Penzance to compare them with those baked by Grandma Carne and my ma, but my wife Judy reminded us that her ancestors on her mother's side included Cornishmen. She said some of them, the Rowes, came from St. Austel, a city east of Penzance. Judy added that it had been told to her that the Rowes operated a pasty shop in St. Austel and that if we purchased any pasties, she wanted them purchased at Rowe's pasty shop. Although it was raining and we were unable to confirm it was the same Rowe family, we found a Rowe pasty shop in St. Austel and enjoyed our pasties. More about pasties later.

As I photographed the lighthouse shrouded in fog and gentle rain at Land's End, I imagined that Grandma and Grandpa Carne had looked out to sea over a century before from the very spot where I stood, discussed the iron, copper, and gold that had been discovered in the Upper Peninsula of Michigan and formed their plan to migrate to America. Before we left England, Fred and I and our wives drove to Plymouth. After watching the America's Cup yacht race in the harbor, we walked to the spot from which the Pilgrims sailed to the United States. The thought crossed my mind again while I looked out to sea at Plymouth that the voyage Grandma and Grandpa Carne took to America in 1903 with their daughter, Aunt Mae, was not unlike the Pilgrims' voyage of 1620. Grandpa Carne, though, may not have sailed to America as the questing adventurer I envisioned him to be at Land's End and Plymouth. I was later informed that whispered rumors had once circulated within the family that he left England ahead of prosecutors looking for smugglers. Of course, I didn't buy it. Not my grandpa![41]

But the land to which they migrated was swiftly developing. As mining operations increased in the Copper Country and on the Marquette Range, other institutions quickly sprang up. In 1885 the Michigan College of Mining and Technology opened in Houghton, Michigan, and became Michigan Tech, a leading technological college and later university. Northern Normal College opened in Marquette in 1899 to train teachers, and it too developed an excellent reputation, expanded its curriculum, became Northern Michigan College, and, later, Northern Michigan University. The Peter White Library was established in Marquette and a Carnegie Library in Ishpeming.

The Northwest Ordinance had provided that "Schools and the means of education shall forever be encouraged." That message was heard and scrupulously carried out as K-12 public schools, and Catholic schools were built and staffed in Marquette, Ishpeming, Negaunee, and the neighboring communities. The children and grandchildren of the immigrants became the beneficiaries—I among them. These schools and colleges produced a number of graduates who achieved national recognition, including Glen Theodore Seaborg, who participated in the Manhattan Project and had a radioactive element (Seaborgium) named after him, and John Voelker, an attorney who wrote novels under the name Robert Traver, including *Anatomy of a Murder,* a national bestseller and a movie sensation.[42]

In addition to the railroads and ore docks that served the mines, other businesses were developed that served the iron mining industry. A chemical plant was built in Marquette to furnish charcoal for smelting ore. It later manufactured other chemicals and became a Dow Chemical Company operation. Logging commenced to supply timber, lagging and cribbing to the mines, and pulpwood and lumbering operations expanded. The Munising Wood Products Company began its operations in Munising, and the Lake Shore Engineering Company was established in Marquette to supply castings, scrapers, hoists and other equipment to the mining companies. The Butler movie theater and the Ishpeming movie theater opened in Ishpeming, the Vista in Negaunee and the Delft and Nordic theaters in Marquette. What had been an uninhabited, worthless wilderness quickly morphed into a modern industrial community.

I recently learned off the Internet that Marquette State Prison was completed in 1889 in Marquette, near where the Carp River empties into Lake Superior, at a cost of $200,000. Some of the most violent and dangerous offenders convicted in Lower Michigan were incarcerated there because, even if they escaped the prison's walls, they, like the immigrants, would have a tough time escaping the Upper Peninsula's wilderness and winters.

~~~

Figure 17
The William and Laura Jenkin Carne family.

Laura Jenkin Carne's family at the Jenkin Market in Penzance, England.
Laura's father was Samuel Jenkin and her mother was Elizabeth (Rowe) Jenkin.

Carne Family at Deer Lake circa 1910. [William Carne, Laura Carne,
Elsie at far right (believed to be Elsie, but that hasn't been confirmed),
John sitting in Laura's lap, with unidentified friends in the background.]
Carne Family Photographs

Figure 18

Main Street Ishpeming—1890. TO-ISH-36

Main Street Negaunee—1915. TO-NEG-70

Photographs courtesy of Superior View Studios.

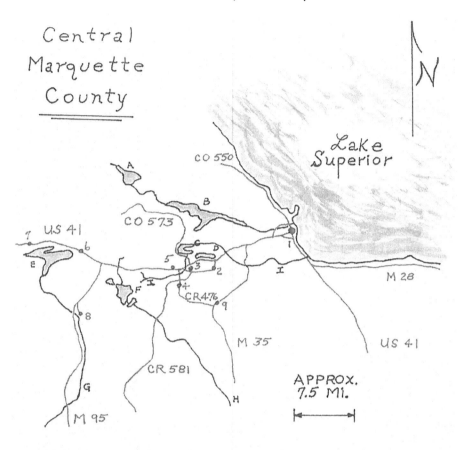

Central
Marquette
County

CO 550

Lake
Superior

N

A

B

CO 573

US 41

7

6

E

C

5

D

3

2

I

I

F

4

CR 476

9

M 28

8

M 35

US 41

CR 581

G

H

M 95

APPROX.
7.5 MI.

Cities & Villages		Lakes & Rivers	
1	Marquette	A	Silver Lake Storage Basin
2	Negaunee	B	Dead River / Dead River Storage Basin
3	Ishpeming	C	Deer Lake
4	National Mine / Tilden Township	D	Teal Lake
5	North Lake	E	Lake Michigamme
6	Champion	F	Greenwood Reservoir
7	Michigamme	G	Michigamme River
8	Republic	H	Middle Branch – Escanaba River
9	Palmer	I	Carp River

Courtesy of Frederick Nelson

Map B
Ishpeming

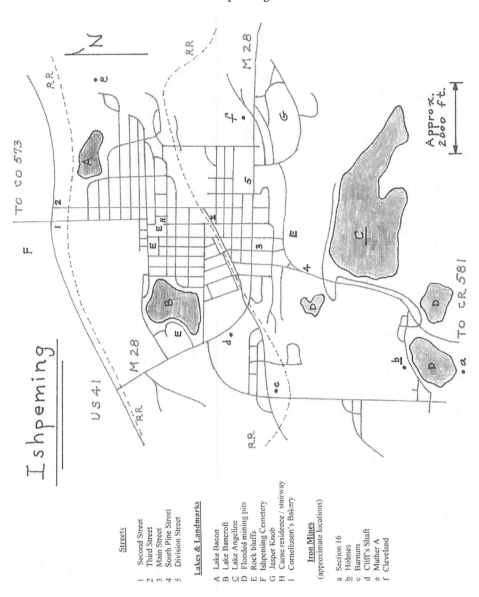

Courtesy of Frederick Nelson

Streets

1 Second Street
2 Third Street
3 Main Street
4 South Pine Street
5 Division Street

Lakes & Landmarks

A Lake Bacon
B Lake Bancroft
C Lake Angeline
D Flooded mining pits
E Rock bluffs
F Ishpeming Cemetery
G Jasper Knob
H Carne residence / stairway
I Corneliuson's Bakery

Iron Mines
(approximate locations)

a Section 16
b Holmes
c Barnum
d Cliff's Shaft
e Mather A
f Cleveland

Map C
Negaunee

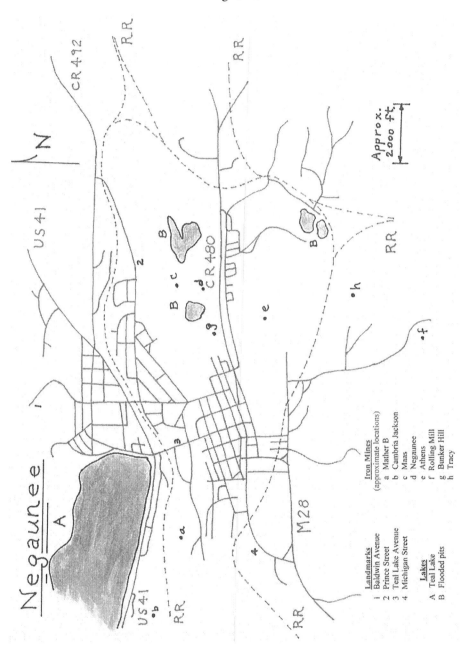

Map courtesy of Frederick Nelson

CHAPTER 5

The Crash of Twenty-Nine

THE PEOPLE WHO walked the streets of Ishpeming when my grandparents arrived came from all over Europe. Proud of their heritage, they maintained the same distance between the nationalities in America as their ancestors maintained in Europe. Gathered on front porches or seated on chairs out on the sidewalks they spoke their mother tongues, cooked their ethnic foods, built and prayed in their own churches, cursed each other, and sought their fortunes. They included "Cousin Jacks," "Herring Chokers," "Finlanders," "Wops," "Frogs," "Polacks," "Swedes," "Micks," and "Krauts." Intensely protective of their Old Country cultures, they became the mining partners and neighbors who drank draft beer in the bars—moonshine when they could get it during Prohibition—fox trotted or polkaed in the bars on Saturday night, and clustered around iron mines in locations like New Burt, Frenchtown, Swede Town, and Finn Town.

Whether they liked what they found when they landed in Ishpeming or not, there was no way any were going back "across the pond." Their offspring married each other's sons and daughters. They became the grizzled miners smeared with hematite who dug iron ore deep beneath the Ishpeming-Negaunee area. They also became the lumberjacks who logged the forests, cut the pulpwood, and supplied the hardwood timber, cedar lagging, and spruce cribbing for the mines. They became the gandy dancers who built and maintained the railroads that carried the ore to Great Lakes ore boats. They came with the hope of riches, a lust for freedom, a compulsion to feed their families, and pride in "an honest day's work." They also came with the perseverance it would take to endure the harsh conditions in Michigan's Upper Peninsula.

My dad was born in 1902, raised at New Burt, and attended school with children of the immigrants at the Old Red Schoolhouse east of New Burt near National Mine. He liked school at first, but not after the spitball fight where he cussed out the kid who hit him and got himself expelled. He never did get past the eighth grade. Maybe, like Grandpa Ole, my dad didn't do well at school, but don't think he wasn't smart. You'd be badly mistaken. I found that out when I watched him mark two-by-fours for rafters for our second barn using nothing but a carpenter's square. He used trigonometry and didn't even know it. Three, four, and five is all he told me.

He told my brother Fred way back in the fifties that electricity could be produced by ocean tides, so he was no dummy. Some folks are trying to do that today. It also showed when he slaughtered a hog or picked beagles for breeding. He once tried to convince my older brother Ken, who worked at the IGA grocery store in Ishpeming—and for a while had his own convenience store—that the future of the grocery business was in large warehouse-style operations. I guess Dad could visualize such stores before they were a twinkle in Sam Walton's eyes.

Another thing I remember about Dad's ingenuity: he was working underground at the Lloyd mine in North Lake when the shift boss asked him to solve a big problem. Water had collected up near the breast of a drift that had been put in wrong and sloped downhill. You got that— the shift boss was asking my dad for help. Electric power lines hadn't been installed in the drift, so the engineers couldn't pump the water out. You may wonder what a breast has to do with iron mining. It's the front end of the drift where the blasting gets done. My dad took care of it with some rubber hoses put there to bring compressed air to the jackhammers—"moiles," the miners called them. He connected the hoses together, put a valve on each end, filled them with water, and had his partner carry one end of that jerry-rigged hose down to the breast through water that came to the top of his boots. On Dad's signal from his headlamp his partner opened the valve on his end and dropped it in the water while Dad carried his end down the raise and opened the valve on his end. Dad siphoned that water out, and it didn't cost the mining company one red cent. My dad laughed when he told that story. Pretty smart, I'd say—smarter than those fancy engineers anyway.

When I tell that story and think of my dad siphoning that water, the thing that brings tears to my eyes is that—like so many things the Great

Depression smashed—my grandparents and my ma and dad never had a fair chance to use their poetry, music, intelligence, or creativity to live their dreams. All of that got buried in the mines and in their quest for survival.

Dad left the books behind and started a career in iron mining in 1916 at the age of fourteen. About that time an iron ore stockpile collapsed and crushed the bones in Grandpa Ole's lower left leg. Grandpa Ole couldn't walk without a cane after that. No one paid you if you got hurt at work in those days.[43] At the same time Dad's older brother Nels went back to Europe to fight the First World War. It wasn't talked about, but my dad had to start supporting himself and pitch in for his family. In fact those circumstances probably played a bigger role in Dad's failure to finish school than the spitball expulsion. Along the way Grandpa Ole had taught my dad how to chew Copenhagen snuff and Peerless tobacco, and how to perform other skills he'd picked up in Norway, including farming, carpentry, tool sharpening, and hog butchering. As it turned out, Dad would need all of them—save perhaps his tobacco habit.

For one of his first jobs, Dad and a friend, I think one of the Fredrickson boys, would walk every morning from New Burt to one of the mines at North Lake, a distance of about three miles. They had to ford the Carp River on foot because there was no bridge. After clearing trees and brush with hand tools all day for the mining company, they would walk back to New Burt, where the usual farm chores awaited them. It was during those years that Dad's commitment to the work ethic was severely reinforced, although I never heard him speak of a work ethic. He always called it "savage amusement" like all the miners did. It was a trait that he would later pass on to his children.

Dad was confirmed at Trinity Lutheran in Ishpeming in 1917. He was very proud of Trinity Lutheran. Indeed, he was also baptized there, married there, celebrated his twenty-fifth and fiftieth anniversaries there, and received the last rites there in 1985. He once showed my wife Judy a picture of his confirmation class and assured her that all twenty—"everyone in that photograph"—were "one hundred percent Norwegian." Later, after Dad retired my brother Ken's son Jeffrey had the altar at Trinity Lutheran refurbished in Dad and Ma's name.

Too young to make it to the first big war Dad later obtained a job mining iron ore underground at the Section 16 shaft just south of

Ishpeming. By the early twenties he had saved enough to buy a Ford coupe—a roadster he called it. Black-and-whites that I saw later told me things were picking up. He'd become a classy dresser and actually a sharp-looking guy straight out of the Roaring Twenties. My dad and Ma met sometime around 1923 when Ma was seventeen. Elsie looked pretty sharp too—in those pictures I mean. She had on a hat that looked like an upside down gladiola and a slinky dress with a low waist. Kinda like a flapper. I guess it was love at first sight, so they went ahead, married in 1924, and promptly started a family.

Later, when the economy turned sour, my dad was laid off at the mine, got in his roadster, and took the car ferry across the Straits of Mackinaw. He found a job building cars for Oldsmobile in Lansing, Michigan. My ma's sister, Aunt Mae, had already married and moved there with Uncle Hank (Toman) and wrote to my ma about it. Aunt Mae wrote that everything there was hunky dory—"gorgeous"— according to my dad. Using money Dad earned at the mine, Ma and their two kids—Marian and Ruth—took the train to Lansing and rented a bungalow. I didn't learn much about family life in Lansing because Dad didn't talk about it and would cut Ma off if she got started on it.

I don't know how gorgeous it was for Aunt Mae, but Lansing didn't work for Ma and Dad because he was not an assembly line or bungalow type guy. In 1928 my dad's mother, Grandma Nelson, went to live with the Lord. She was about fifty. It was some kind of gall bladder operation that went bad. Dad loaded up Ma and the three kids he had then into his roadster, and the five of them drove all the way back to New Burt to attend the funeral. They buried Grandma Nelson in the cemetery north of Ishpeming. From the pictures I've seen she was a beautiful, devout Norwegian Lutheran who took great pride in her family. She died in great pain and way too young.

When they got back to New Burt, my ma decided she'd had enough city life in Lansing, so she and Dad rented some rooms in a small settlement a few miles south of Ishpeming called Frenchtown. Neither one of them was French of course, except maybe a little bit on my ma's side, but they needed a place for Ma and the kids to stay. Dad had to drive back to Lansing because he still had his job at Oldsmobile and didn't dare give it up. Also some of their stuff was still there. I never asked Dad what his feelings were during the ride home from Lansing cooped up in his roadster with Ma, Marian, Ruth, and my brother Ken who had joined the family. Nor did I ask how he liked driving back to Lansing without them, or living there all by himself in a rooming house. I figured if he wanted to talk about that he would have. He did tell my sister Dort later on, and laughed when he told her, that the landlady at his rooming house left each of her boarders twenty-five cents as a Christmas present. It was one of the reasons he didn't like big shots that live in the city.

Whenever my dad talked about Lansing, which wasn't often, all I heard was him laughing at what Aunt Mae had written to Ma, burning himself at the factory, and the Crash of Twenty-nine. He'd picked just about as bad a time as you will ever hear about to go back to Lansing to save his job. Instead he lost it, packed whatever he had into the roadster, and drove back to Frenchtown, cursing President Hoover every mile along the way. He never forgave Hoover. Nobody paid you in those days if you didn't have a job. He never forgave General Motors either. The whole family ended up in rented rooms close to where Dad and Ma were born.

Later, my sister Dort was born in Frenchtown. Dad's the one who called her "Dort." I wasn't there of course, but I saw photographs taken with Ma's Kodak box camera by a neighbor—or perhaps a relative. There it is in black and white telling you everything you'd ever want to know about Frenchtown, those rented rooms and what a great family the six of them had already become before I was even born. I'm damn glad they didn't stop having children. Dad still didn't have steady work, so they must have been living on love and affection, but that's how my Norwegian/English family of Yoopers came to live in Frenchtown.

At eighty-two there's nothing I can do to prevent an economic depression. But I can hope one doesn't happen again and wonder— where do jobs come from? What destroys them? How do you get them to come back? I'd have given a pretty penny for answers to those questions back in the Thirties. I would have told Ma and Dad to watch out. Laid-off iron miners sprinkling salt into ten-cent glasses of beer at the Paradise Bar in Ishpeming blamed the Crash of Twenty-nine on greed, stock manipulators, and highbinders. Those who had doctorate degrees in economics proclaimed that the devastation of the poor wrought by the Great Depression was the result of cheap money, the Smoot-Hawley Tariff, insatiable excesses that roiled up during the

Roaring Twenties, stock manipulators, and farm production that had run amok. Everybody put in their two cents, but was anybody right?

Whatever it is that creates jobs didn't succeed in 1929, at least not where my dad and ma were. Hoover ran for office in 1928 on the promise of a full lunch bucket. After Hoover got in office my dad said he didn't need a lunch bucket so he threw it away. But there they were in Frenchtown—Dad twenty-seven with no formal education and Ma twenty-three with four kids and no prospects—in rented rooms my dad hated—with little more than the roadster, some furniture, a box camera, an axe, a pulp saw, and the clothes on their backs. Ma and Dad didn't cause any of it, so you can't blame them.

My folks liked to work; they were in the prime of their lives and got things done. My dad would have been happy to take a good job and move into a nice house, but that's what a depression is like. No one tells you it's about to happen. All of a sudden there aren't any jobs, and you can't afford things like a house, food, clothing, or medical care. But whatever was going through their heads when the crash hit, I never found out. It didn't show up in the photographs. They were all smiling. They didn't get in bread lines or cry about it.

My dad couldn't earn enough cash to support the family scrambling around for part-time work in Frenchtown or Ishpeming, but he still had the roadster. You could see it in his eyes every time he talked about it. That Ford coupe—he always called it his roadster—had been his pride and joy. I'll always remember him telling about buying it with money he'd earned digging iron ore at Section 16 and driving it through downtown Ishpeming on a Saturday night while people on the sidewalks watched. My ma must have seen him doing that too. Not many iron miners drove cars into downtown Ishpeming in those days. Later on he gave the fishing pole to my older brother Ken. Maybe Ken just took it because it had a reel. There wasn't one for me or my younger brothers, but that was okay. I could take it when my big brother wasn't watching.

I didn't mean to get started on fishing, or everything that happened later, because the way my dad told it, things went from bad to worse in Frenchtown big time during the following two years. The iron mines were basically shuttered. My dad being out of work, out of money and with four kids, would have to do something because Hoover and the politicians weren't doing anything. Dad and Ma were about to discover whether it was more than love at first sight. Recall that the circumstances Ben and Elsie found themselves in during the early 1930s took place in an area brimming with iron and copper and where the streets were supposed to be paved with gold. Also keep in mind that before my ancestors sailed from Europe, substantially all of the mineral rights in the area had been claimed by those who discovered iron on the Marquette Range and were later acquired by the mining companies.

At that time Grandpa Ole found out that a lady who lived in the New England location, Lydia T. Fredrickson Cox, had ten acres of bush land for sale in Green Crick. The parcel was two miles out in the woods south of New Burt and about five miles from Ishpeming. When Grandpa Ole heard about it he told my dad that since he wasn't doing anything else he ought to get going and build himself a house on those ten acres.

I don't know if Dad traded the roadster for the land or if he sold it to get money to buy the ten acres. It was one or the other because Marian, who was seven years old at the time kept telling me that Dad had to get rid of the roadster, and she kept saying that the ten acres cost a hundred dollars. We didn't clear that up until much later when I went to the Register of Deeds in Marquette. It was seventy-five dollars. I still wasn't born when the land was bought, but I sure heard about it. My dad was bound and determined to get land of his own so he wouldn't have to ask anybody where he could live. He vowed never to pay rent again.

Once he got his hands on the deed, my dad went back to Grandpa Ole to talk about building a house on those ten acres. When Grandpa Ole asked him what he intended to use for money, my dad told him he didn't have any. The ten acres consisted of the northeast quarter of the northeast quarter of the southeast quarter of Section 30, T47N–R27W, Tilden Township. That's not exactly the description that was put in the deed that was drawn up—but that's the land it conveyed. It wasn't land leased from an iron mining company. Dad and Ma obtained the title free and clear in fee simple absolute according to the deed dated January 10, 1931. It meant they owned all the legal interests in it, so when Dad and Ma took title they also owned the mineral rights. Problem was there wasn't any mineable iron ore on the ten acres, or any other ore for that matter. The iron lay to the north and to the northeast.

The ten acres had few traces of human activity except some big rotting pine stumps left by timber guys who'd cut down all the really big pine trees years before. Some of the stumps they left behind were four feet in diameter and cut three or four feet off the ground. They were dry as a bone; we used them for kindling. I suspect that lumber from the white pines that had once stood tall on those stumps built the city of Ishpeming. Dad didn't even find arrowheads or circles of rocks for Indian campfires on those ten acres. The Cox family may have cleared a little bit of land up by the northeast corner, but there weren't any houses or barns on it, not even an outhouse for that matter. It was wilderness that had been there from the beginning and was full of wild animals, but it was located on section lines that Burt's crews had surveyed. That was good because later on the Works Progress Administration (WPA) built gravel roads along the section lines that came together at the "corner" just north of our farm.

The only way in from New Burt when the land was bought was a narrow, two-rut dirt road about two miles long. It started close to New Burt at what Dad called the Millimaki Road and came in through the hardwoods. The two-rut bush road became known to us as Flaa's Road because it passed Flaa's sawmill just north of our ten acres. Nobody had ever written that name on a map. If you weren't told, you'd never find it. The Flaas had thrown down logs and built a corduroy bridge across a swamp at one spot, allowing you to cross with a horse or a car, if you had one, because cars in those days rode high off the ground. Once you got to Flaa's sawmill, the road narrowed even further. Even if you had a car you'd have to walk in to the ten acres.

As I said, Dad had to get rid of the roadster to buy the farm, so the condition of the road didn't matter to him so much at first. Ma couldn't drive anyway. They walked everywhere they went—including the five miles into Ishpeming to get groceries. Dad carried them home in a gunny bag slung across his back. It didn't matter if it was summer or winter, raining or snowing, forty below zero or whatever, he'd still have to carry the groceries—tin cans and all—to our house. When Dad had to go into town, Ma of course was left home alone with their kids and worrying about him.

People from the outside might look at those rocky ten acres with a smirk on their faces and tell you it was one hell of place to try digging out of a depression. Some of our relatives might have mentioned that, but they'd never say it to my dad. Sure it was a tough piece of land, but he didn't have a job, hadn't been offered any work, and didn't see it that way. Ma and Dad weren't poor anymore; they finally owned land,

and my ma loved those pine trees. Out of vanity, I guess, they called it their farm, even if it was mostly swamp, trees, ledge, stumps, hardpan, and rocks. Recall that way back in 1815 the land in that area had been described as not capable of cultivation.

Let me tell you, the glacier blessed that place with rocks. You won't find them on big farms you see down state or out in Iowa where one of Grandpa Ole's sisters, the Rystas, moved. No gold, copper, iron ore, or anything else had ever been found there, just rocks. If I had all those rocks with me in the big city where I live now, I could drive around the subdivisions and sell them, but there was no market for them around where our farm was. Everybody there had more than enough of their own.

There weren't any mortgages or bailouts available in those years either, so my dad walked out to the new place from Frenchtown carrying the axe and the pulp saw, cleared a place for a house up on the hill, and sawed down some spruce trees for two-by-fours. Grandpa Ole gave him some carpenter's saws, and somehow he picked up a bigger saw, a crosscut, about that time and that helped—except it was a two-man saw. He had no one to put on the other end except my ma. He needed tall jack pine trees with straight trunks he could cut into logs to put up the house.

The few remaining white pines on the ten acres were much smaller than those that had been cut down by the timber guys, and the place had some Norway pines but not enough. They wouldn't have made good logs to build a house because they were too scrawny, too knotty, or weren't straight enough. Ma's the one who told Dad they weren't straight enough, but Ma loved every single pine that ever emerged from a pine cone seed and didn't want any of the pines on our ten acres cut. Dad had to walk "out south" more than five miles to cut the jack pine logs that went into our house. I think he cut them on land owned by the Flaas because they helped haul them to their sawmill where they were trimmed by cutting slabs from two sides. During 1931 in the middle of the winter, Dad cut down and limbed seventy-two jack pine trees with his hand tools, and said later that when all the logs were on the ground he felt as though his house was nearly finished. Somewhere in that time frame I was conceived in Frenchtown.

Dad explained to me later that jack pine makes good logs and that spruce is good for framing if you forget about the knots, because it's tough. He sure liked things tough. Later on my brother Ken kept that crosscut saw because he wanted one of his friends to paint his own house on it. It now hangs in Ken's living room. I was given the carpenter's ripsaw Dad used, and that was even better for me because it has the farm buildings Ben and Elsie built painted right on it. My nephew Jeffrey Nelson was given the carpenter's crosscut saw Dad also used. It too has the farmhouse painted on it—Dad was included in that one. I think Ma may have asked Ken to have those carpenter's saws painted. If you want to know what the farmhouse they built ended up looking like, just take a look at those carpenter's saws. But again, I'm ahead of myself.

My dad, who chewed snuff, drank strong coffee, and on occasion swore a blue streak, borrowed Flaa's horse and dragged some of the logs he'd cut off our ten acres up the two-rut dirt road to Flaa's sawmill where they were sawn into one-inch boards for the rough flooring, dormers and the roof. The spruce was cut into two-by-fours for framing. I guess the Flaas, who'd also come from Norway, did it to get some of the logs Dad had cut for themselves, but I don't really know how the Flaa boys got paid because that was another thing Dad didn't talk about. He might have worked it off at Flaa's sawmill. Dad always paid his bills—I'll tell you that.

My dad and Grandpa Ole, with the help of my dad's friends, notched and toggled some logs together to erect our house during the spring and summer of 1931. Used bricks were stacked and mortared to build a chimney that was dug down into the ground and stood on the rock ledge right in the center of the house. It had a trapdoor at the bottom for cleaning out ashes and soot. The basement wasn't dug or poured at first. The house was built on cedar posts that were also dug down so that, like the chimney, they rested on the ledge. The house Dad built was about twenty-two feet by twenty-four feet, but with log construction and two floors it worked out to about eight hundred heated square feet—except that the second floor wasn't directly heated.

I never heard Dad call it a log cabin because he'd learned his lesson about putting on airs, although you could tell from the way he talked that he was proud of every spike he drove into it. It was his farmhouse, even if he lacked the money to complete it. To make it livable, my dad and Grandpa Ole salvaged some flooring from an Ishpeming schoolhouse that burned in 1930, the year before I was born. My dad had nothing to do with the fire, although he might have taken some satisfaction out of pulling the floors out of a schoolhouse that burned down.

Dad and Grandpa Ole cut out the worst charred spots, cleaned them up, and laid them down for floors. Actually, the floors were quite good. They put the hardwood maple on the first floor, avoiding any pieces that showed signs of having had a desk bolted to it. It wasn't stained or varnished at all so that when Ma or my sisters scrubbed it, what you saw was the kind of wood grain you find in a butcher block that's been scraped, scrubbed, and washed. There were no vacuum cleaners, you understand, and no electric outlet to plug into if you had one, just an old broom, a scrubbing brush, and a dustpan, but Ma kept those floors swept and scrubbed clean. You could eat off them.

The upstairs flooring was different—a kind of pine flooring—about three and a half inches wide. It probably came out of the gymnasium of the burned-down schoolhouse. It was a good floor too, and it had an orangey, brownish color in it that looked warmer, but it had some burn spots, gave off slivers, and didn't scrub up as well. My ma and my sisters tore up rags, braided carpets, and put them down to spruce it up and give you a warm place to stand without getting slivers in your feet when you dressed.

You had to step real carefully up the stairs Dad built to the second floor because there were no risers, and if your foot slipped you'd probably skin your shin on a sharp edge where bark had peeled off the step. It happened to Ma. I'd never seen her bawl as hard as she did then with those sharp creases in her shins. My dad had some more lumber sawed and installed new steps with risers right after that. It didn't bother me that those floors came from a burned-down schoolhouse. I was proud of them—they made me feel like we were living in a schoolhouse. With Ma there, I guess we were.

My sister Dort told me that the windows and doors were also salvaged from the schoolhouse fire in Ishpeming. Grandpa Ole gave my dad ten dollars to pick them up. Dad got something out of school after all, although at first we had no storm doors. The windows frosted over in winter because there were no storm windows during the first years either. They were added later. When the weather dropped below zero frost formed on the windows in lacy patterns—some like snowflakes— but sometimes in deep swirls that looked like landscapes. I often wondered who created those landscapes and what they looked like to my ma, who liked to look out the windows and used to write poetry about such things. She loved the windows and hand-sewn curtains for them that she kept starched and ironed, but if she ever wrote a poem about those swirl patterns, we never found it.[44]

I'd never have told it to my dad, but the logs, which he didn't have the money to stain or varnish, didn't match up so well. The bark peeled off the corners, and they weren't as straight as you'd like. He had to hurry to get them up of course, which meant that wood strips and rags had to be toe-nailed into the cracks to chink them and keep out the worst of the rain and the wind. Snow, too, would blow in through the chinking, or the cracks in the eaves, and form little drifts inside. My sisters Marian and Ruth developed chapped, raw hands helping to keep those logs chinked in the wintertime. Not all of them agree with me—I think because it might embarrass them—but as a little kid lying in bed, I watched my older sisters and brother carry out snow from the upstairs in cardboard boxes.

Later my dad installed white plaster chinking. It worked better, and I didn't have to carry out any snow or be embarrassed. When Dad earned a few more dollars, he put tar paper on the outside and built a porch. The tar paper had green sand particles embedded right in it so it looked pretty good. Later, he put brown shingles over the tar paper similar to what Grandpa Ole had at New Burt. That looked real nice even though he couldn't afford enough shingles to put them all the way up to the roof line.

Putting down on paper what happened in the early years makes me nervous. I don't want to get it wrong, and my sisters and my big brother keep reminding me that I don't have firsthand knowledge of everything. Of course I don't, but I listened at the kitchen table. Ma, Dad, and the older kids talked about the original building of that house and moving into it many times over the years. I don't think any of them made things up, not even my big brother. I'll admit it hurt not to be part of all the drama they talked about, too young to help and not able to add to the conversation. If I write something that isn't right, I'm sure my sisters or my big brother will straighten me out.

Before I get on with my own story, let's stop and think a minute. Try to put yourself into the circumstances my dad and ma faced. It is October 1931, and a vicious Northern Michigan winter is about to descend upon you. Most of the iron mines are down, and there is no steady work to be had. You have little or no money. There is no unemployment insurance or meaningful welfare. There is no health insurance. There is no Social Security, no Medicare, and no Medicaid. You have four children with one more on the way. The oldest is seven. You are about to move your family to a wilderness where black bears, wolves, and coyotes abound, into a homemade log house, recently built, with cracks between the logs that let the wind, rain, and snow into the house. There is no electricity. There is no indoor plumbing. There is no water well. There is no central heating system. You will live about five miles from "civilization" and there are no decent roads to get there. You do not own a car and there is no other means of transportation except for the legs and feet you were born with. There's very little food or firewood. The Great Depression had reduced Dad's and Ma's lives to an existential quest for survival.

Ma said later that her friends and relatives told her that she would never last the winter in "that place." She and Dad lived there for more than forty years. One of Ma's poems is about "tenacity." If ever there were two people who understood what that word means, it was Ma and Dad.

~~~

Map D
Salisbury Location (Frenchtown)

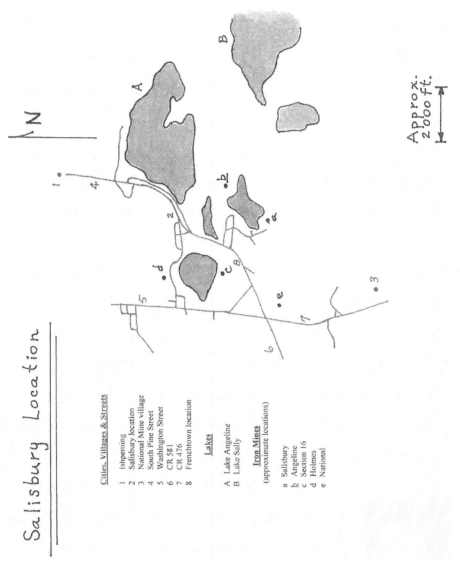

Salisbury Location

Cities, Villages & Streets

1. Ishpeming
2. Salisbury location
3. National Mine village
4. South Pine Street
5. Washington Street
6. CR 581
7. CR 476
8. Frenchtown location

Lakes

A. Lake Angeline
B. Lake Sally

Iron Mines
(approximate locations)

a. Salisbury
b. Angeline
c. Section 16
d. Holmes
e. National

Approx. 2,000 ft.

N

Map courtesy of Frederick Nelson

Figure 19
Old Ish, Section 16 Mine, BarnesHecker.

Old Ish. TO-ISH-60

Section 16 shaft house
Ishpeming, Michigan.
IM-SEC-01

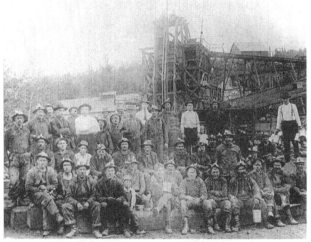

Miners at Barnes Hecker.
IM-BAR-10
(None of the miners in this photograph are known
to have perished in the 1926 disaster.)

Photographs Courtesy of Superior View Studios

Figure 20
Ben and Elsie at New Burt and Frenchtown

Ben and Elsie Nelson at New Burt with Marian and Ruth, circa 1926. Nelson family photograph

Ishpeming High School that burned in 1930. Photograph Courtesy of Superior View Studios TO- ISH-45

Ben with Ken at Frenchtown-1930. Nelson family photograph

Elsie (holding Dorothy) with (L-R) Marian, Ken and Ruth at Frenchtown-1930. Nelson family photograph

CHAPTER 6

Daylight in the Swamp

DAD, GRANDPA OLE, and the Kroon boys used Charlie Kroon's team of horses (King and Queen) and his barn wagon to move what little furniture the family had out to the new farm in the fall of 1931. Dad, Ma, and their four kids moved in with full pride of ownership. Ma was pregnant and must have been worked to death taking care of her kids and helping Dad, but I never heard her complain. My sister Dort told me later that Ma had rickets as a child, a consequence of insufficient vitamin D, but she never complained even about that, and in fact I didn't even know a thing about it until I heard it from Dort. Ma always said that even a poor house is a home if you own it. Besides, it was September and the leaves were turning so the new place must have looked damn good to her. Fall colors in the Upper Peninsula are spectacular. In one of her poems Ma described those colors as Mother Nature "flagrantly announcing" that winter was on the way. We didn't come across that poem until later. Ma was good at hiding her poems, like her fears, in places where they would not be seen.

My dad never flinched where there was work to be done, and when he moved the family out on the ten acres, there was plenty of it. At first most of the physical work involved in building and maintaining the place fell on him. He had no time for golf, baseball, or bowling as young fathers do today—I'll tell you that. Later, as the family grew, everybody had to pitch in to get it all done. Dad used to get us up in the morning to begin the day's chores or a bunch of special projects he had going (like building a barn or a woodshed, splitting wood, raking hay, or digging potatoes) by calling out, "There's daylight in the swamp, time to get up and get going."

The narrow dirt road became a problem when it became time for my two oldest sisters, Marian and Ruth, to go to school. They would have been able to walk a short distance to school had the family stayed in Frenchtown. Tilden Township, where the new farm was located, had built a new brick school in National Mine a mile down from New England Hill near the site of the Old Red Schoolhouse that had also burned. The new school was a two-story, solid yellow brick structure with an auditorium and a gymnasium that stood high on a hill amid piles of waste hematite ore and rock debris from the National Mine. It was surrounded by a black wrought iron fence, and had space for grades kindergarten through twelve. It was an excellent school with an excellent staff. The Northwest Ordinance, along with the tax value of proven reserves of iron ore lying beneath the surface and in stockpiles above, was doing its work, okay, but the roads you had to travel to get to the National Mine School from our ten acres totaled up to a little better than three miles.

Keep in mind that the two-rut road to our new farm was nearly two miles long and passed straight through swamps and hardwoods. Ruth and Marian, who were in the first and second grades that first year, had to walk to where they'd be picked up by the school bus at the Millimaki road. You couldn't drive a school bus over a corduroy bridge across a swamp. Sometimes they rode to school in Mr. Hunganin's horse drawn wagon—or sleigh in the winter I guess—if the bus wasn't running on the Millimaki Road. My ma told me how nervous it made her to send the two of them off to school down that narrow dirt road because of the bears, and how relieved she was to see those "two little heads bobbing along," as she waited on Flaa's hill for them to get back. Even in the wintertime. She also told me how glad it made her to know that Marian was seven years old and able to look after Ruth.

I was born a few weeks after school started and before the snow started to fly. The house didn't even have completed partitions. My sister Dort said you could go from the dining room into the living room by walking between the studs. My sister Marian remembers it. She saw me take my first breath. I never asked her who boiled the water, spanked my butt, or who cut the cord. Years later when I saw my birth certificate I noted that it didn't get recorded until the following January when Dr. Erickson, our family doctor, who apparently worked for nothing, found out about me. There weren't any health insurance plans in those years, so you'd best avoid birth trauma and not get sick. Worse, if you did get sick, you'd get a dose of castor oil. You'd get some of that no matter how poor you were or how deep the Depression was, and don't ask where it came from. There wasn't anything else.

The first light I saw at night came from kerosene lamps and lanterns which had to be carried up the steps when you went to bed. Later, my dad picked up a kerosene lamp with a mantle which gave off better light for doing our homework. That one was not carried upstairs because the mantle was too delicate. It wasn't until the late forties that an electric bulb hanging on a wire lit our kitchen, and by then I was old enough to help put it in.

Our collie joined the family the same time I did. She was named Queen—I guess by my ma—and seemed to be more popular around there than I was, but I was always proud of the fact that Queen, the farmhouse, and I were the same age and celebrated our birthdays together. Queen was proud of it too, and she showed it every time I petted her head and told her our birthdays were the same.

As I mentioned, there were no water or sewer lines serving the farmhouse. Dad built the house up on the hill near where the county might install a road, if they ever did, so it was logical to build on the hill I suppose. But up on the hill there were places where the rock ledge poked up through the hardpan dirt. The well my dad dug north of the house only went down ten feet. It turned out to be bone dry even though Grandpa Ole's willow branch water douser said there was water there. It might have been better in some respects if Dad had built the house and dug the well down on the flat area near Kroon's road where he could have driven a well point. But that area flooded in the spring.

Our ten-acre farm sat on the watershed of the Upper Peninsula. One crick that ran out of the swamp to the north drained out through the Fitch Crick and a series of bigger cricks into the Carp River and emptied into Lake Superior. The Carp drained areas where iron mining operations were conducted north of our farm so the water in the Carp was loaded with hematite. It ran red all the way to Marquette in those days. Neither the Fitch Crick nor the Carp River helped us, but the other crick draining that same swamp ran south across our ten acres and, through another series of cricks and the Ely River, down to the Escanaba River and on out into Lake Michigan. Our water came from that crick. The place where it crossed our farm was marshy ground covered by willows and tag alders. At first, water was collected from the north end of the ten acres near what would become Kroon's Road, but later the collection point was moved near the fence at the south property line.

In addition to fresh air, our farm was blessed with a crick that provided a pristine, pure water system that nobody else but the Flaas and the Kroons enjoyed. I never went back and checked out the topography or geology or anything like that, but there was nobody upstream to pollute it, and the water in that crick was ice cold and crystal clear, even in the hot summer. I just always wished our little crick had a name as fancy as the Fitch. Grandpa Carne lived in Ishpeming where they had indoor plumbing and drank city water they had to pay for that was pumped into their duplex from Lake Sally. He'd come out and hold a glass full of our water up against the sky. He did it about every time he came out to visit in the summer. He declared it to be the purest drinking water on earth. The way he peered into the glass as he held it up and turned it, I guess it must have been. I know I was damn proud of it.

The water in that little crick was the only water available on our farm in the early years. In summer you had to walk carefully across flat stones, slabs, and logs my dad put in across the swampy ground, and sometimes on grass tufts, to get to the crick. By the time I was old enough to collect water there, my dad had cleared out the brush, dug out the crick, installed a dam of rocks, gravel and black muck across it and put a pipe through the dam that rested on top of a big rock. In the summer you could hold a pail under the pipe and fill it up with fresh spring water. But not when it got to be forty below zero in the winter and the pipe froze.

That crick didn't ever completely freeze solid. But, you had to take the small hatchet Dad kept in the snowbank and chop a hole through the ice to get at the water. You had to do it carefully so as not to stir up the sand or the black muck. Next, you'd have to get out the bigger chunks of ice, using your bare hands if you couldn't get them with the little metal dipper that was also kept stuck in the snowbank across the crick. Then you'd carefully dip ice cold spring water into your pail one dipper at a time. You had to skim off small ice chunks if they got into your pail. If ice froze on the dipper you'd strike it on the axe and break it off, but not too hard or you'd dent the dipper. I never saw Grandpa

Carne do that or hold up any glasses of water in the winter. My dad called it running water. "All you have to do is grab a pail and run."

Figure 21

Running Water
Sketch by Richard T. Carne

It sounds primitive to tell it now, but you could do it—my sisters and my brothers did. They taught me how it was done. You'd collect two pails of water, about four or five gallons, and carry them, one in each hand, back over the marshy ground and up the hill to the farmhouse where you filled the reservoir on the end of the kitchen stove. You weren't done because then you had to go back and get at least two pails of drinking water to put on the wood bench Grandpa Ole built that stood in back of the table by the kitchen window. It felt good to know Ma had water she could use to cook, wash dishes, and scrub the floor. On Monday, wash day, we carried in I don't remember how many pails—maybe twenty—and dumped them into a big copper boiler Ma hoisted up on the stove. More buckets were dumped into a galvanized cold rinse washtub that stood on the wooden fold-up wringer rack. In winter Ma would sometimes supplement our water by breaking icicles off the eves of the house and melting them in the tubs. The day Ma washed the clothes involved the kind of "savage amusement" I've already mentioned. My dad liked that expression. I'll explain more about that later.

In the winter the kids liked to grab a pail and ski down the hill to the crick, but my dad said it took longer because you could only carry one pail back up the hill when you had skis on your shoulder. Oh, another thing about that wood bench I forgot to mention. It was the bench my brothers and I used at mealtime, so the water pails had to be taken off and moved onto the floor when we got around the kitchen table and ate. My brother Fred wasn't born until the Forties, so there were only nine of us around that little kitchen table in the Thirties. It was a good solid bench that over the years was painted with whatever color paint Ma selected to paint walls or window frames, so as the paint peeled or wore off in patches, it became multi-colored.

We also used the little crick to fill big wooden tubs my dad put up on higher ground for our cows and our horse. You had to water them on dry land short of the swampy area and get water in the tubs before you let them out of the barn. If they came charging down into the swampy part they'd have crapped all over and trampled the whole setup. One of us would stay up at the barn to let them out, and another would be down by the crick pouring water into the tubs and protecting the crick.

I can still see cows racing across the field with their tails in the air, putting their noses in that ice cold water we'd put in the wooden tubs and pulling it in. I worried about them drinking ice cold spring water, but they liked it. We'd bring the horse down to the crick after the cows got their bellies full. If they got enough to drink down by the crick you didn't have to carry water up to the barn. We got them to go back into the barn by putting bagged cow feed (coarsely ground wheat and bran my dad picked up at Spear and Sons) in feed buckets in their stalls. Sometimes we'd carry full buckets of water into the barn in the wintertime when it was stormy, and let it warm up before they drank it. The barn was heated by the body heat of the animals it housed.

There was an old-fashioned hand pump on Martin Graneggen's land over to the northeast of our farm. His son, Uncle Alden, had married my dad's sister Ann, and moved to Sandusky, Ohio. We used his pump if we were stuck, but didn't go there unless we had to. Uncle Alden called it a camp and only came north to check it out in the summer. The Graneggens didn't have ledge poking out of their land, so they were able to drive a well point deep into the ground. I can't put my finger on it, but there was something about that pump my ma didn't like. It wasn't that you had to pump it by hand—that wasn't it. It wasn't ours, and Ma was a very proud woman who didn't like to rely on others. She used it when she had no other choice. To get to it you had to go down the two-rut road to the Corner, past the mailbox, up Finn Town road a couple hundred feet, and down another winding two-rut dirt road that snaked through the hardwoods to Graneggen's camp—a total distance of about one half mile. They had painted the pump green and surrounded it with a wooden frame built from saplings.

Once when we were pumping water at Graneggen's, a dog came at us foaming at the mouth. I had never seen that before. The dog belonged to a guy who had rented the place. He said his dog had rabies. Ma told us kids to get up on the wooden frame. Queen saved us, but Ma had to hold her back from that dog. Rabid or not there'd have been no way that dog would attack Queen. You don't forget a thing like that, but I don't think that was it either. All I know is that Ma didn't like that water. She said it tasted rusty. Still, there were times when Ma told us to use that pump if a heavy rain or the spring flood made water from our little crick muddy. It was a long way to carry two buckets of water, I can tell you that. By the time you got home, the buckets were no longer full.

Another time, during winter, my ma tried to pull a copper boiler half full of water home from that pump on our big boxy wood sleigh all by herself. She'd done it before if she needed water to wash clothes, but that time she got frostbite on her legs. That sleigh had been hand-built, but I don't know who did it, and if you ever confronted whoever did they'd never admit it. I can't imagine how it ever got out on our farm. The thing was about four feet long, thirty-two inches wide and had metal strips nailed to the bottom of the wooden runners. All the varnish had worn off, and it was nicked and scraped from being used to haul wood. I think it came over on the Mayflower.

Someone had affixed a length of clothes-line rope to the front end so you could pull it, and from time to time the kids tried to use it for sleigh riding—but none of us liked it. That big, bulky, old thing didn't slide well at all. I can't imagine how Ma pulled it all the way to Graneggen's pump and back with a boiler half full of water, because there was deep snow, and like Grandma Carne, Ma wore skirts. I never saw her wear slacks in those years. Now that I think of it, getting frostbitten might have been why Ma didn't like that pump. Dad threatened to saw the old sleigh up for firewood, but Ma wouldn't allow it. I never liked that pump either after that, but sometimes we still had to use it.

Bathroom facilities on our farm were unique in the early days due to the fact that there weren't any inside the house, except a battered old chamber pot Ma kept on the landing halfway up the stairs. No one talked about it, but everyone got to take their turn carrying it out. Dad built an outhouse on the edge of the hill, but when it got real cold outside—like forty below zero, and I don't mean chill factor—you didn't use that.

Figure 22

When Country Wasn't Cool
Sketch by Richard T. Carne

There were no baths except sponge baths, or a weekly dunk in the big round laundry tub set up on the linoleum. Ma had it mailed in from Sears and Roebuck and put it down on the kitchen floor near the wood stove where the water was boiled. That linoleum had a nice bright blue pattern in it just like Grandma Carne's, but it was cold to walk on in the winter. The floor wasn't perfectly even so after a while the linoleum took the shape of the floor underneath it. In winter, of course, the kitchen stove helped keep you warm while you took a bath. I was firmly told that nobody would look, which, when I think about it, is not flattering, but as far as I know no one did. If I saw something I shouldn't have seen I'd not be telling it.

Sometime in the mid-thirties, I'm not certain of the year, a basement was dug by hand to provide a cool place to store the potatoes and rutabagas that were grown on the farm. Since the house stood on posts, Dad had to pour the concrete basement walls in sections between the posts and under the logs. The basement walls weren't all concrete. He couldn't afford that. He put a lot of rocks in the concrete forms he used to shape the basement walls. He had plenty of those. The ledge—he called it the "goddamned ledge"—poked up in the middle of the basement floor after he got it dug, which made walking under the first floor joists in the basement ceiling pretty much of a challenge. He attached a little shed on the west side of the house to cover the entry to the basement once the walls were in place.

The door Dad installed to enter the shed that led to the basement became the place where a kid who was nominated it blinded his or her eyes, counted to one hundred and called out, "ready or not you must be caught," when the kids played hide-and-go-seek, run-chief-run, or kick-the-can. The steel ventilation pipes Dad installed in the basement walls above the surface of the ground became peepholes when the kids played those games. We used them to look through the house to learn when it left the basement door and which way it went, but never confided that trick to the neighbors' kids or to visiting relatives like Donna Mae. We enjoyed stinging Donna Mae with that one.

Dad built cement steps in the little shed, but except for the protruding ledge the basement floor was mostly dirt. My brothers and I helped Dad pour a concrete basement floor in those places where the ledge didn't poke through some years later. The challenge of doing that was to get the concrete floor to adhere to the ledge without leaving a crack where water could enter. Dad accomplished that by roughening the ledge with a cold chisel before the floor was poured. We also installed a cement block wall under the center of the house to better support it.

Telling about the water facilities and laundry tubs reminds me about our kitchen stove. If you live out in the wilderness where temperatures can hit forty below zero, you have got to have a stove. Ma didn't write poems about taking baths, but she wrote a poem about our kitchen stove. The top of it was as black as any other wood stove of course, but the rest of it was two-tone—gray and light blue enamel—and pretty nice as I recall. I knew Ma loved that stove as soon as I saw her poem. There was some shiny metal on it, the oven door had a thermometer you could read from the outside, and there was a warming closet above the place Ma cooked. You could put your bread on top of that stove and toast it if you were careful that it didn't turn black. The oven door was on a spring that helped hold it up. That spring used to break a lot so Dad had to keep replacing it. Once the spring broke while Uncle John was closing the oven door and the door fell off and broke. It had to be welded. Dad was peeved because it left a black mark on the front of the stove. Ma used that oven every day.

I don't know where that stove came from, and I don't know who paid for it. It's something my dad never mentioned. It had the name Kalamazoo on the front so I always thought it came from there. To load it up with wood you'd take the lifter with the silver coiled metal handle from the top of the stove, insert it into the slots in the round lid over the fire box, lift the lid off and place it to the side so you could put fresh wood on the fire. Then put the lid back. Ma said to be careful when you did this. There was even a little door on hinges on the side that you could lift to slip in a small block of wood if the fire died down and there were too many pots cooking on the top. That little door sticks in my mind because once I fell off the big wood box and burned my chest on it. Dr. Erickson had to come out and bandage me that time. The burn healed up well but left a scar on my chest that looked like a triangle. It's faded away now. My dad had built the wood box from scrap lumber, the one I fell off, and one of the things the kids had to do was keep that box filled up without nicking the wall after the walls were plastered. The grates had to be shaken every day and the ashes that collected in the tray below had to be carried out and dumped. You would also have to scrape the compartment that held the ash tray with a little scraper on a wire handle. There'd be burning embers in the ashes so you'd better be careful and not burn yourself or set the place on fire.

Ma cooked and baked all of our meals on that Kalamazoo stove, but would never allow you to drink any hot water from the reservoir that was on the end of it. That was only for washing dishes, clothes or floors. Hot drinking water came from the banged-up kettle on the back of the stove, which she kept full and used to make tea and cocoa.

There weren't things like instant coffee in those days. Ma boiled coffee grounds in a large coffeepot that she also kept on the back end of the stove so it would stay warm. When coffee was poured from that pot you had to use a strainer to collect any grounds that were floating in it. Ma kept flatirons for ironing our clothes on the top of that Kalamazoo. She moved the ironing board in front of it when she ironed on Tuesdays. More about laundry later.

Sometimes while Ma was working in the kitchen we kids would sit around that stove and play word games with her like "I'm thinking of something that starts with." She wouldn't tell you what it was of course—just the first letter, like "S." Other times we played Twenty Questions, but at that time we called that game "Animal, Vegetable or Mineral." They laughed at me one time when I was a little kid because we were playing "Something That Starts With." I had given them the letter "W," and they couldn't come up with the answer. When they finally made me tell them I said, "it's wogs." They were letting me play the game, although I was too young to pronounce or spell "logs." My sisters and brothers never let me forget that. My brothers and sisters were good at those games, and at teasing, I'll tell you that. But even a little pre-school kid could win every now and then if he thought about it. When I came up with the answer all they'd say is that I'd done good, but I always knew they wished they'd got it before their little brother did. I guess I'd have forgotten all about that old stove and those games if Ma hadn't written that poem.

If somebody came out to visit, Ma would prepare coffee, get out her best dime store cups (or those that came in the oatmeal box) and the grown-ups would sit around the kitchen table, drink coffee, eat heavy cake or cinnamon rolls, tell jokes and gab about the damn Depression and the New Deal, which was still going strong by the time I was old enough to go to school. I liked to sit on the wood box by the Kalamazoo stove and listen because, even though I got burned badly there, I liked politics. The kitchen table had leaves hanging on the sides you could lift up to make a round table, so Ma could handle quite a few opinions. You could have written a book right then and there.

In the early Forties, after my dad got a job underground at the Lloyd mine, they'd still sit around that kitchen table and talk, but by then it was about the big new war in Europe and the Pacific, and they had switched over to Zwieback toast that Dad brought home from Meyer's Grocery. Zwieback toast was okay, but I liked Ma's toast better. If I took some Zwieback I dipped it in coffee.

One time my dad told a joke at that table about a guy at the mine who took home a steel eye-bolt from the mine and drilled a hole clean through the kitchen wall of his house, inserted the eye-bolt and painted it inside and out to match the paint on the wall, so he could hang his cuckoo clock there without it falling down like it had been doing. When Dad told a good one like that about a guy doing a ridiculous thing, he laughed till the tears spilled out of his eyes. Or the one he told about the English guy who couldn't read who sat at his kitchen table pointing at a German battleship shown in *The Mining Journal* he was holding upside down while bragging that "John Bull had put another one on her back."

Now, I should explain that the Kalamazoo wasn't the only stove we had. The farmhouse didn't have a basement in the early years so we couldn't install a furnace. To help provide heat Dad set up a box stove on a metal base in the living room. The box stove was maybe four feet long and about thirty inches high if you count the cast iron legs it stood on. It went in when the house was built, but I don't recall any name on it, just some numbers. If it was a patent number the patent must be still pending. It had a metal door on the front that you could open to shove in wood, and it had floral patterns molded into the cast iron sides. When a big fire got going, the floral patterns would glow cherry red. It was a good place for shaking the popcorn shaker, but you better keep the toddlers back. A black stove pipe led from the back of that box stove across the living room and up to the chimney.

Even though there was a gold ring where the stove pipe went into the chimney, Ma wrote no poems about that box stove that I ever saw. One fall, about the year I started school, Ma said the box stove was too dangerous. Dad threw it out, later took it to the junk man, and brought in a shiny, potbellied coal stove with isinglass windows that glowed in the dark. If you tried you could see imaginary figures dancing in the isinglass when the fire was lit, even if your brothers and sisters couldn't see them. That one used hard coal delivered by Spear and Sons that was kept in the bin in the front of the garage. The coal had to be carried in using a coal scuttle. Every day during the winter someone had to turn the top of that stove to the side, which opened two little metal doors, dump the coal into the funnel-shaped hopper, slide the top back, carry in an extra scuttle of coal and put it on the metal base that isinglass stove stood on, then shake the grates and carry out the ashes.

I was constantly told to stay back from the old box stove. We never sat around it. We did gather around the isinglass stove in the winter. With our fronts baked and our backsides frozen we'd listen while our battery-powered Zenith table radio blared out "Lux Presents Hollywood," or Dad listened to Gabriel Heater and the News. There were no stoves upstairs, and while some heat got up there from the two stoves on the first floor, the main source of heat upstairs in winter months came from the stacks of old blankets we slept under, and the brick chimney that ran through the center of the house. Miraculously, we never had a chimney fire.

As I said, I didn't see the place built, except I did see Dad complete the partitions and build separate bedrooms—one for him and Ma, one for my sisters, and one for us boys. It was quite a few years after that before the Celotex walls he put up were plastered and we got electricity. Dad brought out a Swede named Jumbo Peterson to plaster the first floor inside walls. Jumbo was a huge guy who held a mortar board with one hand and slapped on the plaster with the other. He put on two coats of plaster. It made an awful mess that Ma had to clean up. The upstairs wasn't plastered until later; I helped with that.

~~~

Figure 23
The Charles (Charlie) and Teckla Kroon Family

Charles Kroon and his wife Teckla

Front Row: Charles Kroon flanked by his daughter
Adele to his right and his son Elder to his left.

Back Row (LR): Charlie's sons Lloyd and
Ellsworth and his daughter Alice.

Photographs courtesy of Lloyd and Patricia Kroon

Figure 24
National Mine School Bus; The Teacher; National Mine
School that Burned in 1923, and 1925Ford Coupe

Early School Bus—
National Mine School. O-SCB- 03

The Teacher—1880.
O-SCH – 01*

National Mine School
that burned in 1923.
Photograph courtesy of Mary Johnson

A 1925 Ford Coupe
Similar to Ben Nelson's
first car with anonymous driver.
TR-AU – 156

*The school in this photograph is of an early school in Alger County near Munising. There was an early schoolhouse in the Green Creek location that was similar to the one shown. See *Red Dust* (1983, pages 11 and 34).

Numbered Photographs Courtesy of Superior View Studios

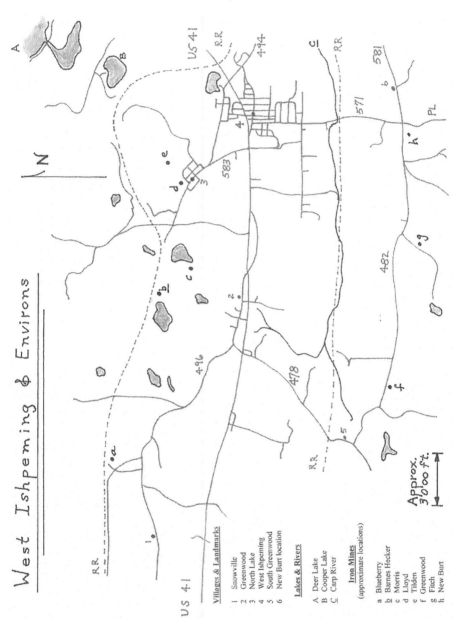

West Ishpeming & Environs

Villages & Landmarks

1 Snowville
2 Greenwood
3 North Lake
4 West Ishpeming
5 South Greenwood
6 New Burt location

Lakes & Rivers

A Deer Lake
B Cooper Lake
C Carp River

Iron Mines
(approximate locations)

a Blueberry
b Barnes Hecker
c Morris
d Lloyd
e Tilden
f Greenwood
g Fitch
h New Burt

Approx. 3000 ft.

Courtesy of Frederick Nelson

CHAPTER 7

The Orange School Bus

DURING MY PRESCHOOL years the bulk of our meager family income came from paychecks Dad picked up from part-time work as a gandy dancer on his brother Nels' section gang at the LS&I Railroad, or as a laborer on Works Progress Administration (WPA) projects that improved the roads that came into our farm.

Uncle Nels' section gang built railroad tracks for locomotives and steam shovels that shoveled iron ore from the stockpiles at the mines into railroad cars. When Uncle Nels returned from the First World War, he hired in at the LS&I Railroad, became a section boss there, and moved to the New England location about a mile east of New Burt, where he and Aunt Lena raised eight children. During the Depression shipments of iron ore from all the companies operating in the Lake Superior District fell from a fifty-million ton annual average during the 1920's to about three-million tons for 1932[45]. Operations were cut back at most of the mines, but since some ore shipments continued Uncle Nels retained his job as Section Foreman for the LS&I Railroad.

Using skills acquired in the First World War, Uncle Nels built and maintained shovel tracks at the iron mines, and also LS&I mainline tracks that carried iron ore from the mines in Ishpeming, Negaunee and environs to the ore docks in Marquette. Years later, Uncle Nels retired as Roadmaster of the LS&I. By then millions of tons of iron ore had flowed to the ore dock in Marquette over railroad tracks he built and supervised. Both my dad and I worked on Uncle Nels' section gang. I'll explain later what that was like.

My sister Marian, who carried lunch to my dad when he worked on the WPA, told me Dad was put in charge of the tool shed when they put in the new roads that led to our farm. But like his job on the LS&I Section Gang, the WPA provided only part-time summer work that generated little income. I don't think his WPA job lasted for more than one summer. In the winter the ground froze solid so no road building took place. His job on the LS&I section crew also only provided summer work because the ore boats that docked at Marquette couldn't get into the harbor when Lake Superior was frozen and the railroads weren't running.

To get cash during the darkest days of the Depression when the mines were down, people like my dad had to pick up whatever money they could. My dad earned some money from slaughtering our calves and selling the veal, working at Flaa's sawmill, or cutting wood or butchering farm animals for our neighbors. Our ten acres did not produce any cash crops. Just about everything Dad raised there was for home consumption or cattle feed. Staples like flour, sugar, salt, navy beans, oatmeal, and pork and beans had to be bought at one of the stores in Ishpeming. That required either cash or credit, both of which were scarce. During his spare time, when he wasn't clearing or plowing our land, Dad used lumber sawed at Flaa's sawmill to build a barn to house a cow Ma called Daisy, a horse he called Belle and some heifers and calves. He also built a woodshed and the outhouse I mentioned earlier.

Later, I learned that free enterprise economists, editorial writers and politicians don't like the whole idea of government-run work programs like the WPA. They call it socialism, even though that term is usually defined as government ownership and operation of the primary means of production. The WPA was certainly not that, but it is true, as Dad often complained, that some of the guys who hired in on WPA projects did little more than lean on their shovels and call it "Whistle, Piss and Argue." My dad didn't call it that, and he didn't lean on his shovel. He needed money. The WPA had made ingress to our farm possible by getting rid of the corduroy bridges and installing corrugated steel culverts—some you could crawl through—and by building two-lane gravel roads along the section lines that bordered our farm. The roads the WPA built into our farm were damn good as far as Dad was concerned, even though the cars that drove past our farm on them kicked up huge clouds of dust.

Dad always bragged about our ten-acre farm and lavished praise on Belle. According to him Belle was so fast that if he didn't hold her back, "the first furrow off the plow would be hanging from the fence."

He used to exaggerate a lot, but when he talked about Belle his eyes got glassy, so you knew she was special. I was sure Belle would have been the first filly to win the Kentucky Derby going away if she was entered. Dad used Belle to clear off the trees, stumps and rocks from our ten acres so he could plant timothy, clover, rutabagas and potatoes.

Ma took over some of it for her garden. Later on Dad sometimes used dynamite to blow up stumps, but in the first years stumps had to be cut and dug out of the ground with an axe and a grub hoe. The rocks were loaded onto a "stoneboat" sled that Belle pulled. Dad built it from maple trees that had a curve at the bottom from growing on the side of a hill. Maple is tough and makes good runners. A plank platform was spiked to the runners. The rocks were loaded, hauled off to the sides of the fields and piled along the barbed wire fences. Some went into the foundation he built for our house, and many were used later as the foundation for a second barn he built in the late forties.

There was no shortage of rocks on those ten acres, or on our neighbors' lands. The glacier had been generous in distributing flat rocks, round rocks, gray ones, white and black speckled ones, and even some that had iron pyrite, or fool's gold, in them. Many were worn smooth, like they'd been in an ocean and rolled around awhile. "Smooth as a baby's ass," my dad used to say. I often wished they'd stayed in that ocean longer and had been ground into sand. They worked up through the soil as you removed those on top, so there was a never-ending supply. Some said the frost pushed them up. We had to remove as many rocks as possible from our fields because you don't want to be holding onto plow handles if the point hits one head on. My dad said it could break the point of the plow. It can also hurt your shoulders.

All I know is that my dad, Ma, and all the kids loaded them onto the stoneboat every spring and built huge stone fences all down the side of the road in and along the south fence line. Later on chipmunks built their nests in those rock fences and Ma wrote poems about them. The rock fences we created are still there. If you're intrigued by looking at rocks, you can walk down Kroon's road to Charlie Kroon's farm. That family built a road across their hay field out of their rocks that went right up to their house, which was also built on the top of a hill. It's all grown back in with brush and trees today and no longer visible from the road.

By the time I started to notice things like rocks, cows, horses and potatoes, my dad and Ma had accumulated shovels, picks, hammers, kegs full of rusty tenpenny nails, pitchforks and crowbars that my dad kept in the woodshed and the barn, and laundry tubs, scrubbing boards, and pots and pans my ma kept in the pantry under the stairs. I don't know where they came from or who paid for them, but I got to use most of them, and they were good things to have around. They got to be part of the place just like Queen, Belle and Daisy did.

Dad put up a barbed wire fence around our ten acres, and pole gates so you could get in and the cows couldn't get out. He also built a pig house and a chicken coop. We got eggs from the chickens and some milk from the cows, but I don't think he was wild about taking care of milking cows. I know I wasn't—they had to be milked by hand two times a day year round. Missing a milking was not an option.

In addition to the calves our cows produced, Dad would go around in the spring and pick up new calves from our neighbors—ones they didn't want. If they didn't become veal, he'd raise the heifers until they were yearlings, take them to the bull on either Kroon's or Millimaki's farm, and then keep their calves and sell them as milking cows. Dad knew when to take them to the bull because they'd start running around the pasture and bawling. He said they were in heat. Any bull calves that came along were castrated by the vet, turned into steers and ultimately became beef.

One year we drove a small herd of cows, three Guernsey and one Jersey, to their new home. As we walked along I asked Dad why we were selling our cattle. Dad told me calves and heifers didn't eat as much hay as cows do and that he could make money doing it his way and buy milk at the store. I don't think that was it though, because Ma was never happy feeding raw, unpasteurized milk to her kids. He fed the milk we did get to new calves and our hogs. We always raised hogs.

There weren't any signs on the roads the WPA built in those days to tell you what they were, but we always called the WPA road that came in from the east the "Finn Town Road," and named the one that went west "Kroon's Road." We never completely dropped the name "Flaa's Road," which came in from the north, but mostly, once the roads were improved and graveled, we just called it the "Straight Road." We called the intersection where the three roads came together north of our farm, the "Corner." The two-rut road from the Corner to our farmhouse was not improved when the other roads were built because the ledge jutted into it at a point just south of the Corner.

Mail service started up a few years after the WPA completed the gravel roads. I don't remember the year, but I do recall that our mailman drove from the passenger side of his car. All the kids thought that was wild. We had gone three to four years without mail, except for some Ma received in care of her at Grandma Carne's house in Ishpeming. Dad put up a mailbox on the Corner. Our mailbox number was 444. When I got to ride the school bus later on I found out that no other kid had three numbers the same. It became my lucky number, and in later years I won a few dollars in the Michigan lottery with it. Our mailbox number was eventually changed to 772 as more people moved into the area. The mailbox kept my dad busy. Every winter the snowplow knocked it down. Ma insisted he put it back up so she could send letters to her sister Mae in Lansing, her brother Dick in Flint and her relatives in Battle Creek—if she raised the red flag.

I can't claim that I had anything to do with the move out to the ten-acre farm, chinking logs, putting up the mailbox or very much of what came later, except to live through it, but I remember the Corner. It was what you saw when you looked north from the dining room window, where the mailman stopped, and the way out. Sometimes you could tell if the mail had come if Ma had mailed a letter, because the red flag would be back down. We also played there. More than that, once the gravel roads were in, the Corner was where the big orange school bus, belching exhaust, came in from the east on the Finn Town road and stopped to pick up my sisters and my brother. It was startling to see that big orange bus emerge from the trees, pull up and come to a squealing stop at the Corner. Not just because it was an old tired-looking vehicle that belched blue smoke. It had to do with the fact that most of the cars that came in from the east on Finn Town road didn't break speed at all because there was a hill that dropped off right at the Corner. You could hear kids screaming when that happened. I found out later that everybody called it "Tickle Belly Hill."

Before I was old enough to go to school I'd stand by the dining room window, look out past the cedar tree across the field where my dad planted potatoes and watch that big orange bus come to a stop, pick up the kids and leave. In the winter of course, there'd be frost on the windows and snowplows would push up snowbanks that blocked my view, but that big orange bus was tall enough for me to blow a peephole in the frost and see the roof. I waited for it every day. I didn't go to kindergarten because the bus didn't pick up kindergarten kids— only kids who lived within walking distance of the school could attend kindergarten for half the day in those years. Ma gave me books like *Algernon, Peter Cottontail,* and *Goldilocks and the Three Bears* that she helped me read at home to keep me current. I also read comic books sent to us by Donna Mae. Comic books taught me to read; they became my McGuffey Reader. One year Donna Mae even sent me a microscope for my birthday. I also used that.

Figure 25

The National Mine

Photograph courtesy of Superior View Studios – IM-NATLMI73

I started my formal schooling in the first grade. I have a vivid recollection of standing on the Corner in September of 1937 and looking up at that big, rattling orange bus on the first day I was to attend the Tilden Township School in the village of National Mine. Like most cities, villages and locations around there that didn't have an Indian name, the village where my school was located had been named after an iron mine. The mine itself had closed before I started school. There were two streets, about thirty residences, a post office that sold confections, and one store (Annala's store) in the whole village. All were coated with red hematite dust.[46] I was wearing brand-new brogan shoes bought at Lofberg's store in Ishpeming and bib overalls bought by mail-order from Sears and Roebuck. I was carrying my brand-new pencil box and some peanut butter sandwiches Ma had wrapped in brown paper and tied up with string. There were five Nelson kids getting on the bus that day, so Ma had to get up early to prepare five lunches. The government had given us the peanut butter.

When I told Marvie about it later he was jealous because he wasn't old enough to go to school. The Jake Kaminen family had moved into a log house further back in the woods about a mile southeast of our farm. When their kids got old enough they walked through the woods to our house and waited for the school bus at the Corner with my big sisters, my brother and me. It's where I met Marvie, his sisters Nancy and Marlene and his brother Paul.

The bus driver, Ted Koski, wore a pilot's cap, a leather jacket, suspenders, and tightly laced high-cut boots that covered his red and black plaid MacMillan britches nearly to his knees. He told me where to sit and to behave myself. In those days everybody told you to behave yourself and where you could sit. I noticed that a lot of the boys on the bus wore high-cut leather boots just like Ted Koski was wearing and that they called him "Ted Kuski." Climbing up on my seat and looking out the windows of that bus back at the dining room windows of our house, where I had stood and looked out, was an adventure of epic proportions. I couldn't see my younger brother Bill looking out the dining room window, but I knew he was there. It was my first ride in a motor vehicle. My dad still didn't have a car when I started school. It was also my introduction to the kids who got on the bus as we completed the circuit. I liked to ride that big orange bus with my sisters and my big brother even though my feet didn't reach the floor. Dad wouldn't let me wear high-cuts and had said they were bad for your legs, but I always wanted a pair of high-cut boots.

Some kids said things to other kids on the bus they would never dream of saying at home. I don't recall specific stories, but I was entranced by stories of families in our locality, the likes of which I had never heard before. It would not be smart to repeat them even now if I did recall them.[47] Phil Hill, who was studious, quiet and only smiled, never told stories. Phil became interested in chemistry after his parents gave him a chemistry set for Christmas one year. Later, Phil became a research pharmacist with the Pharmaceutical Research & Development Division of Abbot Laboratories in North Chicago, Illinois.[48] Robert (Bob) Knievela, who got on the bus with Phil and sat with him, tried to hog the floor with his stories. He used to compete with Robert (also Bob) Lawer to tell the funniest jokes and the biggest whoppers. Their mothers would have wished they hadn't if they'd heard about it.

After a few weeks I worked up my courage and told the kids on the bus about the time my dad complained about Ma not getting up early enough and said he would get an alarm clock with an arm and a fist on it. All the kids laughed, but my sisters didn't. They told Ma about me saying that on the bus, and she was really peeved, even though my dad had actually said it. My dad laughed too, but after that I kept my mouth shut, my ears open, and picked up what I could.

The first day I went to school I learned my first lesson as soon as I climbed down off the bus. I expected all the kids to go right inside the school and get to work. That's what my sisters made it sound like when I listened to them describing school work while they washed dishes with my ma and dried them—going to school was serious stuff. The older kids getting off the bus had different ideas, including my big brother Ken. They fanned out for the apple trees in the neighbors' yards and the bluff just east of the school like swarms of bees. It still wasn't nine o'clock, so they didn't have to be in school, but they were more into picking delicious pear apples and jumping off the nearby bluff than getting to class on time.

Some of the older high school boys grabbed the new high school freshmen boys, with one boy holding his arms and the other his legs, and held them one at a time under ice cold water pumped by another upper classman from a pump at the bottom of the bluff. Each time ice cold water was pumped directly down a freshman's pant-leg, one freshman after the next, the whole bunch of them jumped up and down and yelled like mad. They didn't catch all the freshmen that first day, but their day was coming. Those upper classmen sure had good memories when it came to that pump.

My sisters' classrooms were in the same building as mine. Ma told them to make sure that I put my lunch in the lunch room and that I was in the first grade classroom by nine o'clock. They did. I was assigned a desk three rows from the window and two seats back. The desk had a hole for an ink well, but first graders weren't given pens or ink. We wrote with pencils we sharpened in the pencil sharpener over by the teacher's desk in front of the room. There was a shelf beneath the top of our desks for a tablet, pencil box and books. The seat of the kid in front of me was attached to the front of my desk. My seat was attached to the desk of the kid behind.

Our teacher was Miss Viola Mason. She had graduated from National Mine High School in 1927, later married, and became Mrs. Magnuson. Unlike the way the kids took off from the bus, all the kids seated around me took out their books and pencil boxes as soon as she walked in. I did the same. Miss Mason was young, pretty and strict. She taught both the first grade and the second grade kids in one room—she had to be strict. The first grade sat on the left side of the room facing the blackboard, the second grade sat on the right. Bob Knievela and Bob Lawer, the two comedians I met on the bus, were second graders. They spent more time snickering at the first graders, and me in particular, than they did on their assignments.

Miss Mason had printed the alphabet in white letters, both upper case and lower case, on separate black sheets of paper and strung them across the front of the room above the blackboard. Each day, after we recited the Pledge of Allegiance, the first graders had to print both upper and lower case letters in their tablets. Sometimes a kid would be asked to stand and read the letters out loud in front of the two classes. After a few days Miss Mason passed out readers that contained stories about animals. At the same time she divided the first grade class into Squirrels and Bunnies. When I didn't do so well reading the letters out loud, I got assigned to the dumb Bunnies. The two Bobs couldn't hold it in. Miss Mason had to strike the pointer she was holding on her desk. I got the message and in a few weeks became a Squirrel.

At ten fifteen the kids were instructed to use the bathroom, after which they bolted out the door for recess. They did the same after lunch in the lunchroom and again at afternoon recess. At first it didn't look like much classroom learning would take place. The girls jumped rope, played hopscotch and roller-skated around the school on the sidewalk, and the boys played marbles, softball, touch football and basketball. In the winter they built ice slides on the sidewalk that sloped down to the wrought iron fence and built forts for snowball fights. Sometimes they used inner tubes attached to the fence to launch big snow balls into the forts. When the snow was sticky for making snowballs, they also competed with each other trying to throw snowballs down the big chimney stack on the west side of the school. Paul Juntila in my class threw snowballs down that chimney when he was in the sixth grade. He was the only sixth grader who could. We all looked up to him. Paul went on to become a star basketball player at Negaunee High School, and later a dentist.

The boys also played pump-pump-pull-away. Now there's an unsupervised game that is not for the faint at heart. It started with all participants pushing and shoving themselves into a line on the sidewalk, except for one unfortunate soul who had been selected to be it. The older kids knew how to fairly and squarely make one of the smaller kids it. The one selected to be it had to stand in the middle of the field between the sidewalk and the wrought iron fence.

Yelling, "Pump, pump, pull away, grab your horse and run away," all the guys on the sidewalk took off for the fence and the kid named it was supposed to tackle one of them—usually another small kid struggling to keep up—and put him on the ground. If he did, the guy he tackled had to join him for the next run. It was tackle football with no pads or helmets played by kids of vastly differing ages and sizes. The game continued with the biggest and strongest running back and forth from the sidewalk to the fence while the smaller kids ganged up to tackle them. When one runner was left standing, he was declared the winner. If the bell rang calling us back to class, the first kid tackled (who would be one of the smaller kids) was the new it when the game resumed. I remember being it the first time I played the game.

On some days after lunch Mrs. Gleason would come into our room and take us to the kindergarten room behind our classroom. She taught kindergarteners there in the morning and gave singing instruction, one grade at a time, to all the grades in the afternoon. You could hear them singing from the first grade room. She also trained the High School Glee Club and put on the Christmas Pageant and the Spring Operetta. Mrs. Gleason—Miss Austin before she married Patrick Gleason, the Manual Training teacher—had a piano in her room, which she played even better than my ma or my sisters could. She made us stand up straight and led us through all the verses of "The Star Spangled Banner" and "America the Beautiful." I liked singing. I was better at it than I was at reading, printing letters or pump-pump-pull-away.

Kenny Dymond was in my class. He did not get along with Miss Mason as well as the other kids did. He would not listen and was always in trouble. When I told my ma about things he did she said to stay away from him. One day while we were on lunch break, Kenny told me he could buy candy at Annala's grocery store—which was a mile from the school—without any money. When I told him I didn't believe him he said he'd take me there and prove it. He did. After we picked out Guess Whats, Jaw-breakers, bubble gum, and Mr. Goodbars, all he did was sign his dad's name. I was late getting back to class that day and severely reprimanded. Miss Mason reported me to my big sisters, and they told my ma. I remember what Kenny did that day because I learned the rudiments of credit. It was made indelibly clear to me when I got home, though, that I should never, ever, never play hooky again.

At four o'clock we got back on the bus and were driven down the hill through old iron ore stockpiles, past Annala's store, out past the Hercules Powder Mill (a dynamite factory), through Finn Town, and up Finn Town Road back to the Corner. Once at home we were treated to the cookies Ma baked while we were at school and told to do our chores—carrying in water and firewood and watering and tending the cattle. My sisters worked with my ma preparing supper, cleaning, or darning socks. During the school year, along with all the housework, potato and hay growing and our chores on the farm, the kids were expected to do their school work on time and to do it well.

After a year or two, National Mine got rid of the big orange school bus and bought a red, white and blue one. It even smelled brand-new. By then my brother Bill, who had been born in 1935, was in school and the Kaminen kids got on the bus with us down on the Corner. Bill Dally became our driver. The kids from Ely Township, which adjoined Tilden Township, were driven to National Mine by Otto Anderson. Otto's wife, Andrea, later became the cook at National Mine School. After that we didn't have to carry our lunches. Mrs. Anderson was a wonderful cook who prepared amazing hot lunches for several hundred students and staff using low-cost subsidized ingredients. Her kitchen, smaller than a typical kitchen in a modern family home, had been created by walling off an area in the manual training rooms.

~~~

Map F
Tilden Township

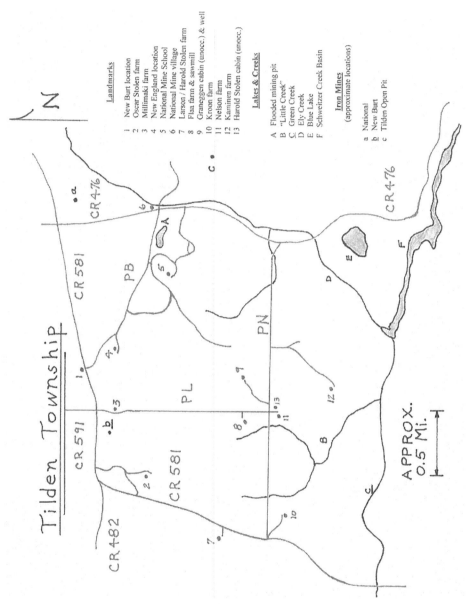

Landmarks

1   New Burt location
2   Oscar Stolen farm
3   Millimaki farm
4   New England location
5   National Mine School
6   National Mine village
7   Larson / Harold Stolen farm
8   Flaa farm & sawmill
9   Graneggen cabin (unocc.) & well
10 Kroon farm
11 Nelson farm
12 Kaminen farm
13 Harold Stolen cabin (unocc.)

Lakes & Creeks

A   Flooded mining pit
B   "Little Creek"
C   Green Creek
D   Ely Creek
E   Blue Lake
F   Schweizer Creek Basin

Iron Mines
(approximate locations)

a   National
b   New Burt
c   Tilden Open Pit

Courtesy of Frederick Nelson

Figure 26

The National Mine School and environs—1930s and 40s.
Photograph courtesy of Marie Flack Keto

Homework by Lamplight—Sketch by Richard T. Carne

CHAPTER 8

The Lloyd Mine, 1937 Ford, and Zenith Radio

I HAD JUST begun school in the first grade when the iron mines started hiring again in 1937. After being essentially unemployed for nearly eight years, my dad hired in as an underground miner for the Cleveland-Cliffs Iron Company—first at the Lloyd mine in North Lake and later at the Mather A in Ishpeming. The Lloyd shaft was near the site of the Barnes-Hecker disaster. Ma worried about that.[49]

Dad resumed his mining career in 1937 as a "Company Count"[50] employee. He was later promoted to a position as a contract miner for which he and his partner were paid to drive new drifts or raises on a piecework basis. To work at the Lloyd mine Dad had to walk about five miles each way, which increased the time he had to be away from his real interest—farming. He used to say, "Talk is cheap. It takes money to buy a farm." He didn't have any. He took the job at the mine because he had no choice. Years later I mentioned to him offhandedly that I was thinking of buying a farm in Lower Michigan. By then he had sold his farm and was living in Sunnyside Estates—a retirement development near Ishpeming. Without a second's hesitation he said, "If you do that Ma and I will come to visit." That said it all because in their later years neither Ma nor Dad liked to travel very far from home. Had I followed through on the suggestion that I buy a farm, I'm sure Ma and Dad would have come to visit.

Let me tell you, in the Thirties there was no time or money to play games. Dad had to work his jobs with the WPA and the LS&I, tend his farm, and grow our own food. The lessons taught by the Great Depression never left him. To work a farm in those days you needed a horse. Now Marvie's dad, Jake Kaminen, our neighbor to the south, bought a Fordson tractor that he used on their farm. I never learned how Jake accomplished that, but he had one. Dad said again and again that he preferred horses, but the fact was that if he couldn't afford a car there was no way he could afford a tractor. The horses Dad bought ended up driving him.

Dad often told a story about a neighbor who kept their horse in the barn, fed it oats, curry combed and brushed it every day and never worked it.[51] That horse died. I heard Dad say it a hundred times— "They killed that horse with kindness." None of my dad's horses or any other critters around our farm would ever suffer a similar fate. My dad said that if a horse really matters to you, it has to have its head and a purpose—something it can do. He loved and treated his dogs the same way.

Dad loved horses even more than he liked to drive a car, which says a lot. You could see it in his eyes when he talked about his first horse— Belle. His attachment to horses didn't mean Dad reveled in being a poor dirt farmer—I'm not saying that. He just liked to put the bit in Belle's mouth, pull the hame straps and belly bands snug, hook the tugs to the whiffle tree, thread the reins though the brass rings and drive her.[52] To Dad a damn good horse with bulging muscles straining to pull a heavy load was a thing of classic beauty. He even enjoyed riveting the harness back together if it broke, although he'd let you know if you were the one who broke it. Horses were in his blood, but he didn't shoe them or trim their hooves; he had to bring the blacksmith out to our farm to do that.

I still hear the instructions he gave me. "Don't you sneak up from behind and poke at a horse, Lee. You'll spook 'em. Always remember that a horse can kick fast and hard. Talk to 'em. Let 'em know you're there—use a firm hand." He always called me by my middle name when he wanted to be sure I understood. It's why I started to think of myself as David Lee. Although Dad treated every horse he owned with firmness and respect, you always knew that Belle was special.

Belle liked to work—she thrived on it. Dad had somehow scraped a few dollars together in the first place to buy her. That was shortly after he acquired the ten acres. I don't know the exact date or where that money came from. I can only relate that Dad had a way of getting things done, and Belle was there. Grandpa Ole gave Dad the harness. After he'd built a barn out of lumber sawed at Flaa's sawmill to house her, he and Belle worked untold late hours clearing the farm, stoneboating rocks, pulling logs, and planting and harvesting hay, potatoes, and other crops. They were a matched team. He loved Belle—why would he sell a horse he loved?

I was six years old when Dad got the job at the Lloyd shaft in North Lake. He told my sister Dort some years later that it had been so long since he'd seen any money he'd, "forgotten what it looked like." But he had to walk five miles due north from our house out past the Millimaki Road to get there. He'd have to put in an eight-hour shift digging iron ore—and maybe overtime—earn about five dollars, and on some days walk into Ishpeming for groceries before he walked back home.[53] It was a walking trip of about twelve miles. When he got home he had all his kids and the farm animals to look after, potatoes to hoe, hay to cut and wood to stack. Without a steady job for nearly eight years, he needed money to make a down payment on a car. It was the job or Belle.

That's how Belle, by then a legend in our family, got sold. Queen, another legend, might have cried because she loved Belle too—used to run and play games with her in the pasture—but my dad didn't cry. I only saw him do that once. That was later when Grandpa Ole died, but it hurt him badly to sell Belle.

I believe it was around February or March because my sister Joanne hadn't been born. I remember deep snow on the ground and that brand-new 1937 Ford two-door sedan. The older kids were in school. I was in the first grade, but I was home sick with a cold. Ma was trying to get me to read *Algernon*, but I was not about to read that day because I'd heard Ma and Dad whispering and knew Belle would be sold out in front of the house. I stayed in the living room with my brother Bill to be close to the isinglass coal stove. We ran from window to window looking out between patches of frost to see what was going on.

Belle, sporting a shiny jet black coat—notwithstanding what Dad said about our neighbor's horse, he used to feed her oats and curry comb and brush her—charged up through the snow snorting, with all her bells and chains jingling like she always did. White frosted breath plumed from her nostrils as she pulled a sleigh. I could be mixed up about the sleigh, but I never saw the sleigh after that, and that's how I remember it. Dad let Belle go with all of her harness. He said the harness belongs to the horse. Like I said, he treated his horses with respect—like a friend. Ma refused to look because of what that horse meant to my dad. Belle came up on the two-rut road in front of our house at a near gallop with Dad running behind with his black Scotch cap down over his ears, wearing Gold Seal boots and an overall jacket, and holding tight to the reins with his chopper mittens. He held her in because Belle liked to stomp around. She was thinking she would get a load to pull and was all ready to go—not knowing she was being sold. She gave the buyer that fierce wild look she had and then turned her head with a quick look back at my dad.

I don't know what he got for her, but it didn't take long before Belle was gone, leaving behind a big empty stall in the barn. Dad had to go back and clean it out. It stayed empty for several years. The Great Depression had taken Dad's job, forced him to sell his roadster, landed him out in the wilderness five miles from Ishpeming on a rocky ten-acre farm facing brutal work, and sent him underground to dig ore at an iron mine. And then it took Belle.

Dad sold all the cattle at the same time to get enough for the down payment. My sister Dort remembers coming home from school, being told that Belle and all the cattle had been sold and thinking we were moving into town. It was tough for Dad to sell all his animals, but he knew he had to do it and hoped that he could replace most of them once he got working at the mine. He could never replace Belle—he knew that.

A few days later Dad drove the Ford sedan home and parked it on Flaa's Road at the Corner against a big snowbank pushed up by the county plow. It was a sight to see from the dining room windows where Bill and I were standing. I stood there for a long time looking out through the frost at that shiny black Ford parked up against the pure white snow with the sun glinting off it, hoping I'd get a ride in it. I'd never ridden in a car.

It was brand spanking new with hubcaps, shiny chrome and a wonderful new car smell. It had an eighty-five-horsepower V-8 engine. Dad bought it on credit for six hundred dollars and was given a coupon book that he took to the Miners' National Bank in Ishpeming every month to make his payments. As much as my ma hated to see Belle go, she cried when she saw that Ford. It meant Dad wouldn't have to carry groceries home from Ishpeming and would have more time to be home.

It also meant Ma could get into town to visit her mother and take a drive on Sundays. My brother Bill was born three years after I was, so Ma had six kids at that time to watch over and too much work to do much walking—although in the summer Ma liked to walk with Queen.

Black was the only color Ford you could get back then, and Dad would never buy a GM car. Not after Lansing. Later, Dad built a garage to house his new Ford, but at first he couldn't drive it up to the house because the two-rut road in from the Corner was covered with snow about four feet deep. It hadn't been improved or graveled by the time Dad bought the Ford, and the ledge still jutted into it down by the Corner. It meant the snowplow couldn't plow our drive. To get the car to our house we had to shovel more than one hundred yards from the Corner. UP winters had a nasty habit of blowing snowdrifts right back in no matter how long it took to shovel the road.

You could see the kind of white pine trees that once grew on our ten acres from the three tall ones that stood in a row like sentinels along the two-rut road in from the Corner, as though a landscaper had planted them. Crows liked to sit on top of them and would raise holy hell if anyone walked anywhere near them. It seemed to me that the three pines would have been excellent candidates as logs or lumber for the house. It was my ma that made Dad keep them there. Once she took a picture of them with her box camera, so I knew they were important trees. She only aimed her box camera and wrote poems when she saw something that was special to her. That was confirmed later when we found a poem she wrote about crows, and another one about a pine tree. There was a fourth white pine, not really in the same line, near where the garage was built.

Several years after Dad bought the 1937 Ford, Marquette County Road Commission guys came by with big trucks and graders and blasted out the ledge at the Corner that we used to play on and built a gravel road into our farm. They told my dad they were taking over the right of way so the snowplow could get in. Ma begged them to spare the three pines, but the County guys said they weren't on our land, and they cut them down. They gave us the logs for lumber. My ma cried so hard she wrote a poem about those pines. That's probably why I still remember them.

But things were picking up. Dad bought the Zenith table radio in 1937 shortly after he got the job at the mine. It had a round top and stood on a little black table in the living room next to the piano. Until we obtained a telephone party line a few years later, it was our only contact with the outside world except for the mailman and the school bus. Sometimes the Zenith made squealing sounds like a short-wave radio, but it usually worked quite well. The day we turned it on was the first time the live voice of a person not on our farm was heard there, although originally the only station that came in was WDMJ in Marquette. Later, WJPD started to broadcast from a radio tower it erected out by the cemetery north of Ishpeming. The Zenith brought the world to our ten-acre farm. We were able to use a radio even before we got electricity because it worked off a car battery that stood on the living room floor next to the black table and had alligator clips attached to the posts.

To charge the battery Dad and my brother Ken, who was about twelve years old then, installed a windmill on the roof of our house. It had a rope you could pull so the windmill wouldn't keep on spinning if the battery was fully charged. That windmill made one helluva racket, I can tell you that. It shook the whole place when those big winter blizzards hit and no one had pulled the rope. When that happened I used to lie awake late at night wondering if all of us were headed for the Land of Oz, because my Aunt Mae had sent me a book about Munchkins, Wizards, and a gal named Dorothy when I had to be hospitalized with pneumonia while in the fourth grade.

The family clustered around our Zenith when boxer Joe Louis fought Max Schmelling for the heavyweight boxing title in 1938. Schmelling had done well in their first fight, although I don't remember who won, and the ballyhoo for the second fight was so great it reached our ten acres and me, a kid seven years old. Grandpa Carne always talked about English fighters and guys like Gene Tunney and Jack Dempsey. He was a nut when it came to prize fighting and would come out to our farm to listen to them. He had a Philco floor model radio of his own at his house, but for reasons not told to me, liked to hear the fights broadcast on our Zenith. Grandma Carne, Uncle John and Uncle Doc brought him out to hear the second Louis-Schmelling fight.[54] Grandpa Carne couldn't drive a car.

They all took their pop glasses and heavy cake, moved chairs from the kitchen and dining room, and huddled in close around the Zenith because no one wanted to miss the fight—not even Grandma Carne.

Everyone expected a long night listening to a staccato blow-by-blow description of a fifteen-round match. Grandpa Carne never drank liquor or beer like my dad did. My ma never drank beer or liquor of any kind. Neither did Uncle John or Uncle Doc. My ma wouldn't let Dad drink any beer when the Carnes came to visit, of course, but Dad had brought home strawberry pop in big bottles from Elson's Bottling Company. He left them alongside a pan of Ma's heavy cake out on our kitchen table, because he knew his in-laws—the Carnes—would all be out for the fight. Dad never mentioned it, but I always knew he was glad Grandpa Carne thought our Zenith was better than his Philco. After they all got in place around the Zenith, I went back to the kitchen to refill my jelly glass with strawberry pop. By the time I got back the fight was over. Louis flattened Schmelling in the first minute of the fight. I was the laughing stock of the evening for missing the whole fight over a glass of strawberry pop. Years later Grandpa Carne was still laughing over that one. My ma told me it was okay if Grandpa laughed because a good glass of strawberry pop, she said, beats a prize fight any day of the week.

Dad had picked up a Victrola somewhere. He put it in our living room over by the stairs. It was about four feet high and housed in a beautiful black cabinet that had wooden slats where the music came out and shelves to store records. The records had red labels on them—and names like "Waters of Minnetonka." It could've come out to the farm on Kroon's wagon when they moved out from Frenchtown. I'd have to ask my sisters about that. It had a picture of a dog listening beside a big horn. RCA I think it said. You had to crank it up to play a record—I don't remember if they were 78's or 33's in those days—and if you didn't crank enough the record would turn real slowly and sound funny. If you cranked too long and moved the little lever the record would speed up and that was worse. All the kids laughed when that happened and would move the lever even if Ma said we shouldn't.

Dad liked to play "Waters of Minnetonka" and "Nicolena" on the Victrola—the latter sung in Norwegian. It went something like, "O Nicolena da da da dee da da-O Nicolena da dee da dee da . . ." And on from there. Slow that one down too much, or worse speed it up, and you have got yourself a riot. Dad listened to it all the time—absolutely loved it right up to the line where the love-forsaken Norwegian singer threatened to jump into the sea if Nicolena left him. I have the distinction of not only moving the lever, but of sitting down upon "Nicolena" and breaking it in two. Nobody laughed that time, unless they did where I didn't see them. It must have been real bad, because it still stands out in my mind. My brother Ken remembered me sitting on that record too, and years later, after Dad had gone to live with the Lord, gave me a tape with "Nicolena" on it. It sure sounds good. I learned later that Dort and her husband Bob recorded Dad singing it and put it on a disc. In retirement Dad sang that song with a joy you can feel, but only he knew.

Along with the improvements to our house our family was growing. My brother William (Bill) was born in 1935, and my sister Joanne (Joanie) was born in 1938. My brothers and I used to play on the Corner. Bill and I used to sail wood boats we'd carved ourselves, and affixed a mast and sail to, in the big mud puddle that formed where the gravel road climbing the hill on Kroon's Road turned sharply up the hill to the north and became Flaa's Road. I was only about seven or eight years old, but I'd been warned to look after Bill and watch out for pulp trucks. As soon as I heard one grinding its gears and gunning its engine so it could climb the hill on Kroon's Road, turn the Corner and continue up the hill on Flaa's Road, something told me to get off the road.

Panic set in. I yelled, "Bill, a pulp truck's coming!" He and I grabbed up a few sailboats and each other and scampered up the bank on the outside of the curve to get off the road. We looked back into the driver's face as he strained to hold his pulp truck on the road as he entered the Corner. Before he could make the turn the whole load of slippery, peeled pulp wood slid off the truck and sent logs flying all around Bill and me. None of them hit anybody. It was a close one the driver said, while he handed me one of our sailboats which was smashed, but mostly he was glad to load up the peeled logs he'd scattered and get the hell out of there—glad he wouldn't be sued I suppose. But hardly anybody sued in those days. My brother and I fixed that one boat and sailed it with the other ones after he left. We never said a word about it to Ma.

That's what it was like; there were lots of close calls during the Great Depression. One day Marvie, the neighbor kid who played with us on the Corner, slipped off the cliff south of our house, fell twelve feet and landed on a ledge. We'd been climbing. Even though he could've been killed he told us not to tell his ma—said he was okay. We didn't tell his ma or ours because Marvie was a good kid to play with, and he could ski jump, catch trout and shoot the head off a partridge with a twenty-two rifle. About 1951 he became a tail gunner during the Korean War. I recall Marvie standing there at the bar at Kip's 41 Club out west of Ishpeming, showing off his uniform and having a few beers with some of our friends the night before he went overseas. The newspaper said his B-29 went down somewhere in the Pacific and that those at home were the lucky ones. I sure do remember the good times we had fishing and playing kick-the-can, and I will never forget the day he fell off the cliff. I wonder what he'd have done with his life if he'd made it back.

One time during the spring melt big chunks of ice slid off the roof of our house. We always accepted those ice slides as a rite of spring. But that time they landed right in front of my sister Joanie, who was three years old and dressed in a brand-new woolly beige snow suit. I mention that snow suit because it wasn't often my folks could afford to buy us clothes. Mostly we wore hand-me-downs. When Ma heard that ice come crashing down and Joanie's scream she ran from the kitchen, grabbed Joanie and hugged her. There were two little footprints in the snow next to those ice chunks. Ma about fainted. That's the way it was for kids in the Great Depression. "Nothing to fear but fear itself," President Roosevelt said during one of his fireside chats. So we didn't.

I was reminded of those days during the Great Depression when my sister Dort and I visited the old place during a family reunion of the kids and their families after both Dad and Ma had passed away. Dort reminded me of the day the ice fell right next to Joanie. The current owner let us in. He was tearing down a wall on the north side to build a new wrap-around porch and had taken down some plaster and Celotex, which exposed logs Dad had cut for the farmhouse. Dort recalled the logs being put up, moving out to the farm, walking between the studs, and then she teared up. Like me, Dort had survived the Crash of Twenty-nine she was born into, but had not forgotten it.

~~~

Figure 27

The Carnes in the 1930s and 40s

William Carne
(Uncle Doc) and John
Carne (Uncle John)
repairing a flat tire
on Grandpa's 1922
Chevrolet (circa 1932).

Grandpa and Grandma Carne at their
camp and garden on land that became the
Ishpeming Sports Club (circa 1938).

Grandma Carne (R)
with Aunt Cretia
Ishpeming, Michigan (circa 1940).

Grandpa Carne (L) and Uncle
John Carne at the Nelson
farmhouse (circa 1940).

Nelson family photographs

Figure 28
The Jacob and Helen Kaminen family
Photographs courtesy of Marie Flack Keto

Jacob and Helen with their children (L–R) Nancy,
Marlene, Paul and Marvin, circa 1941.

Marvin Kaminen in his Air Force uniform (1951).

CHAPTER 9

Lutefisk and Brook Trout

MA ALWAYS SERVED good food on our kitchen table as far back as I can remember, although my sister Marian tells me that was not the case when the family first moved out on our ten-acre farm. The way she tells it, Divine Providence provided our food in the early years. I never fully understood or questioned where our food came from, but it was there. One thing was clear. From wherever it came and whatever it was, Dad never cooked it. It would have been unthinkable for Dad to tie on an apron and cook. He always said that where he came from, "men were men and the women split the wood." So it was up to my ma and my sisters to cook our meals, put them on the table, and clean up afterwards. Ma ran the kitchen; Dad was pleased she did, and so was I.

But Ma wouldn't serve wild animal meat no matter what deprivations were visited upon us by the Great Depression. I heard that some of our neighbors ate bear meat—but that could never happen in our family. Ma did serve partridge during bird season and brook trout and bass during fishing season, okay, but not the meat of wild, four-legged animals. Even in the fall, during deer season, when most of our neighbors shot a buck, nailed their antlers to their garages and ate venison steaks, Ma wouldn't cook it. She said the local venison had a strong wild taste and wasn't at all like beef from the store or deer shot in the Lower Peninsula that had been corn fed in farmers' fields. I tried venison once or twice and agreed with Ma.

Since Ma wouldn't cook wild animal meat—no rabbit or duck for sure—our meat consisted of the pork Dad butchered and hamburger and round steak purchased at Meyer's Grocery or Leffler's butcher shop in Ishpeming. Being an English lady descended from folks who lived near Land's End, Ma would have liked to serve us fancy English stews, shepherd's pies, and seafood. Like Grandma Carne, she believed that the women should wear starched aprons when cooking and flowered hats with veils when they went to town. She told us all about that and showed us pictures. She said the family she came from wasn't royalty or anything like that, but they had class.

Ma's ideal English dishes got somehow mixed up with reality. She didn't like to serve grilled or fried food. She prefried hamburger and round steak, but always added water and served them as meat balls and Swiss steak. We were served Cornish pasties, meat pies, roast beef, pork and roast chicken we'd grown ourselves—sometimes canned sardines—and potatoes, along with rutabagas, carrots, beets, and green beans Ma had grown in her garden. Dad contributed canned goods like soup, pork and beans, ravioli and spaghetti he carried home from the store. Ma and my sisters also canned—"put down for winter"—a lot of wild berries, wild apples, and garden vegetables. In summer months Ma sweated bullets cooking and canning our meals on the Kalamazoo stove. There were no frozen meals or fast food joints she could fall back on.

We usually ate dinner in the kitchen. But on Sundays and holidays, we ate in the dining room at the round table someone had given to us on the cream-colored tablecloth with crocheted trim we got from Grandma Carne. We folded the tablecloth, laid it aside and ate dinner in the kitchen if we had a picture jigsaw puzzle in progress on the dining room table. The main fare stayed the same, but dessert on Sundays and holidays was Jello with whipped cream on top, lemon meringue pie or coconut cream pie.

There were sugar plums, pin cherries, fall cherries and wild crabapples near our farm, but even though Ma talked about making pin cherry wine, she never did as far as I know. She told us not to eat crabapples or wild cherries raw unless we wanted to spend time in the outhouse. One year we tried to use dandelion leaves for a salad. They were okay. We never did take that up. Ma let us pick hazelnuts, but they're hard to pick and harder to shell and peel. Hazelnuts are good to eat, except your fingers turn purple when you peel them. For sure don't crack them with your teeth—crack them between two rocks.

In one area, however, Ma was not boss of the kitchen—lutefisk. My dad insisted that Ma cook lutefisk every Christmas Eve. The way Dad described lutefisk, it sounded like caviar. I was told later that you get lutefisk by soaking codfish in lye. I didn't have to be told it stunk up the place. When Dad walked into the kitchen with a big smelly package of lutefisk that he'd picked up at Leffler's butcher shop—and Ma told him she would NOT cook it—my dad would launch into his lutefisk spiel in which he assured the whole family that lutefisk was a Norwegian Christmas tradition and that it was very good brain food. Lutefisk was Ground Zero where Norwegian pride and English custom collided.

Still, Ma wouldn't cross my dad on a thing as critical as lutefisk, so every year she served it. But she never accepted the idea of putting a big platter of that stuff on her table. It not only made her nervous, it made the whole family nervous each time the scene played out. It had to be boiled just so—dropped in at the precise moment the water boiled and left there for a very short period of time. Then swiftly removed, but carefully, because it's slippery and you would not want that smelly stuff burning on the stove. If it over boiled it broke down into tiny pieces my dad would not eat and the Christmas Eve dinner would be left in shambles. Even after she boiled it just the way Dad asked it really did not taste all that great. Not to me anyway—but please don't tell my kids. As a kid at the table watching the annual rite playing out and hoping Ma would not over boil the lutefisk, you instinctively knew not to laugh and that you were in one of those situations where "a child should be seen and not heard."

Dad got his lutefisk drenched in melted butter every Christmas Eve, just like they did in Norway. At least he said they did it that way in Norway. A large platter of it was put on the kitchen table with gravy boats of melted butter, and we all nervously ate it while glancing at each other. That is if you could keep it from sliding off your plate. "Brain food," my dad kept saying. It made me smart enough not to take any more than I had to. I tried to pass my Lutefisk heritage onto my own kids, but they're not buying it. They won't touch the stuff.

Another entrée Ma cooked was liver. I didn't like it, and in fact couldn't swallow it. Ma and Dad both said I had to because it contained iron. I won't talk about that any more. Breakfast was oatmeal, cream of wheat (lumps and all if you came downstairs late) and something that sounded like Farina. Aside from lutefisk, liver, and occasionally lumpy cream of wheat, Ma was one good cook. As I said, I didn't know at the time where all the ingredients came from because there was no money, but I remember meal after meal coming off that wood-burning Kalamazoo stove. When the kids came running home after the school bus dropped us off at the Corner, there would be peanut butter cookies Ma had pressed with a fork, raisin-filled soda biscuits, or pinwheel cinnamon cookies in the warming closet. They would be gone before Ma could tell us to save a few for the next day. She'd go back, open the warming closet, and look in, but she never said anything. She just smiled.

Ma's chocolate cakes were awesome, but her pies were a special treat. She used wild apples, raspberries and blueberries picked from neighboring trees and fields, white flour kept in a big tin barrel in the pantry, sugar, and lard. After she'd greased the pie tins, rolled and trimmed the dough to the shape of a pie tin, and crimped the edges with a fork, she'd have scraps of dough left over. She put them on cookie trays, sometimes with a sprinkle of sugar, and baked them with the pies. All the kids would hover around the kitchen so they'd be nearby when Ma's pie crust trimmings came out of the oven. Donna Mae and Tommy Carne would too if they were visiting. Doesn't sound like much, I know, but in those days it was a real coup to get your hands on some of the larger pieces of Ma's pie crust before the others got to them.

I found out later that the grocer who ran Meyer's Grocery in Ishpeming had a really big heart. He had extended credit to my dad throughout the Depression. Without the help he gave us, all we would have had for food were the potatoes, vegetables, pork, eggs and milk produced on our farm and wild berries and apples collected from neighboring fields. Sometimes, though, flour and sugar were dropped off by county relief people down at the Millimaki road where the narrow dirt road began. Ma used it but did not like getting anything on relief. One time Dad tried to carry heavy sacks of flour and sugar home during a snow storm. If you have ever tried to walk any distance in deep snow, you will understand why he left a sack of flour in the snow bank to be retrieved the next day. He never found it.

Grown men, and even small boys living around us, got a little dizzy when bird season or deer season opened. A few partridge lived in thorn apple trees south of our farm near the "Big Rock" where we liked to play that stood on what was then Ted Koski's forty. One of the glaciers worked overtime hauling that twelve-foot high monster there. We shot some partridge there and at other thorn apple trees in the area, but not many, and there isn't a whole lot of meat on a partridge. There certainly was not enough to feed a family of ten. There were no wild turkeys around our farm in those years.

We also ate speckled brook trout. The trout we caught were wild trout, not like later when the streams around our farm were fished out and hatchery trout were planted in them by the Conservation Department. Wild trout have more brilliant coloring, more powerful fins, and a stronger body than hatchery fish. You could tell the difference as soon as you hooked one. Wild trout fight harder and come out of the water struggling to be free of the hook and the line. They also have pinker meat and taste a lot better. When it got to be April and trout season opened, all the guys living around us went from dizzy to batty. It was all they talked about. Many shifts at the mine and many days of school were lost as anglers took off for the rivers and streams. There were no fish in the crick on our land, just a few bullfrogs you could catch, but Ma would never cook frog legs. I must say I got caught up in the fishing craze each year like all the other guys, but I was never a good fisherman. Not according to my dad or my big brother.

To catch speckled brook trout we had to hike an old logging road across Ted Koski's land, down along the crick that flowed south across our farm, out past the Big Rock and the thorn apple trees, to where our crick merged with other small streams and became the Little Crick. It wasn't a name you could find on a map—I guess Dad named it himself. It deserved a better name, although it was only a few feet wide. The brook trout that lived there stayed under its banks or beneath logs that fell into it. There were more and bigger brook trout down past the woven fence that someone built across it to contain the beaver, and where the gathering waters of the Little Crick ran into the beaver pond, joined the Green and then fell out to tumble down the big rapids. As a matter of fact, that one—Green Crick—gave the location where our farm stood its name. Sometimes my brothers and I fished the Green all the way down to where it joined the Ely River. That took all day, but a fisherman has no sense of time. He is driven by raging compulsions pulsating through his heart and soul and befogging his mind. He believes that no matter how bad his luck has been, or is, more and bigger trout are waiting downstream.

My brother Ken claims there were schools of fish in those cricks in the early days before I took to fishing, and that the Little Crick and the

Green were full of speckled trout a foot and a half long. Things had always been bigger and better before I came along. Even that Greek guy, Diogenes, carrying his lantern wouldn't find an honest fisherman around our cricks. I never caught any trout more than ten inches long in the days I fished for them. I could sometimes catch a few more than seven inches long—big enough to take—if I worked my worm under a log or the bank or into a swirling pool of black or yellowish water. I'd also get some bites going down the rapids, but mostly that involved sitting on big moss-covered rocks overhung with cedars and birch and watching sparkling water spilling all around me while I ran my line down between the rocks. That worked okay if I was using Ken's telescope pole with the reel. That's the one I told you about that my dad had. Not so good if I was using a government pole.[55] I'll grant it was a helluva place to sit quietly and listen to the birds, eat a pasty and drink coffee from my thermos, but I knew I'd never catch my limit with a government pole.

Now there are a few things about fishing with a telescope pole and a reel, as opposed to a government pole, that you need to understand. As I explain them please remember that while fishing is fun, in those days we really did have to catch some fish for dinner, that swarms of mosquitoes, deerflies, no-see-ums, and horseflies encircle your head as you fish, and that to ward them off, you have to smoke a roll-your-own cigarette against your ma's orders. I am explaining the advantages that follow so you will understand why I swiped my brother's telescope pole with the reel when he wasn't using it, cut me some slack, and not accuse me of thievery.

First off, you can shorten a telescope pole down to about thirty or so inches. That makes it easier to carry it through tag alders than a ten-foot government pole, which enables you to move downstream faster. Second, after you've pulled your telescope pole out to full length, you can stand back from the crick and grab your line with one hand up where it comes off the reel while you guide your pole with the other up to a good fishing hole. That feature allows you to pull your hook with the bait on it up close to the end of the pole, stealthily creep up to the bank, and then slowly let out slack so that your sinker gently and silently guides your bait right down to where you want it without scaring the fish. Sometimes these features will allow you to get your bait into fishing holes where there are a lot of willows, tag alders or tall swamp grass growing on the bank, although not always. If a speckled trout takes your bait, of course, you can give the line you're holding in your hand a jerk and fix the hook. You can't do that with a government pole unless you jerry-rig a reel to your pole. Also, if you snag your hook on a log or under the bank, it's easier to work your line back and forth and break it free if you have a reel and a telescope pole made of flexible steel.

But perhaps the biggest advantage to having a telescope pole comes when you fish the rapids. There you can sit on a rock way upstream without the fish knowing you're there, pull some slack off the reel and let the current work your bait down between the rocks into little pools of sparkling water that collect in the rapids. If at first you don't get a strike, you can let out more slack and let the current pull your bait further downstream while you're hoping your luck will change. Also, if you still don't get a strike you can reel in your line. Most importantly, though, if you do get a strike and hook one while fishing the rapids, you can reel in a wriggling trout beneath overhanging tree branches or underbrush. You can't do any of that with a government pole.

Now to put yourself into the scene, it is critical that you understand the soul of a true fisherman. There is no need to explain if you are one. One of the greatest experiences of life, other than some I'll not mention here, is to hook a trout of some size while you're fishing the rapids with a telescope pole and engage him in a struggle that bends your pole and threatens to snap your line as he fights to be free. You respect a fish like that. But even though there is some solace in having a story to tell about the big one that got away, it's better to land him, add a few inches and tell the guys on the school bus exactly how hard that trout fought.

My big brother caught more fish than I did, but like I said, he had the telescope pole with the reel. He was always bragging about the ones he caught and talking about other guys who filled their baskets. All of them used telescope poles with reels. The way my big brother talked, one of them, a guy named Doily Brown, could come down the crick right after you went through and have speckled trout jumping out of the crick right into his basket. Dad used to laugh at the fish I caught and threatened to tie them in bundles so they wouldn't get lost in the frying pan.

You need luck—that's what's needed. Once when we were kids my little brother Bill came running up behind me and threw his worm onto a sandbar in the middle of the Green where it crossed what later became

County Road 581. I'd been fishing there in some deep water near the bank but hadn't had a bite; Ken was fishing downstream. Before Bill knew what was going on, a goddamned big trout swam past my line across the sandbar, grabbed his worm and took off downstream. That surprised the hell out of him—I had to grab him so he wouldn't fall in, help him pull the damn thing out, and then suffer my big brother Ken's gibes that Bill caught a bigger fish than I did. That ticked me off, because Bill wasn't supposed to drop his line in a fishing hole where I was already fishing. That was fishermen's etiquette. My big brother told me that himself.

We fished those cricks a lot—me and my brothers. We carved our initials into a poplar tree on top of the hill above that big beaver pond where the Little Crick runs into the Green. I liked that hill because you could look down and sometimes get a glimpse of a beaver dragging a log it gnawed from a poplar tree out across the pond to a beaver house that poked up in the middle of the dammed-up water. Arbutus used to bloom on the south side of that hill in the spring, and in the summer blueberries grew all over it. Once you smell wild arbutus or taste wild blueberries you never forget it. I never went back, but I'm sure arbutus blooms on that hill every spring, that it's covered with blueberries every summer and that the old poplar tree is still there.

My cousin Bob used to ride out from New Burt to our house on his red, two-wheeler bike and we'd go fishing on Green Crick. If we traveled to a more remote fishing site, three of us rode that bike holding our fishing poles—one pedaling, one on the carrier over the back fender, and one on the handlebars. As I said, his ma, Aunt Adele, and her husband Uncle George, who worked in town for the power company, lived at New Burt with Grandpa Ole. In addition to the bike, they bought Bob a fancy telescope rod with a spinning reel that had genuine pearl strips glued right into it, a fish basket with leather straps and all kinds of sparkly shiners, leaders and sinkers that he put on his line down by the hook, but that stuff didn't do any good. You needed patience, not shiners. The fish laughed at shiners. When my brothers and I went fishing we used worms. In the first place we didn't have any fly rods, hand-tied flies or know-how to tie them, and couldn't afford to buy them. What you had to do was snake your worm into the water up near the bank or close to a log or a rock where water was swirling and hope your hook didn't snag under the bank or on a root if a trout bit.

We dug up worms from the black dirt at the end of our garden or by the manure pile by the barn, and put them in tin cans that still had the top partly attached. You could carry them that way if you watched out for the sharp edges. Sometimes we found big night crawlers in the grass and saved them. Fly fishermen can laugh all they want, but we wanted the fish for dinner, and worms work if you thread them on the hook correctly and don't kill them. I never did completely understand how to bait a hook for trout myself, though, because those who knew all about that, like my big brother, and caught the big speckled ones wouldn't tell you. I've seen some spit tobacco juice on the worm to make it squirm. I didn't chew tobacco when I was a kid. I'd loop the worm on the hook, not show any barb, and not walk too close to the crick. I'd catch a speckled trout if I got lucky and he didn't steal my worm or snag my hook.

I've read about fly fishing out in Montana. Those guys wear big floppy boots, fancy beige vests full of pockets, buckles and loops, and hats full of flies they've tied themselves, with their fish baskets slung over their shoulders. They never use any bait at all and laugh at guys like us who did. They'll tell you they can cast a line through the tag alders without getting it tangled and just reel 'em in. That's bunk. It's not as easy as they'll tell you. I watched fly fishermen waving fly rods out at Deer Lake north of Ishpeming years ago. I hid behind a big rock so they wouldn't see me. Look out for what those guys tell you—I never saw them catch any fish at all.

While I didn't ever go to Montana, there were no fly fishermen I ever saw in the vicinity of the little cricks out by our farm. That was because our cricks snaked back and forth and were hemmed in by tag alders and willows. It is difficult to imagine the severity of the terrain unless you experience it yourself. You couldn't get close enough to our cricks to whip a fly around, and if you were silly enough to try, your line would get all snarled up in the bushes. Not just that, the fish in our cricks lived under the banks and behind logs in the water and would never see a newfangled fly, even if you did get one near the water. Besides, you needed one hand free to swat mosquitoes, no-see-ums, horseflies and deerflies. You have to step real carefully approaching a crick if you want to catch trout. If they see you waving a fly rod around or feel vibrations when you step too close to the bank, they won't bite—they'll be gone.

Sometimes when we were casting for trout we'd catch chubs. If we pulled in a sucker we threw that back, but we cut chubs up for bait on a windfall using our jackknives. For some reason that worked if it was raining. In fact, once on the big beaver pond on the Porcupine Crick upstream from where it empties into the Green—just below the rapids I mentioned—my big brother and my friend Marvie reeled in eight or ten big speckled trout during a rainstorm using chub meat. I was there and saw them do it. I'd have got some too, but I didn't have a reel, and my government pole broke off with all my line when I tried to pull one in. They laughed at me for breaking my pole and falling off the pine log into the beaver pond while I was trying to grab hold of my line. They asked me why I fell in, and I tried to explain that I started to fall so I jumped. I never finished what I'd tried to say to them because in my opinion all trout fishermen are a little dizzy. It was raining and they got as wet as I did, except they had fish.

We carried the fish we caught on forked willow sticks shoved through their gills. That way you can stick them back in the crick to keep them from drying out. We laughed at the guys carrying trout in baskets stuffed with cedar boughs. Some of them had more cedar boughs in their baskets than fish.

Because of all the things I've just explained, growing up I always wanted my own telescope pole with a reel just like the one my dad gave to my brother. In fact, Marvie and most of the kids around there had access to a telescope pole with a reel. Unless you were there, it is near impossible to imagine the frustration of a kid not so equipped. Then I caught a break. When I was about twelve years old I came across an advertisement a seed company had put in *The Grit*, a local tabloid type magazine my dad used to bring home from Meyer's Grocery. I won't mention the name of the seed company even if it comes to me as I explain what happened, but I was ecstatic. The ad offered to mail a new fishing pole with a reel to anyone who sold the number and type of vegetable garden seed packets listed in the ad—and it even had a picture of the pole with the reel attached. With Ma egging me on, I mailed in my entry form. When I received my allotment of seeds, I proceeded to sell them to all the neighbors and relatives in the Green Crick area happily informing each one of them that I was competing for a new fishing pole.

Everybody in the Green Crick area was wrapped up in trout fishing, and greatly pleased to buy their seeds for spring planting from a little kid striving to own his own fishing pole with a reel. They smiled when I showed them copies of the ad and practically begged them to buy seeds. I also told them the seed company had good seeds, and that the seeds I was selling were the best ones they had. Once all the seeds were sold, I mailed in the proceeds and ran to the mailbox each day to see if my new pole was hanging from it. After a week or so, the pole arrived. Upon tearing open the carton I was stunned. It was a metal pole all right, as advertised, but it was not telescopic, only about thirty-two inches long, and the reel was, to put it charitably, a ridiculous piece of junk. It most certainly did not have any pearl strips. Still, the new pole was mine, and it did have a reel, however tacky. When my brother Ken laughed at it, I loaded the reel with line, attached a hook and sinker, dug up some worms, and took off all alone down the path to Kaminen's house. I intended to show my new pole to Marvie and ask him if he would head down to the Green with me to help me try it out.

It was spring, early May as I recall, and most of the snow had melted. While I was walking the trail through the bush to Marvie's house, I suddenly heard the powerful beating sound generated by the wings of a mother partridge. It was her brooding season, and she was protecting new chicks that were scattering to hide. She was also headed straight for me and coming in fast at face level. Dad had warned me and my brothers that a brooding mother partridge will go for your eyes. I instinctively raised my new pole to ward her off, and to strike her if I could. I got in a pretty good whack that knocked her down before she got to me, but the act of striking with my pole worked my line loose from my new reel.

Somehow my fishing line got itself tangled around one of the mother partridge's legs. She flew up from the ground where I'd knocked her, but, convinced her chicks were by then well hidden, she abandoned the attack and took off with her wings pounding the air. With my new reel spinning wildly all of my fishing line went with her as she flew away between the trees. I never found out if she ever disentangled herself. That is a true story no matter how hilariously funny it struck my dad, my brother Ken or Marvie. Not seeming to care if my new pole and reel were ridiculous, all my fishing line was gone, or if my eyes were pecked out, they never let me forget that my first official catch with my new pole was a partridge. I never did use that damn pole after that. I stored it in the woodshed for a while, then threw it away and tried to forget about it. Nobody uses a thirty-two inch fishing pole unless they're trolling or ice fishing. I never sold seeds again either.

I didn't mean to get started on fishing, because in 1937 Meyer's Grocery filed for bankruptcy. That was a sad, sad day. We weren't the only ones that had bought groceries on credit. Once he got back to work at the mine my dad paid back every cent he owed to the bankruptcy trustee—every cent. He made his payments down at the bank where he made his car payments. You have to pay your way, my dad said. Later, I wondered if the owner of Meyer's Grocery was ever thanked or rewarded for his benevolence.

~~~

Map G

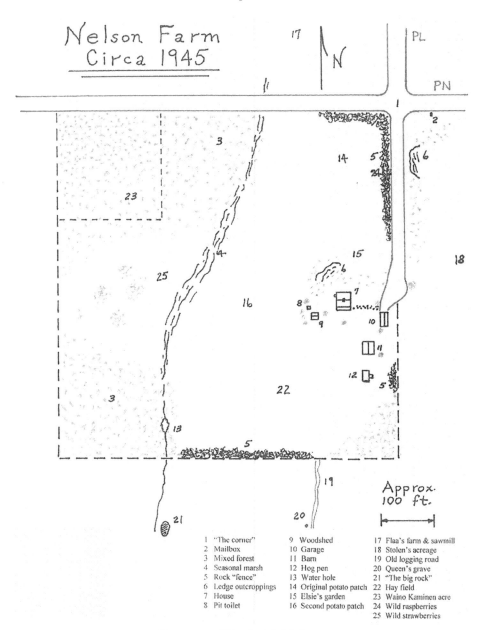

Nelson Farm
Circa 1945

17   N   PL

PN

1	"The corner"	9	Woodshed	17	Flaa's farm & sawmill
2	Mailbox	10	Garage	18	Stolen's acreage
3	Mixed forest	11	Barn	19	Old logging road
4	Seasonal marsh	12	Hog pen	20	Queen's grave
5	Rock "fence"	13	Water hole	21	"The big rock"
6	Ledge outcroppings	14	Original potato patch	22	Hay field
7	House	15	Elsie's garden	23	Waino Kaminen acre
8	Pit toilet	16	Second potato patch	24	Wild raspberries
				25	Wild strawberries

Courtesy of Frederick Nelson

Figure 29
Painting of Ben and Elsie's Farm with carpenter's ripsaw

Painting of Ben and Elsie's Farm in Tilden Township.
Reproduced with the permission of Roger M. Junak, a family friend.

Carpenter's ripsaw Ben used to build the farmhouse, barn and
woodshed, with one of Ben's beagles emblazoned on the blade.
Reproduced with the permission of Kathrine Savu, a family friend.

CHAPTER 10

Hog Slaughtering

YOU GET TO understand where food comes from a little better when you're raised on a small farm—particularly on days when Dad slaughtered the hogs. It usually happened around Thanksgiving, but we had no electricity and therefore no freezer, so it depended on the arrival of freezing temperatures. Grandpa Ole had picked up the trade in Norway, brought it to America with him and taught my dad how it's done. Dad got good at it. Most of the neighbors used his skills to slaughter their animals.

When Dad announced a hog slaughter everyone had to get up early, haul in the water and load plenty of good hardwood into the wood box to keep the fire going nice and hot in the Kalamazoo, because two boilers of freshwater had to be boiling before you got started. The two copper boilers—one borrowed from Grandpa Ole—were hoisted up on top of the Kalamazoo stove and each was filled with about fifteen gallons of water. When you saw those two boilers on top of the Kalamazoo you knew it would be a hectic day, and you better pay attention.

My dad kept the double edged stabbing knife Grandpa Ole gave him wrapped in butcher paper on top of the cupboard in the kitchen, and no one was ever to touch it except him. No one ever did that I heard of, but later, once the garage got built, Ma made him keep it out there. He'd go get it, carefully unwrap the butcher paper so as not to tear it because he planned to use it again, and run his thumb down both of the edges. If it wasn't sharp enough for his taste he'd take the whetstone to it. When the water was boiling he'd load the single shot twenty-two and walk down to the hog pen where we'd fed those hogs and made straw beds for them all through the spring and summer.

Ma never went with him. She stayed back in the kitchen with my sisters to keep the water boiling and to prepare the meal we'd need when it was all over. A couple of White Giant roosters—killed, plucked and dressed the night before—had to be roasted, carved and spread out on platters with corn, mashed potatoes and gravy on the round dining room table. Ma always said that when you worked out in the cold the best thing for you is a hot meal. I've never tasted anything that good since.

In late November there'd be snow of course, and some would collect in the troughs where the hogs ate. Dad took the feed bucket we used and dumped some into the trough on top of the snow. The hogs went wild as soon as they saw that bucket. They thought it was feeding time so they came bounding in shoving, grunting and oinking—looking up at us with dirty faces—as they always did. Then "pop" and one would fall with a twenty-two bullet dead center in an X between its eyes and ears. The others scattered. Hogs have small brains so it had to be a good clean shot at the specific angle that dropped the hog with the first shot. You didn't want the bullet penetrating the meat or a wounded two-hundred-fifty-pound hog running around the pen scaring the wits out of the rest of them. It was always a good shot because my dad knew where their brains were. Out of respect for the hogs he was swift.

Before you knew it my dad was over the wooden slabs that formed the pen with his stabbing knife in one hand and a rope with a small noose in the other. Sometimes my big brother Ken handed him the rope. He'd slip that noose around the hog's front leg up behind the hoof, ram his knee in behind the hog's shoulder and pull the leg back tight. That hog was not getting up. He'd take his thumb and measure off a depth on the stabbing knife that would bleed a hog of that size, and with one smooth stroke drive the stabbing knife into the neck of the hog so that it entered between the jugular veins. The hog's bright red blood poured out and bubbled on the white snow as he pulled out the stabber.

My dad told me it was critical that the stabber not sever the jugulars because if severed they would "knot up" and cut off the flow of blood. He wanted every drop drained out before the heart stopped. I wondered about that because he chopped the heads clean off our roosters. Dad would ask me to come along to help out as a water carrier and scraper when some of our neighbors hired him to butcher their hogs. Some of them wanted him to collect the blood in pans for blood sausage. He'd do it if they asked, but my ma wanted no part of that.

Once bled, an iron hook with a handle was inserted into the dead hog's jaw and it was pulled out over the slab fence and dragged over to the scalding area in back of the barn. As soon as it got there a metal spreader was placed between its back legs through knife holes made before the tendon at the knee. The hog was hoisted up with a block and tackle chained to a pole that extended from the back of the barn to the crotch of the maple tree behind the barn. A large wooden barrel Dad had picked up at the bakery shop was then wheeled under the hog, and my dad called for the scalding hot water.

The two copper boilers of simmering water had to be taken from the kitchen, carried down the porch steps and then down a hill to the scalding area. The dirt trail down that hill was narrow; it had rocks in it, and by November was slippery from new snow. If you were one of the kids carrying a boiler you had to be careful not to slip. There'd be a kid or my dad on each end of a boiler. The one downhill had to hold their end up and the one uphill had to carry their end low. You were forbidden to spill any water, and you had to get it down to the big wooden barrel as fast as you could before it cooled. You can't scald a hog with tepid water, and you couldn't put your boiler down in the snow or interfere with the two carrying the other boiler right behind you. Some might look at that whole process and say it was dangerous as hell, but we never spilled a drop that I ever saw. Telling about it, I'll have to admit, makes it sound scary, but it was like what Harry Truman once said about an S curve on a winding road in Missouri. It was so dangerous it was safe.

When you got your boiler to the scalding area, my dad took over from the one in front, lifted his end and placed the boiler handle on the edge of the barrel. There were flanges on the handle that let him hook it there. The other end was tipped up and the scalding water went into the barrel one boiler at a time. I never found out if that's how they did it in Norway, but that's how we did it. Then my dad took off his gloves and with a bucket of cold water in one hand, he'd splash the other hand into the water to test the temperature, spill cold water in and test again until he said it was right. It was the kind of thing he knew but couldn't tell you, so I never did learn how to do that. It was done the same way every year until he got arthritis. That's when he drove into Jackson's hardware store and picked up a thermometer on a string that bobbed when he threw it into the barrel.

When the hog was lowered with the block and tackle into scalding water that was just the right temperature, the hair and the first layer of skin would come off, sort of like when you peel a banana. We used hand-held round scrapers to clean away all the excess hair and skin. The scrapers had wooden handles with a large sharpened cuplike disc on one end and a smaller one on the other for the tight spots around the eyes, ears, and folded skin. My dad took great pride in his work so you had better scrape carefully, not knick the skin or leave round scraper marks. If you did you'd hear about it. He wanted the rind pink and clean with no hair or marks on it, even though all he did with the rind was to cut it off later and let the birds peck it clean. It was how he did things.

First the front end was dipped and then the hog was dropped on wooden planks placed across the top of the barrel, turned and rehoisted with the hook in its lower jaw and lowered in again. If Dad was scalding two hogs at once you had to get the first one scalded and moved onto planks on the sawhorses beside the barrel before the water cooled down. There'd be one set of scrapers working the hog on the planks across the barrel and another doing the one on the sawhorses. You couldn't wear mittens or gloves when you used the scrapers so your hands might get cold. My dad instructed us that if they did, we could dip them into the barrel of hot water.

Once the scalding and scraping was completed, the barrel was dumped and the hogs were hoisted, one at a time, with the spreader in their back legs, gutted and halved. Some of our neighbors didn't like seeing their hogs gutted when Dad was working a hired job. I can't say that I enjoyed it, but I watched. The insides of a hog are quite similar to a human's. You could see the bowels, pancreas, liver, heart, lungs and windpipe fall right out as Dad made a clean, even cut and severed the diaphragm. The smell was bad. The only part of the insides he saved was the liver. The rest was thrown into the woods and eaten by wild animals. As far as I was concerned he could've thrown the liver there too. Some of our neighbors kept the intestines as casings for blood sausage.

Butchering hogs is not the nicest thing to talk about, but that's how it's done, whether you do it yourself or it's done at a meat packing plant. At the end of the day there would be two, maybe four, halves of fresh, clean, wholesome pork hanging in the woodshed, where they froze as solid as the planks on which they had been scraped. There wasn't a drop of man-made chemicals in that meat.

Later, they'd be taken one at a time and cut on the kitchen table into hams, pork loins, spare ribs, bacon and pot roasts, enough to take us through the winter. My dad didn't have enough meat hooks so he'd punch holes in the cuts, put hay bale wire in the holes and hang them back in the woodshed. There is no bacon anywhere that tastes as good as the fresh bacon we raised on our farm, and the pork chops were even better. Bacon grease was saved and used in place of butter on the bread my ma baked, but during the War the government wanted the grease for munitions, so we collected it in tin cans and turned it in. Strips of leaf lard extracted from the area of the hog's tenderloins was rendered for baking. Ma took some of the suet and hung it outside on the trees for the birds. She sure did love those birds.

You can talk about the food served in fancy restaurants all you like. Let me tell you Ma's bread was delicious with or without fresh butter or bacon grease on it. I've never tasted or even seen any bread like it since. It didn't matter if it was a square slice from a long loaf or one from a round loaf baked in a pie tin because she didn't have enough bread pans. It had a golden crust and each and every loaf had body to it. Not like the white paste sold in plastic bags at stores today. It stuck to your ribs and made you feel good inside and out, particularly with peanut butter and strawberry jelly late at night when you had school work to do. You could spear a slice with a fork, hold it over the Kalamazoo stove to toast it, put fresh butter on it, and dunk it into a cup of cocoa—even better yet if Ma put raisins in it.

You haven't lived until you've seen Ma melt yeast in a jelly glass, knead that bread dough on flour spread all over the oil cloth on the kitchen table, let it rise in the big dishpan with a dish towel over it, knead it some more, cut it into loaves, grease the pans, let it rise some more above the warming closet and then put it into the oven of that Kalamazoo stove. She never bragged about it, but later on I found a poem she wrote, so I know she loved baking bread. She wrote no poems about hog butchering that I ever saw.

Another thing she baked she'd learned from her mother. We called it heavy cake, but to me it was like flat bread with raisins in it. It was started in England I guess. You couldn't get enough heavy cake, saffron buns, seedy buns, or pies and cakes she baked. I guess, though, the best of all were the Cornish pasties. I've tried to make them myself, but she never gave me a recipe, and I couldn't do it like she did anyway.

Despite what the Finns tell you, pasties had been invented in England to meet the need for a lunch a miner could tuck in his shirt. You can buy them in Cornwall today. All they consist of are cubes of potatoes, carrots, rutabagas, onion, suet, and either cubes of round steak or hamburger, seasoned and rolled up in pie dough and baked. Ma's pasties were even better than those baked by Grandma Carne. Hers weren't as brown as Ma's. Ma cut up the ingredients, shaped them on a rolled-out pastry crust, folded the crust to fit in one half of a pie pan, crimped the edge, and punched three holes in the top to let the steam out. Two at a time were baked in a pie pan. When they came out of the oven and cooled off you could hold one right in your hand and eat it. They weren't just brown, they were golden brown and delicious hot or cold. I ate hundreds of them.

These days you can buy dried-out frozen pasties from the store, but not like the ones she made. Along with pasties she cooked homemade vegetable soup, pea soup with chunks of ham in it, meatballs, deep-dish meat pie, meatloaf and beef stew. I could go on. Ma put some of her pie crust across the top of her meat pies. Everything she had went into what she cooked and stewed and baked, including all of her love and her soul. That's where food comes from. Like I said, you'd understand better if you were raised on a hardscrabble, ten-acre farm and read her poems.

CHAPTER 11

Firewood Chopping and Stacking

ABOUT THE TIME Dad got the job from Cleveland-Cliffs and was assigned to the Lloyd shaft in 1937, Harley Fisk rented the Graneggen place. Harley also worked at the Lloyd mine. Things were picking up at the mines, so Dad traded in his 1937 Ford and purchased a maroon 1940 Ford sedan. Then World War II broke out and gas was rationed. To save on gas Dad and Harley used to trade off driving to work. But Harley's tires were always going flat. We were kept busy jacking up Harley's car and patching his inner tubes so the two of them could keep their agreement to ride-share and still get to work. Sometimes Harley's tires went flat on the way to work. We put patches on top of patches, because new tires and inner tubes were not available to civilians during World War II. If a tire split we put a "boot" in it.

When I think of Harley renting the Graneggen place, I recall one time when Harley wasn't at home. Dad had bought eight piglets at a big discount and moved them into the brand-new hog house and pen Harley had built on Graneggen's land, but hadn't yet stocked. Dad intended to build a hog pen and hog house for the new piglets on our ten acres, but hadn't done so and forgot to tell Harley. When Harley heard all eight piglets squealing for food he came running over to our house and announced to Dad that an act of Divine Providence had stocked his new hog pen with eight piglets, and to get right over and take a look. Dad laughed, assured Harley that the Almighty had nothing to do with the delivery of those piglets, and explained what he'd done. Once Harley got the story he didn't mind—he laughed. Folks helped each other in those days and expected to do so.

The two-rut road that led to the Graneggen place cut across Olaf Stolen's land. That road has always reminded me of Ma's frostbitten legs. It also reminds me of cutting firewood, filling the wood box alongside our Kalamazoo stove, and hauling out the ashes. Dad built our woodshed a hundred feet west of the farmhouse about the time he built the barn. It sheltered the only source of heating and cooking fuel we had in the early years. Twelve feet square and built of unpainted pine lumber, it's still there. It was nothing spectacular, but it held eight or nine rows of wood about eight feet high—a little better than twenty-four face cords, more if you threw some up on top where the spruce joists crossed. That worked out to about seven full cords because we had to save some space up front for the pork Dad butchered and the tools we kept there.

To feed our Kalamazoo, we had to cut a never-ending supply of firewood, sawed to length, split and stacked in the woodshed so it would be there and dry when we needed it. Particularly in winter months, but also during summer when rain would drench any firewood stacked outside. Still, some firewood had to be stacked outside to take us through the winter because the woodshed didn't hold enough to do that. My brothers and I spent a lot of time working in and around that woodshed. We carved our initials on the front of it with our pocket knives to remind people we'd been there. Some years later after Dad and Ma passed, I went back to see what the old place looked like and found our initials still there, although considerably weather-beaten. On one of my trips back home the then current owner, Jimmy Pietro, offered to let me remove the board they were carved into and take it with me. I wanted to do that, but I felt my brothers would want that board left there as a sort of monument to mark the place where all the firewood got cut and stacked. Later, Jimmy Pietro or one of his sons, removed it anyway and told my brother Ken to give it to me. My dad sawed that board with his carpenter's saw. If you lay a square on it you'll see it was cut squarely. My brother Fred framed it and turned it into an heirloom.

Figure 30

The plaque on the above states, "BOARD FROM BEN NELSON'S WOODSHED BUILT CIRCA 1932 INITIALED BY HIS SONS KEN, DAVE AND FRED 1940 – 1957"

Like I said, collecting firewood was a chore that had to be done all year long, or we'd have had no wood to cook our food or to heat the house. My dad wanted hard maple, cherry, oak and ironwood, if you could get it, because hardwood makes a hotter fire that lasts longer, and is less likely to create soot in the chimney that might cause a chimney fire. But hardwood is tougher to saw and split, particularly if it's already dry. Like I said, Dad liked work that was tough, so that didn't bother him. We cut wood wherever we could, but we never cut anywhere without permission. Sometimes we'd find an ironwood windfall on a neighbor's land and carry that home too. Ironwood burned hot, and its embers lasted, but that never amounted to much. Ironwood windfalls were scarce. While Ma, of course, loved all trees—not just pine trees—and didn't like to see any tree cut down, we needed firewood.

After we'd cut all the good firewood on our ten acres, the Stolens—who owned the forty off to the east and had good hardwood maple—asked us to clear some of their land, burn the brush, and remove the wood. We also cut hardwood on Uncle George's forty up in Greenwood out past the Fitch because Uncle George also wanted his land cleared. One time while we were cutting wood there, I was shaking a dead maple to knock it down when the top came off, hit me on the head, and knocked me out. I woke up as we drove home on top of the load of wood piled on Uncle George's Model T truck.

It started with chopping a notch into the bottom of a tree with an axe—to establish the direction it would fall—sawing the tree down, limbing it, sawing it into eight-to ten foot-lengths, and then hitching up our horse to skid the logs up to the woodshed. Smaller trees or limbs large enough to saw into firewood were dragged up to the woodshed in bundles. The brush from limbing was stacked in huge brush piles. During winter when it was bitter cold and snow protected against forest fires, my dad burned the brush piles. Huge flames and sparks shot thirty to fifty feet in the air, melted the snow down to the bare earth, and reddened your face if you stood nearby. The acrid smoke of burning balsam, pine and spruce branches would fill your nostrils with smoke from three or four piles of brush burning all at once. When it's your job to gather bundles of freshly cut spruce limbs and then walk into the heat and throw your bundle on the fire, it stays with you.

After the main burn the embers had to be raked together so that we'd leave as little unburned brush as possible to clean up in the spring. We used to set potatoes down by the embers and roast them for lunch. We had no aluminum foil in those days, so some would turn black on the outside. Dad said if you kept them back from the coals and broke them open real carefully the insides would be pure white and delicious. If not the first smoked potatoes on the planet, they were the best.

After Belle was sold, my dad had to borrow Flaa's horse and bring her down to our place to skid our firewood. Later, he found another horse, Babe, and bought her hoping against hope she could replace Belle. But Babe was no Belle. She was a small saddle horse and useless around work, although my brother Ken liked to saddle her up and ride her. When Dad brought out the blacksmith to have Babe shod, the blacksmith couldn't get her to hold her right back leg up and said she was stifled. Dad sold her. It was one of the few times I saw Dad make a mistake on an animal.

Then Dad bought Nellie, a draft horse with no prospects for the Kentucky Derby whatever. She was bigger than either Belle or Babe, about sixteen hundred pounds, but her primary mission in life was to eat all the hay and oats that were put in front of her and to create manure. Nellie's proclivities for eating were enough to doom her too, but her neck arched like a circus horse, she had a beautiful rich brown coat, a black mane and tail, and she could pull. Nellie, a plodder, was not a flamboyant, dynamic animal like Belle. Not at all. But she was alert enough. She perked up when you called out "Giddap" or "Whoa."

The larger logs were dragged up in front of the woodshed and piled up there, and the smaller ones were stood on end against the maple tree next to the woodshed. Dad said they'd dry better standing up. We'd end up with huge stacks of wood by the woodshed that had to be hand-sawed into lengths suitable for the Kalamazoo stove—about fourteen to fifteen inches. In the early years Dad had to do all the sawing, splitting and stacking, but gradually my brothers and I took over. As we did we wondered how Dad ever did it by himself. We used Dad's pulp saw on the smaller logs and his crosscut on the larger ones—one kid on each end of the saw. Dad didn't sharpen his saws himself. He had to use a guy in Ishpeming to keep his saws sharp. "You can't saw with a dull saw," he reminded us. "And I can't keep paying to sharpen them so don't run them into wires or nails."

Sometimes it took several brothers to lift a log up on the sawhorse. When we got it up there we'd saw off one block at a time moving the log forward as we did. If the log was too heavy for us to lift up on the sawhorse, we raised it with crowbars, put wooden blocks under it to raise it, knelt down on the ground and sawed it into blocks there. The larger blocks were thrown into a separate pile for splitting on the chopping block, the smaller ones went directly to the split pile for stacking outside on two poles laid parallel to keep the firewood off the ground when it rained. Dad taught us to sink the axe deep into the freshly sawed end of a block that was tough to split, and to then raise the axe with the block attached to it and slam the back of the axe blade down on the chopping block. The block's own weight would split it. Sometimes there'd be two brothers sawing and one splitting the blocks. Once the axe cut my brother Ken's hand real bad while he was splitting wood. He bled all over the chopping block, and ran all the way to Flaa's dripping blood. They took him to the hospital in Ishpeming where his hand had to be stitched. Several years later I did the same, but mine wasn't as bad.

If we couldn't get blocks split to firewood size by just using axes, because there were too many knots, we used wedges and a sledge hammer to break them up. We had to use all the wood we had. Pine knots with pitch in them were separated because they made great kindling wood. Firewood was stacked first outside, bark side up, so the sun and wind would dry it, but before the snow started to fly, we'd restack as much firewood as we could in the woodshed to keep it dry. It was an annual chore that took many weeks.

My brothers and I became skilled in the use of saws, axes, splitting wedges, and the lost art of firewood cutting and stacking. Later at college, when they held a Paul Bunyan contest for Northern's Homecoming, I and a one-armed college friend, who'd had similar experience, won the log sawing contest by sawing off a sixteen-inch diameter slice of log in twenty-eight seconds and beating out a bunch of football players who thought it only took muscle. It was a piece of cake. My dad told me to use smooth even strokes, not to force the saw and to give the teeth a chance to do the work. "You won't tire as fast," he said.

Sometimes, but not so much after my brothers and I got older, my dad would have Uncle George come out with his gasoline-driven circular saw and cut our firewood into woodstove lengths to help us out. It was kind of like a hog-butchering day in a lot of ways, except we did it to the woodpile. My Uncle George, who had rigged up his Ford Model T truck to power a circular saw, would drive the Model T into our yard, jack up the back end on blocks, and put a long rubber belt on the right back wheel. He said that was the wheel with power on it. He'd built a wooden cradle that rocked back and forth in a frame that he and my dad removed from the back of the Model T and staked to the ground about eight feet behind the Model T. The belt was then stretched over a pulley wheel installed on the same axle that held the circular saw blade, and the whole apparatus was tightened up.

When Uncle George cranked up the Model T and put it in first gear, it engaged the belt and the circular saw started to spin at an outrageous speed. The belt would ripple and smack together, but it usually stayed on the pulleys. Uncle George always cranked the Model T himself. He told us kids that if we ever cranked a Model T we must keep the thumb and all four fingers of our hand together on the same side of the crank. Otherwise, the Model T might backfire and break our thumb. I looked at my thumb and grabbed it when I heard that because I had already tried to turn the crank.

Figure 31

Uncle George's Model T Ford circular saw—
Sketch by Richard T. Carne

Logs were taken from the woodpile and lifted up on the wooden cradle—it had to be operated by two men—and slowly tilted against the whining saw blade. That was accompanied by even higher-pitched screaming and sawdust flying in all directions as the circular saw cut through the log and produced firewood lengths. The even higher-pitched zinging sound the saw blade gave off just as a cut was completed and the saw broke free is still imprinted in my memory—sort of like an opera singer moving up to high C—along with the pungent smell of sawdust mixed in with cigarette smoke and the gasoline, oil and exhaust of the Model T.

Uncle George and my dad couldn't push the log into the saw blade too fast or the belt would fly off. The operation required a block pitcher to catch the blocks and throw them on the cut block pile. If they came to a really big log the block pitcher had to help lift it up on the cradle. Until my older brother got old enough to lift up the logs or pitch blocks, Dad would ask some of his friends to help out. When he did, Ma invited them in for dinner and jokes.

There were no guards on the circular saw and nobody wore safety goggles, so it was about the most dangerous thing you'd ever see, and you had to be in your late teens to work the cradle or pitch the blocks. I never advanced to that stage, but my brother Ken did. My Uncle George also told us kids to stay away from the belt in case it slipped off—and not to throw anything on the belt that could fly and hit somebody. Younger kids like me who might do that were kept busy carrying smaller pieces from the woodpile over to the saw. My dad put them on the cradle in bundles and sawed three or four of them at once. The block pitcher would end up with his hands full.

That circular saw got the job done though, and no one talked about it being dangerous because if it was used right and you worked at it, a whole big pile of logs would be reduced to firewood-sized blocks in one day. Even though there'd be a huge sawdust pile to remove, it was worth it to get the winter wood sawed. Also, if they set up the Model T saw a day early you'd get to play on the leather seats, turn the steering wheel, aah-ooga the horn and move the gear shift. It had a smell to it—old tired leather, wet horsehair upholstering, gasoline and motor oil—but the big thing about that Model T was its isinglass roll-down windows. It was a great place to play. There was no danger that kids could start it up because to do that you had to set the choke, the spark and gas levers, put the belt on the pulley wheel, and then crank it. My Uncle George and my dad could hardly do all that themselves.

Uncle George's circular saw was set up right next to our kitchen porch one year because we had stacked about eight or ten cords and didn't have time to saw it by hand. That's full cords, not face cords, mind you, and we hadn't left enough room to get the Model T saw down close to the woodshed. The circular saw screeched all day right next to our kitchen door. That drove Ma nuts and created a huge sawdust pile. I could see that Ma was mad about the way Dad set it up because she didn't want sawdust in her flower beds, but she never said anything.

Carl Farm used to stop by at our farm on Sundays. Carl was a boyhood friend of my dad's. If we were sawing wood on Uncle George's saw when Carl came by, Dad would ask him to pitch blocks, but Carl spent most of his time telling jokes, juggling small rocks or snowballs and playing his harmonica. My dad never went for that, although he'd laugh at Carl's jokes. The kids loved when Carl came by because he taught us to juggle, and he could juggle three rocks—or three snowballs—and play the harmonica all at the same time. Later, he was drafted into the infantry during World War II and came back wearing khaki Army pants that he tucked into his Gold Seal boots. He told us he'd been assigned to an antiaircraft gun in Belgium, and that the lower lobe of his right ear had been shot off. The bullet or shrapnel that hit him came close to ending his life. He came back from the war still juggling and playing his harmonica, although the jokes he told were ones he'd heard in the Army. He won the Purple Heart in the war, but he had already won our hearts. Clarence, another friend of my dad, used to stop by, but he and his wife would be all dressed up and coming from church, so I never saw him pitch blocks.

After Uncle George took away his oily, screaming circular saw we had to split the bigger blocks into firewood and pile it for drying just as though we'd sawed it ourselves. If you split a lot of wood you'll get in good shape, my dad said. That was a gross understatement. My brother Bill took a lot more pride in making his woodpiles than I did in mine. Bill always seemed to have a special God-given knack in that regard. He'd keep all the face ends lined up, turned all the uneven or ragged cut faces away from the front side, and worked his blocks till they were neat and even as though he was building a masonry wall. It looked great, and he got a lot of compliments, but I thought it was silly. When Dad told me I should stack firewood like Bill did, I got up from my knees where I was piling, held my hands out at my sides—palms facing forward—and informed him that Bill's piles got burned in the Kalamazoo stove just the same as mine. That's when my dad turned his fierce face on me, said it would help if I learned from my younger brother, and that we'd get more wood in the woodshed doing it Bill's way. He added that, "Wood stacking is good discipline," paused for effect and went back to his old stand-by, "Anything worth doing at all is worth doing well." I tried, but nobody stacked wood like my brother Bill.

Actually, as I learned later in life, firewood stacking is not a frivolous subject to a Norwegian, though it may seem that way to the uninitiated. It was reported on page A-4 of the prestigious *New York Times* as recently as February 20, 2013, no less, that differing theories on how one should stack firewood have split Norwegian firewood choppers into two warring camps. Indeed, As the New York Times reported Lars Mytting, a Norwegian, published a book on the epic battle of the axe men, entitled *Solid Wood: All about Chopping, Drying and Stacking Wood—and the soul of Wood-Burning*, that stayed on the nonfiction best-seller list for more than a year. Mytting's book, which is available on the Internet, evolved into a twelve-hour Norwegian television production watched by millions. Now that certainly is not frivolous. Anyone wishing to delve more deeply into the Norwegian tradition of splitting and stacking firewood should get themselves a copy of these sources and read up on it.

When I read the coverage I was astonished because I had never looked upon firewood cutting, splitting, and stacking in the manner Lars Mitting and the New York Times described. But I must say, the detailed coverage contained in those sources knocked my socks off because back at our woodshed during the Great Depression my dad insisted firewood be stacked bark up, and he had sided with Bill who, once I became aware of Lars Mitting's book and the news coverage, seemed to possess a special Norwegian gene I knew nothing of and didn't inherit.

Not all of the trees we cut were used for firewood. Some pine trees were cut to make lumber for the second and bigger barn my dad built, and one winter we cut a number of spruce, balsam and poplar trees for pulpwood. We didn't have our own horse that winter. My brother Ken borrowed Flaa's horse to drag the pulpwood over to the pole gate leading to Kroon's Road on the north property line. The Flaas were glad to let us use their horse to give it some exercise. If my dad conned them into it with his old line about not killing a horse with kindness, I didn't hear it. I've forgotten if that horse had a name, but it got plenty of exercise.

Throughout that winter Dad, my brothers and I, along with cutting firewood, also cut pulpwood in eight-foot lengths, stacked it and later skidded it to the big pile over by the pole gate. The trails where the logs were dragged became icy as the winter wore on and it was quite a sight to see my brother Ken hanging on to the reins and riding two logs behind Flaa's horse. In the spring the Kroons helped us load it onto their pulp truck. The pulpwood was hauled to a railroad siding near Frenchtown where it was loaded on a railroad car and shipped to the paper mill. We didn't have enough spruce, balsam or popular to fill a whole boxcar with any one of them, so we stacked what we had cut separately on one gondola and shipped a mixed load. It took a major effort to get that done, but we were all glad to see my dad make a few extra bucks. Then we went back to chopping and stacking firewood.

Other than that there aren't a whole lot of good things to say about cutting wood, skidding pulpwood and clearing land. Well, I shouldn't have said that. We used to cut Christmas tree (balsam and spruce) branches and sell them to down-state and Wisconsin strawberry farmers who used them to cover their plants. I also forgot to mention the time we were clearing Harold Stolen's land east of our house and my ma asked Dad to save a large oak tree.

It was unusual to see an oak with only one trunk because most of the oak trees that grew around our farm had several trunks in a cluster. The one Ma liked was about sixty feet tall and as straight as an arrow. Grandpa Carne said it looked like a big umbrella when he saw it. I guess it got that way growing up amidst all the other trees that had been there that we cut down. My dad said it looked like good straight oak lumber to him and wanted to cut it down for the lumber it would produce, although he told Ma the wind was going to blow it down anyway since it was standing there all alone on top of the hill. Ma put her foot down that time and got her way.

One winter after all the leaves had fallen we had a midwinter ice storm and all the trees were coated in ice. I saw it when I was walking up from our crick carrying a pail of water with my skis on my shoulder. The whole scene was bathed in sunlit ice. I'd seen that before, but this time the sun had come up right behind that oak tree, illuminating the frosted ice that covered it and shooting off a halo of glistening sunshine in all directions.

I don't know if Ma knew that would happen, but when I told her about it that morning—and she came out on the porch to take a look—the sight of that oak made her smile. The good Lord had thanked her by turning that oak tree into a sparkling piece of crystal sixty feet high. I'd have written a poem about it myself, but I wasn't very good at that. Later on I asked my sisters to look for a poem that might be named something like "Crystal Oak." I'm sure Ma wrote one because she wrote them about pine trees and put them in old sugar bowls, but if she did, they never found it. Even my dad, as much as he wanted the lumber, would've been forced to admit that the ice storm justified Ma's decision to save the Crystal Oak.

By the time I had graduated from high school and moved on to college, we had cut all the trees off five of our ten acres, three acres of our neighbor's land, and an acre or two of Uncle George's forty. It was all burned in that Kalamazoo stove along with waste slabs from Flaa's sawmill. My dad got rid of the isinglass coal stove in the living room and installed a fuel oil furnace in the basement in the early fifties. By then he was making good money as a contract miner at the Mather A because they worked a lot of overtime. The Michigan Gas and Electric Company (later UP Power) extended the electric lines out to our farm in the late 1940s, but we still used a wood burning stove in the kitchen for cooking. Matt Keto, an electrician, wired our house. It's difficult to install wiring and electric plugs and lighting fixtures in a log house because the walls aren't hollow. I know—I helped. But we got it done. I'll never forget the day when an electric light bulb hanging on a wire lit up our kitchen. A couple years later my sister Ruth, who had hired in at a secretarial and bookkeeping position at Michigan Gas and Electric Company, brought home an electric kitchen stove. Not only Ma, but the trees that remained appreciated that.

Cutting firewood didn't only supply heat, teach Bill how to build masonry walls, and put us in shape physically; it was looked upon as good for family togetherness. As I mentioned, one year we cut hardwood maple from Olaf Stolen's land alongside the two-rut road that led to Graneggen's camp. It was September. My dad and my brothers and I had worked until late on a Sunday afternoon cutting and piling hardwood amidst a riot of brilliantly colored falling leaves. Bone tired we piled the wood we'd cut, put our axes on our shoulders and headed home to a dinner of White Giant roosters with all the trimmings prepared by my ma and my sisters. Ma's fresh roasted chicken, mashed potatoes, stuffing, gravy and pumpkin pie with whipped cream were always delicious, but on those special days when the bunch of us trooped home from cutting and piling maple hardwood, exhilarated from all the work and fresh air, Ma's dinners were as good as it gets. It's too bad you weren't there.

~~~

CHAPTER 12

A Time to Work—
A Time to Play

I DON'T WANT to leave the impression that Ma and Dad were drudges who worked all the time. What with all our chores and school work, though, it is difficult to explain how we had time for any fun at all. I can only relate that in our spare time the family laughed, played games, and had plenty of fun. During the winter months we played games with Ma like Monopoly, Parcheesi, Chinese Checkers, regular checkers (on the black and red board), and card games like High-Low-Jack-and-the-Game (Smear) and Authors. It all happened in the dining room around the big round hand-me-down table where we did our homework and ate Sunday dinners. At night, before we got electricity, the kerosene lamp with the mantle lit up our faces and our games.

Ma liked to play Authors. It helped her to introduce her kids to writers and poets like Tennyson, Poe, Longfellow, and Wordsworth. Sometimes Ma would recite their verses from memory. I remember the writers and poets depicted on the Authors cards as being unsmiling old men wearing dark old-fashioned suits, with long hair and beards. It didn't seem likely to me that the faces on the cards would encourage one to become a writer or a poet, but Ma enjoyed shuffling and dealing out every one of them as she recited their verses. My dad didn't usually participate in Authors or board games, but he did like to play Smear and reveled when he could throw down his cards and yell out, "high, low, jack and the game!" We played Rummy sometimes but not as much as the others.

The family also worked jigsaw picture puzzles on the dining room table. We received them second hand from a relative or as a Christmas present. One large jigsaw puzzle depicting a Conestoga wagon pulled by four horses being driven west by settlers with their cattle and their dogs stands out. Some settlers were mounted, others were on foot. The whole entourage was moving west past a purple mountain under a big, partly clouded sky. I may be wrong on some details (it's been about seventy years), but it was a huge puzzle with a thousand pieces that occupied the dining room table for a couple of weeks. Sometimes the family did jigsaw puzzles depicting famous paintings or sailboats. We always did the edge pieces first. Each kid would assemble portions of the puzzle and move segments into the main body as the picture emerged. Ma said it was easier to insert a piece in the puzzle if you studied color and shape. Sometimes finding a difficult piece created a bit of sibling rivalry and arguments over who found what piece first, and what blue went with what segment. But placing the last piece in the puzzle was a real big deal. Each kid competed to be the one that did, and would hide pieces so they could. The urge to see the completed picture would usually bring the hidden pieces forward, and if it didn't Ma saw to it that the missing pieces were produced.

Using the bushel basket Ken nailed to the garage, we played basketball on the dirt and gravel driveway in front of the garage year round. We didn't stop during the heat of summer or the snows of winter. When he got into high school my brother Ken made a steel hoop in Manual Training that we erected in place of the bushel basket. We also played baseball, softball, and football in the summer. I think another one of our games was called pin ball. We played it out in one of our hay fields in the spring or in summer after the hay had been cut. The object in pin ball was to bat, field and then throw a spongy ball at a batter running the bases and try to hit him before he reached the next base. If you hit him he was out. We carved our own bats out of maple wood. Kick-the-can was a variation of hide-and-go-seek. In that game the players, who had hid themselves from being discovered by it, were saved from being it in the next game if they ran home, kicked a can, and yelled "kick the can" before it saw them, ran to the cellar door and yelled, "You're it!" Once Marvie missed the can and kicked a pitchfork lying nearby. In winter months we ski jumped—more about that later.

After Dad bought the 1937 Ford he would drive as many of the family as would fit in it up U.S. 41 past the village of Champion to Van Riper Park, also known as Champion Beach, for Sunday picnics and swimming. The park is located on Lake Michigamme. He also drove us to plays, operettas, declamations and orations, and basketball games at the National Mine School. In the summer he took us into Ishpeming for ice cream cones he bought at a place on Main Street named something like Dreamland or at Petry's—a convenience store on Division Street. Sometimes we stopped for ice cream cones at either Nault's store or Sarvello's in Frenchtown. There were no fast food places in those days. Dad also drove the kids to Ishpeming on Saturday afternoons so we could see "cowboys and Indians" or the Green Hornet at the Ishpeming Theatre. Dad once told us that when he was a kid his family couldn't afford to go to the movies. He claimed he and the kids he grew up with didn't have the advantages lavished on us, and had to walk to the Ishpeming Theatre on Saturday nights so they could look at movie ads on the wall outside. He laughed each time he told that story until the tears streamed down his face. But Dad used to exaggerate a lot (when he was a kid the movies were "Silents"), so I never knew when to believe him.

After all their kids were raised Ma and Dad used to drive to a roadside park on the way to the Copper Country. They called it "The Tioga." Ma took along a pasty for each of them, along with a thermos of coffee and spread a tablecloth on the picnic table by the little Tioga Creek waterfall. Even when they got up in years the two of them would drive there with their picnic basket and enjoy a couple of Ma's pasties.

Sometimes they drove to a little roadside spot they'd found on U.S. 41 where it passes Teal Lake near the old Cambria mine shaft—not far from the monument where iron ore was discovered. The beautiful Teal Lake vista, that had been part of the hunting lands of the Ojibwa, also had a picnic table, was closer to home and a cluster of white birches grew there. Ma loved the flowers that bloomed there in the summer. Teal Lake had become Negaunee's water supply, so no power boats or bathing were allowed there in those years. Ma said it was quiet—calm. She liked the serene feeling it gave her and wrote poems after they drove home. There was not much time for serenity or poetry in the early years. It's a good thing my sisters found at least some of Ma's poetry.

Now my dad was different. In a lot of ways they were opposites. He drove Ma to Teal Lake, or the sixty miles it takes to get to the Tioga, to please her. But he couldn't stand things being quiet. He was a pedal to the metal type guy. Sometimes on a straight-away, if Ma wasn't in the car and there were no posted limits, he'd push the speedometer toward a hundred miles an hour.

Uncle John used to drive Grandma Carne out to our house to pick up Ma and take her for rides in their four-door 1922 Chevrolet touring car once in a while. After Dad bought the 1937 Ford, Grandpa Carne bought a gray 1940 Chevrolet four-door sedan. I don't think it was because the gear shift lever had been moved to the steering column—he didn't like the idea that Dad had a newer car than he did. Uncle John drove it out to our place. That one was a beauty. It had the wonderful odor of a brand-new car and plush gray upholstering, but it created a lot of discussion between my dad and Grandpa Carne in front of our garage when my dad told Grandpa Carne that his Ford had a V-8 with eighty-five horses and that all the Chevy had was a straight six. Grandpa Carne shot back that the V-8 in the Ford was no good at all because the pistons were lying on their sides and would wear and cause the engine to burn oil. He held up one arm at an angle and rubbed the inside of it when he said that. My dad was not a person you raised your arm at or told things to—relative or not. Neither was Grandpa Carne. They never settled that one that I know of, but V-8 engines became the gold standard in the car industry for many years.

Sometimes one of Grandma Carne's friends, Mrs. Laver or Mrs. Harvey, would get dressed up and drive out in the Chevrolet with them. Grandma Carne was a sight to see perched on the back seat of that sedan. We loved when she came to our house. She had the most beautiful silken white hair you will ever see, and she wore it in combs under hats that had veils. Grandma Carne was a beautiful woman, but then so was my ma—even in her bandana. Ma never wore a hat out on the farm. Once they drove Ma to the Pictured Rocks Park in Munising. Another time my dad drove Ma down to Pembine, Wisconsin, to visit relatives. Those were special days for her and for us because we knew she needed them. They didn't happen a lot because of us kids and all the work. On most days the only rest Ma got came from her poems and the piano.

Grandma Carne gave my ma some red, blue and gold Indian blankets to put in our Ford. She told Ma they'd help keep her warm in the winter. One year Dad drove us into Ishpeming in his new Ford for the Christmas tree lighting ceremony. It was special because we had all drawn names, were given two dollars and went shopping for presents at Woolworth's Five and Ten Cent Store, Newberry's and J.C. Penney's. Then we lined up with the other kids for popcorn balls and oranges that were passed out by policemen when the big Christmas tree lit up near "Old Ish," the statue of an Indian brave in the town square. Dad bought my sisters some sheet music that Christmas. They had taken piano lessons at school from Mrs. Gleason, our music teacher, and had some Stephen Foster stuff they kept in the piano bench and some old hymn books, but nothing modern. Later, a WPA piano teacher came out to our farm and gave my sisters lessons playing classical études, and they learned to play the Stephen Foster stuff real well. My older brother Ken didn't like the piano so he took up the harmonica and later tried to learn to play an old banjo we got from Uncle Dick.

Buying that sheet music wasn't something you expected a wood chopper, a farmer or an iron miner to do. Although, when he first heard about my sisters learning to play at school, he was the one that scouted around, picked up an old player piano, and put it in the living room. The bench came with it. Actually, it didn't all fit in the living room so it sort of jutted out through the arched doorway into the dining room. You could insert paper rolls that had a lot of square holes in them, pump the big pedals, watch the keys go up and down as you held onto the front of the piano and pumped, and play beautiful songs perfectly without knowing one thing about music. My dad thought it was amazing and liked to pump it because he couldn't otherwise play a piano, but my ma didn't like it. She wanted my sisters to learn to play by themselves. Dad had a piano tuner take out all the player apparatus and tune it. My dad put the player parts in the garage and moved the piano into the far corner of the living room. Ma put a lace doily and a bunch of family pictures on top of it.

Even with that I was surprised that Christmas when Dad picked up "Harbor Lights" for my sisters along with another song in a green and white jacket. I'd forgotten the name of the last one and thought it was "Santa Claus Is Coming to Town," but my sister Marian tells me I'm wrong about the green and white jacket and that it was "Alice Blue

Gown." I couldn't argue that one with her because she still has the sheet music. I really can't picture my dad picking out that one either, although I still recall those black and whites of him from the Roaring Twenties. The Depression had suppressed a lot of the things people like to have in their lives. I discovered on that Christmas trip into Ishpeming that my dad was no different.

I was even more shocked when Dad started singing "Harbor Lights" while we were parked on Main Street by the snowbank across the street from the Chocolate Shop, which was all lit up with high school kids milling outside. It sounded okay to me, although Dad was not ready for prime time. All the stores and restaurants were decorated in red and green and lit up for Christmas. I was in the back seat of the Ford and looking out at the street where Dad had driven his roadster years before and where he and Ma met. Snow was falling soft and gentle, and it was the first time I had heard him sing that song, or seen anything like it. Later, I heard him sing something like, "I can't begin to tally you . . ." Something like that. My sister Marian tells me that in the early years he used to sing "Oh What a Friend We Have in Jesus" in Norwegian. I never heard him sing that one, but he liked to speak Norwegian. Ma and my sisters used to play "Harbor Lights" for him on our piano.

My ma insisted that I take piano lessons from the WPA guy, but it didn't take. He smelled like a pack of cigarettes, and put me in a concert at our school. I have no idea what I played. It had to be real bad. As far as I can tell I didn't get past "Peter, Peter, Punkin Eater." But I was amazed to learn on that Christmas that Dad liked music and even liked to dance.

My ma was a different story altogether when it came to the piano. She played "by ear" according to what Ruth, one of my older sisters, told me. Ma could hear a new song she never heard before on the radio and just sit down and play it, chords and all. I think she added some of her own to it, and it sure sounded good. Her hymns did too. Better than the radio as far as I was concerned. I sure couldn't do it. Ruth told me Ma heard notes like "do," "re," "mi" and knew where they were on the keyboard, but to me it was like magic.

She played songs like that many years later in the dining room at the Mather Nursing Home. Even though everyone there liked to hear her play and said so, you could hardly get her to do it because she never had lessons and didn't consider herself to be a piano player. If they pressed her to do it she'd put one hand to the side of her face like she always did and shake her head. It sounded good enough to me, and if you ever saw her do it at home when no one was watching you'd know for sure she loved to play the piano. She'd take all the music off the rack and put it in the piano bench while she was dusting and then sit down and play with a flair that told you she loved it one hell of a lot more than dusting. None of us was smart enough to tape her, so it's all gone.

Our music teacher, Mrs. Gleason, would put on a Christmas pageant each year in the auditorium at the National Mine School. In those days you could perform Christmas plays in public schools. It was the same big stage where the high school kids put on the senior play and the high school boys played basketball. All the parents would come to see their little kids dressed up in costumes that had been sewn by the girls in Home Economics classes, wearing rouge and singing Christmas songs. It was a spectacular pageant that required every ounce of patience Mrs. Gleason had and involved every teacher in the school. The guys in Manual Training were in charge of the scenery under the direction of her husband, Mr. Gleason, who was also the basketball coach and later became the driver training instructor. Everybody knew that Mrs. Gleason would put on a good Christmas pageant, and every year, no matter how bedraggled it made her, she did. My sisters usually had leading roles. Ma used to drill them in their parts.

Each Christmas, the day after the pageant was over, all the kids at school would queue up and receive a brown grocery bag down at Mr. Bath's office—he was the Superintendent. The bags were full of stuff like Cracker Jacks, peanuts, hard candy, a popcorn ball, an orange and an apple. That would really get us going because on that day the bus took us home early and would be filled with kids carrying not only the usual armload of homework but big brown Christmas bags and singing carols from the Christmas pageant. Some had pretty good voices— almost as good as the Cracker Jacks. For some families the brown bag was the only Christmas present the kids would see.

But tough as things were, Christmas at our house was special. Somehow, Christmas came every year no matter how poor we were. Dad would find a perfect spruce tree, usually two or three miles back in the woods, drag it home, nail it to a wooden stand, and put it up in the living room in front of the window between the piano and the radio. He didn't care whose land it came from if it was seven feet high and had a perfect shape. Later on my brothers and I did it. We had no electric lights in the early years, but we'd string silver tinsel and gold roping on it, put the star on the top and get out all of the balls and tree ornaments Grandma Carne gave us. One year my brother Ken made a Yule log. Another year my dad, who had some kind of a streak in him, got in real trouble with my ma when he took my new cork gun and started to shoot Christmas tree balls off our tree. He was showing us what a good shot he was, but Ma didn't appreciate the results.

On Christmas Eve, Grandpa and Grandma Carne would visit, along with Ma's brothers, Uncle John and Uncle Doc. They wanted nothing to do with lutefisk, so Ma had to serve it and clean it up before they arrived. We'd gather around the isinglass coal stove and open presents. There'd be fruitcake baked by my ma, strawberry and orange pop from Elson's Bottling Works, together with all sorts of cookies, nuts, chocolates, and Christmas candies. The kids had all drawn names, and Grandma Carne and Uncle Doc brought out gifts so we'd have presents to open. I usually got new socks or mittens, but one year I got a new wallet with places for photographs. The year I drew my sister Ruth's name I gave her some Mum deodorant. Ruth was embarrassed when all the kids laughed as she opened that one, but Ruth understood that I meant well.

Later, Marian, my oldest sister, moved to Flint after she graduated and got a secretarial position at AC Sparkplug. She sent us a big box of presents every year. Ma opened that box on the dining room table and gently put all the presents under the tree—one at a time. You knew Marian's presents were special because of how carefully they were wrapped, but also because you were told not to open yours until Christmas Eve.

We were told about Santa Claus, and hung up our stockings—some with darned toes—but I was probably eight years old when that one got blown away. My brother Ken, who was three and a half years older than I, had maple skis that were six feet long, and that didn't sit well with me and my younger brother Bill. Ken used to take them up to Flaa's hill where he and the Flaa boys had built a ski jump just to the north of our farm. You couldn't jump far on that hill, maybe fifty feet tops, because it didn't have a steep enough in-run to the bump nor a long enough landing. But you could look out of the windows in the dining room of our house and see my brother and the Flaa boys jump that hill. For an eight year old and his little brother wanting to jump, that looked as good as anything could be.

Bill and I understood that Dad could hardly afford more skis, but we had asked for, and were expecting, Santa Claus to bring them for Christmas. No one said he wouldn't. My dad, who provided everything but rarely bought any presents himself, saw the problem, I guess, and went into town. I don't know where he got them, probably Jackson's Hardware Store, but he brought home five-foot maples for me and four-foot maples for my brother Bill. It was all the footage he could pay for. He hid them behind the Kalamazoo stove in the kitchen so that Santa Claus could deliver them on Christmas Eve, and they'd be there under the tree when we came down the stairs on Christmas morning. But Dad couldn't take the pressure of waiting for Santa Claus. He sat fidgeting in his chair at the head of the kitchen table near the Kalamazoo stove. When he had something going it showed. Three days before Christmas he got those skis out and gave them to me and my brother Bill. What a day that was.

Now you have to understand that the skis he gave us didn't have binders, just leather straps you put your toes through. After we waxed them up with my older brother's wax—which he had taken from the wax Ma used for canning—Bill and I cut rubber bands from an old inner tube and put them around our ankles. We put our toes through the straps on the skis and pulled the rubber band over our toes. If the band broke one of us tied it back together with string while the other stretched out the part to be tied. We got real good at doing that. A lot of kids on the bus wore three or four inner tube binders around their ankles, so we knew how to do it. Some of them called them "Firestone binders."

It took a few years before Bill and I were able to jump Flaa's hill, but we did. I don't have a recollection of the first time, but I'd have been scared when I took off from the rocky bluff where the icy in-run started on those five-foot maples wearing Firestone binders, hunkering down through Flaa's apple orchard and building speed until I straightened out, took off from the bump and tried for a "red wing landing" like the kids who had metal spring binders talked about on the school bus. Landing was a different thing than they talked about because of those Firestone binders and the ruts in the landing. But we got pretty good at riding Flaa's hill with Firestone binders.

My cousin Jack's hill in the New England location, though, was a whole lot bigger. Jack was Uncle Nels' son. Both of my binders came off in midair the first time I rode it, and I landed without skis. Don't try that one. Later on my brother Ken got eight-foot hickories with spring binders and he let me use them. I won the jump Marvie held on his hill the first time I used those hickories.

I never graduated to the big ski jumps like "Little Bluff" in National Mine and certainly not "Suicide Hill" east of Ishpeming—just off M-28 on the way to Negaunee. I can't say I'd have jumped those hills even if I had the equipment, but I'd like to think I would've. The big meet at Suicide usually took place on or near Washington's Birthday. If the weather was too windy or stormy the meet would be postponed, but it was held every year. At Suicide, jumpers made jumps that measured over two hundred fifty feet. It attracted ski jumpers from all over—including the "Flying Bietala" brothers from Ishpeming, Dave Freeman from Iron Mountain, and jumpers from Lake Placid, Norway, Sweden, Finland, and Austria. If the jump took place on a school day just about all the kids took off for the afternoon and found a way to get to the big jump at Suicide. At the bottom of the jump, stands were set up to vend popcorn, coffee, hot chocolate, hot dogs, hamburgers, and of course beef pasties. It was one hell of a day.

I recall the year in the late 1940s that a stocky round-faced Norwegian jumper, whose last name I believe was Kongsgaard, came to the Suicide meet. Kongsgaard was already famous for jumps he'd made at Hollmenkollen in Norway and at other venues in Europe. Out-of -town jumpers stayed in Ishpeming; I'd expect at the Mather Inn. Dad approached a group of strolling ski jumpers on Main Street in Ishpeming that year, introduced himself as the son of Norwegian immigrants, and asked Kongsgaard for his autograph. Dad said later that although Kongsgaard was very friendly, he was astounded when Dad could produce nothing he could sign except a five dollar bill. Later, Dad proudly displayed the five dollar bill all over Ishpeming and laughed as he described how flabbergasted Kongsgaard had been to meet "such an extravagant American."

On the day Kongsgaard was to compete Dad took time off from work to attend the meet, but became concerned there'd be no jump that day when a severe winter storm rolled in with high winds. After meet officials haggled back and forth, Dad about popped all the buttons off his chambray shirt when Kongsgaard was the one asked to do a trial run to determine if Suicide was safe to jump. In those days ski jumpers held their arms forward, not down and back like they do today, but have no doubt—once airborne a jumper becomes in effect an airplane wing. He must maintain lift during the jump and fight off crosswinds. Kongsgaard, clad in a navy blue tassel cap with black numbers on a white tie-on covering his ski sweater, and ski pants tucked into his ski boots, pushed off the scaffolding high above the trees, plunged down the in-run, leapt from the take-off, stretched for distance in heavy wind and snow, executed a perfect red wing landing, and slewed to a stop at the bottom of the out-run with a huge grin on his reddened face. The crowd roared. Kongsgaard had established that Suicide was safe to jump, and Dad had yet another Norwegian story that he told for years. The afternoons we spent at the Suicide Meet were always very special days, but for my dad the day Kongsgaard jumped in a snow storm was the best of all.

Still, if you were honest about it, severe snow storms in February were no novelty around Ishpeming. Shoveling snow off the road in from the Corner was another story altogether. We'd all get involved in that. I recall taking a square snow shovel, cutting one foot cubes and clearing out our drive with my brothers and sisters. You'd get it cleared and before you could turn around the wind would drift it in again. You expected that.

In the legendary "Winter of Thirty-eight," a huge snowstorm left drifts six feet high in places. Ishpeming was buried in snow. My dad had to leave his Ford at Millimaki's gas station more than two miles from home when that one hit and then walk home through drifts up to his waist. Someone took pictures that showed a dozen or more cars and trucks parked at Millimaki's gas station with their roofs barely sticking out through the snow. Others were completely buried. We were snowed in for over a week, and all the kids loved the fact that there was no school. That time the county came with a Caterpillar tractor snowplow that was twelve feet high with tiers of yellow blades in front of it and that ran on treads. It was hard to get that thing in on our drive because of the place where the ledge jutted out, but somehow they did. My ma got out her box camera and took a picture of snowbanks ten feet high that it pushed up in front of our house. I don't remember if it knocked down our mailbox, but we found out later that spring that the county's tractor snowplow had knocked over our fence and left scrape marks on the ledge down by the Corner.

There's something exciting about a big snow like that. Everything changes for a while. There is adventure in just living through it. Dad had to take Ken's skis and go into town for groceries because we were socked in. My ma waited in the living room, blowing on the window to melt the frost to make a peephole so she could look out to see if he got through. Finally, she saw a black speck coming in on skis. It grew until she saw the burlap bag over his shoulder. The kids knew it when she yelled out that Dad had made it through. It was a good thing we had a woodshed full of wood and pork, potatoes and preserves in the basement, coal in the bin in the garage and hay in the barn when that storm hit. The "Winter of Thirty-eight" became a legend as stories about it grew. It was as though we had all climbed Mt. Everest. Mother Nature had reminded all of us that no matter how tough it may be to dig out of a Great Depression, she could always ask for a little more and expect to get it.

Later, after our road in from the Corner was finished, the regular snowplow was able to plow all the way in to our garage once the main roads were cleared, so the amount of shoveling was cut down. But the winters remained severe. We still had to clear snow left by the plow off the driveway up to the garage, and dig two parallel paths out to the Corner for Dad's Ford if he had to go to work and the plow hadn't plowed our drive. On some days the snow blew in so fast there wasn't time to shovel. When that happened two or three kids would get behind the Ford and push it to get it going. While Dad spun the wheels, we'd rock it back and forth until he built up the speed he'd need to blast his way through newly fallen or drifted snow all the way out to the Corner with kids laughing and pushing from behind. After he left, the kids would clear the two ruts and hope they didn't blow back in. Winter lasted from November to May, so there was a lot of snow shoveling. We even had one snow storm in July.

~~~

Figure 32

Cleveland Avenue, Ishpeming, Michigan—
after the Blizzard of 1938. - TO-ISH- 108

Photograph courtesy of Superior View Studios

Cool Country—Sketch
by Richard T. Carne

Running Water on Skis—
Sketch by Richard T. Carne

Figure 33

Ski meet at Suicide Hill in the 1940s (SP-SKI 21)

"The Flying Bietalas"

(L–R) Leonard, Roy, Ralph & Walter (SP-SKI 13)

Photographs courtesy of Superior View Studios

CHAPTER 13

The Discipline of the Rows

MOST FOLKS WHO drive by farms with cultivated fields and a big red barn don't understand farm work. It isn't just milking cows, curry-combing horses, feeding chickens, collecting eggs, slopping hogs, carrying in firewood or water, or even shoveling snow—which are nothing but daily chores. You have to do those jobs even if you have homework or orations at school, a basketball game, or if there is other farm work to do. A lot of farm work is seasonal, and it's hard work. Remember that.

I've already explained firewood cutting and hog butchering. Our farm is grown back in with trees now, but when I lived there we grew hay, potatoes, and rutabagas on that place. We didn't have a lot of space to do it in because part of our ten acres was swampy. Also, my dad sold one acre out on the west side to Marvie's uncle, Waino Kaminen. Waino needed a place to put his house trailer and we needed cash. Actually, we couldn't use the west side because it was so full of rocks and stumps you couldn't get a plow in the ground if you tried. The soil back there wasn't good anyway. Not like the loam we had up front. I'd say we had five tillable acres altogether once most of the stumps and rocks were dug out and removed. I don't have any idea how Dad farmed the place before his kids got old enough to help, but our fields told you he did.

It was always made clear to me growing up that while the good Lord created grass and clover, if our cows and our horse were to eat in the winter, "You have to make hay when the sun shines." You can laugh all you want, but I was actually told that along with a lot of other stuff like "Don't cry over spilled milk," "Children should be seen and not heard," and "Honesty is the best policy." The grownups kept bringing up stuff like that along with our high school principal's favorite—"W-O-R-K = S-U-C-C-E-S-S." That one was printed in chalk in big white letters on the blackboard in front of the Large Assembly, never erased, and sometimes read out loud before classes held there. It was presented like an algebraic formula (thus immutable and irrefutable) that set forth the work ethic in big chalk letters. If you didn't like the shape of the world imposed by these and other adages too numerous to list here, you would be told that, "What can't be cured must be endured." I was also pointedly told that haymaking was not just work—it was hard work. But I already knew that because all the work that I could see around our farm was hard. The part I didn't get at the time was that hard work was good for kids because it helped to build their character.

My dad planted timothy and red clover in among the rocks that were too big to move and the stumps he couldn't get out right away. He said growing hay would help rot the stumps. The timothy and clover came in good, though not like what you see pictured in the seed catalogs. Some shorter white clover came up too, along with daisies, dandelions, buttercups, Indian paintbrush and quack grass. If the good Lord planted those, He did it without any means to separate them from good grass and clover, so it all got harvested together and became hay for our cattle and our horse whether the sun was shining or not. They would separate out what they liked right there in the barn. We used the stuff they didn't eat for bedding. If it rained and the grass got too wet to cut, you would not be bored because you could always sharpen an axe or a scythe blade or cut and split firewood. My dad was good at starting a new job before the old one got finished.

Ma liked daisies, dandelions, and buttercups, and even the blazing-red Indian paintbrush that grew in our fields. Sometimes, if she found a minute or two, you'd see her sitting in the lawn chair my brother Ken made in Manual Training at school, transfixed by flowers waving in the wind across our fields. She even wrote poems about them, although I never saw any poems about quack grass or Canadian thistle. Marvie's dad used to complain to my dad about having Indian paintbrush in his fields. The stuff grew all over and ruined his hay fields just like it was doing to ours. My dad laughed and said, "Don't worry about it, Jake. That stuff grows where nothing else will." That was the truth. On our farm it grew in hardpan even if you didn't put any fertilizer on it at all, and the cows would not eat it. Go figure.

One of the first needs you will have if you make hay on a small farm is a sharp scythe. I know it would've been better to have a mowing machine that Nellie could've pulled, but we couldn't even afford a grindstone to put scythe blades or noses on, and anyway, we had too many rocks and stumps in our fields to run a mower through them. At first, Dad used to take our scythe blades back to Grandpa Ole's place in New Burt and sharpen them there. In fact he sharpened all his tools there, except saw blades. You can't sharpen a saw on a grindstone. I liked to go to New Burt with him and my brother Ken because my cousins Bob and Jerry, Aunt Adele, and Uncle George lived there with Grandpa Ole. Aunt Adele, who always wore crisp aprons, smiled and gave me a "baloney" sandwich with Miracle Whip every time I went there. We never had Miracle Whip at our house.

Grandpa Ole kept his grindstone in a dusty little room leading into his barn. It smelled real bad from his cows, and most people would have seen it as being dirty and cluttered up with tools and horse harness. But it was the grindstone that dominated the room. It was a huge thing for a little kid to look up at—about thirty inches in diameter and four inches thick with a big metal handle on the end. It turned on ball bearings and rested in a trough of water. The water drained down off the grinding surface as the grindstone turned, which prevented the tool being sharpened from heating up or losing its temper. A lot of tempers could get heated up and lost when that grindstone was used. A kid standing on the little stool Grandpa Ole kept there could take hold of the handle and turn the grindstone at whatever speed my dad called for as he expertly concentrated on holding a blade to the grindstone. You were not allowed to stop while he was grinding. My dad said Grandpa Ole made the little stool especially for kids to stand on when they turned the grindstone.

At first my big brother said that I could come along, and he'd let me watch while he took the handle and turned the grindstone because it took strength, character and grit to stand for hours turning that grindstone at a smooth, steady speed while my dad sharpened his tools, and that I didn't have it yet, but could acquire it if I watched and didn't play around or bother the cows in Grandpa Ole's barn. That's what he told me. I have to admit that made me jealous at first, and made me want to be the one selected to turn that grindstone, but there came a time when I would've been happy to let my big brother get picked and watch him turn that grindstone all day long.

I figured out later that I'd been lured in and that the Miracle Whip sandwich was bait, because you would have to turn that handle for several hours while my dad sharpened his tools. My dad, who normally didn't talk a lot or hand out advice on what he was doing while he was bent over concentrating on grinding, did not hesitate to remind me what good eyesight he had, that he'd turned that handle for Grandpa Ole while standing on the same stool I was on, and how important it was for a young kid to develop into a tool sharpener with character who could grind away bad metal, avoid a wire edge and produce a sharp tool. More bait. Later on when my older brother suddenly became expert enough to work the grinding end, my younger brother Bill and I turned the handle. I lured Bill in just like I'd been.

We sharpened scythe blades in late June or early July when the grass got high enough to cut. Once we got the blades razor sharp and back home, one blade would be bolted to the scythe handle Dad took down from the maple tree by the garage and honed even more with a whetstone. Oh, what a stroke Dad had with that whetstone. It was a thing of beauty to see him holding the scythe handle erect in front of him and stroking the scythe blade on first one side of the edge and then the other, over and over in one continuous fluid motion. He reminded me of a violinist. The other newly sharpened scythe blades were wrapped in butcher paper and put between studs in the garage to be whetted and used later. If you asked Dad why he put a whetstone to a blade he had been grinding for more than an hour, he'd tell you he had to make sure the wire edge was gone—a wire edge, like any wire, will break if you bend it back and forth.

I couldn't see wire edges as well as he did, but you'd have to admit, even if you didn't really want to, that my dad had sharp vision and was the world's best guy with a whetstone. He always said he was, and when he officially announced that the scythe was ready to cut, he could shave off timothy, wildflowers, and even short clover with smooth rhythmic strokes of the scythe that left an impressive sheared cut in front and neat windrows to his left and behind as he moved forward with a step-pause-step-pause gait. He said he could've shaved the fuzz off the face of a fourteen-year old boy going through puberty. My ma asked him to shave off the grass and clover around the house. The blade wouldn't stay sharp without repeated use of the whetstone, so it and a mason jar full of water to soak and cool the whetstone had to be moved along as the windrows lengthened. If the scythe blade contacted hay bale wire that shouldn't be there, a rock or a pile of dirt left at a groundhog hole, it went back to the grindstone along with one of the kids.

Before too long I was taught the intricacies of the scythe, but I never did master the art of sharpening blades even later when my dad brought home a brand-new grindstone you could sit on and pedal like a bicycle. The water dripped from a little can onto that one. I didn't like that grindstone either but for a different reason. It wasn't a bicycle. I had never owned my own bicycle, nor did any of my brothers, and I didn't know how to ride one. In fact no one in our family had a bicycle until my sister Dort bought one after she graduated from high school and got her own job at Michigan Bell Telephone as an operator and needed transportation to Ishpeming. But that was a girl's bike, so my brothers and I never used it. A bicycle grindstone seemed like an insult to me.

Like most field work you do on a farm, scything down a field of hay gets to be a row after row kind of thing—finish one row, turn, walk back, scythe the next row. My dad said the whole thing involved discipline. It was a word he frequently used; and a word he always pronounced "Dis-Cip-Line" with great emphasis placed on the middle syllable. My mother-in-law, Lois Olson (Loie), who attended college and came into my life much later, would have pointedly told Dad, as she did me with respect to words I mispronounced, that he was placing the em-PHA-sis on the wrong syl-LAB-le.

After the scything was finished and the hay was lying in windrows, it had to be spread with a pitchfork and later turned over so it wouldn't dry wrong. Then it had to be stacked. To do that you'd have to undo the spreading you'd done a day or two before and rake all the hay back into windrows using a rake that had wooden teeth—another row after row kind of thing you did while walking on the sharply cut stubble that was drying out. If you had holes in your shoes you'd better plug them with cardboard or folded newsprint.

New, of course, a new hayrake has wooden teeth that are factory made, firmly seated about three inches apart along the crossbar, and quite perfect. However, wooden teeth are prone to loosen out in the sun and apt to break if you're not careful when you're pulling hay into windrows. If your hayrake hits a snag and you jerk too hard, a tooth can break off. On real bad days you'd find yourself bringing a rake back to Dad that looked like a hockey player's smile. At that point you'd hear, "Can't you even pull a hayrake?" Dad would get on you real good because he'd have to carve new teeth and drive them into the crossbar. If that isn't done just so, the teeth will fall out again and you will be blamed. It didn't take Dad long to train us to replace the broken teeth ourselves, which he said would help avoid breaking them.

I never took to raking hay or to putting new teeth in a hayrake. The best part about it was Ma squeezing lemons and bringing a pitcher of lemonade out to us that we poured into jelly glasses and drank right there in the hay field. We didn't have a refrigerator so there'd be no ice, but she always used cool water from our crick with lemon rinds and pieces of the lemons floating in it and told us not to work too hard.

Once it was stacked, the hay had to be transported into the barn. We couldn't afford a hay wagon either, so we used our maple clothesline poles. They were long, slender, strong and available. Two of them could be easily slipped under a haystack so that with one kid on the front and another on the back, the whole haystack could be picked up and carried up to the barn where we used pitchforks to lift it up into the hayloft. One kid on the bottom lifted up a forkful of hay, and one up in the hayloft door sunk his pitchfork in and pulled the hay into the loft. The one on top had to avoid the wasp nests up there and be careful not to snag the pitchfork of the kid below and pull it out of his hands. It might fall and hurt him.

Once in the loft the hay was pushed across the floor and dropped into the hay barn that Dad built behind the barn where the cattle and our horse were going to eat it. None of us ever told Dad that I know of, but sometimes his kids, including me, used to take a run across the floor of the hayloft above the barn where the cattle were housed and summersault into the new hay in the barn behind. If he found out he'd have said, "You don't play in the hay, dammit! It's food for the cattle."

One of the more exciting things about making hay is getting it into the hayloft ahead of a rainstorm. There might be as many as twenty or thirty haystacks scattered out in the field when the leaves on the trees began to show their white backs, the wind came up and a sudden summer rain storm threatened to move in. There were no Doppler radar reports in those days. Suddenly you'd hear my dad, brother, sister, whoever yelling, "Rain's coming! Get the hay in the barn," and we'd all spring into action like firemen going to a fire. It was up to the kids to pick the clothes off the clotheslines if there were any there and throw them in the clothes baskets, and to then get the clothesline poles under the stacks—which were carried up to the barn by two running kids—and then hoisted into the hayloft before the rain hit. Rainwater makes hay rot so there is a need for swift action. I still see kids running with haystacks on clothesline poles across sharp stubble left by Dad's scythe while black thunderheads came rolling in from the west.

Because our land could not grow enough hay to feed our cattle and our horse, we also got permission to harvest hay from our neighbors' fields. They liked having us cut their fields, and it didn't matter to them if I was the one that had to scythe them down or not. Even with that, in the spring before the snow melted our hay supply would run out, and each year we'd have to buy a ton or so of baled hay from Spear and Son and have them deliver it with their truck. If my dad wasn't there the driver would ask me or my brothers to sign pink delivery receipts he laid on the truck bed and then peel out and hand us a carbon copy to give to Dad. They used real carbon paper in those days. It even smelled official.

In the summer our cows were allowed to graze in our neighbor's field to the west of our farm and didn't need a lot of hay. They knew where the good grass was and would walk there by themselves down through the pole gate to the path outside the fence on the south property line. At feeding and milking time in the evening, when you heard tinkling and clanging cowbells, you'd know they were walking home with Queen trotting after them. We knew which of them was coming by the sound of each bell. Sometimes we would have to go to the pasture and recover a calf that got left behind.

In the winter though, our cattle and our horse depended on the hay we'd cut the previous summer. Part of our evening chores involved taking hay from the hay barn and placing it in mangers in front of them. To do that you lit a kerosene lantern, walked through snow down the path to the barn with Queen trotting behind, lifted the big iron hooks on the Dutch doors, and hung the lantern on a tenpenny nail in the joists in the ceiling. Queen was never allowed in the barn because she might spook the cows, but if she'd been given a choice she wouldn't have come in anyway because of the smell and the manure. She wouldn't want to mess up her feet.

I can still picture Nellie and our cows munching hay after their stalls had been cleaned, new bedding was laid down and they had been watered and then fed middling or cornmeal. I still see orange light from a gently swinging lantern that rippled shadows from its frame throughout the barn. It was a time of peace when you knew that the animals depended on you, that you'd done the best you could for them, and that they were warm and contented.

Potatoes were planted on the northeast corner of our ten acres at first, and then Dad converted that area to hay and clover, except for a little piece my ma took over for her vegetable garden up near the house. Later, he selected a potato field, about two acres in all, southwest of the farmhouse. When you become dependent on a potato crop, you tend to believe that the whole world ought to grow them, and that if they did it would solve world famine. Whatever you might think about that, bringing in a potato crop was big on our farm. It was important that you knew how to grow them. They don't take long to grow actually, but while they are in the process of doing that you will have more hard work to do. That didn't seem to bother my dad because he was addicted to hard work and wanted his kids to be the same.

Starting in late spring, after the last of the snow had melted, the potato field was plowed, then harrowed, any additional rocks the plow might have thrown up were picked and whatever horse we were using at the time would pull the banker through the field and create a series of trenches about eight to ten inches deep and three feet apart. All of that is easy to say, but not so easy to do if you're the kid picking rocks, holding the plow or bobbing along behind the banker.

On planting day, Grandpa Ole sat on a wooden chair Dad put on one end of the potato field with the seed potatoes in bushel baskets by his side. The sight of Grandpa Ole cutting our seed potatoes lingers because the manner in which he did that was inscrutable—unbelievably difficult. He'd roll each seed potato in his hands before he deliberately took the knife, selected a line and cut it in two. At one point I thought he might be blessing the seed potatoes. He insisted on doing it himself, not because he liked to sit in a new potato field, but because, as he said, Dad could only afford so many seed potatoes, and it is critical that the pieces you end up with each have at least three eyes. That's where the stems come from. I think he said three. My brothers might remember it differently. I was never entrusted to cut seed potatoes—I didn't have the wisdom or the knack for it. After Grandpa Ole went to live with the Lord, my dad cut the seed potatoes.

You could use whole potatoes, but to create more stalks, they were always cut. The kids took buckets full of the cut potatoes and placed them in the trenches one step at a time, cut side down and about fifteen inches apart. If we had any cow manure left over after fertilizing the hay fields it would be thrown into the trench. Horse manure would never be used if that could be avoided, unless our horse dropped it there by accident. After that the banks from either side were manually pulled in over the seed potatoes. To get that job done we had to employ as many kids as were around and all of our rakes, hoes and shovels. It was important to create a hill or hump down the line where the potatoes were planted to give the new potatoes enough soil for growing and to mark the row.

In a few weeks the blessing took hold and new potato plants emerged, together with a whole batch of dandelions, Indian paintbrush, milkweed, quack grass and Canadian thistles that hadn't been blessed or intentionally fertilized, but grew much better than the potatoes did. This necessitated weeding and hoeing. There were no chemicals to kill the weeds. The fun seemed to go out of it at that point because weeding and hoeing a row of potatoes the way we did it is a humbling experience. We didn't use Nellie or any of the horses I've mentioned to pull the banker or a cultivator through the rows and plow the weeds under like you might see in a newsreel. That was because the horses we were using hadn't been trained to do it, we had no time to train them, and they'd have stepped on too many of the potato plants or pulled the banker or cultivator into the planted rows. We could not afford to lose any sprouting potato plants.

My dad said it was a hands and knees job that required discipline, and had to be performed out in the hot sun while the soil was dry without disturbing the potato plants and by leaving the pulled weeds between the potato rows behind you for later pickup as you crawled along. The Canadian thistles were the worst because you had to dig your fingers in down under the roots. If you came upon a rock that had been missed you took that out too. When some of us kids asked if it might be better to use the cultivator or the banker anyway, we were told by my dad that you can't just bank the weeds under. "You have to get the roots or they'll come right back." When we pointed out that they did that anyway my dad said, "It'll be good discipline for you."

When your row was finished you turned and did the next row down from the one your brother or sister was in until the patch was weeded. Then the rows were hoed one by one to loosen the soil so it would retain water better and not dry out. I got to thinking about potato weeding and hoeing, as well as the other work we had to do on our farm, as the discipline of the rows.

Weeds are bad things to have in a potato patch, but potato bugs are worse. If they get in and you don't do something they'll destroy the whole crop. I don't know where potato bugs get their information, but they don't bother dandelions, Indian paintbrush or Canadian thistles and have a knack for finding a potato patch freshly planted by poor people out in a remote wilderness and then inundating it. It's as though they're mad at potatoes, if not the poor people who plant them, and seek them out.

One remedy that doesn't involve any chemicals is to examine the leaf backs of all the potato plants in the field one by one for the orange eggs that are the telltale sign that the first stage of a potato bug attack has commenced. You can either remove the leaf or destroy the eggs with your thumbnail. That is not an efficient method to protect a whole field because you will not find all of the eggs, and potato bugs have a habit of coming back even if you do, and, take it on faith, you'll never see a potato bug laying eggs. Or you could go through the field and pick all the potato bugs off the leaves once they hatched, put them in coffee cans, pour some kerosene on them and burn them. No one ever saw that method work either, so chemicals had to be used to kill the bugs—either Paris Green or, I guess, arsenic. That worked.

First you made a wand out of stalks of straw or timothy hay that were tied together with string and looked sort of like a round whisk broom. Then, after you waited to make sure it wouldn't rain for a few days, the wand was dipped into the bag holding the powdered, poisonous chemicals and shaken over the potato plants one by one so that the poison would fall on the leaves. No one questioned the wisdom of doing this without a mask or of putting those chemicals into the soil in those days, at least not on our farm, because if you wanted potatoes in the fall that's the way it was done. Grandpa Carne did it that way at the cottage he leased north of Ishpeming, and we simply had to bring in our potato crop every year.

After you got through potato bug season, the field would be weeded and hoed several additional times before harvest. A tough job my dad would say, and then stand proud up there on the hill in late August looking down on the potato patch when Grandpa Carne came out.

If you came up by them you could hear Grandpa Carne saying, "Just look at those tidy green rows of bug-free potatoes will ya." He'd say something like that every year, and my dad would just smile as though he'd done the whole thing all by himself. It's best if a kid says nothing at a defining moment like that and just appreciates the discipline of the rows.

In late August Ma would ask for new potatoes so a few plants would be dug up for her to see how the crop was doing. Then in early September the whole field would be hand-dug. Here again we didn't use our horse and the banker because that would crush, pierce or cut those precious damn potatoes in half, which I sometimes thought might be a good idea. When we asked Dad about that he hitched Nellie to the banker one time and proved you couldn't do it that way and end up with many potatoes you could eat.

First you pull the plant, remove any potatoes that come out with it and throw them behind between your legs. Then you hoe to either side of the center so as not to spear any potatoes and then pull the soil away from them. Hoe one row, turn and do the next row down from your brother or sister. We were told that there is great pleasure in doing this carefully, and in finding big, white, mealy potatoes that you haven't speared with your hoe. My brothers spent the day looking for bigger ones than I found and holding them up so I could see them as if they'd grown them all by themselves. If I found a big one I'd keep it to the side and wait for them to hold up theirs and then nail them with it as soon as they did. Usually, there would be eight to ten potatoes of good size from each plant and a larger number that were smaller or marble sized. The latter, and any that were cut or speared too badly, were boiled up and fed to the hogs.

We always tried to remove the crop on a sunny day so the surfaces of the potatoes could dry in the sun. They couldn't be left out overnight on top of the soil because a heavy dew or frost could spoil them. The dried crop had to be bagged in gunny bags or put in bushel baskets and placed on the stoneboat. Nellie, who up until then had stood in the barn creating manure, could then be used to pull them up to the entrance to the basement where they were carried down the basement steps and stored on a wooden platform for winter use. We'd end up with forty or fifty bushels. What I'm trying to tell you is that potato digging was hog butchering and firewood splitting on steroids. Sometimes before we got around to harvesting the rutabagas and carrots the ground had become partially frozen.

I'd have to say though that as tough as those days could sometimes be, it made you feel good. You might think me crazy, but the year we asked Harold Stolen, our neighbor to the east, to let us use his field to plant our potatoes stands out. He was happy to get his field plowed, harrowed and weeded. Later, he planted timothy and clover there, but the soil was more adapted to a potato crop. We proved that by producing a bumper crop the first year we planted there. Harold's field was on the hillside to the east. It got good sun.

During the harvest that September I stood on the road in from the Corner and looked up at our potatoes drying on the hillside in Stolen's field. It struck me then that potatoes played a huge role in our diet. But, I also felt those good, warm feelings that come from working hard, growing your own food, and knowing that Dad and Ma were growing more than potatoes.

~~~

Figure 34

Ben surveying his farm with one of his beagles circa 1950. The barn shown here is the second barn he built. This painting is taken from a painting placed on a carpenter's crosscut saw used to build the farm. It was painted by Kathrine (Waters) Savu and is reproduced here with her permission.

Figure 35

Main Street, Ishpeming —1940. TO- ISH- 47

Miners at the Lloyd Mine in North Lake—1940s. IM-LlOY- 03
Photographs courtesy of Superior View Studios

CHAPTER 14

Women's Work

MA DIDN'T DO field work, tend livestock, or saw and split firewood, although she helped raise baby chicks and kept a vegetable garden up by the house. Ma, assisted by my sisters, did the housework, cooked our meals, cleaned the house, helped with homework and, of course, washed, ironed, and sewed our clothes. In those days, a man's work and a woman's work were completely separated at our house. Dad liked it that way. Ma used to quote an old adage to my dad: "a man works from sun to sun, but a woman's work is never done." When she did, my dad would repeat the line, putting strong emphasis on *never*. He then laughed—another one of his bad jokes. Then he'd tell Ma that he had been raised, "where men were men, and the women split the wood." Ma would laugh at that as we all did, but she knew none of that was true. While my sisters were called upon from time to time to help carry in water or firewood, rake hay and carry it to the barn, weed and dig potatoes, carry out the ashes, or shovel snow, Ma mostly stayed with her housework. But she worked as hard as—or harder than—Dad did.

In the early years, Ma washed clothes using a folding wooden frame that had a wringer attached to its midsection. Each Monday, wash day, the leaves on the kitchen table were dropped; it was moved to the side, and the wooden frame was set up in the kitchen. One tub of hot water was placed on the part of the frame jutting out on one side of the wringer, and another tub with cold rinse water was placed on the part jutting out on the other side. Water was heated in the copper boiler on top of the Kalamazoo stove and then dipped out by the bucketful and dumped into the hot tub. Fels-Naptha, a yellow bar soap, was used along with a scrubbing board. Either Duz and laundry detergents hadn't come on the market, or we couldn't afford them. The clothes were separated by colors, white first. They went into the hot tub and got stirred around with a sawed-off broom handle. Then each piece was scrubbed on the scrubbing board by hand before being run through the wringer and dropped into the cold rinse. The wringer was turned by hand, and you would be smart to keep your fingers clear.

Rinsed, the clothes would be put back through the wringer again and tossed into bushel baskets we used for laundry. Items that needed starch, like a white shirt or the dickeys my sisters wore under their sweaters, were put aside in a separate pan. I don't remember if that came after they went through the cold rinse and had been wrung. My sisters could tell you. Then the colored clothes were run through. The real dirty stuff like barn clothes, field clothes, or socks went through last. It took Ma about three hours to run the clothes through for all of us.

Dad's mining clothes were not done every week—they were washed separately on a morning devoted solely to that purpose. They were not run through the wringer, I'll tell you that. Ma wouldn't permit that. They were wrung partially dry by hand. It was always a bad scene with red hematite water all over the place. I don't want to talk about that except to say that the year Joanie was born, 1938, Dad washed his own mining clothes while Ma was at the hospital. My brother Bill, who was three or four years old, fell off the chair Dad had put him on (and told him to stay on), right into the tub of hematite water. I heard some words that day that I had never heard before and was forbidden to repeat. So I won't.

When my sisters got older, they did their own personal stuff and dried them between two towels. Their sweaters were a whole different thing. They had to be dried between two towels and spread out just so on papers on the floor so they wouldn't shrink or go out of shape. Ma made them do that for themselves. It's a lot easier to wash clothes for a boy. Being a boy also had the advantage of not having to do any of it except to help carry water in and out and sometimes turn the wringer and take clothes off the line if Ma had a cold or wasn't feeling well. Normally, washing clothes just wasn't a man's work. I always liked that part of it.

Once the clothes had been washed and the bushel baskets were full, the water had to be carried out and dumped and the clothes had to be hung outside on clotheslines to dry. There were several lines just outside the kitchen strung between wooden posts. On Mondays, they'd be full, and the little basket Ma used to hold the clothespins would be empty. Forked maple clothesline poles (the ones we used to carry haystacks) were used to prop up the lines so the laundry wouldn't drag on the ground. It was quite a sight to see our sheets, towels, and whatnot, blowing in the wind on a bright summer day—including bloomers and my dad's long johns—squeaky clean and hung out to dry for all to see. Once dry, the clothes were picked off the lines and put back in the bushel baskets. If rain came, they had to be hung up again inside in the dining room on a wooden folding rack that stood in the corner.

Ma insisted that the laundry be hung out to air no matter how cold it got or how hard it was to set the clothespins. Lanes had to be shoveled under the clotheslines in the winter. To get a better understanding of Ma hanging the clothes out to dry in the winter as opposed to tossing them into a gas or electric dryer, visualize her standing in a lane dug in the snow—with temperatures below zero—beside baskets of wet clothes placed on the snowbank, to be pinned on the lines with wooden clothespins, and doing it with bare wet fingers. To be sure that the item would not blow off the line, she'd make a small fold before she set the pin.

When hung out to dry in the winter months, our clothes froze solid, and then, stiff as boards, they were collected for hanging on the wooden rack. My dad's long johns would be stood by the side of the rack until they thawed out enough to be hung. After drying, the clothes that needed to be ironed were separated and the rest put away. My brothers and I were assigned one small and one large drawer in a metal chifforobe in the boys' bedroom. It had once been part of Ma and Dad's bedroom set. They kept the dresser.

Ironing was done on Tuesdays—also in the kitchen. Flatirons were kept on top of the Kalamazoo stove. A metal device with a wooden handle was dropped over them, and they'd be lifted off the stove for ironing. It all had to be done carefully because the irons were sizzling hot, and if one was left on top of the ironing board, it would burn a brown spot the shape of the iron in the ironing cloth. When an iron cooled off, it was put back on the stove and another picked up to replace it. Ma kept a pan of cold water nearby so she could dip in her hand and shake water on the thing she was ironing if she couldn't get a wrinkle out.

Sometimes, to get out a tough wrinkle, Ma had to slam the iron down on top of the thing being pressed, and you'd hear the thump when she did it. Even in the summer, the kitchen stove had to be kept going so she could heat the irons. She'd be sweating bullets while she hunkered down over the ironing board slamming those irons. She taught my sisters how to do it, and as we got older, my sisters did a lot of the ironing. Looking back, I wish I'd have helped her, but she'd never have let me do it even if I asked—which I didn't. There wasn't any boy capable of doing Ma's laundry.

Later—I'm guessing in 1940—Dad brought home a gasoline-driven Maytag washing machine that was the latest thing out there. Marvie's ma already had one, and his dad, Jake, told my dad to get one. Neither of our families had electricity in 1940. It looked real good when it wasn't running and stood in the corner. It had an agitator in the tub and a wringer that would help simplify the process. That is, if you could get the damn thing to start. My dad put the kitchen storm window on hinges so that when Ma used the Maytag, she'd raise the inside window, shove the storm window out, and drop the flexible exhaust pipe out the window. She had to be sure to get that part right, or we'd have been asphyxiated with carbon monoxide.

The machine used a gasoline and oil mix, and it was very temperamental. The worst part was setting the carburetor and cranking the thing to get it to start. It had a black lever with corrugated ridges on the part you shoved down to start the thing. Or if you were afraid of a backfire that might break your arm, you could put your foot on the black lever and ram it down. If you didn't get that done "just so," it would flood. If it did, you had to wait. I can't say I ever heard Ma cuss, but if she ever did, it would have been when she tried to start the thing.

Once the Maytag was started, it would put out a steady *rat-a-tat-tat* while the clothes were being washed. The Flaas could hear it all the way up in their house, a quarter of a mile away. Ma got pretty good at operating it though, and it did help. Not with the water—that still had to be carried in and heated on the stove, and the clothes still had to be hung out to dry. It was a blessed day when we finally got electricity and Dad replaced our gasoline Maytag with a new electric washer and dryer. Ma couldn't believe it. All of that happened after the war when the power company brought the electric lines out to our farm. Once the house got wired for electricity, we installed an electric pump to bring water into the house, and Dad installed an electric water heater. I'll talk about that later.

Dishwashing was different altogether. A dishpan of hot water drawn from the reservoir on the end of the stove was put on the kitchen table, and dish towels that had once been cattle feed bags were handed out. Don't get me wrong, my ma and my sisters did the dishes. One would have her forearms submerged in the dishpan washing, and the others would dry.

I used to sit on the wood box by the Kalamazoo stove, keep my mouth shut, and listen because when the dishes were being washed, dried, and put away, it was more like conversation than it was work. Sometimes, I became concerned that the dishes were not being washed, dried, and shelved properly because Ma and my sisters would become immersed in stuff they'd never bring up otherwise. Sometimes it involved something that had happened to some girl at school and what kind of girl she was, but mostly the conversation involved schoolwork. My ma loved literature of all sorts, particularly poetry. As my sisters worked their way through the lower grades and then high school, they would bring their English assignments home and discuss them with Ma. About the only time available was dishwashing time, but Ma was in her glory whenever that happened. They were so wrapped up in dishes and literature, they didn't even realize I was listening. I paid attention because I knew that someday I'd be taking those same classes, and I had better get ready.

I heard them recite Portia's mercy speech from the *Merchant of Venice*, Sydney Carton's last words on the guillotine from the *Tale of Two Cities*, Marc Antony's funeral oration from *Julius Caesar,* and passages from *Ivanhoe*. Who were they most like: Rebecca or Rowena? Ma loved the English poems in their literature textbooks and loved American writers like Whitman, Emerson, and Thoreau. She read those textbooks as much as, or more than, my sisters did. I can still hear their voices rising and falling there in the kitchen as they washed, dried, and softly debated who or what the raven represented in Poe's "The Raven." Was the writer mad? What did it teach us? It was a pretty heavy load for a little kid sitting on a wood box.

Sometimes, my dad would also be sitting in the kitchen reading the *Mining Journal* when things were being discussed. He never joined in or commented on English writers as a rule because my dad wasn't into literature. One dishwashing topic though, was boyfriends and how one could know if he was Mr. Perfect. My sisters wanted to know. I tuned in on that one because I had always wondered if in fact I was destined to be Mr. Perfect, and I wanted to hear what it would be like. One time, in the course of such a dishwashing conversation, one of my sisters—I can't remember which one—asked my ma to explain to her how she would know when she had met the right one, the perfect guy that she would marry and live with happily ever after. While my ma paused to give that one some thought so she could deliver the ultimate answer, my dad groused from behind the *Mining Journal*, "When you don't have to ask that question." I got up off the wood box and left because I didn't want to burst out laughing right there. That ended the conversation on that subject for the night, but I have always believed Dad's answer would handle that question for a lot of people.

Sewing and darning socks was a whole new ball game. Baskets for sewing, darning, and knitting were kept in the dining room and the front room. A hole in an article of clothing wasn't a reason for discarding it in those days. Darning socks seemed simple enough. Ma and my sisters would put a jelly glass in the toe or heel of a sock that needed it and stitch a crisscross pattern over the hole. That took time, of course, and provided another reason to discuss the subjects they'd already worn out while the dishes were washed and dried. They also crocheted doilies and knitted sweaters and socks. I'm not prepared to elaborate on any of that.

I should explain the incident involving the Singer sewing machine. One summer afternoon during World War II, a guy drove out to our farm in an ancient pickup truck that had a brand-new Singer sewing machine in the truck bed. Not a table model, you understand—the thing stood about three feet high. The guy had on a dirty white shirt and a suit and tie that looked like they needed to be worked over with one of Ma's flatirons. He introduced himself to my dad, who was sitting in the lawn chair Ken had made in Manual Training at school, mentioned it was very nice day, and then pointed to the sewing machine in the bed of his truck and began to describe it to my dad.

The Singer was a magnificent piece of equipment, there could be no doubt of that. The guy assured my dad that if he would let him set it up in the house, he could demonstrate the many features of this incredible machine and explain how it would make Ma's work a breeze.

My dad got up from the lawn chair, carefully explained that he had no need for such a contraption, that he could not afford it, and that there could be no way that he would ever permit the damn thing in his house. When the guy backed away and then came back holding his hands out, explaining that it wouldn't take very long at all to make his demonstration, I began to fear that Dad would go and get one of the flatirons and work the guy over with it.

It was getting pretty hot when Ma came out of the house to see what the racket was. When the guy saw her, he quickly moved over to the porch, took off his hat, and began to explain that he was just a poor sewing machine salesman trying to rescue farm women from the drudgery of hand stitching. He went on to say that if she let him bring the sewing machine into our farmhouse, he'd show my ma what a miraculous boon it would be. No need to buy it, you understand, just a demonstration of how it would sew anything she might want—including leather belts and wooden roof shingles. When my ma said it would be okay if the guy did that, my dad went speechless. It was the first time I'd ever seen him do that. He turned, walked over behind the garage, and let go a stream of tobacco juice while Ma held the door open and the guy lugged the sewing machine into our dining room all by himself.

It was the kind of sewing machine that had a foot treadle you pumped to make it work. In a flash, the guy was showing Ma how to insert the bobbin, work the treadle, and thread the needle and had her operate the machine while he let loose a continuous barrage of sales talk. He whipped hot pan holders out of his case she could practice on. It must have taken him weeks to memorize his spiel. Singer was the best there was; this particular machine had been out in the market for years, was sold all over the country, and, in fact, was the key to marital bliss. Ma would not only be buying a fine machine, she'd be getting an heirloom that would be in the family for years and become the subject of conversation at family gatherings for years to come. "Look at the golden cast in the finish on the cabinet," he said, assuring my ma it was a fine piece of furniture and came with a bench. "Keep it a few weeks," he said. "No charge—try it out." While this was going on, my dad came in and out of the dining room, glared at my ma, and kept going back outside to spit tobacco juice.

An hour or two later, with no sign the guy would leave no matter how many times he was told there'd be no sale, my dad came back into the kitchen and sat down close to the flatirons. Dad announced that the demonstration was over and that the guy had better pick up the goddamned thing and get it the hell out of our house if he knew what was good for him. At that point, my ma said, "Hold it, Ben. I've always wanted a machine like this." The guy quickly whipped out an aluminum clip with a filled-in order blank from his case and put it on the dining room table, explaining to Ma that it would only require fifteen dollars down, with payments of five dollars a month, and that she could sign on the line at the bottom.

It proved to be a wonderful addition to our house. Ma and my sisters used it daily and made all sorts of things with it, including broomstick skirts my sisters sewed from old feed bags. They were quite the rage at the time. My dad would have nothing to do with it. The guy never gave us his name and never came back with the free patterns he promised— he mailed them.

<center>~~~</center>

CHAPTER 15

National Mine School

AFTER SPENDING TWO years in Miss Mason's room, I moved down the hall to the third grade. That is where I was introduced to cursive writing. I still get panic attacks even thinking about that because penmanship was not my strong suit then and still isn't. I put it right down there on the bottom of my list of not-so-favorite subjects—one notch below spelling. We did push-pulls and ovals every morning on lined white paper right after the Pledge of Allegiance. Our black pens were the type that required you to push the pen point into them, and they had to be dipped with great care into the inkwells on our desks. We were instructed to stay within the lines and that *we better not spill any ink!* Some of the boys in my class got into real trouble when they dipped the braids of the girls in front of them into their inkwells. That didn't happen very often, and I'd never admit I did a thing like that—even now. I did take some pen points home with me because my brother Ken had taught me how to tie them to a matchstick with a rubber band and turn them into darts. I proved to be much better at making darts and paper airplanes from the paper we used than I was at cursive writing.

Whether you were right-handed or left-handed, we were taught to keep our index fingers straight and to hold our pens between the index finger and thumb so that the pen was parallel to the index finger all the way up and crossed at the large knuckle. Not above, not below—but at the large knuckle. Not too tight either because cursive writing must flow freely like the strokes of an artist and all uppercase and lowercase letters, which we also practiced every day, had to be formed exactly as depicted in the red booklets that described the Palmer Method. In case you wonder what a room full of kids sitting upright at their desks looks like when writing according to the Palmer Method, compare it to how kids today scrunch up their writing hands, hold their ballpoint pens upright, and hunch their face down close to their pens.

Some kids were able to do it, but my index finger cramped, and I was firmly told by my third grade teacher on several occasions that it was not appropriate to hold one's pen with a cramped index finger like you might hold a pencil. (Damn, I wish I could remember her name.) You had to sit with both feet flat on the floor, with your back straight, and with your writing hand resting gently on the heel of your hand with the other hand lying palm down above and across. We continued these writing exercises, burning through reams of ruled white paper, through the third grade and on into the fourth and fifth grades. You'd think I'd be able to write perfectly today, but I never did master the Palmer Method like the girls in our class did—with all their push-pulls precisely parallel and their ovals and letters gracefully and perfectly lined up within the lines. I still can't write like that, although I don't cramp my index finger anymore.

The fourth grade and the fifth grade were taught in one room by Miss Fannie Millimaki. A portrait of George Washington hung in front of the room with a painting of a farmer strewing seeds by hand off to the side. Miss Millimaki, who had been raised near New Burt, did not tolerate any monkey business at all. No one dipped braids into inkwells in her classes. Any kid dumb enough to make a racket in the clothes closet in front of her room could expect to feel the sting of her ruler when she called them out of there. Miss Millimaki was born with a normal left arm and a short stub for a right arm. Her wooden ruler was usually tucked under her short arm, available at a moment's notice to be snatched by her left hand and administered to the unsuspecting miscreant. Nobody questioned a little corporal punishment in those days.

When I developed pneumonia in the fourth grade and missed about two weeks, the kids in my class sent me letters written in ink according to the Palmer Method. They were priceless. I wish I still had them. One revealed a classmate really straining to get his penmanship just so as he wrote, "Dear Dard, Hope you're better. Friday was an airy day." By the time Dr. Erickson was called, my temperature was down, but I was hospitalized at the Ishpeming Hospital to make sure I recovered.

That is where I was introduced to toast from an electric toaster, poached eggs, and orange juice in a glass. I didn't need an oxygen tent like Marvie when he landed in the hospital with pneumonia. Aunt Lily and Aunt Adele told my dad that I had caught pneumonia because my big hand-me-down corduroy sheepskin coat had worn thin and didn't have enough buttons on it. They bought me a woolen Mackinaw winter coat that was the envy of all the kids in my class when I got back to school.

In addition to penmanship, Miss Millimaki relentlessly drilled us in multiplication, division, fractions, decimals, spelling, and geography. We were also exposed to art. Carl Hemmila once drew a horse pulling a wagonload of hay using only his pencil and Crayolas that was so perfect Miss Millimaki posted it on the bulletin board with thumbtacks. It stayed there for months. It scared me. Where did a kid get that kind of talent? I gave it my best shot, but had difficulty drawing a realistic stick man, so none of my stuff got posted anywhere.

In the fifth grade, Lorraine Saari, a girl in my class, won the dictionary in the spelling bee. It was the first of four dictionaries she collected—that girl could spell. She outspelled all the kids in grades five through eight. I asked her years later at a class reunion how she ever got to be such an excellent speller. She said, "You have to go slow." While pondering that, I painfully remembered that I got knocked out in the first round in the sixth grade when I put two *c*'s in *across*. Maybe I'd been spelling too fast.

While I was in the fifth grade, the Japanese bombed Pearl Harbor in a surprise Sunday attack, and the United States entered World War II. On Monday, a group of high school boys who knew they were subject to the draft gathered and threw snowballs at targets drawn with snowballs on the brick wall of the school. It was next to the rooms where Mr. Gleason taught manual training and where they would later carve and paint airplane models for use by the United States Air Force and Navy to identify enemy airplanes. Their carefully carved black silhouettes that were hung on strings from the ceiling produced an aerial dog fight right there in the Manual Training room.

During World War II, all the kids at the National Mine School collected savings stamps in booklets handed out at school. When a savings stamp booklet was completed, it could be turned in for a twenty-five dollar war bond that sold for $18.75 and cashed out in ten years. One year, I sold savings bonds to our neighbors. We were also asked to write letters to the boys in uniform. I wrote to Norman Korpi, who rode on my school bus and served in the army. He wrote back. During the war, a poster was placed in the hall down by the lunchroom that showed Uncle Sam pointing his finger and stating, "Uncle Sam Needs You." It was kept there throughout the war with other posters that described the four freedoms: freedom from want, freedom from fear, freedom of speech, and freedom of religion. A number of National Mine boys who threw snowballs that Monday were later drafted or enlisted. Small red, white, and blue flags were hung from gold, braided trim in front windows to denote a serviceman or servicewoman lived there. There was a star on the flag for each man or woman from that home who was in the service. I saw some flags with five stars. For those who would not be coming back, the flags bore a black border and a black star.

My sixth-grade classroom was on the second floor by the Home Economics department. Our teacher was Miss Thomas. I think it was Miss Thomas. I know her nickname was J. Webb, but I don't remember where that came from, and I'm sure she wasn't told about that. She was young, beautiful, and wore skirts and sweaters. All the guys noticed that. When she walked down the hall, even upperclassmen—*particularly* upperclassmen—let go a low whistle. I guess they were starting to feel their oats. I never whistled at her, but I don't remember a whole lot about what I learned that year.

Junior high school at National Mine consisted of the seventh and eighth grades. The homeroom for both classes was the Small Assembly, which was across and down the hall from the sixth grade. Mrs. Coughlin was our homeroom teacher, and she also taught science courses. The thing that stands out in my mind from those years was a skit some of the seventh graders had to enact in front of the two classes. The skit was about a court trial. I was assigned the role of an attorney. I liked playing that part, and for some of my assignments, I began to spend time with the *Collier's Encyclopedia* down in the Large Assembly where I read up on Abraham Lincoln and other famous Americans who had been lawyers. In the seventh grade, I decided to become a lawyer.

There was a hitch in my plan. Before I would ever be a lawyer, I would have to get past Mr. Annala. He taught geometry to the sophomores, world history to the senior class in the Large Assembly, and English to all classes, including my eighth-grade class. A lot was expected of teachers in those days. Mr. Annala had graduated from the

National Mine High School in 1920. My sisters warned me that he was from the old school, but I already knew that. When he taught pronouns, you ate at the table of pronouns. When you submitted a short story or essay, it came back with check marks in the right margin at the ends of most of the lines you had written. There'd be no explanation of the errors you had committed in that line, but for sure they'd be there—and the neophyte scriveners better find them, correct them, and resubmit their papers. The papers kept coming back with more check marks until all errors were corrected, which hopefully happened before report cards came out.

Mr. Annala once asked Virginia Flack to write one of her sentences on the blackboard so he could critique it in front of the whole English class. In doing so, Virginia spelled the word *catch* as *ketch*. Now that may be what Virginia heard while playing hopscotch during recess, but it was not an error you wanted to make in Mr. Annala's English class. Mr. Annala did not hand out a lot of accolades, so I thought it quite unusual when he complimented one of the girls in my World History class who he'd asked to stand and read a passage from Greek history. Mr. Annala smiled and asked the whole large assembly, not just the World History class assembled in front, to note how the word *Peloponnesian* had "rolled off her tongue." I was glad I hadn't been sent to the blackboard or asked to read Greek history because I had lousy spelling skills when a dictionary wasn't nearby, a fear of cursive writing that still panics me, and a terrible time pronouncing Greek names.

~~~

Figure 36

National Mine School Faculty Shown: (A) Walter
Bath, superintendent, (B) George Annala, principal,
(C) Patrick Gleason, manual arts, coach, driver
trainer, (D) Dorothy (Austin) Gleason, music teacher,
and (E) William Tonkin, band director.

Nelson Family and Marie (Flack) Keto Photographs

Red Dust

The National Mine School first opened in 1900 on the site where
the building pictured above now stands. (See figure 24). On November
20, 1923, the original building burned to the ground. The building
pictured above was dedicated on June 24, 1925, as a K-12 school. All
of the Nelson children graduated from this school. A project known
as "Red Dust" began in 1983. It had two components. The first, *Red
Dust*, consisted of booklets of family histories published annually by the

eighth grade. The second was the National History Day Competition where students competed with other schools in categories entitled project, performance and media. The first level of competition was held at Northern Michigan University in Marquette, Michigan, and winners there travelled downstate to compete statewide. A National Mine team went downstate each year they competed. Annually, two winners in each category at the state level went on to compete in the national competition held at College Park, Maryland. National Mine teams placed second in the nation once, third twice, and were in the top twelve every year except one. Francis Ruesing was National Mine's Principal during the Red Dust project. The teachers who vigorously promoted the project included Sharon Richards, Bobbie Ameen, and Maxine Honkala. In 1990, National Mine was recognized as one of 15 exemplary schools by the State of Michigan Superintendent of Public Instruction and the Michigan Department of Public Education. The 1996–97 year was the last full year the National Mine School remained open. See, *Red Dust* "Commemorative School Edition", 1997, pp. 70-97.

Figure 37

(L–R) David, Dort, Bill, Ruth, and Ken being greeted
by Queen on the way home from school—with Elsie's
pine trees in the background— Circa 1943.

Nelson family photograph

CHAPTER 16

The Legend of Coon Lake

THE DAY I was told that Uncle John was going to take me bass fishing on Coon Lake, I walked proud. I believe the first time was the summer when I was twelve years old. Uncle John worked for the city of Ishpeming in the public works department, had huge biceps that he liked to flex, and came out to our farm on the Fourth of July every year and shot off fireworks. He also laid foundations for headstones at the Ishpeming cemetery, did carpentry work, and was a meticulous man in all the work he did. Once, at the duplex on Second Street while Ma was visiting Grandma Carne, he showed me how to operate the clutch and move the gear shift lever through an *H* pattern to change gears in Grandpa Carne's 1922 Chevrolet touring car. Uncle John always drove that car because Grandpa Carne either couldn't drive or didn't want to. If Uncle John thought I was ready for bass fishing, I'd hit it pretty big.

For several years, I'd watched Uncle John, Uncle Doc, and Grandpa Carne leave with my brother Ken on bass fishing trips to Coon Lake. I became jealous and anxiously awaited my own invitation but believed it would never come. It didn't help that on his first trip Ken had caught an eighteen-inch smallmouth bass, the biggest fish of the day, and was extravagantly praised for having done so. I was reminded of that catch each time bass fishing was discussed. My own son Dan was later confronted with a similar situation when my wife Judy's parents took my oldest son Dave on a trip. Rubbing tear-filled eyes, Dan told Dave as he was about to fly off to Disney World, "I hope you have a rotten time."

Epic accounts had been given at our kitchen table of loons—which I had never seen—landing on Coon lake, how to put a crab on your hook so a bass won't see the hook, and how bass fishermen landed the really big ones. The stories that Grandpa Carne and Uncle John told about bass fishing, that Uncle Doc chuckled over, and that Ken repeated after they took him along were the stuff of legend. It brought tears to the eyes of a skinny kid sitting on a wood box striving—as I was—to elevate himself from the lowly status of trout fisherman using angleworms to that of a renowned bass fisherman who fished with crabs. Coon Lake was located about sixteen miles west of Ishpeming near the village of Michigamme, so if it happened, it would be an adventure at least equivalent to that of a safari. I'd never been on a fishing trip anywhere near that long nor to any place where legends had been created. I was as hyped up as a twelve-year-old kid could get.

I should explain that by the time I got asked, Uncle John had traded away the 1922 touring car he'd purchased from Grandpa Carne when Grandpa Carne bought the 1940 Chevrolet sedan. Uncle John replaced it with a secondhand Chevrolet coupe that had been converted into a pickup truck when the prior owner removed the trunk lid, cut the body down a bit, and added a truck bed purchased at a junk yard. When Uncle John drove it out to our farm to show off his new wheels, all of us kids thought a coupe-truck was quite an oddity. Had it belonged to anyone but Uncle John, we might have laughed. Grandpa Carne, who didn't think Uncle John could do anything wrong, assured us that actually it was a unique forward-looking vehicle that might catch on if mass-produced, and in fact some of today's Cadillac SUVs employ the concept.

But the truck bed became a problem when Uncle John went to buy license plates. People at the secretary of state's office told him he'd have to buy more expensive truck plates. The truck bed extended six inches more than was allowed out over the back bumper of the coupe. Uncle John returned home, took a blowtorch, cut off the offending part of the truck bed, and bought passenger plates. I tell you this so that you'll understand that when Uncle John took us bass fishing to Coon Lake, he and Grandpa Carne would sit inside with Uncle John driving. Uncle Doc, Ken, and I sat in the truncated truck bed with our feet on the back bumper—no seat belts, of course—where we could look straight through the windshield of the car behind and smile back at the damn laughing fools in it who didn't realize what a forward-looking vehicle we were riding in.

In the period leading up to the trip, it was explained to me over and over that bass fishing required much more acumen than trout fishing because bass are heavier to pull in and land. My expectations kept building, together with my doubts that I could meet this test. My excitement rose to a near fever pitch when my brother Ken told me that Uncle John, Uncle Doc, and Grandpa Carne had gone to Teal Lake down near Negaunee and collected four dozen or so crabs. He told me Grandpa Carne and Uncle John were going to take me bass fishing. Ken and I were driven to Grandpa Carne's duplex the night before, where I was shown crabs squirming backward in several oval-shaped aluminum pails. Like I told you in chapter 4, they originally were miners' lunch buckets that Grandpa called tins. I was fascinated by the crabs but did my best to not show it. Ken and I slept at the duplex, which was an adventure in itself. I did not play on the wooden steps that went up the nearby bluff because for a bass fisherman, that was kid stuff.

Grandpa Carne always embarked on fishing trips early in the morning, so my first trip to Coon Lake began on a beautiful, sunny Sunday in June while sparkling dew was still fresh on the grass. I was wearing brand-new overall pants—Levi's you'd call them today—and I was still enjoying the new smell of them. One of the belt loops was wide and made of genuine leather. It had a cowboy with a lasso burned into it. I put my newly sharpened jackknife in the holder I'd cut from the side of a worn-out high-cut boot I'd found and threaded it to my belt. Grandma Carne came out while we were loading up the coupe-truck, handed me my jacket, and told me to be sure I wore it. She said if I didn't, I'd take a chill.

Our bamboo fishing poles were tied to the driver's side of the coupe-truck, and red handkerchiefs were tied to the ends. Uncle Doc and my brother Ken also brought along telescope rods with reels. The telescope rods were put inside the coupe-truck on the shelf by the back window. The fish box went into the truck bed so it wouldn't smell up the passenger compartment. With tins of crabs squirming backward, two more large pans—Grandpa also called them tins—to boil tea and hotdogs over the campfire, tackle boxes, and a grocery bag of hotdogs, buns, tea, Eagle Brand milk, and heavy cake stashed in the bed of the coupe-truck, we were provisioned to take off for Coon Lake. I squeezed into the truck bed along with Ken, Uncle Doc, the fish box, and the provisions.

When we hit the open highway, I was glad I was wearing my jacket like Grandma Carne said and my baseball cap, which I held by the brim, because an early morning in June in that country can test the courage of a fledging bass fisherman hunkered down against the wind in the bed of a coupe-truck. When you are commencing an adventure of that magnitude, you can't be concerned about your cap blowing off in the wind, so you hang onto it, just like Uncle Doc said. We drove on for miles past farms, forests, villages, rivers, and lakes. As we went, I wondered why we couldn't fish in the lakes we were passing, but I assumed that the legend of Coon Lake would never have gotten started if it wasn't the greatest lake of all.

Finally, Uncle John pulled the coupe-truck up into a dusty turnoff beside a steep wooded bluff. Uncle Doc exclaimed his glee as he alighted from the truck bed, that there were no other cars in the parking turnout, which meant there'd be no other fishermen on the lake. Uncle John pointed to a spot on the other side of a windfall where he said the only known route to Coon Lake began, but there was no visible trail or path there that I could discern, just underbrush and trees. When I pointed that out, Grandpa Carne laughed and assured me that there was a trail there all right and that, in any case, true bass fishermen didn't need a trail.

As I picked up the gear assigned to me and looked up at the bluff, it struck me that there was going to be a whole lot more to bass fishing than legend. Recall that the whole area had once been described as worthless wilderness and that no one except the Ojibwa would ever live there. We began our trek loaded down with tackle boxes, the fish box, crab tins, bamboo poles, telescope rods, our food, and the tea and cooking tins. We pushed into the underbrush and hardwoods, snaking the bamboo poles ahead of us through the brush, and proceeded to scramble over rocks and windfalls up a huge rocky bluff that stood between us and the lake. As we proceeded, Uncle Doc warned me to be careful climbing so that I didn't drop anything. He didn't seem to mind that dirt and moss were getting all over my brand-new overall pants, but I began to wonder what Ma was going to say about that.

Grandpa Carne always insisted on hunting or fishing in remote places—the more remote, the better—but never without tea. The rarely used trail leading up the bluff told me that not many people knew Coon Lake held bass or that it even existed. Finally, we cleared the top of the bluff and stepped into a small clearing. There it was—Coon Lake—a crystal clear, fresh-water lake ringed with cedars at the water's edge and hardwoods festooned with new growth covering the sun-drenched hills behind it. Misty early morning vapors were still rising from its placid surface. As Uncle Doc predicted, there were no boats on this lake, no swimmers, and no cottages or camps on its shores. It was a wild, utterly quiet lake known only to bass and bass fishermen—and very few of them. I wondered how the bass ever found it. We put down our gear to rest before proceeding down to the shore.

Ashes in a fire pit made of rocks announced the spot where we'd finally be able to lay down the heavy gear we'd packed in over the bluff. We had arrived at the legendary fishing site described to me so many times, which Grandpa Carne had discovered and dubbed Coon Lake because he once saw a raccoon on the shore. You won't find that name on a map. It looked to me like Grandpa Carne may have been the first human to ever see it. Directly out in front was a group of large black rocks sloping into the lake, and about one hundred feet off to the right was a large weather-beaten trunk of a cedar tree the wind had toppled into the lake many years before. Sparkling, dark blue water washed over it. Because of the high bluff behind us and overhanging trees, the shore of the lake was shaded and cool.

Uncle Doc swiftly baited up and took up his fishing site on the large black rocks in front of us, and Ken joined him there. Both of them used their telescope poles with reels and wasted no time arranging gear. They wanted their bait in the water. Grandpa Carne and Uncle John took their bamboo poles and moved over to the large cedar windfall and took up fishing sites on either side of it. Almost on cue, a loon labored across the lake and landed on the opposite side, while crows as black as ebony screamed their rage from pine trees on top of the hill across the lake. Chicken hawks and seagulls soared overhead. We had intruded into their environs. I was assigned a spot on a sloping gray rock between the others—my very own bass fishing Nirvana.

Uncle Doc and Ken were standing expectantly watching their floats with their bait already in the lake when Uncle John instructed me to collect firewood and to then come back for a lesson on the proper way to prepare my line. I would be using a bamboo pole. After I'd hurried to gather as much dry wood as I could, Uncle John half-hitched heavy bass fishing line at several of the ridges on my bamboo pole and then neatly wrapped a ball of line at the end of the pole, leaving about twenty feet of line to be cast. Then he placed a heavy sinker about eight inches above the hook and a cork floater about six feet up from the sinker. You don't put too much line between the sinker and the float, he explained, because you don't want the crab to hit bottom and crawl under a rock. With that done, he picked up a crab and explained how I should put it on my hook.

Uncle John was a methodical guy who spared none of the details even though I had heard all about the art of putting a crab on a hook while I sat on the wood box by our Kalamazoo stove. But when I told him that, he looked the other way. You pick them up with your thumb and index finger from behind and away from their pincers. Then you insert the hook—much larger than a trout hook—into the back end of the crab's tail from above, turn it, and bring the barbed point up through the tail again from the underside of the crab so that the point of the hook faces the rear of the crab. If it's done right, your hook won't kill the crab, your line won't prevent it from working its pincers and attracting bass, but most importantly, a bass won't see the hook.

The crab will be attacked from the front, Uncle John explained, so it's essential to place the hook properly. When I asked why a bass attacked from the front and how he knew that, Uncle John waved his good index finger (the other index finger and parts of other fingers had been amputated after being caught in a train coupling when a careless engineer released the brake on a steam engine) and patiently explained that I'd better be thinking about casting my line into the lake without losing the crab and not take my eyes off my float. If it disappeared under the water, I'd have to pull the bass in and land it in the rocks behind me, so I'd better be ready. I was also told not to grab a bass with my hands if I landed one because they are not trout—they have sharp spikes on their backs. With that explanation, I cast my line, set my bamboo pole in the fork of a birch stick somebody had driven into a crack in the rock I was on, sat down on my jacket, and commenced my bass fishing career.

Uncle John rigged his pole and set it on his side of the windfall opposite from where Grandpa Carne had already set his. They always sat on their own side of the windfall, and, except for meals, stayed there all day watching their floats. All I heard from them were faint murmurs when they talked, which wasn't often.

After waiting to see if he'd get any quick strikes, Uncle John came back to light a fire in the fire pit and to brew the first tin of tea. Grandpa Carne would watch his and Uncle John's floats while Uncle John brewed tea in a tin that had been permanently blackened by many legendary bass fishing trips. As he approached my rock, Uncle John explained that any bass caught on his pole was his whether Grandpa Carne landed it or not. I guess the law of bass fishing had made that a binding rule. Once brewed, the hot tea would be sipped from tin cups we'd carried to the fishing site inside the blackened tin. Then Uncle John broke out the heavy cake and put it on a flat rock near the fire.

While Uncle John immersed himself in lighting the campfire and hanging a tin of fresh lake water on a tripod of sticks he'd set up over the fire, my brother Ken hooked a bass and began to reel it in. Ken was leaning back with his telescope rod straight up and his line taut when all at once he pulled in a bass with a mighty heave, and it flew in Uncle John's direction over by the fire and bounced around in the rocks. Ruffled, Uncle John sharply told Ken to watch out for the heavy cake and to land his bass in some other direction. Then he went back to brewing tea.

No damage was done, but Grandpa Carne came over to observe all of the excitement and to examine the bass Ken had landed to see how long it was. As he trudged past the tin of boiling tea, Grandpa Carne grumbled, "John, that tea is way too strong."

Uncle John shot back, "It'll lighten up when I put the milk in." They broke out in wild knee-slapping laughter over that one with Uncle John holding his crippled hand to his face to hold in his false teeth. Uncle Doc looked back from his own float down by the lake and chuckled his agreement. I was to learn that these lines were a ritual and reenacted every time Uncle John brewed tea on fishing trips. Even though it was a lousy joke I knew I'd better laugh, and that I'd never get a better tin cup of tea. Ken's first bass that day didn't come in at the eighteen-inch level he'd established on his first trip, but as I remember, it was close. As Grandpa Carne walked back to the windfall to tend his line, he took time to carefully explain to me that if I sat on my jacket on the slanted rock I was on and got up, my jacket would fall into the lake.

By the time Uncle John announced it was lunchtime, I'd killed off a half dozen crabs without even a nibble, although I wondered if despite what Uncle John told me, the bass were hitting my crabs from the side. Ken and Uncle Doc had landed a few, and Uncle John brought in one close to twenty inches. Chains were put through the gills of the bass they caught and tied to a stake driven in among the rocks so that the catch could be submerged in water and kept fresh.

At noon, Uncle John hung another tin of fresh water over the fire and boiled our hotdogs. We took turns eating lunch so that all the floats could be watched. The hotdogs were legendary, even without ketchup or mustard. Finally, during lunch, I got a strike, jumped up, and landed a sixteen-inch bass. My jacket fell into the lake. As I retrieved it, Grandpa Carne turned his stern face on me and looked away in disgust.

After that, we fished into the afternoon without much luck. Grandpa Carne called over that the sun was getting too bright for the bass. As I sat watching my float, my mind wandered back to trout fishing on the small streams by our house. Trout fishing is a lot different from bass fishing because when you fish for trout, you carefully walk down the stream from hole to hole and stand back. You go after the trout as I explained before. And you certainly don't walk right up to the stream and look into it. With bass fishing, you don't give a damn if the bass see you or not. You boldly step right up to the lake and cast your line into the lake with a bobber on it, leave it there, and wait for the bass to come to you. One lesson learned that day was that waiting for a bass to bite can get tiring, even for legendary bass fishermen. The murmurs from where Uncle John and Grandpa Carne were sitting on their jackets were fewer and fewer.

By two o'clock, we weren't getting any more strikes and I was getting drowsy from looking at my bobber. My mind began to stray from Uncle John's instruction that I keep my eyes on it and not take them off it. I began to wonder why some ripples on the lake moved in one direction and some another and what figures I could make out in the fluffy white clouds. I studied the line between the deep green of the pines on the opposite shore and the blue sky and the whirling seagulls. There were a lot of nice little flat rocks lying near the shore that would have been ideal for whipping out onto the lake to see them skip, but a hidden voice warned me that skipping rocks would not enhance my standing as a bass fisherman.

Finally, Uncle Doc called over to Uncle John to say that it didn't look like there were any more bass on our end of the lake—which is what I was thinking. Grandpa Carne gruffly called back, "Oh, they're in there." That produced new rounds of false teeth guarding and laughter from all sides. Another tradition that the new recruit had better get up to speed on had been observed. We'd caught a total of nine bass, which were placed between cedar branches in the fish box. Then we trekked back out over the bluff.

On the way back to Ishpeming, Uncle John stopped at an Asselins ice cream stand and bought us all cones. I didn't hesitate to order the strawberry twirl I liked. Grandpa Carne never said a word to my ma about my jacket falling into the lake. Ma was glad to see us get home safely and happy to have fresh bass she could fry for dinner. She was not happy about the condition of my brand-new overall pants. Then I carefully started my own legend with my little brother Bill, providing him with all of the details involved in landing that bass. When you have been invited into a legend you don't include details like carrying the gear in over the bluff or your jacket falling into the lake. I've since ordered sea bass in fancy restaurants all over the country, including the West Coast, but none tasted even close to the bass we caught that day.

~~~

Figure 38
Candid shots of Ben and Elsie's kids growing up.

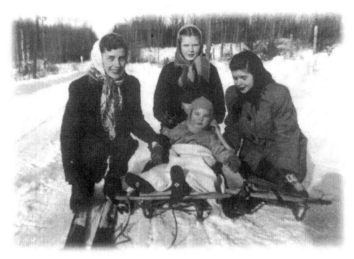

Dort kneeling on skis, with Joanie and Ruth teaching
Fred how to sleigh ride (circa 1948).

Ken at Coon Lake with his wife-   Elsie and Dave at the
to-be Loraine Bath (circa 1949).   Nelson Farm (Circa 1952).

Nelson family photographs

CHAPTER 17

Horse Wisdom

EVEN AFTER BELLE was sold, Dad liked to watch horses pulling huge loads. He'd pile as many kids as he could fit into his 1937 Ford sedan and drive down to the Upper Peninsula State Fair in Escanaba to watch horse-pulling contests. He'd do the same at the Dickinson County Fair in Norway, Michigan. Ma said she didn't like the fairs, but she really stayed home so more kids could fit in the car. While Dad said he was just doing it to give us a day to enjoy the carnival they always had at the fairs and to ride the Ferris wheel, something about horses plunging into their collars and using all their might to move huge heavily laden stoneboats turned him on. That and to look at humungous beef cattle and dairy cows. He used to say while driving to the fairs that "horses don't pull their loads, Lee." He'd look at me and then laugh, "they push 'em." It took me a while to figure that one out. It was kind of like the question of whether the bottom of the tire on a moving car is stopped relative to the road.

During one summer in the late forties, after electric power lines were installed on the right of way to our house, we decided to dig up the big round ceramic tiles Dad had used to put in the well just to the north of our farmhouse—the one that proved to be a dry hole. We intended to reinstall the tiles in a new well to be dug down by the crick, install an electric pump in the new well, and pump fresh water into the kitchen. Dad said it made sense to dig the new well down by the crick. We'd been carrying our water from there for more than fifteen years and knew there was water there. We couldn't install a gasoline-driven pump in the basement or underground so we couldn't pump water into the house until we were connected to the public utility power line.

It was a simple idea perhaps, but it proved to be a big job. In those days, we didn't have the money to hire the job out, so like everything else, if we did it at all, we'd have to do it ourselves. For openers, we had to build a tripod over the old well so that we could use Dad's block and tackle and hoist the heavy three-and-a-half foot wide ceramic tiles out of the ground without breaking them. Dad showed us how to tie three poles together with a chain and then raise them to form a tripod. Once we got the tiles out of the ground, we had to fill in the hole. The project hit a snag when the guy who was selling the electric pump came out to our farm, looked over the tiles, examined the proposed site for the new well, and told us we had a problem. We couldn't pump water by suction more than, I think he said, twenty-eight feet in elevation. It meant we couldn't put a pump in the basement so it wouldn't freeze. Nor could we put a pump in the well and push water up to the kitchen because they didn't have submersible pumps in those days.

That put the whole idea on hold, but still a new well down on the flat would give us a better supply of drinking water than the small pipe poking out of the earthen/rock dam Dad installed in the little crick. We took a whole slew of measurements, but nothing could alter the fact that the elevation of a faucet installed in our farmhouse kitchen, in relation to the level of a new well site down on the flat, exceeded the permissible limit. The guy selling the electric pump said we'd have to dig six feet down into the side of the hill between the well and our house and install an insulated concrete block pump house to protect the electric pump and pressure tank that would be installed there from freezing in the winter. When Dad mentioned to the pump guy that we might hit ledge on the side of the hill, he shrugged his shoulders and said that would be too bad, but that there was nothing he could do to change the elevation of our house. In addition, he said the new pipeline would have to be dug in at least four feet deep, or better yet six, to stay below the frost line. Bottom line—by the time the pump guy left, the project was pretty well stymied. But that couldn't be. There simply had to be a way we could pump water into Ma's kitchen.

My brother Ken had taken a job at Robbins Flooring Mill in Ishpeming. From the point of view of Bill and me, that put the two of us in charge. So one sunny afternoon, we got some shovels, crowbars, and picks from the woodshed and decided to jumpstart the project. We wanted to prove to my dad once and for all that his younger sons were fully capable of accomplishing things all on their own. Bill and I went to work and dug a trench extending out from the house about fifty feet long and three feet deep before Dad and Ken got home from work. The trench we dug was in hardpan soil that was full of boulders, but both Bill and I were good diggers. Dad had taught us that the secret of digging a trench is to keep a clean bottom—and not stand on dirt you've broken loose with your pick. "Keep your work out in front of you," he'd told us time and again. "Don't stand on it." It was only a small start, but Bill and I were as proud as two kids could be when Dad got home from work.

As Dad climbed up on the pile of dirt we'd created and looked at me and Bill smeared with dirt and leaning on our shovels down in the trench, he didn't seem to be as astonished as much by the trench we worked so hard to dig before he got home as he was by the realization that now he would have to complete the project. With the terse remark that we had, "bit off a whole lot more than we could chew," he spit some tobacco juice and pointed out that the ditch for the waterline would have to be dug uphill for about two hundred fifty feet and that we might hit ledge. He mentioned that we had overlooked the fact that the ledge poked up in the middle of our basement. Then, spitting more tobacco juice, he pointed to a huge rocky outcropping that was mostly underground but poked up through the surface down by the site for the new well. It had been there for thousands of years. "How," Dad said looking me and Bill right in the eye, "are you going to dig your trench through that? Don't the two of you have any wisdom at all?"

After Bill and I examined it, we at first concluded it probably was part of the ledge because the ledge poked up in a lot of places around our farm. If it was a boulder it had been rounded off by the glacier, so we'd have a hard time getting a chain around it that would stay, and it was way too big to roll onto a stoneboat. Our horse Nellie could never have moved a boulder that size if it was a boulder, and it would have been dangerous to blast it because fragments could reach the house. What to do? With fifty feet of trench already dug, Bill and I were again hopelessly stymied, and Ma was dismayed.

A few days later, my dad told Bill and me that he had punched some holes around the thing with a crowbar and concluded it was nothing more than a big boulder and not the ledge. He said that he'd asked a guy he called Blackie, who kept some horses in his old neighborhood in

Frenchtown, to come out with his team to pull it off to the side. Then he instructed Bill and me to dig out around it. When Ken got home from the Flooring Mill that night, he helped out. I never heard Blackie's last name, or if I did, I've forgotten it.[56] All the while we dug out around that boulder I wondered why Blackie was going to do it because he had to drive his team four miles out to our farm, and he knew my dad could not pay his normal rates.

I can only relate that a few days later Blackie arrived at our farm driving a matched team of draft horses as black as his nickname, wearing shiny black harnesses with silver bells on their bridles and creating a cloud of dust as they dragged their whiffletrees, evener bar, and chains in the dirt behind them. Blackie was running beside his blacks with two hands full of reins as they thundered down the hill to where my dad, Ken, Bill and I had dug out all around that boulder.

Once the blacks were in position stomping their feet and blowing their noses, my dad, who seemed to instinctively know where a rock's center of gravity was, placed a chain around the boulder between ridges and valleys only he could see and asked Blackie to "tighten 'er up." A chain affixed to a rock of any size or shape by my dad seldom slipped. If you asked him how he knew where the center of gravity was, he would have given you that fierce look and sharply told you, "Wisdom". It was another word he liked and frequently used. The way he looked at you and spat it out reminded you that he had it, and you didn't.

That team of blacks was totally under Blackie's command as he slowly moved them forward to first tighten the tugs, then the chains that led to the whiffletrees, next the evener bar, and then the chain that engirdled the boulder leapt up and went taut. Blackie was on his heels holding his blacks in when he looked at my dad and nodded. As my dad stepped back, Blackie let them loose with a "Hi-ay-hi!" loud enough that our neighbors heard it.

When the two blacks felt the weight of that rock, they hunkered down with their leg muscles bulging and their bellies almost on the ground, and then they took off in unison, one powerful leg after the other. That big boulder leapt clean out of the hole we dug and went swinging from side to side behind the blacks, cutting a deep trench in the dirt. Blackie held them in tight at the bit, but there was no stopping those blacks until the boulder was over by the fence. My dad ran after them, laughing all the way, slapped the two blacks on the rump, and rubbed their noses to let them know they'd done real good. My dad handed Blackie something, but I didn't see what it was. Blackie unhitched, laughed in the direction of my dad, and left running after his team of blacks as they charged out in a cloud of dust. It had been a tour de force.

Figure 39

Blackie's Team—Sketch by Richard T. Carne

Like I said, I never found out why Blackie did it. I've always suspected that it arose out of a discussion he had with my dad at the Paradise Bar where—knowing my dad—he probably assured all the guys at the Paradise Bar over a draft beer that Blackie's blacks would never move that boulder. Considering that my dad was a guy who would drive all the way to Escanaba to watch a team of Percherons pull a stoneboat, seeing those matched blacks pull that boulder from his own field beat anything he'd seen at the fairs and was reward enough for him. He kept telling that story years later, adding a little each time he told it. Whatever anyone thought of him bragging about those blacks, the boulder was over by the fence, and the most it could have cost was five dollars.

That accomplished, my brother Ken and Dad joined Bill and me in the digging end of it; my sister Ruth helped Dad with the money needed for the pump house, pump, pressure tank, and pipes; and Ma, Dort, and the whole family pitched in. Thankfully we did not hit ledge, but to get the pipeline into the basement we had to dig beneath a three-foot-thick concrete and rock basement wall Dad had installed beneath the farmhouse. Then we dug an eight-foot-by-eight-foot cesspool out south of the farmhouse. Sixteen years after the farmhouse was built, the electric, water, and sewer lines were in place and all the ditches were refilled. The decision Bill and I made to start the project, wise or not, was vindicated. Our reward came from the smile on Ma's face when a stream of fresh clean water gushed out of the tap we installed on the new sink in her kitchen. Later, we added a water heater and extended the waterline to the barn. After I left home to attend college during the 1950s, Dad and Bill installed a bathroom in a portion of our dining room and installed a septic tank to the west of our house. The family was going modern.

The Blackie story sticks in my mind because a few years before that, about 1945, my dad had bought Nellie and told me it was my job to take care of her, and he explained exactly how I should do that. I was about fourteen years old. After I'd looked after Nellie for a while and learned to harness her and hitch her up, I began to consider myself a pretty good horseman, but I was humble about it. I was no Blackie, of course, but I was getting pretty good, and Nellie and I got along. A few years later, I kept looking at a big pine log in the middle of a new hay field we were clearing not far from the original site of the boulder Blackie's blacks had pulled. We'd cut it too low to the ground, and the bottom of it flared out. There was a crotch at the top end of the log we'd cut, so the top flared out too. It meant that no matter which end you hooked on to, that pine log would dig into the ground. It was too big to roll onto a stoneboat. Dad tried to pull it out of there himself and told me it couldn't be pulled. The damn thing was an eyesore right there in the middle of our new field.

Without mentioning anything to my dad, one winter afternoon, I harnessed Nellie and drove her down to the log and hitched her up thinking the fact the ground was frozen would help and that the log would ride out on the snow if I got it going. I decided not to involve my dad. You don't have the same problem hitching up to a log as you do a boulder because the chain won't slip. I certainly had enough wisdom for that phase of it. All the while I was doing it, I kept remembering the day Blackie had been out. I'll admit I had a lot of pride in what I was doing. I intended to prove to my dad, who came out and stood up on the hill by the house with a big smile on his face, exactly how his second son had grown up to be as wise and capable as he was and fully able to rid his new field of that big nasty pine log.

I got Nellie to pull the chain taut just as Blackie had done and then eased off a bit to be sure everything was in order before I gave Nellie the "Hi-ay-hi." Then I gave Dad a quick glance to make sure he was watching. I don't know if the neighbors heard me, but I scared the hell out of Nellie because she took off, and when she did the bottom hame strap that I had just put new rivets in broke in two. You do not need to have that happen because when the hames sprang loose from the collar and flew back up against the back saddle, they sliced off both reins as soon as they hit the brass rings on the saddle. The two lines went as limp as spaghetti and dropped into the snow with me holding the other ends.

When Nellie didn't stop, even with me yelling "Whoa" at the top of my lungs, the belly bands broke. At that point, everything, and I mean everything, including the tugs, the back saddle, the hold-back straps, and the rear breaching was stripped off Nellie, and she took off for the barn wearing nothing but her bridle and collar, leaving me holding the severed reins. Later, back at the barn, with two pieces of Nellie's shattered belly bands in my hands, I looked at Dad and humbly asked him to explain where I'd gone wrong. I got the fierce look—"Wisdom." When I asked where I could go to get that, he shot me another one. "Give it time." Then he helped me repair Nellie's harness, all the while laughing and telling stories about horses pulling big loads that he had seen. Once the harness was repaired, he told me to find my brother Bill and saw the pine log into firewood.

He was still telling that story years later when I came home from law school to visit. By then he was saying that "the snow was peppered with pieces of harness." I'd have laughed too, but damn it, I'd riveted that hame strap real good. The only thing I got out of it was the wisdom, confirmed later at law school, that an argument is only as good as its weakest link. Now that I think about it, that's exactly what Dad told me as we riveted Nellie's harness back together.

I was glad I saw Blackie's horses pull that boulder myself though because Dad could tell exaggerated stories about powerful horses pulling humungous loads and guys possessed of enormous strength. He left you wondering whether they happened or not, even though a kid is apt to think everything his dad tells him is the God's truth. Like the one about the English guy (I don't remember his name either) who Dad said was the strongest man in the county. Dad told outrageous tales about the guy's strength, including the time the guy and his buddies decided to build a deer camp way back in the woods and needed to haul a kitchen stove out to their new camp. Dad said they put carpets on the English guy's shoulders and tied the stove to his back so that the oven door was in back. Halfway out to the deer camp, Dad began to laugh, the guy behind decided the bag of canned goods he was carrying was too heavy, so he opened the oven door and threw them in. At that point in his story, leaving the English strongman plodding along, tin cans and all, laughter came bursting out of my dad until tears came streaming down his face. I'd never actually accuse Dad of making stuff up, but I never did believe that one.

Another story Dad told about the English guy involved a newborn calf the guy bought and carried home on his shoulders. Each day, when he went out to his barn after that, Dad would say, the guy would lift the calf onto his shoulders. After a year or so, the calf grew up until finally the guy was hoisting a full grown steer. Dad was so serious and convincing as he related this story, and then laughed with tears pouring out of his eyes, I was dumbfounded. What an interesting but wildly crazy image. In the end, I didn't believe that one either, but who would think up a story like that? Since everyone else laughed each time Dad told his English strongman stories, I did too.[57]

~~~

CHAPTER 18

Queen, King, Rocky, and Labaan

I F YOU FOLLOW the old bush road that leads away from the pole gate on the south side of our farm, it'll take you to Queen's grave. It's the same road we took to go trout fishing, and it crossed the path where Queen had driven our cattle home from Kroon's pasture. It was fitting that Queen's final resting place was close to that path. She'd have liked that. I was thirteen and about to enter high school when Dad put her down. It was an excruciatingly hard thing for him to do. Particularly because of Ma. Queen wasn't just a golden, classic collie with a pleasant face and one that was good around cows. She was good with everything, and she had personality. But Queen was more than that. She was a good-looking, reliable watchdog that all of us loved. Queen was special. If I'm honest about it, she had a rough go of it too, and I don't just mean stuff like porky quills, but she never complained.

Times were different from today, when pets are treated like toys. Queen had a purpose—a job to do. But that didn't get her in the house. None of our animals were allowed in the house, except for the baby chicks that had to be kept warm in the spring and Ma's no-name cat. The cat was only allowed in to catch field mice that worked their way inside, so she also had a job to do. We didn't keep tomcats. Years later, Ma explained it to my wife Judy as Ma waved her hand over the kitchen doorsill, "They never crossed the kitchen door. When it was cold, they could come in the shed."

In the early years, Queen slept on the porch where she'd ball herself up if it was winter. It didn't matter if it was forty below zero—she'd be there on the porch covered with snow. When she woke up, the ball exploded and Queen shook herself off. Later, in the early 1950s, when the porch was replaced with a shed to shield the kitchen door from the elements, our dogs slept in the shed until Dad built a doghouse for his beagles. If Ma baked a cake or pies and put them outside to cool on orange crates kept on the porch, not even a chickadee was allowed to come near. Queen would see Ma coming, get up, go over and lie right there, guarding whatever Ma put out to cool. She and Ma could communicate without talking.

Queen had a look that told you she knew what was going on and that she was boss of the porch. She was on her own and wouldn't wear a collar or a leash. If Ma went for a walk, Queen would quietly get up and tag along wagging her tail, letting Ma know she was protecting her. If you were there, you'd have loved Queen. She was fed table scraps because that's all we had, but Ma always sneaked in something extra when no one was looking and made sure it was good to eat because Queen was Ma's dog.

Queen attacked whatever wild animals might venture onto our farm, even coyotes and in particular, porcupines. You don't need to see a dog with a mouthful of porky quills. Those damn quills are layered like fish scales, which allows them to easily work their way in but makes them difficult to extract. They had to be taken out with pliers. You just simply had to do it—if they were left in they could've penetrated a vital organ and killed her. Quill removal is unbelievably painful, not just for the dog, but also for the two people needed to pull them out. Queen's head had to be firmly held because you had to be sure not to break the quills off and to get all of them out—even those inside her mouth. If one was missed, a large ugly pus bag would form around the quill and after a month or so, it would burst. If that happened what was left of the quill usually came out with the fluids, but it left a serious injury and a threat of infection or blood poisoning.

The summer a porky came after our chickens, Queen drove it up the maple tree just outside our kitchen door. Porkies had already hurt Queen badly so she knew all about quills and that she should stay away from them. But she wasn't about to let a porky scare her off or go for the chickens. Ma said she kept faking runs, scrunching down, paws forward, belly to the ground, backing off and barking until it scampered up the maple. It was the first time I'd heard of a porky in a tree. Queen could put on a vicious face and intimidate when she wanted to.

Ma was home alone with my youngest sister Joanie, who was only a few years old, leaving it up to Ma and Queen to keep the porky from getting into the chicken pen. Also, Ma didn't want Queen to wind up with another mouthful of quills if the porky came down out of the tree, so she got out Dad's twenty-two rifle—which she otherwise was afraid to touch—and joined Queen in the attack.

When Bill and I drove up with Dad, Ma was in her kitchen apron out under the maple tree blazing away with empty twenty-two shells scattered all over the ground and Joanie huddled up on the porch. Ma had hit it several times, but she was not a good shot. The porky was clinging onto a branch high up in the maple tree when Dad took the twenty-two from Ma and, with one shot, blew its head off. Ma hated doing anything to hurt that porky because she loved wild animals and even wrote poems about ants, but there was no way she'd let that porky get into the chicken pen or hurt Queen.

Queen was frequently exposed to serious injury. Once she was kicked in the head by a horse. She recovered by licking her paw and transferring saliva to her wounded head. Another time, Queen got her front paw caught in a leg hold trap and walked around for several months carrying that paw off the ground—a three-legged dog. It didn't stop her from chasing after wild animals or from being a good watchdog. She could run at a pretty good clip even on three legs. Over the years, her injuries healed, but she bore their scars.

In her thirteenth year, Queen became sick and used the little energy she had left to chase after cars that came near our farm. She'd bark like hell at them and try to bite their tires. It was as though she knew the end was coming but didn't want to abandon her job as watchdog. Confused, Queen once went after Marvie and tore his pant legs. When my dad saw her dragging herself on the ground trying to get in front of a car, he knew what had to be done. No matter how bad it hurt, he did it.

We brought Queen down the old bush road alongside the big bluff south of our farm, pulled back the moss, and dug a grave in the soft loam. I remember it being surrounded by wildflowers. Ma transplanted some more flowers by the grave. There used to be a fallen pine tree by the grave, but it's rotted away now. I'll never forget that lonesome mound. Ma put a big rock by it to mark the spot. It didn't have moss on it when she put it there like it does now.

We didn't have a dog for a while after my dad put Queen down because there was no way that Queen could be replaced. It stayed like that for about six months. That was when Mr. Torreano brought out a beagle pup that he wanted us to board. I was in high school—probably a freshman. Mr. Torreano must have paid my dad something, but I never found out what it was. He explained to my dad that some guys were starting up the Ishpeming Beagle Club just up the road past Flaa's sawmill. They intended to run beagles on snowshoe rabbits. Mr. Torreano wanted us to board and train his pup so he could enter him in field trials at beagle clubs around the Upper Peninsula. He expected his new pup to get in a lot of practice driving snowshoes through the swamps around our farm. What he really wanted was a beagle he could put out to stud.

We called him King, although I don't know what fancy name Mr. Torreano wrote down on the AKC papers. It was my brother Ken's responsibility to look after King, and we kind of looked upon him as Ken's dog. Ken turned him into a great rabbit dog—in fact a fantastic rabbit dog—by running him on snowshoe rabbits and giving him his head. Ken understood that a dog that is able to run free will turn out better than one that's penned up. We all loved King except Ma. I don't think any dog would ever replace Queen in her mind, but I knew from the start that that wasn't it. Ma didn't want Mr. Torreano's beagle on our farm. King would've been glad to be adopted into the family—and we kids would have welcomed him in—but he never was.

With all the black, white, and brown markings of a pure-bred beagle—and AKC registered—King was perfect in every way but one. The Beagle Club only allowed two height classes—a thirteen-inch and a fifteen-inch class—measured by a metal bar at the shoulder when standing flat-footed. You might get an extra quarter inch if your beagle didn't stand up on his or her toes, but King didn't have a chance. He stood sixteen inches at the shoulder, and he rarely, if ever, stood flat-footed. When Mr. Torreano tried to enter King in his first field trial, he was rejected. King would have become a field champion and inducted into the beagle hall of fame, but it was not to be. King was too tall. I've often wondered what would happen if there was a similar rule for basketball players.

To please Ma, Mr. Torreano had to take King back, so we didn't have him for long, but it was long enough for us kids to love him and for him to love us. About a month or so later, Mr. Torreano brought King along on a rabbit hunting trip to a large cedar swamp near Palmer and turned him loose. The swamp was twenty miles southeast of our farm. If Mr. Torreano believed that a month was enough to pen King up, feed him, and have him forget about Ken and us kids, he was badly mistaken. King made a beeline through the swamps, brambles, and hardwoods to our farm where he showed up on our porch the next morning. His tail was wagging, but he was spent, and his feet were bleeding from sharp rocks and underbrush. He laid himself down next to my brother Ken who was sitting on the porch. No one explained how King found his way across the wilderness, through twenty miles of tangled swamps and rocky hills, straight to our house, but he did. That was the day when he won Ma's love as well, but of course, he wasn't ours. Heartbroken or not, he had to be returned to Mr. Torreano.

As they say, when one door closes another opens. King had shown my dad an opportunity. Uncle George had already picked up Dewey Lake Sister—a beagle bitch sired by field champion Tumbleweed Tumble—and joined the Beagle Club. Once Dad heard that Uncle George had bought into a field champion bloodline, they started talking beagles, and one thing led to another. Dad was never shy about priding himself on picking bloodlines and would remind you that he had picked Belle. It wasn't long before he went to Norway, Michigan, and picked up a little runt of a beagle pup for fifteen bucks, brought him home, and named him Rocky. Ma didn't like that either—and not just because the new pup looked like a little black weasel. She could see that Dad's purpose was commercial, and she didn't see dogs that way—rabbits either for that matter. She would have preferred if Rocky was just a pet. She called him Rocks and the rabbits bunnies.

Rocky was out of Mighty Mite, another purebred beagle some breeders thought might become a field champion. Somehow, you tell me, Dad had heard about him. Maybe at the mine—at that time Dad worked at the Mather A. It could have been the Paradise Bar. Rocky's sire's name was Jim's Smoky and his dam's name was Bill's Bubbling Over. Rocky would have no trouble making even the thirteen-inch height standard. He grew up small but wiry, sinewy, and tough. He didn't have classic beagle colors—some scattered brown, but mainly shiny black with mottled white on a very broad and deep chest. He came with AKC papers and a broad head with eyes that bulged out, which would become a problem later on when he drove snowshoe rabbits in cedar swamps. Dad said he liked his colors, said they were balanced and that his broad head meant he was smart. Rocky had more than color, brains, and a deep melodious voice. That dog could hunt. He had a nose and heart that wouldn't quit.

Rocky grew up driving snowshoes in the swamps around our farm just like King had done, but Dad built a doghouse for him and he ate better than Queen or King ever did. Dad fed him raw eggs and brought home canned tuna fish packed in oil, cod liver oil, canned dog food, and vitamins that Rocky lapped up—all in the hope that Rocky's skinny body would fill out. Dad said that fish oil would develop and loosen up his muscles. He also picked up a tube of, I think, mercuric oxide to be applied if Rocky's eyes got red from the brush. It didn't improve Rocky's relationship with Ma because the only things she'd had to feed Queen were table scraps. Rocky may have been eating better than her kids.

In the spring after the year we bought Rocky, Uncle George drove out to our farm and suggested we enter Rocky in the thirteen-inch class in a derby field trial to be held in Palmer, the place where King had taken off for our house. Dad had to join the Beagle Club. Rocky wasn't a year old and still quite small, so he qualified as a first year or derby entry. We'd never penned Rocky up or tried to train him to be in a field trial. He'd been allowed to run free as a bird just as Queen and King had been. But we knew from hearing his voice booming deep out of the swamps around our farm that he could drive a snowshoe. What we couldn't figure out is where such a little runt got such a big voice.

My dad, Uncle George, my brother Bill, and I climbed into the Ford with Rocky, drove down to Palmer, and entered him in the derby as Uncle George suggested. By then, we'd received AKC registration papers in the mail that listed his registered name as Trigger XVIII. The name Rocky may be a good name for prizefighters, but it was too plain a name for the AKC. Purely by chance, Rocky (Trigger) was given the number 22, but the guys registering him in the field trial had difficulty rolling yellow paint onto his sides to display his numbers because he was small and thin-waisted. As I lifted Trigger up on the measuring table and watched his numbers being rolled on from wood blocks, I observed that they almost came together at his back.

One guy looked at him and called him a runt—but I knew that. Thinking him to be some sort of smart-ass, I told him Dad was only entering him at Uncle George's suggestion to see what he'd do. I turned from him, picked up a doughnut and a paper cup of coffee, and led Trigger up to where the gallery was collecting. Trigger approached the starting line oblivious to all the other derbies being entered, with his leash as tight as a bowstring and working the ground as he searched for rabbit scent. The guy who'd called him a runt had followed us and stood watching. I found out later that he was a judge.

It was to be a three-hour field trial as I remember, which meant three hours on game. Trigger didn't know he was a runt and, all heart, immediately took over the pack. He led it all day, demonstrating again and again to the three judges who ran with the pack through those big cedar swamps his ability to stay on scent and to check without barking when he lost it—including the guy who smarted off to me.

If you've never seen a beagle field trial, let me explain. Snowshoes are different than cottontails. The latter make a beeline for their hole when they're flushed. Snowshoes think they're smarter. They use powerful back legs and long leaps to take off in a large circle ahead of a pack of snuffling beagles and lead the pack around the swamp back to the point where the drive began. It's a trait that must pass through their genes. Every snowshoe I've ever seen flushed tries to create a zigzag circle of scent maybe a half mile wide and then leap far off the circle at a later point, maybe onto a log or a patch of bare ledge, to create confusion in the pack as to which line of scent to follow. At that point, the snowshoe might take off for its den or, if it had young there, create a new line of scent on the old circle and do it again and again. Snowshoes leave scent not only on the ground, but on the bushes and grass they brush up against as they run. What's needed is a beagle with a discriminating nose. You don't want your beagle to continue baying down a line of snowshoe scent if the snowshoe has hopped off the line. Of course, if you were hunting snowshoes, you'd go to the point where it was rousted out because you'd know the snowshoe was coming back. In that case, you stood to the side of the circle because you didn't want to shoot toward the pack of beagles if they were closing in.

The key in judging a field trial is to determine which beagle follows the snowshoe's scent. Another key is to see which one will stop baying when scent is lost and then wheel and circle until it's picked up again.

The latter is called a checkpoint or more simply a check—it's critical that baying stop at the checkpoint because clumsy baying will lead the whole pack astray. But it takes more than that. The best dog in the end is the one that goes out front and stays there ahead of the pack and will drive away any dog that tries to usurp his leadership—or hers if they're running bitches. It's a beagle thing.

Some beagle owners don't understand the elemental fact that you don't teach beagles how to drive rabbits. It doesn't help to threaten them if they take off after squirrels or to pick them up and throw them at a rabbit. I've seen both done. They either have it or they don't. My dad understood it. So did Uncle George. He confided to my dad while we were waiting for the derby pack—which was in full throat—to come through that Trigger had been sneaking away from our farm and running in practices down at the Beagle Club where he led packs of fifteen-inch dogs. He knew that the judges were taking numbers, that points were assigned to each beagle as the drive continued, and that Trigger was piling them up. Uncle George, who had also sat on the school board at National Mine, had been a judge, but Dad, Bill, and I were too new to the game to know what was going on.

When a snowshoe is rousted and the whole pack goes on game, the sound of twenty or thirty beagles puts out one helluva racket as they circle the swamp, but I knew Trigger's baying and could pick it out. It was deep and rhythmic with an enduring quality. You couldn't mistake it. I knew from his voice when Trigger had good scent when he hit his checkpoints and the quickening that came when he picked up scent again. I also knew he was leading the pack. My dad just looked at me and Bill and smiled.

About fifteen minutes before three hours on game was up, the snowshoe came onto the logging road where we were watching the drive with Uncle George, one of the judges, and the rest of the gallery. Right behind him, Trigger came crashing through the brush leading the pack. Before I could see what was going on, Trigger slumped to the ground. His back legs were stiff—useless. When the pack finally came out and went charging past him, he tried to get up and pull himself after them using only his front legs, but he was spent. I looked quickly at Dad, ran, and picked him up. He tried to squirm away, but I held him tight. He was done for that day, but hey, he was just a runt.

Dad, Bill, and I took Trigger back to the car to massage the cramps out of his back legs, calm him down, and get some water into him.

We'd reward him with a good meal, but not until he'd rested. We were dabbing mercuric oxide on his eyelids when Uncle George came and told us that Trigger had won his first field trial. He didn't go the whole distance, but he had led in every category for the whole day and piled up enough points to win the blue ribbon and the trophy going away. I didn't need those guys telling me that Trigger was blue ribbon. I also knew on that day that my dad had an instinct about bloodlines.

Trigger grew stronger after that derby trial, always wore the number 22, and seldom lost a field trial. We ended up with a shelf full of ribbons and trophies he'd won. Dad put some on the back shelf at the Paradise Bar where Blackie Nault displayed them with bonded whiskeys and trophies of all descriptions. The *Mining Journal* sent a photographer to our farm and took pictures. Trigger made the Saturday "green sheets" before I did. We still called them Green Sheets even though the *Mining Journal* had changed to peach for weekend sports.

Once Uncle George saw what Trigger could do, he suggested to my dad that they breed his beagle, Dewey Lake Sister, to Trigger. My dad wasn't sure about that, but finally they agreed to do it. It would unite the blood of two field champions—Tumble Weed Tumble and Mighty Mite. Since my brother Ken had by then moved to Flint, I became the oldest boy at home and was selected to see to it that the union took place and to then look after the pups and get them started on snowshoe rabbits. I never asked either of them to do it, but Uncle George and my dad promised me that if I did what they'd asked, I would have my pick of the litter. When Dewey Lake Sister went in heat, I saw to it that the union took place.

There was only one male in the litter, so it didn't involve a lot of choice—I wanted a male. As an aside I should explain that by that age—about sixteen and a tenth-grader—I had been given the nickname Dagwood. Even my dad called me that, and my brothers and sisters in particular relished the chance to name me after a comic strip character who appeared with his wife Blondie in our funny papers.

It happened at a birthday party Ma gave me when I turned thirteen. Although Ma always baked a cake to celebrate our birthdays, this time Marvie, his brother Paul, and his sisters Nancy and Marlene, along with cousins Bob and Jack, and some neighbor kids were invited for candy bars, cake, and pop and to play games. The crew of them raised holy hell playing run chief run, kick the can, bows and arrows, pinball, and other games. I doubt that our cousin Donna Mae was there. My birthday party was in October, and she went to school in Flint. My thirteenth birthday party almost destroyed our farm. My present was a jackknife I could use for making slingshots, arrows, guns that shot rubber bands, toy sailboats, and government poles for fishing. It was a damn good folding knife with a pearl white, S-shaped handle I could carry in my pocket or in a pouch on my belt. I'd be like Tex Ritter or Gene Autry with that knife on my belt. I could also use it to punch leather if my belt got too tight and needed a new hole. I learned later my dad had won it on a punch card he played at a gas station. I cut my finger the first time I tried it out and was promptly given the nickname Dagger. When all the kids at my birthday party busted out laughing over my new nickname, it morphed into Dagwood before Ma could bandage my bleeding finger. You know, kids can be mean. I still have the scar.

You understand that nicknames are not something you get to pick, and once you get one you can't get rid of it. My big brother's nickname was Tixie, and other kids had nicknames like Bipper, Tooner, and Weiner. Another was called Gully Gus. They even dubbed our high school principal Bitty. The superintendent of schools was Snuffy, although I doubt that either Bitty or Snuffy ever heard about that. I learned later that my dad's nickname was Barney. My dad would never have allowed us kids to call him that, but the way I saw it, a lot of important people had nicknames. It was a kind of status thing. Not everybody had one—not my brother Bill. If your name is William, you will be called Willy, Will, Wills, Billy, or Bill. Even if some people might think it demeaning to be nicknamed after a bumbling comic page character, I figured I'd been singled out to have a nickname and that the kids at my birthday party must've been thinking I'd amount to something. No one else had been nicknamed Dagwood. I felt like I had been accepted into an exclusive club. But no matter what I thought, it became my nickname. Later, I discovered that gandy dancers and miners had nicknames more imaginative than anything I ever heard. I shall not repeat them here.

It might sound like apologizing to my dog, but that's partly how he got named. It might've been better if he'd been named Green Crick Ripper or Pile Driver from Hell or something like that. The rest of it came from my dad, who liked to use Norwegian words, in some cases mongrelized words he thought were Norwegian words. Soon after I brought my new pup home from New Burt but hadn't yet named him, Dad saw him lying spread-eagle on the porch in the sun. He exploded, "Look at that Labaan! Is that all that big, fat, lazy son of a bitch can do is lay out in the sun?"

I tried to explain that puppies are roly-poly and fat and that he was just resting. But from the way he kept looking away and then back, my dad knew my pup had potential. He bore the coloring of Tumble Weed Tumble, but he had the brain and nose of Mighty Mite, and we could both see it. The bloodline picker liked him. There's no way to sugarcoat it. Dad, who had refused to take a bitch from the litter, was jealous. But he and Uncle George had made a deal and given me my pick of the litter. I could see right away from my brother's experience with King that Labaan would be a great beagle. The nickname Lazy Labaan stuck; he answered to Labaan, and no other name would ever do. When we applied for the AKC papers he became Dagwood's Labaan. I wondered about that one because they'd rejected the name Rocky.

Trigger taught his son Labaan the art of picking up and holding scent and driving snowshoes, except Labaan grew bigger than Trigger and just cleared at fifteen inches. Labaan had another thing—a distinctive baritone voice that was even more melodiously sorrowful than Trigger's. Once they heard it, no beagle man could ever mistake it. I joined the Beagle Club and took the two of them there to practice with dogs of the other members. I was still just a kid, but they welcomed me in. Swatting mosquitoes and deerflies, we'd gather at a small fire on the old railroad grade that cut through the Beagle Club's land in the swamp north of our farm, listening to a Detroit Tigers' ball game and music from a pack of beagles in full throat. Sitting on windfalls and stumps out on the railroad grade, those guys taught me a lot about beagles—as well as baseball, Grain Belt beer, and dirty jokes for that matter.

Both Trigger and Labaan had the nose, the brain, and the heart of a champion. They were soul mates. Just as Trigger took over the thirteen-inch class, his son Labaan took over the fifteen-inch class. Ultimately, they both became field champions, and today, their names appear in the pedigrees of several AKC-registered field champions. My talented cousin, Tommy Carne, Uncle Dick's son, painted their heads in father-son silhouette with me in the background. I still have that painting.

One winter, Trigger and Labaan followed me way back in the woods south of our farm down past the Green. I had snowshoed in looking for fox tracks. My Uncle John had asked me if there were any red fox there. He used to trap them for their pelts but told me the state of Michigan was paying a bounty on them and asked me if I could find a den. Foxes lay their tracks down in a straight line. Their back legs use the same spots as their front legs, and in winter there is no way to tell which way a fox is headed unless you see him—which you won't—because all they leave is a line of dainty holes, sometimes with a line from a dragging tail.

Uncle John, who as I said was a trapper, told me that if I came onto any fox tracks, the fox would have smelled me coming and would've laid its tracks purposely to lead me away from the den. He didn't think female foxes would be roaming that time of the year but would be back at the den protecting her pups while the male went hunting for food. He told me that I'd have to backtrack if I wanted to find the den and collect a bounty on the pups. That, of course, presupposed I could tell which way the fox was going. On this day, I found some tracks that looked just like those Uncle John had described. While I was trying to figure out which way the fox had gone, Trigger and Labaan found a snowshoe and started to drive it. In late winter, some crust had formed on top the snow in the open areas, and an inch or two of fresh snow had fallen on top of the crust. Otherwise, the snow was about three feet deep, making the going pretty rough for the two of them except where the snow was crusted.

After an hour or so, they came lunging down off the hill to my right with two snowshoe rabbits hightailing it on top of the snow in front of them. I could have taken out both rabbits but I didn't, even though I was carrying the sixteen-gauge shotgun Uncle John told me to carry in case any foxes took unkindly to my looking for their den. It was tough to break up their fun, but I had to. That deep snow was too much for them. Trigger was spent. Labaan might have handled it, but he was pretty well gone as well. Foxes and rabbits would be safe for the rest of that day. Halfway home, Trigger and Labaan climbed on and rode my snowshoes where there was no crust. I didn't complain. They were entitled.

We took Trigger and Labaan to field trials all over the Upper Peninsula. They continued to pile up trophies. It was during a field trial at the Ishpeming Beagle Club that Labaan showed his home club the champion he was. The gallery was gathered on Flaa's Road near Flaa's sawmill when the snowshoe came out of the swamp and scampered onto the dirt road. It was the same road, now graveled, that my sisters had walked to meet the school bus years before. Startled by the gallery, the snowshoe wheeled away and bounded up the middle of the gravel road for at least a half mile where it suddenly made a ninety-degree turn and went bounding off into the swamp. When the pack broke out onto the road in full voice Labaan was in the lead as he always was. In the swamp, there'd been a line of scent on the bushes and grass the snowshoe had brushed against, but not on the gravel road. There would only be patches of scent where the snowshoe landed on the gravel.

When Labaan hit the gravel road his baying stopped, and he began to circle with his nose pressed tight to the ground. The main body of the pack came up headlong out of the swamp in full voice, passed Labaan, and went charging across the road. Their baying continued after they crossed into the swamp on the other side. Not Labaan. He made his check without one yip, circled all alone back out on the gravel road, and as soon as he hit the first patch of scent in the dust, he resumed his powerful baying and, with some of the pack beginning to straggle after him, followed the patches of scent right up the middle of the gravel road, baying as he hit each patch to the point where the snowshoe had leapt into the swamp. Then he stopped baying to make another circle until he picked up the scent again on the other side of the road, and with the gallery of beagle men from all over the Peninsula standing in awe, went plunging into the swamp again in full voice with the pack gathering behind him. It was classic. He made me just about as proud of him as I could be, although it wasn't the first time I'd seen him do it.

Before Trigger became a field champion, Dad sold him. He was offered two hundred fifty dollars, and in those days, that was a lot of money. I held out and kept Labaan, but when I enrolled in college I'd have no opportunity to take him to field trials. My brother Bill took care of him for a while, but I knew that Labaan was a champion and that the only way he could reach his potential was with an owner who could afford to take him to field trials around the Peninsula and out of state—and had the time to do it. I also received two hundred fifty dollars, which gave me a huge financial boost toward an undergraduate degree at Northern Michigan College, as it was known at that time.

Both Dad and I have been criticized for selling our dogs, and when I think back on how loyal and trusting they were, I still wonder about it. I think we made the right choice. With the financial backing of his new owner, Labaan met a lot of female beagles he'd never have met otherwise and got his photograph plastered all over the *Mining Journal* and the AKC monthly magazine. He fulfilled his potential and became a pedigreed field champion with several more field champions populating his family tree just as Trigger did. I ended up with a law degree, but that's a whole 'nother story.

~~~

Figure 40
Queen, Trigger XVIII, and Dagwood's Labaan

Trigger (front) and Labaan in a father-son silhouette with Dave restraining an eager Labaan.

Painting by, and printed with the permission of, Richard T. Carne of Ishpeming, Michigan.

Joanie in her beige snowsuit with sled and Queen (circa 1942).

Dave with Dagwood's Labaan.

Ben and Fred with Labaan.

Nelson family photographs—1942 to 1949

Figure 41
Trigger XVIII and Dagwood's Labaan

Fred quizzically studying
Trigger XVIII and trophies.

Bill with Labaan and Ben with Trigger XVIII.

Ben displaying Trigger
XVIII and his trophies.

Bill with Trigger XVIII.

Nelson Family Photographs—1945 to 1949

CHAPTER 19

The Glory of Basketball

I BECAME A freshman at National Mine High School in September of 1945 not long after my dad put Queen down. President Franklin Roosevelt had died of a cerebral hemorrhage in May and was given a state funeral. World War II ended in August when atomic bombs exploded over Japan. Labor unions were flexing their muscles, and the GIs were coming home—but not all of them.

I was initiated into my freshman year with ice-cold water from the pump over by the bluff and assigned a seat in the Large Assembly on the second floor. It was the homeroom for grades nine through twelve. My freshman classmates were scattered throughout the Large Assembly. I sat two rows in from the right and about six seats from the rear. It was my homeroom seat for the next four years. My brother Ken sat two seats behind me, and my sister Dort sat to the left over by the window and up toward the front. Marian and Ruth had already graduated with honors.

The principal, Mr. Annala, sat at the desk in front of the Large Assembly and monitored the room. He assured us that his title, principal, meant chief, that it was spelled differently from the one that meant rule, and that he *would* monitor the room. Mr. Annala's office stood at the top of a high, narrow staircase down the hall that led only to it. If you saw a student coming down those stairs, you knew that kid was in deep trouble. My sisters told me that Mr. Annala did not summon kids there to give them accolades and that I had better not be seen coming down those steps.

When classes were taught in the Large Assembly because there weren't enough classrooms and teachers to go around, students who didn't have an assigned class elsewhere would study there—and they better be quiet! I found it to be a good place to bone up on classes I'd have to take later on. I was intrigued when the "Chief" or "Bitty" Annala, as we called him behind his back, or Mr. Bath, led discussions of *The Merchant of Venice, Julius Caesar, Ivanhoe, A Tale of Two Cities* and the English and American writers and poets. It was kind of like hearing about them when my sisters helped Ma wash dishes or darn socks at home.

Every year, the senior class enacted a play in the auditorium. Their class advisor directed the play, and Mr. Gleason was in charge of the scenery—which of course did not change much from year to year. There was an outdoor scene that could be rolled down from the ceiling for the Christmas pageant. An indoor scene for the senior class play was created by bringing folded scenery stacked out in the hall onto the stage and tying it together with ropes.

One year, Lloyd Kroon, Kroony, and one of the Kiiskila boys, Bipper, both seniors, were assigned to pull the big brown curtain that separated the stage from the audience for the senior class play. They decided during a rehearsal to have some great fun grabbing each other by surprise and rolling each other up in the curtain. But things got a little dicey when Kroony, a big kid who cut pulpwood and starred on the basketball team, sprang out holding the curtain in front of him, grabbed who he thought was Bipper, and rolled him up while yelling "Gotcha!" only to find that his victim was our superintendent, Mr. Bath. If it had been Bitty Annala, Kroony would never have graduated, but Mr. Bath was more tolerant, and besides, Kroony was a great center on the basketball team. During my senior year, our class play was *Meet the Middletons*. The playbill made it sound like a soap opera. Pauline Felt played Gladys. I played Edwin Westrate, Gladys' husband.

Figure 42

"MEET THE MIDDLETONS"

By ROBERT ST. CLAIR

Presented By

SENIOR CLASS OF THE NATIONAL MINE HIGH SCHOOL

NOVEMBER 17, 1948, AT 8:00 O'CLOCK

CAST OF CHARACTERS

Myra Middleton—The widowed mother, 47....Janet Maki
Elinor—Her oldest daughter, 22...............Virginia Flack
Gladys—The middle daughter, 20...............Pauline Felt
Teddy—The youngest daughter, 17.........Patricia Pietro
Johnny—The oldest son, 18...............Maurice Hansen
Allen—The youngest, 15 ....Carl Hemmila
Cynthia—Myra's sister-in-law, 50...............Rachel Juntila
Merle Potter—Elinor's husband, 25.......Kenneth Larson
Edwin Westrate—Gladys' husband, 22........David Nelson
Bobby Haines—Teddy's boy-friend, 17....Donald Lukkari
Enid Oakley—Gladys' girl-friend, 20..Joanne Trebilcock

I did well enough in high school to finish second in my class. Kenneth "Rudy" Larson, who was not tall but was a very good basketball player, finished first. Rudy and I sometimes practiced basketball at his house near New England Hill at lunchtime. His dad, who was our family barber and cut hair for fifty cents, had erected a pole with a backboard near their garage. Rudy also played the piano at our get-togethers and got excellent grades. He and another of our friends, Donald "Erkie" Lukarri, who did not sing so well at our get-togethers but also got good grades, later went to Michigan Tech. Rudy graduated from Tech with a major in forestry, and Erkie obtained a degree in geology. The three of us, along with Maurice "Hussey" Hansen, Fred "Freezer" Magnuson, and Allen "Adu" Alderton, played together on the basketball team through junior high school and high school and went out together in Ishpeming on Saturday nights. We hung out with guys from the Ishpeming basketball team.

Mr. Gleason coached basketball. Our colors were blue and gold. Rudy made the first team in our freshman year. We played "race horse" basketball—when we fell behind we picked the other team up man-to-man all over the floor. It won us quite a few games. I made the varsity team midway through my sophomore year and played left guard. I'd have done better at right guard because I'm right-handed, but I was privileged to make the team at all, so I did not bring up small points like that. I proudly pulled on number 10 and took my seat on the bench. There were only eleven kids altogether in my sophomore class counting the girls so, although I strutted around awhile when I made the first team that year, the truth was that any male kid able to walk without help had a good chance of making the team. Still, Coach Gleason produced good teams, although I received three personal fouls the first time he put me on the floor at Trenary.

We did well in 1948 as juniors against our nemesis, Champion, and against Republic. We finished second in the Class E district tournament. A vivid picture of the championship game is indelibly imprinted in my memory. We played Michigamme on the Ishpeming court. We may have beaten them during the regular season, but if we did, the score would have been close. The district championship was a seesaw game. With just a few seconds left on the clock, National Mine was ahead by one point, and our cheerleaders were going berserk in their snappy skirts, bobby socks, and white gym shoes. Then with what looked like the entire population of National Mine in the bleachers, Michigamme's Phil Numinen, whom I was guarding, let go a two-hander from center court. I leapt as high as I could and swatted at the ball, but it just cleared my fingers, arced toward the basket and, with no more than two seconds left on the clock, went swish. He got nothing but net. In those days, there were no three-point baskets, but those two points were enough to deprive us of the trophy. I have never forgotten that night because, had I blocked that shot, we'd have been district champs for the first time in twenty years, my name would have been plastered all over the green sheets of the *Mining Journal*, and maybe, even at five feet ten, I'd have been launched into a lucrative basketball career. Instead, Phil got the press, and I had to face our cheerleaders. Later, at Northern Michigan College, Phil and I became good friends.

Still, I earned a letter in 1948. The next year (1949) when we were seniors, we won 14 of 16 games during the regular season. During my senior year, Marvin Kaminen "Marvie," Bob Anderson (Otto and Andrea's son), Ralph Helsten, Ronald Toy, and some other juniors were also on the basketball team along with Ralph Keto, a sophomore. Bob had bloodied my nose one time when we were down in the grades, but we got over that—I had done the same to Jackie Pietro with a lucky punch. We beat Champion twice during my senior year and split with Michigamme. If you total the scores of those two games though, Michigamme only beat us by one point.

We also beat John D. Pierce from Marquette twice. Pierce was Class D, and we were Class E in a class system that ranked the largest schools in Michigan Class A.[58] We beat them 40 to 34 on their court and then 46 to 35 on our floor. That's when we started to get more press because Pierce was the training school for teachers attending Northern Michigan College. My wife Judy and her sisters, her father, and all her aunts and uncles on her father's side went to school there, but I didn't know Judy or her family then. I'm glad I didn't have to play basketball against Judy's uncles because that family had nine boys, and they were all great athletes—although their primary sport was hockey. Judy's Dad, Wackey, played and coached hockey in Marquette and was later inducted into the Upper Peninsula Sports Hall of Fame. He invented the kick shot, which was later determined to be deadly and banned. One of her uncles, Eddy, played professional hockey and was later inducted into the U.S. Hockey Hall of Fame. Marky, who played hockey at Michigan Tech, and was an expert logroller, was also inducted into the Upper Peninsula Sports Hall of Fame. Teddy played hockey at Michigan Tech with Marky. Weldy played hockey at Michigan State in the fifties and was a member of the U S. Olympic Hockey Team that won the silver medal at Cortina, Italy, in 1956. He was also on the U.S. Olympic Hockey Team that beat the Russians at Squaw Valley in 1960 and went on to win the gold medal there. They were a family of athletes.

All the local sporting events, including high school basketball games, were reported each weekend in the *Mining Journal* so all the scores are enshrined there for posterity. One of those games happened the night our team walked proud on January 27, 1949. That's the night we beat Class D Negaunee St. Paul on our court. St. Paul's coach, Mugs Gingrass, always put a good team on the floor. He liked to beat National Mine—relished it. St. Paul blew us out on their court 57 to

36 in the first game that year. They had played Greenland Mass (Mass City) from the western end of the Upper Peninsula the week before our second game and had broken a sixty-game winning streak that Mass City had piled up, which included several Class D state championships. In short, Mass City had become Class City and was plastered all over the green sheets of the *Mining Journal* every Saturday. Bottom line, it was expected that National Mine would take another drubbing.

I must say that in those years, any team playing on our court was playing at a disadvantage because those who planned the architectural scheme for the National Mine School had placed the auditorium— where senior class plays and Mrs. Gleason's Christmas pageants and spring operettas were held—right next to the basketball court. We played basketball on the stage built for the auditorium, and its numbered seats became the bleachers. A net had to be placed between the basketball court and the fans when basketball was played to keep players from flying across the stage and out into the auditorium where the cheerleaders led the cheering and the fans were roaring. It usually took a while for visiting players to keep from flying into the net. In addition, several rolls of scenery were hanging over the stage adjacent to the basketball court and somewhat overlapped it. Those rolls helped the home team because it took visiting teams a while to realize that our scenery could block a good shot at the basket.

We were ahead of St. Paul by five points with three minutes left, but St. Paul, exhorted by Mugs Gingrass, put on a furious rally and took the lead back 49 to 47. That's when Ralph "Gully Gus" Helsten scored with a minute to go. Soon after Hussey Hansen, who played forward on our team, sank a free shot. We stalled the rest of the way to secure the victory. We beat St. Paul that night fair and square, no matter what complaints Coach Gingrass might have expressed about our facilities. A *W* is a *W*. Yeah! Coach Gingrass—we beat the team that beat Mass City! I personally scored twelve points, which was my highest point total for any game. By way of footnote, I took most of my shots from the side and somehow avoided the scenery. I had four personal fouls.

We beat Chassell on our court in my senior year and then played them on their court in February of 1949. When we played in the Copper Country, we usually stayed at the Douglas House in Houghton and ate at Nelson's Restaurant (no relation) next door, or we ate across the Portage Canal at the Golden Pheasant or at the Venice Café in

Hancock. What a trip—what meals we ate! Houghton and Hancock were still booming little copper mining towns in those years. The stores were loaded with copper souvenirs. I picked up an ashtray for my dad. After beating Chassell in the second game and a rollicking good time in the Copper Country, the basketball team was caught in a huge snowstorm on the way back to National Mine.

We had traveled to Chassell in two cars, one driven by Coach Gleason and the other by Mr. Bath, with five boys and their gear in each car. Unable to get us all the way back to National Mine, Coach Gleason and Mr. Bath put the whole team up at the Mather Inn in Ishpeming and blew a big hole in the basketball budget. All the mining executives who came to town stayed at the Mather Inn. It was a classy place—we'd become celebrities by being trapped in a snowstorm. The next morning, we ate breakfast at Auntie's Café across the street. We had another blast. Our party line telephone had been installed by my senior year, so I was able to call home. My dad drove in from Green Crick and picked me up at Auntie's later that morning.

In 1949, we won the Class E district championship, which was held at the brand-new basketball court built at Michigan Tech in Houghton, Michigan. Ours was the first district championship played there. Ma and Dad were celebrating their twenty-fifth anniversary in Ishpeming, but I couldn't attend their celebration because we were in the district championships. It had been a banner year. The girls in home economics cooked us a hot meal before we left for Houghton—as they always did for out-of-town trips. Mocking a then-current song, Erkie Lukkari sang in the brand-spanking-new locker room at Houghton that we had come to the district championships to "see the sun go down on Dollar Bay." Like I said, Erkie was not our best singer, but we played hard and made Erkie's lyrics come true. We trounced Winona in the first game and Dollar Bay in the second.

We were smokin', but we still had to face—you said it—Michigamme for the title. The game, played on March 7, 1949, was close and hard fought throughout. In the course of it, I committed four personal fouls. Michigamme was ahead by one point at the end of the first quarter, but we were ahead by one point at the half. At the end of the third quarter, the two teams were deadlocked. In the fourth quarter, Michigamme went ahead 28 to 22. At that point, we picked them up man-to-man all over the floor and stole the ball right under their basket. Bob Anderson scored on a layup, and Addu Alderton followed with a free throw to bring us within 3 points. I sank a long shot, and Addu came back with another free throw to tie the game with a minute remaining.

Five seconds later, Rudy Larson (who scored 13 points that night) intercepted the ball, dribbled in, and scored again. The basket was disallowed because Larson had been fouled before he took the shot. He made the free throw, and National Mine took a one point lead with less than a minute remaining. We went into a stall, and Michigamme fouled four times in that minute, but we had reserved our time-outs and took the ball instead of the free shots. You could do that in those years. The score at the end of the game was National Mine, 29—Michigamme, 28. Bedlam broke out with National Mine fans going berserk in the Copper Country. After something like a twenty-year hiatus we avenged our loss to Michigamme the previous year and hoisted a trophy for our trophy case. Best of all for me, Phil Numinen, the guy I was assigned to guard, did not score one point.

Since we were playing the districts on the campus of Michigan Tech, we were given a tour of the rock museum it housed. The museum contained exotic rocks of all kinds and was an exhibit of the mining industry itself. I got a brief glimpse of college life and was hooked. Also, on our way to Michigan Tech, we visited a model village Henry Ford had built at Alberta. Coach Gleason, who was also our manual training teacher, wanted us to tour the sawmill Ford operated there, which was devoted primarily to creating wood paneling for Ford station wagons. But the unique feature that our coach wanted us to see was that all its waste slabs and damaged lumber were burned on site to create the electricity that powered the plant, drove the saws, and lit up the village—a self-sufficient plant and village.

Unfortunately for the high school girls, they had no interschool sports in those years and did not get to go on long trips to out-of-town venues like the boys' basketball team did. As a consequence, they didn't go to rock museums or model villages. If our out-of-town game was closer to home, like in Champion or Republic, practically the whole high school rode to the game on our school bus. Bill Dally drove. He was a great fan of the basketball team; he came to all our games whether we played home or away. Bill played on the 1930 National Mine team that won the Class E state championship. On the way back from our games, we always sang our fight song, "National, National raise our voices, fling the banner high . . . sons and daughters ever loyal shout this battle cry, N-A-T-I-O-N-A-L fight, fight, fight . . . " Or popular songs with lyrics like "With someone like you, a pal good and true, I'd like to leave it all behind and go and find a home that's known to God alone." Some of those kids really could sing. We had a blast! Mr. Bath came along but did not sing.

We lost out to the Alpha team in the Class E state final championship in our senior year.[59] We won the first game of the state championships by beating out Grand Marais 63 to 23. Hansen scored 18 points in that game, and Larson scored 14 points. I had 8 points but got thrown out of the game with 5 personal fouls. That put us up against Alpha for the state championship. They were a team of big, tall farm boys from the southern part of the Upper Peninsula down by Iron Mountain. We called that area the banana belt. All Class E teams were located in the Upper Peninsula, so the Class E championship game was played at Northern Michigan College in Marquette—not at Jenison Field House in East Lansing where Classes A, B, C, and D played their state championship games.

I think Coach Gleason had us in the locker room too early for that one. By game time, we were a bit edgy. No excuses, but some of our players had the flu. It was a bigger floor than we were used to, and the Alpha players were a whole lot bigger than we expected. While we could have claimed fatigue—emotional if not physical— following the championship trip to the Copper Country, the dog-eat-dog victory over Michigamme, and the blowout against Grand Marais, Alpha flat outplayed us. Because of the size of the floor and the flu, we didn't go to racehorse basketball. It was a great disappointment. There was one state championship Class E trophy in the National Mine trophy case—and a picture of the members of that legendary team—right opposite the Large Assembly, and our guys wanted to put another trophy and our picture there. You don't get to tell the coach how to play the game, but if I ever had the chance to play that game again, I'd have asked Coach Gleason to let us use all our subs and play them racehorse style. Our guys could run—we'd have beaten them good. Instead we lost 50 to 33 and took home the runner-up trophy. We played 21 games in my senior year including five tournament games. We won 18 of them. We scored a total of 835 points against 627 points scored by our opponents.

My senior year in basketball proved to be a banner year despite our loss to Alpha in the final game, and became even more so later. Let me tell you why. C. C. Watson coached the Ishpeming high school team in those years and National Mine used to scrimmage his first team. They were Class B, and we were Class E, so we never played them in competition. We played the Ishpeming second team in competition, but we scrimmaged against the first team. We never beat Ishpeming's first team in our scrimmages, but we were competitive enough to give C. C. Watson the willies and every player on his team fits when he bawled them out. C. C. Watson, who was very good at raking players over the coals, also put some pretty good teams on the floor. Tommy Sullivan, whose short stature didn't stop him from being very big as Ishpeming's center, usually led the scoring for Ishpeming with a wicked spinning underhand shot and a jumper and layup that wouldn't quit. In those days, no one was tall enough to tip the ball in. Lindberg on the Ishpeming team might have been—we called him Stretch. Coach Gleason would never have been able to tip one in—he was short and we called him Hubbub behind his back—but he never bawled a player out in front of the team. He wanted us to be men and treated us that way.

Some of the Ishpeming guys we scrimmaged against—Stretch Lindberg, Tommy Sullivan, John Junti, and Don Doney—were on the Ishpeming team that won the state Class B championship in 1950 at Jenison Fieldhouse in Lansing by knocking off River Rouge. My God—River Rouge! Rudy Larson reminded me recently that Terry Thompson may have played center for Ishpeming that year. River Rouge had a star player named Spoelstra. Rudy also recalled that Stretch Lindberg defended well against him. I still remember when the Ishpeming team returned home like conquering heroes. Everyone had followed them on the radio and in the *Mining Journal*. We National Miners basked in their reflected glory knowing, though it never reached the green sheets, our Class E team had scrimmaged against them with considerable success. Our claim to fame was that we won eighteen games; we beat St. Paul, won the district championship, finished second in the Regional, and scrimmaged an Ishpeming team that took home a state Class B championship the next year. Talk about walking proud.

After our senior season ended, Coach Gleason took the team to the Beau Chateau restaurant in Negaunee. Although it finished off what was left in the basketball budget, we enjoyed a great dinner there, which Erkie Lukkari dubbed "the Last Supper." Erkie liked to clown around. My basketball years were some of the best years I can remember. I was blessed to be part of a great group of guys who played for the love of the game and with a young-spirited joy in their hearts. None of us went on to college ball, but for our time, playing Class E ball, we had about as much glory and pleasure as any sport can ever deliver. I put my Class E championship medal in my chifforobe drawer knowing my basketball days were over.

I took my final exams and graduated from the National Mine High School in June of 1949. I didn't need to take the bus on days when there were finals. My brother Ken had found a shortcut for walking to the National Mine School. It went through the hardwoods behind Graneggen's camp and came out just west of the school (see Map F at the end of chapter 7). On the day of my last exam that June, I walked through a forest of maples adorned with newly minted leaves that reflected a golden sun and through trilliums bursting from the forest floor. I was about as exhilarated as one kid can get.

In those days, there were two ceremonies—baccalaureate and commencement. I wore the brand-new, brown, double-breasted, pin-striped suit my dad bought for me at Lofberg's store to both ceremonies. It was the one I had my graduation picture taken in at the Child's Art Gallery in Ishpeming. Just like those of all my sisters and brothers, Ma framed it and put it on the piano. In fact, it was the only suit I had. The first ceremony was a religious affair they probably can no longer have in a public school. At the second ceremony, the glee club sang, and we received our diplomas in the auditorium where we put on the senior class play and played basketball.

At graduation, and even more so later, I noticed that none of the other guys were wearing brown, double-breasted, pin-striped suits. Their attire was more attuned to what guys were wearing at college and probably purchased at Stern and Fields in Marquette. Although I didn't ask them where they bought their suits, I did notice that their ties, like mine, were also tied with four-in-hand knots. My brother Ken taught me how to tie a Windsor knot in 1950 so that I could be best man at his wedding to Loraine Bath, who was from Negaunee.

Thanks to the grit of my family, the excellence of the National Mine public school, and basketball, I had come a long way from that skinny little kid who sat on the wood box by the Kalamazoo stove and blew holes in the frost on the dining room window to see the old orange school bus. I had been given a chance.

~~~

Figure 43

The National Mine High School Basketball Team—1949 District Champions and Runners-Up in the Regional Championship Game

Back row (L-R) Ralph Keto, Marvin Kaminen, Coach Patrick Gleason, Ralph Helston and Ronald Toy

Front row (L-R) Maurice Hanson, Donald Lukarri, Allen Alderton, David Nelson, Kenneth (Rudy) Larson and Robert Anderson

Photograph supplied by Ralph and Marie Flack Keto

Figure 44
Nelson Graduation Photographs

Graduation photographs of Ben and Elsie's kids:

(A) Marian—1942, (B) Ruth—1943, (C)
Kenneth—1946, (D) Dorothy—1947,
(E) David—1949, (F) William—1952, (G)
Joanne—1956, and (H) Frederick—1964.

There were four valedictorians and two
salutatorians among them.

Nelson family photographs

CHAPTER 20

Making Hay, Icing Doughnuts, and Gandy Dancing

I WAS NOT able to obtain full-time employment the summer I graduated. I was still only seventeen years old. Hussy Hansen hired in as an iron miner at the Cleveland- Cliffs Mather A shaft and was soon driving a shiny navy blue 1948 Ford four-door sedan. Rudy Larson and Erkie Lukarri were on their way to Michigan Tech that fall, and, while I wanted to go with them, I needed some time to put money together before I could enroll in college. Putting it bluntly, I was penniless, and Ma and Dad were in no position to help me.

Notwithstanding the depleted state of my finances, I had by then decided on prelaw, and for that, Northern Michigan College in Marquette was starting to look better. That summer, I worked mainly on Stolen's farm helping Oscar harvest hay and weed his potato field. My brothers also worked there during their first summers out of high school. I also took a correspondence course in solid geometry that summer that was supervised by National Mine's superintendent, Mr. Bath. I loved geometry.

Oscar had the most peculiar team of horses I had ever seen. One was a big white horse with small patches of mottled black in his coat and one clouded eye. His teammate on the right was a short stocky brown. They were nothing like Belle or Blackie's matched team. In fact, they reminded me of Mutt and Jeff. Oscar worked, I believe, at the Cliffs Shaft iron mine in Ishpeming for his day job. He harvested hay on his farm with a horse-drawn mower, which eliminated the need for scything his crop down, except for some patches around rocks and at the edges of his fields. My job was to rake it into windrows and stack it. When Oscar was off shift, I drove his team of horses and pitched the hay up to him on the hay wagon. He spread it across rope slings he layered on as the wagon filled. The slings were used to pull the hay up into his hayloft.

After the wagon was loaded, Oscar drove the team over to the barn—a weather-beaten hip roof structure. There he unhitched his team from the wagon and hitched them to a rope drawn through a pulley tied to a post at the side of his barn. He instructed me to drive his mismatched team as hay was lifted up into the hayloft one sling a time. I had to keep those two horses moving in unison lest a sling of hay plummet down upon the hay wagon and possibly Oscar. Once a sling of hay was lifted up to the rail at the peak of the hayloft, it hit a dolly on the rail and scooted on in. At that point, I was to stop the team while Oscar pulled a rope that released the sling and dropped the hay into the loft. As I turned the team and drove them back to hoist another sling, Oscar pulled the empty sling back down. It was a much better system for putting hay in a hayloft than the one we used at home. It was work I liked and was used to because I had harnessed and driven Nellie, but it didn't pay a lot. Still, I had found part-time work that first summer, even though it included weeding Oscar's potato patch and the discipline of the rows.

In September, I learned that Carl Corneliuson, whose son Tony had played on the Ishpeming basketball team, needed a packager and handyman at his bakery in Ishpeming. I wouldn't be eighteen years old until October and wasn't old enough for full-time employment, but I applied in September and was given the job. Bakeries start their workday early. I'd have to walk the two miles to New Burt and take a bus from there into Ishpeming to get to the bakery on time. In the winter, my coat was covered with frost when I arrived at New Burt. It brought home what Dad had gone through during the Depression, although he had to walk all the way into Ishpeming. There was no bus for him. At the bakery, I earned four dollars a day for a nine-or-ten-hour day during the week and six dollars on Saturday—twenty-six dollars a week in all. Ma insisted that her kids pay room and board when they found outside employment, so after taxes and room and board, I netted about seventy dollars a month. To protect my clothes from sugar and flour, Carl told me to buy a brown divided apron that strapped to my legs. I had saved enough from my work at Oscar's farm to handle that. On my first lunch break, I opened an account at the Peninsula Bank in Ishpeming to save up for college. My sister Ruth had lined me up with her dentist in Ishpeming, and I also needed funds for that.

My job at the bakery was a far cry from working on the ten acres or at Oscar's farm. The work was more genteel than, say, mucking out a barn. It involved icing and then wrapping or boxing Danish rolls, doughnuts, jelly buns, and long johns among other pastries. Dirty fingernails were not allowed. It also encompassed wrapping whatever else was baked for the retail stores. I was the only one in the wrapping department during the week, so I did it all. It was a nonstop job, but one that had been performed previously by a young woman. That was sobering. On Saturdays and the day before a holiday, Carl brought her or another wrapper back in to help me out. I'm sorry; I've tried but can't remember names.

I also ran the bread slicing and wrapping machine and prepared trays of baked goods to be displayed at retail stores. The trays I prepared were taken (along with packages of rolls and boxes of wrapped white bread, rye bread, Pullman loaves, and Finnish Limpu bread) to local stores by Billy Woods in a panel truck bearing the Corneliuson logo. His brother Tommy Woods delivered to outlying communities in a larger truck with the same logo. They devoted their early morning hours to razzing me, telling jokes, and making sure I got their trays ready on time.

I was required to prepare about twenty trays daily—more on weekends and holidays—exactly as described in retail orders that hung on a wire above the wrapping table and to have them ready by the time the trucks left, one at eight and the other at nine o'clock. If they weren't prepared correctly or if I was late in having them ready, Billy, Tommy, and their customers would bitch. After that, I packaged hotdog and hamburger buns for display in the store in front of the bakery and then sliced and wrapped a rack or two of bread using the bread machine. The Pullman loaves had to be sliced lengthwise for weddings and anniversaries.

The bread machine gave me fits. Once I threw the switch, it put out one hell of a racket, shook the whole building, crushed as many loaves as it sliced, and mangled many more as it wrapped. The first time I saw that machine crush and mangle loaves of bread, I thought I'd be fired on the spot. I did clean, oil, and try to fix the damn thing as did Bob the handyman, but even Carl himself couldn't tweak that antiquated thing enough to get it to operate right—except that the girl who trained me as her replacement, and whose name I've forgotten, could. She had a gentle touch. The bread slicer and wrapper responded to her, which made Carl look quizzically at me. She did quite well with that machine, although she too mangled a lot of bread and wasted a lot of wrapping paper with it. I still see her pulling mangled bread out of that thing.

The rest of my day involved getting Billy Woods' trays and boxes ready for his afternoon run, cleaning the trays he and Tommy brought back from the stores, and cleaning my wrapping table, racks, and work area to get ready for the next day. Bakeries are fierce for depositing loose flour, sugar, and whatever else all over the floors, racks, and wrapping tables. I was commended by the bakers for keeping my area clean. My dad had taught me to always keep my work out in front of me and to keep a clean bottom.

But the best part of my job at the bakery was listening to the wild and sometimes raunchy jokes that Billy and Tommy Woods brought back from their runs. I won't repeat the stories they told here, but, boy, did they tell them. Bob the handyman joined in, as did Spencer Felt, who had served as a cook in the navy and made glazed doughnuts and baked bread and rolls in the big ovens. Billy and Tommy Woods, as well as Spencer Felt, were from National Mine, so at times it felt like a mini-reunion. Once, Tommy told me I should learn to speak Finnish to a Finnish girl, Vera, who also came in to help with packaging on Saturdays. He gave me a question I was to ask Vera in Finnish, her native language. It sounded like "Auna Mauna Nussea," but I didn't speak Finnish then, and I don't to this day. By then, I had caught on to Tommy's tricks, so I didn't bite. Had I done so, I learned later, I would have had my face slapped.

On Saturdays, Carl would put several rings of bologna in the big oven and serve it with fresh hotdog and hamburger buns to all of the help. I had more than my share. One Saturday, Carl baked meat from a bear he had killed. Carl knew how to use spices, so it came out of the oven tasting delicious. That surprised me because Ma would never cook bear meat.

The strangest work assignment I received while at the bakery involved a Shetland pony, if you can believe that. Billy Woods had located one near Gwinn and asked me to help him haul it to National Mine in the back of the bakery panel truck. Carl and Billy were on good terms, so if Carl didn't object, how could I? I never inquired if the health department or the Society for the Prevention of Cruelty to Animals objected because it was to be a birthday present for one of Billy's kids. Billy knew I had experience handling cattle and horses because I'd once told him about me and Dad transporting a bucking Hereford whiteface steer home to our farm in the back of Dad's 1946 Ford pickup truck. Still, I wondered why Billy didn't ask his brother Tommy.

After we took all the racks out of the bakery truck and drove down to Gwinn to pick up the pony I found out why he didn't ask Tommy. I have no idea how we got that Shetland into the bakery truck, but we squeezed it in. That done, we discovered that there were no adequate restraints in the panel truck between the cargo space in back and the bucket seats where the driver and passenger (me) sat up front. There also was no place to tether the Shetland. Billy solved that problem—he told me to hang onto its halter. On the way back to National Mine, there would be three sets of eyeballs looking through the windshield, and let me tell you, that Shetland was one curious pony. For a while, it looked like it wanted to take over Billy's seat and drive the truck. I can only relate that we made it back to National Mine without the Shetland trying to buck, but as we drove along it insisted on thrusting its head forward between Billy and me, while I clung to its halter with all my might to restrain it from leaping through the windshield. I guess his kids liked having a new pony, but after cleaning the truck and restoring the bakery racks, I was not inspired to initiate a career transporting Shetland ponies in bakery trucks.

After a few months at the bakery shop, I bought a 1931 Model A Ford to drive into work. It cost me one hundred and fifty dollars. Once I got the Model A, I was able to drive into Ishpeming on Saturday nights where I patrolled the streets between Auntie's Café and the Chocolate Shop with Rudy Larson, Erkie Lukarri, Freezer Magnuson, Hussy Hansen, and guys from the Ishpeming basketball team.

I must say, though, that my beat-up 1931 four-door Model A sedan was nothing like my dad's roadster from the early twenties, even though I polished it and installed new carpets and covered the back seat with an Indian blanket. I also put in new spark plugs and distributor points. When I finished installing them, I discovered the Model A wouldn't run unless I also timed the engine. The exhaust was coming out of the carburetor, the engine was running backward, and my dad was laughing like mad. I did not know how to time a Model A engine, nor did he. My brother Ken pushed me into Juntila's garage in Ishpeming with his car, where I was taught the intricacies of the timing wheel on the front of a Model A four-cylinder engine.

It was a great car in snow during the winter because it stood high off the ground, but the heater worked off the manifold and provided little heat. It had no defroster, so I had to scrape the frost off the windshield as I drove. But, that was one tough little car. Once, I accidentally hooked bumpers with a 1948 Chevy. His was bent all out of shape, and mine wasn't even scratched.

In the spring of 1950, my uncle Nels offered me a job working for the LS&I Railroad. Carl agreed to keep me on at the bakery on Saturdays, and sometimes, I worked at Oscar's farm on Sundays. Originally, Uncle Nels had mentioned that I might be assigned to work with the engineers, so I went into Lofberg's store in Ishpeming and purchased a pair of leather boots of the type I thought an engineer might wear and oiled them with Neat's-foot oil. Headed for the big time, I wanted to be properly clad, but no slots opened with the engineers. Instead, I spent the summer working as a gandy dancer on Uncle Nels' section gang. It was the same job my dad had occasionally worked during the Depression.

Working on the "Section" paid more than the bakery, but it was much harder work. The section crew I was assigned to consisted of eight or nine guys in addition to my Uncle Nels. To take us to our work sites at the iron mines, Uncle Nels sat up front operating a gasoline-powered car equipped with steel wheels to run on the railroad tracks. Some of the old timers on the crew sat on the lead car with him. The rest of the crew sat back to back on benches down each side of the car that followed him with our shovels, pinch bars, spiking mauls, wrenches, and other tools under our feet or on the flatcar that brought up the rear. They all knew I was Nels' nephew.

My first day was a sunny day, but not all of them were, so the ride down the LS&I tracks to the Athens mine in the fresh cool May air was exhilarating. There was still some snow on the ground. I tucked the pant legs of my bib overalls into my engineer's boots just like all the other section guys so that they kind of ballooned at the ankle. In doing so, I noticed that the crew was wearing steel-toed work shoes after one of them pointed to my shiny new engineering boots, and they all laughed.

I had heard about gandy dancing from my dad the night before. Dad explained that two gandy dancers stand opposite each other on the railroad ties right next to the rail, and, with another gandy dancer pinching a tie up against the rail with a pinch bar, pry rock ballast under the railroad tie with square No.2 shovels in order to level and support the tracks. Surprisingly, you can raise a set of railroad tracks that way. But that is not how shovel tracks are built. Although the members of Nels' crew were called gandy dancers, I didn't get my introduction to actual gandy dancing until later when the crew worked on the main line.

Shovel tracks were constructed so that they could be repositioned by the section crew beneath the trestles at the iron mines alongside stockpiles of iron ore that had been hoisted and dumped there during the winter. The shovel tracks had to be moved as cuts were dug from the stockpiles by a steam shovel. Shovel tracks, at that time, consisted of two sets of tracks—one for the locomotive and one for the steam shovel that was used to load railroad cars pulled behind the locomotive. The two tracks were separate and parallel and could be as long as two or three football fields. Each was constructed by supporting the ties that held the rails with hardwood planking that was placed right beneath the rails. Stacks of hematite-coated planking—some tapered and sawed to a variety of thicknesses—were piled near the shovel tracks and used from year to year.

When we arrived at the Athens mine, we found the tracks where they had been left the previous fall—shoved off to the side of a stockpile of iron ore that had been dumped there from the trestle during the winter just ended. Our task was to move both the steam shovel tracks and the locomotive tracks up next to the stockpile, align and level them, and build up under them with wood planks. We used our pinch bars to heave the tracks. Four Section guys would line up on one rail and four opposite them on the other rail, with their feet between the ties and their pinch bars spotted beneath the rail. Upon hearing "Heave!" from Uncle Nels, they would heave the track in unison a section at a time—with all the rails bolted together and the ties attached. First, one set of rails, then the other, and then back a little if they had been heaved too far. It soon became apparent that it is best to wear steel-toed shoes when this is done. The process was continued until the two tracks were moved almost intact to their desired location. Then the ties were examined, and any that broke or became unstable while being heaved were replaced, and loose ones were respiked. If necessary, loose or broken spikes were extracted using our pinch bars, the spike holes filled with wooden plugs, and the rails respiked. A gauge was used to maintain the distance between the rails. If any angle bars that connected the rails broke while being heaved, they were also replaced.

I was instructed that a spiker must not hit the rail with the spiking maul and that when a spike is driven, it must stand erect in the plate placed under the rail with the bottom of the head of the spike flush against the slanted flange at the bottom of the rail. It is not easy to miss the rail, hit a railroad spike on the head every time you swing the spiking maul and still have the spike stand up straight. Some of the spikers were very good at it. My spikes weren't erect or flush enough for Uncle Nels, so I was assigned to pinch ties up against the rail with my pinch bar while they were spiked by others. I found out later that I was nearsighted and needed glasses.

Once the heaving and spiking was complete, Uncle Nels directed the crew to line up the two tracks, level them, and support them with wood planks. To level them, heavy jacks were inserted under the rails, the tracks were raised, and wood planks were inserted under the ties. The varied thicknesses of the planks and the fact that some were tapered allowed Uncle Nels to level the tracks using a level that fit between the rails. To align and level the rails, particularly around curves, he also used a gauge that fit between the rails and two wood blocks. One was a truncated triangle with a peephole near the top. The other was triangular.

Uncle Nels did not have access to a civil engineer with a transit or a sighted level. I understood how his level worked, and I could see that the gauge gave him the distance between the rails. But Uncle Nels never explained what he was doing when he placed the two wood blocks on one of the rails, lay down on the ties, and sighted though a peephole in one of them at the pointed tip on the other to bank the tracks around a curve. I can't provide more particulars; I have no idea how he did it. Uncle Nels must have picked up that skill laying tracks across France during World War I while dodging bullets. I can only relate that when the locomotive and shovel tracks we built were finished, they were parallel, level, aligned, and properly elevated so that the inside rail was lower than the outside rail to handle the curves.

If there were no existing shovel tracks alongside a stockpile, we created them by leveling a bed with our No. 2 shovels and then hauling in ties and rails on the flatcar. Because of my experience working on our farm, I was very good with a No. 2 shovel. For short distances, we moved the car down the rails by hand, laid out the ties in the bed, and placed rails on them as we went along. When tie tongs were available to carry the rails, pairs of men with tongs lined up on each end of a rail and moved it into place. The rails were usually sixty-pound rails (that meant sixty pounds per foot of length) and thirty feet long. If we weren't using tongs, four to five men would line up on each end of the rail and kneel to pick it up. Once we had all positioned our hands to lift, Uncle Nels called out, "Ball to the belly!" We then lifted the 1,800 pounds in unison, turning the rail as we lifted so that the ball (top) of the rail turned to our bellies. Once lifted, the rail was carried over to the ties. When we heard Uncle Nels' "Hands on the ball!" we placed the rail down on the ties. Sometimes, we lifted eighty-pound rails. The guys doing the lifting watched down the line to make sure there were no floppy elbows and, if any were seen, called out, "Hey, I see elbows flopping." I knew that first day they better not be mine and learned the meaning of pulling your own weight.

The litmus test for the new shovel tracks we laid came when we leaned on our shovels and spiking mauls and watched a belching steam locomotive push a steam shovel out on to the track nearest the stockpile and then spot empty ore cars on the parallel track. The tracks had to carry the weight of the steam shovel, the locomotive with a string of eight or ten ore cars, and then the weight of loaded ore cars. Uncle Nels was a first-class section boss. Our tracks always passed the test. No locomotives, steam shovels, or ore cars derailed from his tracks. They wouldn't dare.

The creosoted black ties we handled were the worst because they were a lot heavier than untreated ties, and when you handled them, you ended up with creosote all over your overalls and your gloves. But all section work is tough on footwear and clothes. The crushed rock where we laid the tracks tore the hell out of my boots. On my first day, Uncle Nels stood by the shop after we came back to the yard after a ten-hour shift to put our tools away. He had a big smile on his face and laughed as

I stumbled to my Model A to head home. I still don't believe it—Uncle Nels was laughing. The soles of my new boots were cut to ribbons and my overalls were in tatters. I must have been a sight. It was tough work, but my dad and my cousin Jack, Uncle Nels' son, had done it. Besides, on my first shift "workin' on the railroad" I earned "time an' a half" for two hours overtime. By the end of the summer, I had helped lay shovel tracks at quite a few of the mines and had worked repairing the main line. I was in great shape, wearing steel-toed boots with tough soles, and was even allowed to spike. I had become a full-fledged gandy dancer.

Gandy dancers never bragged about it or even mentioned it for that matter, but the shovel tracks they built were a vital link in the movement of ore cars from the mines at Ishpeming and Negaunee out to the main line of the LS&I Railroad and then to the loading docks in Marquette. Ore trains began to roll to Marquette as soon as the snow and ice melted on Lake Superior; ore boats could dock there, and the shipping season began. Section gangs of gandy dancers worked all through the shipping season relocating shovel tracks at all the mines on the Marquette Range. I was proud to be a gandy dancer. We were a vital link in the chain.

During that period, I also helped my dad at home. After the war ended in 1945, Dad had decided to spend some of the money he earned at the mine during the war on a new Ford pickup truck and to build a new and better barn. He still wanted to be a farmer no matter how many rocks we picked or what the mine paid. My brother Ken moved to Flint around 1948 where he worked for Farmer Pete's Supermarket as a meat cutter. My sister Marian already lived in Flint where she worked at the A.C. Spark Plug Company as a secretary and bookkeeper, my sister Ruth worked at the Michigan Gas and Electric Company (later the UP Power Company) in Ishpeming as a bookkeeper, and Dort had taken a job in Ishpeming as a telephone operator at Michigan Bell Telephone Company—"Number please."

Once I took the job at the bakery and later at the LS&I, my brother Bill was the oldest boy left at home, so he took over most of the haymaking, potato hoeing, and wood-cutting work, and he finished the second barn my dad was hell-bent on building. It had a concrete floor, cement block walls, a much larger hayloft, and it was painted red, as a barn should be. As it was built, the first barn was torn down to cannibalize some of its lumber. I helped out, but Bill did most of the work. The barn Bill built proved him to be a very good carpenter and mason, although Dad marked the rafters for cutting. By then though, my dad had reverted to bloodline picking and had taken up the breeding and running of beagles. But that's a story I've already told you about.

~~~

Figure 45
Athens Mine and Cliff Shaft

Miners installing and spragging
timber Athens Mine, Negaunee,
Michigan IM - ATH – 05

Shaft house Athens Mine,
Negaunee, Michigan
IM - ATH – 16

Athens Mine, Negaunee,
Michigan Electric motor,
motorman, and brakeman
IM- ATH – 12

Cliffs Shaft Mine Ishpeming,
Michigan, IM –Clif-19

Photographs Courtesy of Superior View Studios

Figure 46
Gandy Dancers and LS& I Shovel

Gandy dancers, Hancock, Michigan RR-152

LS&I Shovel, Ishpeming, Michigan IM-Misc-65

(Note: In the early days the shovels were steam
shovels that ran on railroad tracks).

Photographs courtesy Superior View Studios

CHAPTER 21

Out of the Frying
Pan into the Fire

WITH SEVEN HUNDRED Fifty dollars saved from money I'd earned at the bakery, work at Oscar Stolen's farm, and as a gandy dancer with the LS&I Railroad, I quit the section gang, left the farm and Labaan behind, and entered Northern Michigan College in Marquette in the fall of 1950, not knowing if such a venture was sensible or not. No one in my family except Aunt Ann, my dad's sister, had ever attended college. Aunt Ann attended Eastern Michigan College in Ypsilanti, Michigan, and became a grade school teacher. She later married Alden Graneggen, who graduated from the engineering school at the University of Michigan. He was from the same Graneggen family that owned the camp by our farm. If they could do it, why shouldn't I give college a try? But I was just a rough-hewn farm kid—I'd never lived in a city where they had sidewalks, streetlights, laundromats, city water, and plumbing with showers. I had never been down from the Mountain of Iron or lived out on my own.

Northern—now a university—is situated twenty-five miles northeast of Ishpeming in a city named after Père Jacques Marquette, a French Jesuit missionary who was one of the first to come to the region. Père Marquette's contribution to the area cannot be overemphasized. His statue now stands at the east entrance to the city of Marquette on a small bluff commanding a view out across Lake Superior. The latter, which the locals bill as the greatest freshwater lake in the world, is a dark blue body of water that on a clear summer day takes your breath away, but on a stormy, wintry day can destroy you—as it did the Edmund Fitzgerald lake freighter decades later.

When I enrolled there, Northern consisted of Kaye Hall and two adjoining sandstone buildings, together with the John D. Pierce Training School for teachers, the Lydia Olson library, Lee Hall (a cafeteria and conference center) and Carey Hall (a girls' dormitory). It had no dormitory for boys. Boys from out of town stayed at rooming houses around town or at the two fraternity houses.

Northern's campus was located on historic soil a mile or so south of the dock where iron ore, dug by miners from the Mountain of Iron, was loaded on ore boats at the LS&I dock. It was near the spot where a century before Abraham Williams had built two cottages on the Dead River about the time copper and iron were discovered on the Peninsula. The shore of Lake Superior was still wilderness then and a whole lot different from the one that greeted me when I arrived in Marquette.

Just past the iron ore docks, Presque Isle rises out of Lake Superior. Dad had driven the family there during summers for Sunday picnics. Preserved as a public park and loaded with history, Presque Isle became part of the legacy of the Shiras family, a prominent Marquette family devoted to conservation. The name Presque Isle is old French for "almost an island." It contains the grave of Chief Kawbawgam. Attached to it is a concrete and stone breakwater that forms the harbor where ore boats dock, and a tree-tunneled lane and bike path encircle it. It is famous for The Cove where silver had been discovered years before and Sunset Point where the sun sets across a bay of Lake Superior in a blaze of glory behind hills that lead to two mountains—Hogsback and Sugarloaf. It was where young college men took Northern coeds to watch brilliant sunsets and to tell their dates they were there to "watch submarines race." But there would be little time for any of that during my freshman year.

When I enrolled in prelaw I knew that to stay enrolled I'd have to pick up part-time work after the first semester or sell my Model A. I had driven from Ishpeming to Northern's campus with three or four guys. Names escape me. We planned the trip at Auntie's Café the night before and arrived about eight o'clock in the morning because I wasn't sure if the tires on my Model A would carry that many guys that far. After picking up some coffee, we lay down on the big grassy heart landscaped into the lawn in front of Kaye Hall, reminisced about our summer jobs, and talked about the Korean War, which was heating up. After about a half an hour, one guy got up, glanced at Kaye Hall, and announced he would hitchhike back to Ishpeming. He had decided not to matriculate. As I watched him walk away, I wondered if I had made the right choice.

I selected economics as my major because it was listed in the catalog as a prerequisite for my prelaw program, but I also hoped to nail down the cause of the Great Depression I'd just lived through. With LS&I hematite still under my fingernails, and after wading through lines of students paying their tuition and enrolling for the fall semester, I picked up my ancient history, sociology, zoology, composition and rhetoric, economics, and speech textbooks. To say the least, they were markedly different than the tools of a gandy dancer. Then I went to the library and excitedly cracked open my economics textbook even before classes began and learned that economics is a science. That had not been mentioned in high school, at the Paradise Bar, or even on the section gang. It sounded like higher education to me.

Eureka, it's like physics, chemistry, and biology, the textbooks said. I was hooked. The swings of the business cycle could be analyzed and brought under control through rigorous application of fixed principles and mathematical formulas. Just wait until I mastered the formulas, returned in triumph, and explained to my old section gang at the Paradise Bar that economics is science and that there would never be another Great Depression. That thought produced a smile. It brought back memories of a grizzled old gandy dancer with hematite on his face, who stared into the face of a man in a blue uniform who came into the Paradise Bar in defiance of his religious scruples and asked the guys at our table to make a contribution to the poor. The old-timer slowly twisted a glass of draft beer, forked over a dollar and said, "Goddamn it man—we *are* the poor!"

After renting a room in the home of Mr. and Mrs. Pascoe on Park Street, I sat down at the dinner table at Lindberg's Boarding House that first evening with some football players and upperclassmen who had enrolled under the GI Bill. They lived at the Tri Mu House but ate their meals at Lindberg's. I had a prank played on me the first night—someone had dropped a plastic angleworm into my soup. It clinked and rolled to the surface as soon as I dropped my spoon into the soup to stir it. Recalling Tommy Woods' high jinks at the bakery shop, I announced how excited I was to be dining on the newest thing out there—angleworm soup. That broke up the room and no one played high jinks on me at Lindberg's after that.

But the whole dinner table at Lindberg's broke out in uproarious guffaws after I excitedly announced to them my newly minted knowledge that economics is science. One of the guys, a bright-looking veteran named Jack Rousseau, smiled and said, "Don't pay attention to these guys. If you want credit hours toward your major, you better believe that economics is science." He added, "Another thing, this isn't high school. Hard work may not be enough—it has to be smart work. It's more important to study your professor than it is your textbook." Although I didn't like to hear criticism of Bitty Annala's work ethic or my own, I paid strict attention to what Jack said because I'd heard he had good grades, and getting good grades in undergrad was essential to admission to law school.

As I progressed through my textbook, it wasn't long before the wheels came off. Each succeeding chapter and the footnotes therein brought out fundamental lines of cleavage among the scholars. Footnotes—wow. I never read footnotes in high school. "What do you mean they don't agree?" I thought. In fact they rarely agreed. Instead of science, economics was an argument among the well-off academic elite to whom it did not seem to really matter whether they were right or wrong. Oblivious to Lincoln's admonition that a house divided against itself cannot stand, economics was passing itself off as science despite two diametrically opposed schools of thought that came roaring out of the Great Depression I'd grown up in and sprang off the pages of my textbook. How could I go home and tell Ma and Dad—after all they'd been through—that not even the economists had answers?

I discovered later that the schism in my first textbook continued through my advanced courses, permeated the editorial pages of major newspapers, legislative halls and media talk shows, and endures to this day. The rift produced a boiling pot full of economic theories, laws, business regulations, and taxation that wildly gyrated from election to election. I also discovered that the advocates of the two schools of thought were so wedded to their ideas that they very politely couldn't stand each other.

After contemplating the advice Jack Rousseau had given me, some classmates and I cornered Dr. Albert Burrows, the chairman of the economics department, after class one day following a contentious debate over our textbook's claim that economics was science. He laughed, "Some claim if you laid all the economists end to end they wouldn't reach an agreement." He chuckled again as he picked up his lecture notes, closed his textbook, and added over his shoulder, "In fact, if you laid all of them end to end it might be a damn good thing." Later, I omitted the word *damn* and used that line as a member of Northern's debate team, where the question was whether the United States should impose price and wage controls, which had happened during the War and was a hot national issue at that time.

When it became time to enroll for my second semester, I received a college deferment from the draft, but my own economic situation was proving to be not scientific at all, and soon my money would run out. That's when I sold Dagwood's Labaan. I was in the same fix Dad was in when he sold his Roadster and later Belle. Still, if I didn't find better employment than the odd jobs I was able to pick up in Marquette—washing walls, mowing lawns, or painting or doing windows—my college career would soon be over. That's when I heard that Cleveland-Cliffs Iron Company was hiring part-time people at the mines in Ishpeming and decided to apply there. I passed my physical for underground work and hired in at the Mather A where my dad worked.

I would be able to work underground on Fridays on the afternoon shift and Saturdays and Sundays on the day shift. I would also be able to work during vacations and the summer. I sold the Model A for one hundred fifty dollars—the same price I'd paid for it—and picked up a used 1937 Ford sedan, just like the one my dad bought new, because I would have to drive back and forth between Marquette and Ishpeming to attend college and work at the Mather A at the same time. It didn't take much to move up to the '37, although I'd also need money for gas, new tires, and mining gear. My schedule would be tight, but if I could handle it, I'd be able to stay at Northern. I threw my Indian blanket on the back seat of the 1937 Ford, hopped in and returned to the Mountain of Iron.

~~~

Figure 47
Marquette Sites

Statue of Father Marquette
Marquette, Michigan
TO-Marq-380

Aerial View of Upper
Harbor Marquette,
Michigan. TO—Marq-83

Longyear, Kaye and Peter
White Halls Northern
Michigan College—1950.
TO—Marq-373

Presque Isle Park—1880
Marquette, Michigan.
TO-Marq- 226

Photographs Courtesy of Superior View Studios

CHAPTER 22

Savage Amusement in the Bloody Bowels of the Earth

B EFORE WE GOT on the "Cage," an elevator that would drop me with the day shift down the Mather A shaft, I pulled off my street clothes, hung them on hooks dangling from a chain on a pulley and pulled them up to the ceiling on the clean side of the "Dry." The latter was a brick building near the Mather A shaft where miners changed into digging clothes, and showered and got back into their street clothes when they returned to the surface. It was the mine where my dad still worked. He was forty-eight years old and still a long distance from retirement.

Once undressed I picked up the towel and soap I'd need when I got back from underground along with my new mining gear and walked buck naked into the dirty "Dry" where my "digging clothes" would be hung to dry between shifts. I found another chain hanging from the ceiling that had been assigned to me and pulled on thick underwear and socks, a denim shirt, bib overalls, a wide leather belt and my brand new knee-high, steel-toed rubber mining boots. I looked around and then carefully folded my boots calf-high like all the other young guys getting dressed to go underground. The older miners wore their boots up to the knee. While I was pulling on my overall jacket one of the supervisors came over from the timekeeper's office and handed me a battery powered headlamp, a hard hat, safety glasses and a brass tag etched with a number. I think it was 117, but I could be wrong. I was instructed to wear the hard hat and safety glasses at all times while underground.

I hung the six-pound acid battery from my leather belt and, as instructed by my dad the night before, took out my pocket knife and cut a notch to hold the cord to my headlamp in the left brim of my hard hat. I positioned the battery on my left hip and clipped the headlamp to my hard hat. "You're right-handed," Dad had tapped my chest, "you don't want that damn cord in the way." Every direction I faced my headlamp illuminated the way before me. It was about to show me what the insides of an iron mine look like.

Figure 48

My hard hat from my days at the Mather A

I clipped my ID tag and my army surplus water canteen to my belt as proud as a new recruit could ever be, grabbed my dinner bucket, and was fully equipped to go underground on my first shift as a "company count" iron miner. That's how the miners said it. It meant I'd be working on the Company's account at an hourly wage and not as a contract miner. I sauntered outside to watch some miners pitching horseshoes. One of them, who drove in every day from Covington up in the Copper Country, tossed his shoes with a sweeping loosey-goosey stride. His shoe made the same flat turn every time he tossed one. Like my brother Ken, the guy was really into horseshoes. He got a ringer or a leaner almost every time. None of the guys threw their shoes flip flop like I did, so I didn't join in the game. Then I walked down the corridor to the shaft with the day shift. They were smiling at my clean digging clothes and talking baseball, women and dirty jokes.

After the miners coming up from the midnight shift pushed through the day shift on their way back to the Dry, the day shift lined up in the Cage like bottles in a case of beer. The guy next to me nudged me and said to hold my mouth open. With my ears popping the Cage dropped us about 2300 feet straight down a shaft that had been blasted into solid rock. At the sixth level the first cage of the day shift shouldered off and assembled in the main drift to get work assignments from Willie Wigg, our Shift Boss.

A guy, whose battered hard hat and worn knee-high boots told me he was an old-timer, sauntered over, identified himself as Two Beer Tony, and told me I was assigned to work with him. He pointed to my battery and told me to be sure to rack it in the battery rack for recharging when we got back to the surface. He also told me to be sure I hung onto my brass ID tag and to drop it through the slot at the timekeeper's office on the way back to the Dry. They'd need it, he said, to figure my pay and to identify me if anything, "God forbid," should happen.

Like my dad did year in and year out to support our family, but unlike the stories that circulated in the family about Grandpa Carne, I found myself in the bowels of the earth with some guys I never met before, ready to help dig iron ore from deposits that had been there for millions of years. I turned to study the main drift as the day shift got their assignments and supplies, and groups of "partners" walked into the mine. I was comforted to see solid rock and that, unlike early iron mines I'd been told about, the main drift was lit with electric lights.

A narrow-gauge railroad track curled away from the shaft into the main drift, and from it a spur track ran off to the side into another drift. I asked Two Beer to explain the purpose of the spur track. He ran his headlamp down the spur and said that the tramcars that carried the ore out to the shaft were unloaded there. When I raised my hands palm up to indicate I didn't understand, he explained that the tramcars had a fifth wheel that contacted a ramp when a train of tramcars was pulled through the spur. When the tramcar's fifth wheel went over the ramp, it lifted one side of the tramcar and spilled its load of iron ore into a large trench from which it was scraped into a skip that lifted the ore to the surface. As he spoke, an electric "motor" with a train of about ten loaded tramcars entered the spur.

After Willie Wigg instructed us to stop at the first crosscut, Two Beer motioned to me to follow him in. As we started down the narrow-gauge track l turned to study the unloading spur, but Two Beer told me to hustle up because the electric motors that pulled trains of ore cars and flatcars loaded with supplies on the narrow-gauge track we were walking on moved at "a pretty good clip." He said I should keep an eye out for them, and that if I heard one coming I should try to get to a wide spot in the main drift or into a crosscut drift to let them go by. There wasn't much room between the trains of cars and the side of the main drift. At the same time he explained that getting to be a motorman was a good thing because when the trains were running, motormen "sat on their ass all day" pulling trains of ore cars out to the shaft.[60] I noticed that there were few wide spaces in the main drift and that a ditch full of hematite-laden water ran on one side of the narrow-gauge track.

Two Beer relished his role as my mentor, particularly since I was a college kid. As we walked further into the workings of the mine he launched into his lecture. A mine shaft should not be sunk directly into the ore body because hematite ore sometimes crumbles and wouldn't support a shaft. Pointing, he explained that up ahead the main drift and crosscuts branching off it would take us into the ore body. To sink the shaft I'd just descended, miners had drilled straight down into granite and jasper, blasted it loose and then using No. 2 shovels "mucked" (shoveled) the broken rock into a skip that hoisted it to the surface. They also bolted together the steel rails that guided the cage and skip up and down the shaft and installed electric, water and air lines. Two Beer took the strap holding up his bib overalls in one rubber-gloved hand, flicked a piece of mud that had fallen off a timber onto his headlamp with the other and laughed, "It's what we call 'savage amusement'—like digging into a barrel of nails."

I checked my light for mud and continued after Two Beer down the main drift. Although I'd never have admitted it to him or anyone else, I noticed cracks in the granite and jasper, and I saw that some of it had fallen into the drift. Timber and cribbing had been installed to hold it back, and in places steel beams had replaced broken wooden timber, and bolts had been drilled and hammered into the broken rock to hold it in place. Strangely, none of that frightened me. I drew strength from knowing my dad had worked underground for many years.

When I asked Two Beer about that he laughed and changed the subject. He pointed to pipes hanging in the main drift and assured me that fresh air was blown into the mine and blasting gases blown out. He also warned me not to touch the thick bare electric wire that ran above the railroad tracks. He said it furnished electricity to the narrow-gauge railroad motors, and that if I touched it I'd be "knocked on my ass."

As we clumped along in our mining boots for over half a mile, Two Beer kept repeating that the ore body was just up ahead. It wasn't horizontal, he said, "It's on an angle." When we finally reached the first crosscut he led me into it, climbed up into what he called a "top timber job"—a space about twenty feet square and six feet high—and pointed to a "raise" that had been erected off and above the crosscut. He thought we'd be assigned to hoist timber up the raise. As I walked over to the raise, Two Beer nervously ended his lecture, started to climb back down from of the top timber job, and said he couldn't show me everything right away because he'd spotted a light coming into the crosscut. He thought it might be Willie Wigg.

After we climbed back down from the top timber job to wait for Willie Wigg, Two Beer sat down on a narrow-gauge railroad flatcar parked in the crosscut and explained that parallel drifts had been driven from the top timber jobs above the crosscut, and that from them raises and more drifts were installed under the ore body. When I pointed to some rocks that had fallen into the crosscut he chuckled. "Don't worry; the whole damn place is lined with hardwood maple timber, spruce cribbin' and cedar laggin'." Cut from the surrounding forests, it was holding back cave-ins and supporting the drifts, top timber jobs, raises and crosscuts. Some of it was moldy, rotting and broken.

I asked Two Beer where the water dripping into the drifts and running in the ditch in the main drift alongside the railroad tracks emptied. He said it ran out to the shaft. He assumed it was pumped to the surface. I learned the purpose of the ditch when Willie Wigg, whose bobbing light had followed us into the crosscut, walked up and asked what the hell we were doing in the crosscut. Willie Wigg led us back to the main drift, picked up a couple of buckets lying on the side of the drift, handed them to Two Beer and me and instructed us to scoop hematite-laden muck from the ditch. It looked like chocolate cake batter.

Willie Wigg also pointed to hematite-encrusted rubber suits hanging on the side of the drift and ran his headlamp beam down the ditch, "I'm not running trains today after nine o'clock so I want all that damn muck scooped out. Two Beer will show you how it's done. The motorman will drop off a car for you. If it's too stiff for the bucket, use your No.2 shovel. Put on a rubber suit (he motioned) so you don't slop that shit all over those fancy new overalls." Scooping muck, while sweating inside a rubber suit, became my savage amusement. It was a far cry from my erudite life as a freshman on Northern's campus sporting leather elbow patches on my new tweed sport coat.

But I digress. A few shifts later, after I mastered the art of scooping muck, Willie Wigg took me to one of several top timber jobs built above the first crosscut. As Two Beer explained while we were scooping muck, a drift had been installed above and at a right angle to the crosscut so that iron ore blasted loose by the contract miners could be scraped into tramcars. As the reader has probably surmised, a "drift" was a tunnel the miners had blasted through the rock or in some cases into the ore body itself. In some mines drifts are placed at a steep angle, but at the Mather A the main drift and crosscut drifts were only slanted enough so that water would drain out of the mine.

A top timber job had been cut into the rock above the crosscut and lined with timber. As Two Beer had described, there were several of them about sixty feet apart above the crosscut. Top timber drifts (the miners didn't describe them as such, but I'll use that name here) began at each top timber job and proceeded at right angles to and above the crosscut and under the iron ore body. The one I was being assigned to was dripping with water. They were smaller than the crosscut we'd walked in on, but were also framed with hardwood timber and cedar lagging to protect against cave-ins.[61]

Willie Wigg gave me a more detailed description of stope mining than Two Beer had given to me. The hole in the rock and ore formation that was created above the top timber drifts when ore that had been blasted loose fell down through the mills into the top timber drifts was called a "stope." The whole process, he said, involved "sub-level caving." As the ore on one level of the mine was blasted out of the ore body using the sub-level caving method, and scraped into tramcars, new levels of the mine were blasted out below that were about two hundred feet apart. New main drifts, crosscuts, and top timber jobs were established for each level of the mine as the shaft was sunk deeper. Willie Wigg said that at that time the Mather A had seven levels and that as each level was mined out the stopes (caves) would grow larger.

Contract miners had already drilled "long holes" through the cedar lagging in the ceiling and into the iron ore body from the top timber drift next to the one I was assigned to. These long holes had been drilled in a series of semicircles about eight feet apart, one after the other, down the length of the top timber drift. The long holes had been charged and fired one ring at a time, and the ore above the top timber drift had been blasted loose over a period of several months by the time I got there.

When I nervously asked Willie Wigg if it was safe for me to work beneath a body of loose ore, he assured me that the dynamite sticks the contract miners had shoved into their long holes with a charging stick had been placed deep in the long holes they drilled. He pointed at the cedar lagging in the ceiling and said that a ceiling of unblasted ore was in place above the cedar lagging that protected the top timber drifts from collapsing. "It's like a great big box of kitchen table salt with a whole lot of spouts," he said as he walked me past a series of "mills" punched into the upper corners of the top timber drift. "Gravity drops the goddamned ore through these mills. I want you to scrape it back up to the top timber job."

Willie Wigg warned me to be careful working around the mills and that chunks of ore could unexpectedly drop from the stope above and fly out of the mills into the top timber drift. I already knew about that because my dad had been hit by such a chunk and his upper lip was severely cut. Once the ore fell into the top timber drifts it was scraped by electric "tuggers" and dropped from the top timber jobs through a grating of iron rails known as a "grizzly" into tramcars the electric motor pushed into the crosscut below. The ore was then pulled out the main drift to the shaft where the skip lifted it to the surface for stockpiling.

I discovered later that sometimes, depending on the slant or position of the ore body, "raises" were built above the top timber jobs and additional drifts were driven under the ore body sixty or so feet above the top timber jobs. In that case the ore was scraped across a grizzly and dropped down a raise into the top timber drift. From there it was scraped again into the tramcars.

Willie Wigg told me it wasn't necessary for me to know everything there was to know about stopes and sub-level caving, in order to run a tugger and fill ore cars. The tugger consisted of a large electric motor attached to two reels that held wire "ropes." The wire rope on one reel ran down the drift to a pulley attached to the "cap" on the last set of timber in the drift and then came back down the drift where it was attached to the back end of the scraper. The other reel driven by the tugger pulled the scraper back to the grizzly. It was a drag line whose reels were activated by two handles that operated in opposition on top of the tugger. Pull the left handle and you would pull the scraper back into the drift. Pull the right one and the scraper would pull a load of ore back to the grizzly. It looked simple enough and lots better than scooping muck. I was to follow instructions from a light bulb that would blink three times and tell me that the motorman had pulled an ore car below the grizzly and the chute below it, and was ready to receive ore. "And don't scrape any damn ore into the chute if there's no car there. If that light comes back on—STOP!"

I was also instructed on the technique top timber tugger men used for cutting and reattaching the steel wire "rope" that connected the scraper to the tugger if it should break. "And keep your head down. That screen in front of the tugger doesn't always work. I don't want that damn rope messing up that pretty face."

As iron ore peeled off in the stope above us and dropped through the mills into the drift, I was to scrape it up close to the grizzly so I'd be ready to scrape it into ore cars when the light came on. If chunks of iron ore plugged a mill I'd have to get a contract miner to help push a "five-by-five" dynamite charge tied to a pole up the mill, press it against the chunk, light the fuse and run like hell. "Blast 'em out," Willy said, "but don't set off five-by-fives if miners in the next drift have packed their long holes for blasting because you could set off their dynamite and blow the place to hell." I learned some time later that that did happen. Two good men I knew, both contract miners, had been taking a five amid half-emptied boxes of dynamite sticks after charging their long holes and were blasted to bits.

On other days I was directed to hoist timber, steel beams and girders, kegs of bolts and spikes, cedar lagging, and spruce cribbing from the crosscuts up into the top timber jobs, and then through a series of drifts and raises to contract miners who were driving a new drift, blasting out a new raise or repairing existing workings.

Supplies were pulled into the crosscuts on flatcars, and spotted at a trap door leading into a top timber job or at a raise that went up from the crosscut. Two company counts were assigned to hoist the timber and supplies. One would tie a wire rope to the thing to be hoisted, and the other would work above running a small air-driven tugger that hoisted the timber up into the top timber job or directly up a raise to a drift fifty or more feet above the crosscut. Sometimes the wire rope would break or slip so, again, there was danger. A good friend of mine, after attaching a wire rope to a large timber, was severely injured when the rope broke and a piece of timber he was hoisting up the raise fell and pinned him to the side of the crosscut.

The contract miners, who worked in pairs, liked to visit with company count guys. It gave them someone to talk to. As you introduced yourself you might hear one of them laugh back, "Are you bringing me a son of a birch or a son of a beech." Or you might hear one of the contract miners try out a new joke. "Hey, did you guys hear about the army guy being shipped out to Korea who ran and hid under a nun's habit? When he began to explore things he found that some private parts hanging above him were not female and heard a deep voice from above, 'Keep your goddamn hands off—I don't want to go to Korea either!'" My dad never told stories like that around me, but it gave me a story I could tell to the football team at Lindberg's boarding house. Over time I learned that my dad was one of the funniest story-tellers at the Mather A. It was a persona that stayed at the mine.

George Collins from Negaunee, who played on Northern's football team, sometimes ate lunch at Lindberg's, and belonged to the Tri Mu Fraternity, worked with me. George was an adventurous soul. One day while we were hoisting timber up a raise he told me he had found a way to look inside the stope and took me up a raise that led to a drift high above where we were working. Once there I followed him to the end of the drift where we shined our headlamps into blackness. It was the stope, but we could not see ore or rock in any direction. We were standing at the end of a drift high up on the edge of an ore body that was peeling off into the stope. Had the drift subsided into the stope at that moment, as it eventually would, it would have ended two college careers then and there. I decided when we reached the surface afterward that peering into peeling stopes was not for me.

Another night when I showed up for the midnight shift because I had exams the next afternoon, I was assigned to watch the pumps at the bottom of the shaft. The water from the ditches on the various levels collected there to be pumped out. I assumed it was pumped up the shaft, but I was never told where it was pumped. My job was to listen to the pumps, and if they stopped pick up the telephone and call it in. I had nothing to read so I sat through that shift all alone about 3000 feet down at the bottom of the Mather A shaft contemplating a thesis I was writing for Composition and Rhetoric and the next day's economics exam. While I listened to the steady throb of the pumps, I recalled the Barnes-Hecker disaster and hoped the pumps did not fail that night. I also hoped I would not fail my exam the next day.

Because no one could smoke cigarettes underground a lot of the miners chewed either Peerless tobacco or snuff. If you were caught smoking you would be fired because of the fire hazard smoking created. If you did smoke the shift boss could smell it. Simple as that, iron mining underground had curbed the smoking habit.

As our mining careers progressed George Collins and I were given the job of sitting on our asses running the electric motors that pulled the ore out to shaft. During one midnight shift George was assigned as motorman and I was his brakeman, although my primary duty was throwing the switches that directed the train into the crosscuts or back out to the main drift that led to the shaft. About an hour into the shift George pulled a snuffbox out of his pocket and offered me a chew of Copenhagen. My dad chewed that and Peerless all the time, but I had never chewed. My ma forbade it, but that night in a spirit of reckless abandon I put a pinch between my cheek and gum and learned why she did. When I reached up to guide the pole onto the overhead wire, I touched the wire, and it knocked me off the motor on my ass and into the ditch—just as Two Beer had warned. With my head spinning I brushed myself off with as much dignity and bravado as I could muster in the face of George's hysterical laughter. I don't know if it was Ma's disgust with tobacco, George's laughter, or landing on my ass in the ditch, but I never chewed the stuff again.

Another time I was assigned to work on the trestle on the surface. It was the trestle from which ore hoisted in skips was dropped onto stockpiles. I liked working on the surface much better than at the bottom of the shaft three thousand feet below. From the trestle I could look down on the stockpiles where I helped build shovel tracks while with the LS&I Railroad.

I worked at the Mather A for a little better than two years as a part-time employee. I never had the experience of working as a contract miner like my dad did, so I can't tell you in any detail what that was like. Those guys were paid according to their production and worked their asses off. If they were driving a new drift or a raise, the contract miners began their shift by scraping out the blasted rock and debris left by the prior shift and by repairing any damage from the blast the prior shift fired. Then they erected a new set of timber and lagging, or cribbing in the case of a raise, in the space just blasted out. That done they drilled holes about six feet deep into the breast of the drift, or the roof of the raise, charged them with dynamite and blasted out the new cut before their shift ended.

If instead of driving a drift or raise they were drilling long holes through the ceiling of a drift into the ore body, the contract miners started their shift by scraping out any ore that fell into the drift from the blast fired by the shift that preceded them and repairing any timber or lagging damaged by that blast. Then they braced a steel post into the drift being worked and attached a pneumatic drill. By rotating the drill on the post they drilled about ten long holes as deep as twenty or thirty feet in a semicircle right through the lagging in the roof of the drift. That done they dismantled and stored the drill and charged the holes with dynamite and electric fuses. All company count men were cleared out, and as the shift ended the charged holes were fired, leaving behind the smoke, loose ore, and debris the next shift would clean up. The holes they drilled had to be designed and charged so that their blasts did not blow out the roof of the drift, but would break loose ore from above that would then run out of the stope from the mills located in the upper corners of the drifts. By the time I went underground, handheld steel bits had been replaced by drills with carbide tips, and the steel mauls that had been used to strike the bits were replaced by a pneumatic drill powered by compressed air and manipulated by two miners.

Contract miners depended on each other and on the partners who worked the shifts before and after them. They were self-motivated guys. It's how they made their money. They worked at the ends of drifts or raises in the bowels of the mine, seeing only the company count men or the shift boss during their shift. With the risk of serious injury or even death at their shoulders, their success or lack thereof showed up in their paycheck every two weeks. Like buddies fighting a war they became fast friends. My nephew Jeffrey had a bas-relief with the heads of my dad and Jeff's wife Paula's grandfather struck. They had both worked as contract miners at the Mather A. That bas-relief now hangs in the Cliffs Shaft Mining Museum in Ishpeming among numerous artifacts collected from mining iron ore underground.

I discovered while working at the Mather A that those who demean iron miners as hillbillies don't know anything about them. Aside from a very few, they were rock solid, intelligent guys like my dad who supplied an honest day's work in exchange for a few dollars so they could feed, house and clothe their families. Chapters in my economics textbooks dealing with restraint of trade, time and motion studies, supply and demand, labor unions, worker's compensation, and Social Security took on a whole new meaning as I shuttled between Northern Michigan College and the Mather A.

While fame and fortune rightly came to those who conceived and built the corporate world of the iron mining industry, credit must be given where credit is due. The brave men in clunky boots and overalls with battery-powered lamps clipped to their hard hats that I worked with were a mighty cog in the machine. They were the foot soldiers who supplied the savage amusement it took to drive shafts, drifts and raises, blast out stopes, and lift millions of tons of iron ore to stockpiles on the surface for transport to steel mills. They and the families they supported carved an existence out of the "worthless" wilderness to provide their children a better life. Without them the river of iron would never have flowed.

After about two years I lost my part-time job at the Mather A along with all the part-time guys. I never learned why. It could have been an economic downturn—or it might have been complaints from union guys that we were taking their jobs. It seemed wrong to me. Not just because I was depending on my job to attend Northern and to save up for law school, but because the part-time work offered by the Cleveland-Cliffs Iron Company provided a genuine opportunity for the kids of miners to acquire a college education. Since then I have looked back and wondered whether it would be better for all concerned if the business community provided college kids who needed it good, honest, part-time work, rather than having banks loan them money they would have a difficult time ever paying back.

I went back to wall washing and gardening around Marquette, working for peanuts. One summer I hired in with several Tri Mu guys as a construction worker. The city of Marquette was building a sewage disposal plant at the mouth of the Carp River. We built forms and scaffolding for the concrete walls that went into that construction. Carl (Buck) Nystrom, who played football as a lineman for Michigan State, showed up on the first day and told the construction boss he wanted the heaviest and hardest work they had because he was getting in shape for the fall season. Buck had quite a football career as a lineman at Michigan State. Nick Menghini, a fellow Tri Mu I drove to work with, told the boss, "And I would like the lightest and the easiest." Nick kidded about a lot of things. He shouldn't have said what he did. Buck was assigned to sit on his ass and drive cement buggies, and Nick was handed a No. 2 shovel.

Between my junior and senior years I landed a position with the Duluth, South Shore and Atlantic Railroad (DSS&A) in the Engineering Department. I did some work on engineering reports stored in Marquette, but spent most of the summer riding a small gasoline-driven railroad car and cabooses at the end of trains as an aide to a senior engineer who was inspecting all of the culverts, bridges and tracks between Marquette and the Copper Country. It was a good summer job that paid the minimum wage and exposed me to railroad engineering, although I spent quite a few nights away from home.

In my senior year at Northern I took the LSAT test for law school and passed it. At Northern I had been Class President, a member of the Debate Team, President and later House Manager for the Tri Mu Fraternity, and President of the Social Science Club. I loved my history classes and finished with enough hours to qualify for two minors in history and one in sociology. I graduated summa cum laude completing my major in economics. Had I not been accepted at the University of Michigan Law School, I would have pursued a career as a history professor. History has always fascinated me.

My work at Northern was good enough to land me a scholarship that covered my tuition at Law School. I had put aside about seven hundred fifty dollars for books and room and board at law school. It was the same amount I had at the Peninsula Bank when I entered Northern. I again knew as I enrolled at Law School that while I had sufficient funds for my freshman year I would need to find more part-time and summer work if I intended to practice law. Fortunately, I was hired as a waiter at the Michigan Law School dining room and later in the dining room at the Michigan Union. I spent my summers back in Marquette where the DSS&A provided me with work on their section crews. I also borrowed about five hundred dollars in my senior year so that I could finish in three years.

Law school was a whole new story. I was well prepared, although I didn't know it. I entered believing I had little chance of getting past my freshman year. I did better. I made the staff of the *Michigan Law Review* and gained a battery of friends who would become lawyers. I graduated in 1957 and practiced law for fifty years. The Law School's use of the Socratic method of instruction was as fine an experience in learning that I can imagine. I am today a proud alumnus of Ma's kitchen, National Mine High School, Northern Michigan College (now University) and of the University of Michigan Law School.

I met Judy at Northern in 1953 and married her after my law school debt was paid in 1960. Our three children and two grandchildren celebrated our fiftieth anniversary with us in 2010. I got a lot of breaks, but I always understood that for a hillbilly to get ahead he would need row on row discipline. My opportunity to attend college and law school brought home to me the full meaning of the clause in the Northwest Ordinance that provided, "Schools and the means of education shall forever be encouraged"—may it never be otherwise.

~~~

Figure 49
The Mather A and Mather B Mines

Mather B mine Negaunee,
Michigan.
IM—Math-02

Mather A Miners
Ishpeming, Michigan.
IM—Math-08

Mather A shaft house
Ishpeming, Michigan.
IM- Math- 01

Break-through—A and B Shafts
Mather Mine, June 6, 1950.
IM- Math- 04

Photographs courtesy of Superior View Studios

Figure 50

The engineering drawings of the Sixth Level of the
Mather A and Mather B mines shown here were published
in The Mather Mine (1979) by the Marquette County
Historical Society, pp. 72-25. They are reproduced here
with permission of the Marquette Regional History
Center and the Cleveland-Cliffs Iron Company.

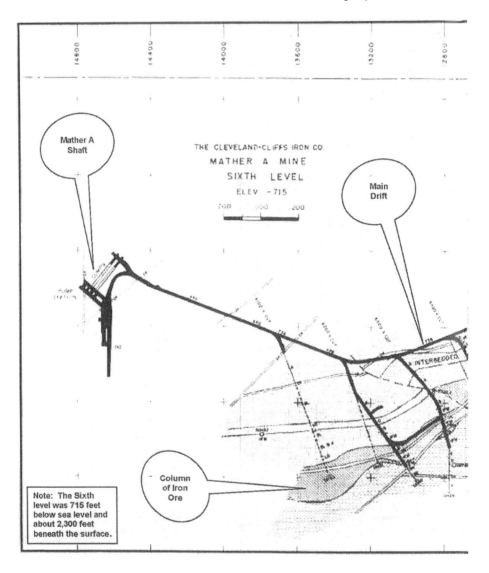

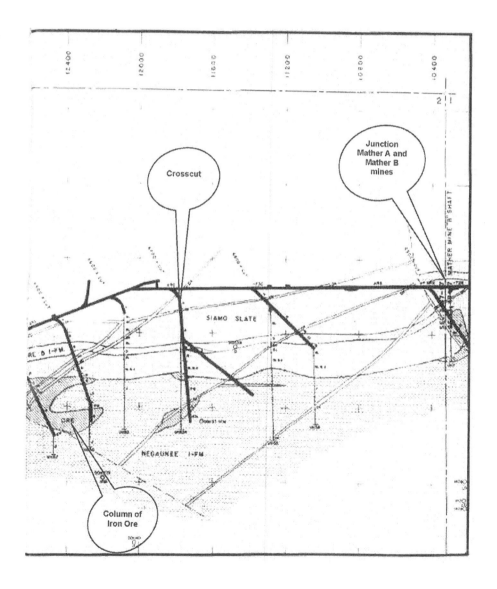

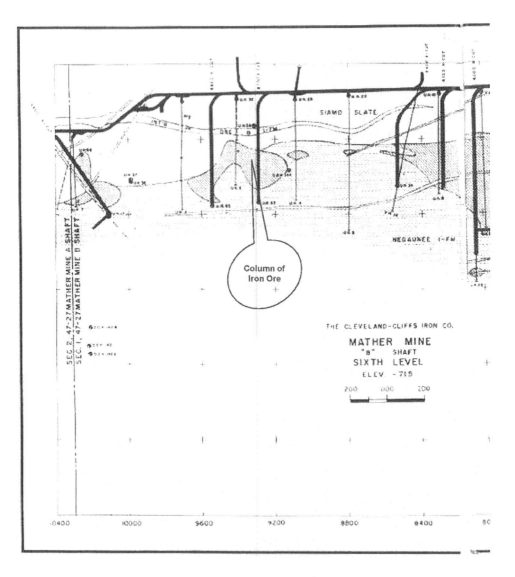

Figure 50 continued

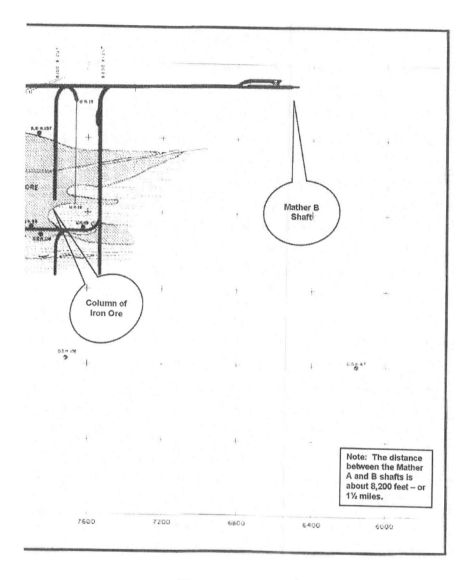

Figure 50 continued

CHAPTER 23

River of Memories

IN BIBLICAL TIMES it was written that man was placed in the Garden of Eden to work it and care for it (Genesis 2:15). It was also written that man should not "make gods of cast metal" (Leviticus 19:4). When you enter your golden years you ponder things like that. You become concerned that a stranger poking through your childhood experiences (and adult escapades, I might add) will ask if you have observed the foregoing biblical injunctions, along with a whole slew of others. While I have enjoyed work throughout my life, as I was taught to do, and still mow my own lawn, clip my hedge, and maintain a few rosebushes and flowerbeds, I have to admit that I haven't done much to care for the Garden, nor have I always observed biblical injunctions. Worse, the coins I've accumulated in my pockets, and more particularly those I finger through and stash in a jar, might be looked upon by the Almighty as cast idols. I extracted iron from the Mountain with full knowledge that others would cast it into steel. I have been complicit, but I didn't create gods. I simply tried to make a living and survive.

I got into this memoir thing when I asked a speaker I met at a writers' conference to explain the craft to me. He didn't. Instead he said, "Write a novel—writing a memoir is dangerous." Then he asked why I wanted to do it in the first place. I blurted out that I wanted to know why poor people migrate across oceans to faraway mountains so they can dig iron and copper from the bowels of the earth—only to find that they have become mired in a Great Depression that devastates their lives. He looked long and hard at me and then at his fingernails.

He told me there are two different types who would do something like that. First, there are those who will dig iron from a mountain with great vigor, sell it at a profit, and then, if opposed by do-gooders or environmentalists, explode "What in hell are a few fish?" "Then," he said, "there are dreamers who travel to mountains to observe their wonders, paint them, protect them, and write poems about their pine trees, chipmunks, and even ants." He told me to look for good in both. But what was the purpose of any of it?

I left my family and the Mountain of Iron to study law, raise my own family, and seek my fortune with the city slickers in Detroit, Michigan, where among other things, they built the Ford cars my dad drove. When I arrived there to practice law, a senior law partner handed me a book to read, *Detroit Is My Own Hometown*.[62] He said it would help to introduce me to my new environment. Now I did take time to read the book as I was instructed to do, and wine and dine my wife-to-be at the Ponchartrain Wine Cellars, the Rooster Tail, Baker's Piano Keyboard Lounge, and the London Chop House. I also visited Belle Isle, the Detroit Institute of Arts, and Greenfield Village, and as years went by I did my best to love the Tigers, Lions, Pistons, and Red Wings and become a Detroiter. Trouble was, I never really left the Mountain. I couldn't. Its magnetic force, Ma and Dad, Judy's Mom and Dad, class reunions, and family gatherings kept drawing me back. So did family illness, marriage, death, and a million memories they stirred. There are gold mines in California and Alaska, iron mines in Minnesota, copper mines in Montana, and fantastic sunsets in Hawaii. There are lands that don't drift with snow, become bitterly cold, or suffer winter storms. Like many Native Americans who used stones to pound metals into weapons and jewelry, I could have been attracted elsewhere. I wasn't.

I returned with my family at least once a year, often two or three times. If I accept a thousand miles per round trip (each trip exceeded that) as a reasonable estimate, and an average of two trips per year for fifty-eight years, I have driven approximately 116,000 miles—over four and one-half times around the earth at its equator—to and from the Mountain of Iron. It's been quite a ride. Each trip home, each picnic, each sunset brought back memories of days long passed. Judy and I visited with our families, returned to the old haunts, and laughed and retold family stories again and again. I didn't spend time logging memories in a notebook or digging into the nitty-gritty of life in the Great Depression. My dad died in 1985 and my ma died in 1999, so I'm coming back to it late in life. I can ask my brothers and sisters for help, but it's not like hearing it from Ma and Dad.

I have considered inventing a machine that could be affixed to me in some fashion that would not only bring back all the old memories but, indeed, bring the folks I grew up with back to life so I could talk to them. Not even my dad came up with anything like that. I'd like to hear more of the nitty-gritty. You know, "How does one mark two-by-fours for rafters with only a carpenter's square, Dad? And please, Dad, please don't tell me to give it time, how does one obtain wisdom?" Or "Ma—how does one play the piano by ear? Can you teach me to do that? Tell me how to write a poem?" "Uncle Nels, what were you doing with those two blocks you put down on the rails?" Or "Mr. Annala (I would not call him "Bitty" or "Chief" to his face even now), why didn't you explain when we made errors in our essays?" (When I write I still wonder if someone will come along and put check marks in the margin). "And what's with that work-equals-success crap you kept popping off about? Who thought that one up?"

Instead, on the many times I returned home with Judy to visit my family at the farm, or later at Sunnyside Estates after they moved there, I mostly brought up banalities while sitting on the edge of a chair in their kitchen. Like "Nice to see you, Ma. How's the arthritis, Dad? Are the winters too hard for you, Ma?" I never dared to delve into their feelings or bring back the tribulations they endured during the Great Depression. Of course it was nice to see them, not one person I ever met enjoys arthritis, and after ninety or more Upper Peninsula winters, Ma did not need to be reminded about them. Nonetheless, it went that way from year to year because I was afraid to dig into the hard stuff. They were, too. We exchanged a string of niceties, certainly nothing that would upset anybody or explain the Crash of Twenty-nine. But pensioned off, graying (balding in my dad's case) and shrinking from the weight of time, they were survivors of the Great Depression. They harbored a load of memories. I picked up some of it, but I let a lot of it slide away—shame on me. I should have taken a tape recorder like Dort did and dug for more.

Figure 51

A retired Ben and Elsie relaxing
at home on the farm (circa 1968).

Nelson family photograph

I did work up the courage to ask them if it was okay to take a spruce seedling growing in what was left of an old hay field near the logging road where we buried Queen. I also took a black-and-white speckled rock from the stone fence on the south property line for my flower garden and salvaged some old photographs. Ma and Dad were quite protective of their farm and their photographs even then, and wondered why I'd make such foolish requests. The spruce grew into the power line serving my Dearborn Heights home and had to be removed, but I still have the rock. It brings back memories every spring when I pick it up, study its texture and color, and wonder how far it had travelled on its journey to me and how it got so smooth. As I study it, I also wonder if I had been the one who put it in the rock fence. Then I brush it off and relocate it among my flowers. I have a few more artifacts. My brother Ken arranged to get me the carpenter's ripsaw Dad used to build the farmhouse. It has the farmhouse painted on it. He also gave me the board with our initials carved in it from the woodshed Dad built with that saw. And I have the painting of Trigger XVIII and Labaan.

When my sister Marian gave me some of the poems Ma wrote while I was growing up, I chuckled a bit, and then tucked them away for a time when life would be more serene. I shouldn't have. Later, I stumbled upon Ma's poems while rummaging through a cardboard box in my basement. As I sat on the basement floor and read them in the light of advancing years, it struck me how critical it was for Ma to take time from her family and the burdens of her life to scribble down what she saw, experienced, and felt. Without Ma's poems, much of our family life would have been lost forever. I keep the originals in Ma's handwriting in my safe deposit box. After Dad passed away, we published Ma's poems together with family photographs, and gave a copy of *Wandering Verse* to her at the Mather Nursing Home near Ishpeming while she was still among us. My sister Dort wrote a prologue and an epilogue that captured Ma's life. As I recall the smile on Ma's face I am most grateful that we did.

Her poems tell you a lot, but Ma was not talkative at all about her poems. Not to me anyway. I sometimes had to guess what they were saying about her, her family, the clapboard duplex on Second Street, and the ten-acre farm in Green Crick where she spent most of her life. I tried to visualize her sitting down and writing them. I never actually saw her do it. Even after we got those of her poems that survived bound into a book and presented them to her, I didn't ask about her feelings when she wrote them. She'd have just looked away. I guess that's not a proper thing to ask a poet. She saw and heard things in life that I didn't. In her later years my brother Fred asked Ma if she still wrote poetry. She thought for a moment and then replied, "No, you have to have profound thoughts to write poetry, and I'm not feeling very profound right now."

I have learned, though, that when I start scouring for old stories and dredging up memories I should take fully into account that other biblical commandment that one ought not to bear false witness. I first heard about that at Sunday school at Trinity Lutheran. When you start telling stories about your childhood you'll bump up against that one— big time. But it's not just lies that will nail you; it's even more dangerous to bring up the truth. Once when invited to speak at a National Mine all-class reunion, I told some stories of my school days. I'd spent the whole day in my motel room writing out notes of things to bring up— inject a little bit of humor—get a few laughs.

Although I probably did wax a little bit eloquent on the podium, I did not intend my remarks to be a tell-all speech. All I did in one little anecdote was suggest that on occasion the boys' basketball team walked the streets of Ishpeming trying to pick up girls. Now I did mention some names, so it probably wasn't the smartest thing I've ever done. Particularly with some of the by-then retired faculty in attendance. The women were dressed to the nines. Their men were suited up, and some wore boutonnieres. All were seated with their spouses. It was a rather elegant affair. Later, after I got down from the podium, an old classmate took my bit about chasing girls as an improper disclosure of things people do in their youth that ought to be kept private. I tried to point out that it had happened fifty years before, but he emphasized his position by pointing out that his wife objected to it, and that she had mentioned their children. He let me know he recalled no such thing ever happening, and that he never spoke of things like that even if it did. I apologized and assured him I was out of line and that he was absolutely correct.

Even at family gatherings there is great danger in reminiscing—in fact, especially at family gatherings. After a family matinee dinner at the Northwoods Supper Club in Marquette to celebrate Dad and Ma's fifty-fifth anniversary in 1979, the family gathered for pictures and dessert at my brother Ken's house (he and his wife Loraine called it their ranch), which was seven or eight miles north of Ishpeming out past Deer Lake. After the whole crew filled up Ken's living room, some began to tell stories of the old days. I just loved it, although I did not get out my note pad or a tape recorder. After a while, Ken asked my ma, who had never before had anything to drink stronger than wine as far as I know, if she wanted something to drink, thinking she'd like some strawberry pop. Ma, to the astonishment of all, briskly said she'd like "scotch on the rocks." The party was loosening up. It looked to me that the occasion had finally arrived where it would be appropriate for a story most of them had heard a few things about— but not all the details. I forgot the lesson I'd learned about telling family stories on the bus ride to the National Mine School.

When we were kids my dad had won a pocket knife with a pearl handle on a chance he bought on a punch board at a gas station in Ishpeming. There was a well-developed nude on the handle. Not wanting Ma to know he had a knife like that, my dad gave it to Ken and told him not to use it, and to keep it "safe and secret." Instead, Ken took it on a fishing trip and lost it when it fell into Green Crick. We waded into the black muck trying to get it back, but we couldn't.

When Dad later asked Ken for the knife, Ken told him it had accidently fallen through a hole Dad had left in the wall at the top of the stairs and was down between the studs. When Dad couldn't retrieve the knife with magnets, he broke holes into the wall at the bottom of the stairs in a futile effort to recover it. Ken insisted that somehow the knife had lodged between the studs on the way down. Dad did not discover the knife's whereabouts until I mouthed off in a cheerful spirit of now-it-can-be-told at his fifty-fifth anniversary. I was trying to stir a few laughs—that's all. Dad didn't laugh. He spent the rest of the day glaring at Ken; Ken spent it glaring at me, and I was left to wonder why I'd been born.

On still another trip back home one of Northern's professors, a retired critic teacher who had taught student teachers how to teach at Northern's John D. Pierce Training School, which Judy had attended, stood before an all-class reunion of John D. Pierce students and extolled the virtues of his cream-of-the-crop students. Nothing wrong with that. Except that in the course of his lavish praise, he paused, smiled, and said, "Of course, then there were the swampers." If he was trying to inject a little humor, it didn't work for him either. In fact, some of his former students did come from low-lying areas near the Training School, and had not been well-to-do at all. That professor got lambasted by some "swamper" graduates who'd done quite well, thank you.

My wife Judy was raised in Marquette. When we went home this usually created tension over which family we would visit first and for how long. Judy's dad, Wesley Olson (Wackey), and her mom, Lois Olson (Loie), lived on Third Street in Marquette. It was where I had kissed Judy good night when we were dating. Judy's kid sister Wendy told me years later that she sometimes hid in a tree nearby and watched us. I have lots of memories of Third Street, and particularly of the night Loie turned on the porch light while Judy and I were parked on the street out in front talking politics. After we were married and started our own family, we usually drove home over the Fourth of July and stayed with Wackey and Loie.

Each summer the city of Marquette held a Fourth of July Parade with bands, twirling batons, floats, and a host of American flags. It all marched with great fanfare right in front of the Olson home, up Third Street, and down the steep hill to downtown. We all had ringside seats along with friends and relatives who sat with us on the front porch, draped themselves down the front steps, or stood in the front yard. There were always friends and relatives visiting at Loie and Wackey's house. It was a great spot from which to listen to the bands, pay respect to the marching veterans, and enjoy the red, white, and blue festooned floats that carried girls with banners and smiling local dignitaries, followed by a bunch of howling kids—some with firecrackers. It became a ritual we did every year. One year my oldest son Dave was asked at Show and Tell what he did over his summer vacation. He reported that he had gone to Marquette to visit his grandma and grandpa because "they hold a parade there every year for our family."

On a few of those trips in the 1970s I pulled a travel trailer and parked it in the Tourist Park on the Dead River Basin just north of Marquette. My daughter Julie's eighth birthday party was held on a sandy strand of beach along the Munising Highway (M28) where we swam in Lake Superior, played games all afternoon, and picnicked near the spot where Père Marquette first came centuries before. That night we slept in sleeping bags on the beach beside a huge bonfire and beneath a sky full of brilliant stars, a full moon, shafting columns of the northern lights, and a shower of Perseid meteors (shooting stars that occur in August each year at the time of Julie's birthday). Not many kids have things like that at their eighth birthday party. Loie had us sign our names on a smooth piece of driftwood she found on the shore. I took it home and shellacked it. We still treasure it.

During our trips home, Judy and I drove with her family and our children hundreds of times to Presque Isle, which is on the north side of Marquette. Yes, I did mean to say hundreds—we went there several times on each trip home. When we were kids, my dad used to drive us there. Presque Isle is attached to Marquette by a narrow neck of land near the harbor where ore boats are loaded. As I've explained, its name means "almost an island," but locally it is, and forever will be, "The Island." It is where the river of iron collides with Mother Nature. Judy once described it as "One of God's Cathedrals." It is a place to reminisce, meditate, and wonder.

To get there you drive down the shore of Lake Superior on Lakeshore Boulevard. It isn't really a boulevard, but it's called that. If you drive there at night, Lake Superior may try to seduce you with northern lights dancing on her waters, but like Jezebel, she frequently changes her personality. It's wise to study her mood before you set out for The Island. On a stormy day in early October, Lake Superior becomes a spurned mistress that crashes huge whitecaps over breakwaters protecting her harbors, and relentlessly pounds her fists on the shore along Lakeshore Boulevard. Throughout the year you may find her waters cold. But in winter they are frigid, and her shoreline is a forbidding moonscape festooned with slabs of ice. When summer thunderstorms strike, she becomes violent—then slate gray and sullen as the storm subsides. But on a pleasant summer day she becomes a calm, deep-blue temptress with seagulls whirling above lapping waves that sparkle with sunshine. You will be seduced forever.

Sometimes we began our trip to The Island at Lighthouse Point, a rock outcropping on the shore in the center of Marquette. There's a Coast Guard Museum there, and a red lighthouse has stood there as a "Beacon on the Lake" for years. We usually drove along the shore to the beach at Picnic Rocks. We wore our swimsuits beneath our clothes. At that time there was a sandbar between the shore and first rock. I marveled at the clarity of the water and the visible stones and rippled sand at the bottom. I didn't dive from the rocks like Judy and my kids did, or try to swim out to second or third rock. I swam near the shore because I was never an accomplished swimmer, and I'd been warned about the strong currents. Judy held a lifesaving certificate, and had taught Julie, Dave, and Dan to be good swimmers. I recall the crisp, clean, cool sensation that Lake Superior's waters left on my body when the swim was over. When we left Picnic Rocks we drove through two columns of stately Lombardy poplars on either side of Lakeshore Boulevard. Loie loved hiking to The Island between those Lombardies. But they're gone now.

Not all of the drive was scenic. The Island helps to form a natural harbor for the ore dock, and there is only one road you can take to The Island. It goes over the bridge at the mouth of the Dead River, past the electric power plant with its huge stockpile of coal, and under the trestle that carries railroad cars to the ore dock.

Once you are on The Island the boulevard carries you past a harbor of sailboats and pleasure craft bobbing at their moorings, to a little park engirdled with pine logs where a concrete-and-stone breakwater is anchored. A small memorial honoring hikers who were swept off the breakwater to their deaths during a storm warns that there is danger to those who walk out on the breakwater, but on a few of our trips we took that challenge if the skies looked clear.

The first stage of the breakwater is a concrete pier, so it is not too difficult to navigate, but the second stage consists of huge stones (riprap) that lead to another lighthouse at the end of the breakwater. The stones are sharp, slippery, have gaps between them, and sometimes slant sharply into the lake. If an ore boat was being loaded at the dock across the bay, we heard the sharp scream of iron ore pellets sliding down the chutes. It is a constant reminder of why the Europeans came. But once at the lighthouse at the end of the breakwater, we forgot that and reflected on the wild beauty of Lake Superior, and the immensity of her blue waters. The lighthouse reminded us of the vulnerability of the men who sail her. It has been said that Superior never gives up her dead, so we watched our steps as we climbed over the rocks back to shore.

Then we resumed our drive past a gazebo where weddings are sometimes performed at dawn, past Chief Kawbawgam's grave up on the hill, and headed through the tunnel of trees to the Cove where silver was discovered centuries before. We parked at Sunset Point and always waited for the last speck of sunset on the hills that lead up to Sugarloaf Mountain and Hogsback across the bay, so that we could feel the coolness and calm it left behind and experience the pulse of The Island.

If we got out of our car, Judy told our kids to use caution—there is an overhang. The rocky shore is continuously undermined by storms off the lake. As we reluctantly left Sunset Point we drove past an old road, now mostly washed away, that once carried cars closer to the shore. It's too dangerous to drive a car there now. Fragments of the road and stumps of trees swept away by wind and tide reminded us that The Island is at once wild, vibrant, and vulnerable.

There used to be a little zoo that contained black bears and whitetail deer over by the Pavilion on the southwest side that my kids loved, but that too is gone now. The Pavilion has been rebuilt on the other side of the road. The bandstand where local groups perform is still there, though, offering a pleasant interlude on a summer's evening where so many times the cares of our day drifted away.

On the west side of The Island you will come upon a large piece of glacial float copper. "Floated along" by the last glacier that once covered the area, it is a dramatic exhibit of mineral deposits that permeate the

Upper Peninsula. Discovered on a farm near Calumet, Michigan in 1997, it is the largest piece of glacial float copper ever found. It weighs 28.2 tons and is much larger than the Ontonagon boulder discovered in the Ontonagon River in the 1800s—now on display at the Smithsonian—which is estimated to weigh 3500 pounds. (See, C. Fred Rydholm's book, **Superior Heartland** p. 119). The late Mr. Rydholm, widely acclaimed as Marquette's historian, working with the landowners where the specimen was found and some of his former students, was instrumental in moving the boulder to Presque Isle in 2010. Efforts are currently underway by the Marquette County Community Foundation, Superior Watershed Partnership and the Rydholm family to raise funds to purchase the boulder and give it a permanent home at Presque Isle. From there the boulder will continue to provide school children, geology students, and tourists with a globally unique specimen of the Upper Peninsula's rich geology.

Figure 52 Fred Rydholm and the copper boulder he helped move to Presque Isle.

Courtesy of Superior Watershed Partnership and June Rydholm

Judy and I purchased pasties in Marquette and enjoyed them with our family at picnic tables at The Island, along with Jilbert's ice cream cones from the ice cream stand where Judy once worked as a teenager. They were huge, delicious cones of strawberry twirl, butter pecan, or maple nut ice cream churned by the local dairy that challenged you to eat just one. Loie and Judy's Aunt Ethel loved those cones.

While Judy was growing up, her mom and dad frequently cooked family breakfasts of scrambled eggs, bacon, and coffee at barbecue stands on The Island. They arrived early to watch the sun rise over Lake Superior. Judy said Loie thought that was special because Wackey did the cooking. Like her family, Judy and I never tire of circling The Island, of calmly sitting there, and never will.

In 1940 Thomas Clayton Wolfe published his famous book, *You Can't Go Home Again*. That's true. All the trips we took back to the Mountain of Iron, home to the farm, and to The Island, indeed my whole life, convince me that Wolfe got it right. You can never again return to the experiences of youth—not even at a family gathering or a reunion.

There is no way one can again capture the delicious fear of racing through an apple orchard to a ski jump on five-foot maple skis with wind-driven snow in your face, the reality of a hog slaughter, fishing the rapids on Green Crick, clustering around an isinglass coal stove, my ma playing the piano by ear, or my dad singing "Harbor Lights" in his 1937 Ford on a snowy street in Ishpeming. Nor will I ever again ride that big orange bus to the National Mine School and laugh at the tales spun along the way, play pump-pump-pull-away, fill orders at the bakery, install shovel tracks at the Maas Mine, or drop down the Mather A shaft. But I can carry memories of my childhood home and of my family along with me as I travel along life's journey. I can keep them nearby, use them as guides, and experience the joy of recalling them and writing about them.

Unlike material things that become obsolete and rust away, memories endure. They are, to be sure, but fragments of time drawn from a failing ability to recall them, but in the end, memories are more than a string of stories about building one's shelter, harvesting food, enjoying games, getting an education, finding a job, or even uncovering a philosophy of life.

My river of memories, like the "sparkling stream" Ma wrote about in one of her poems, is not just about metal flowing off a Mountain of Iron—it's about surviving to be sure, but mostly it's about family.

~~~

Figure 53
Bas-Relief of Oscar "Skippy" Arseneau
and Bernard "Benny" Nelson

This Bas-Relief of Oscar "Skippy" Arseneau and Bernard "Benny" Nelson, both of whom worked underground at the Mather A Shaft, now hangs in the Cleveland Cliff's Iron Mining Museum near the Cliff Shaft mine in Ishpeming, Michigan. It was commissioned by Jeffrey Nelson, Ben's grandson, and is reproduced here with the consent of Roger Junak, of Ishpeming, Michigan, its creator.

Obverse and Reverse of Mather Mine
Fifty Millionth Ton Medallion.

Figure 54
Ben and Elsie's Children, Grandchildren, Great-grandchildren

The daughters
of Ben and Elsie
(L-R) Dorothy,
Marian, Joanne,
and Ruth—1995.

The sons of Ben and
Elsie (L-R) Dave, Fred,
Ken, and Bill—1953.

Some of Ben and Elsie's children, grandchildren and
great-grandchildren at the Northwoods Supper Club to
celebrate Ben and Elsie's fifty-fifth anniversary—1979.

Photographs from the Nelson family collection

CHAPTER 24

Reflections on Great and Important Things

DURING MORE THAN fifty years practicing law, I occasionally thought about but never reflected very deeply on what Ma and Dad had been through. They had always brushed adversity aside as just something you live with. I began to reflect on that more seriously when I came across the beat-up cardboard box in my basement marked "Ma's Poems." My sister Marian had given them to me and asked me to "get a load of these" several years before. At first glance they appeared to be nothing more than a few lines Ma had scribbled down now and again onto scraps of paper. I stashed them away. I had too much important stuff going on in my life to be bothered with them. I was too busy for frivolity. But in retirement I suddenly had time for the frivolous and little else, so I began to smooth out some of the crumpled sheets and spread them on my basement floor. Ma's poem about anthills caught my eye. Another one did too. Ma had named it "Seniority." It was about her golden years. Chastened by my earlier offhanded dismissal of Ma's poems, I slowly read it right on through the last two lines:

> No longer to pine for the great and important,
> Finding abundance in the real and the small.

It was then that I reentered Ma's life through a crumpled, handwritten poem with the rest of her verse scattered around me. I picked up a few more poems and glanced at them, but I kept coming back to those two lines—struck by nagging questions. What "great and important" things had you pined for, Ma? She'd never talked about anything like that to me. She was always focused on us, her family, the next meal and not any great or important things that she pined about. What had she given up to raise me and the rest of her kids? Would I ever find that out? It was kind of late to ask. Then the last line came crashing down on me like a meteor out of the void and brought forth a tear.

Ma experienced a whole lot of the real and the small, and she always found abundance in such things. All of us knew that. It was who she was and had always been. But now a few simple, elegant lines scratched out in Ma's shaky handwriting at the twilight of her life burst off the page. She had shelved the things she pined for to raise us kids, but her difficult circumstances had not dimmed her positive twist on things, nor did they interrupt her search for meaning. As I sat on my basement floor and began to sort Ma's poems into groups, I resolved that as best I could, I would chronicle what I witnessed while growing up. I would leave a record of what confronting the Great Depression on the Mountain of Iron meant to my family and our neighbors.

It soon developed into a family effort to preserve and print Ma's poems along with some yellowing family photographs. In helping with that project I discovered that family photographs are not enough. They are a platform of knowledge to be sure, but their significance cannot be fully grasped without written words that convey the inner feelings behind the smiling faces. The why of it all is hidden from the photographer behind the smiles. It lies beneath, and only poetry, art, music, and the written word can unmask and preserve it. How wonderful it would be to have a written description of the feelings of the Ojibwa and their Chief Marjijesick as they turned their backs upon the Mountain of Iron. They sought to live in harmony with their environment—not to confront it or tear it apart. Ma was like that. A verse in Ma's poem "Over My Shoulder" reads as follows:

I know a place where the trembling wildlife
From tree and bower is heard,
While the brisk running stream 'neath the rusted bridge
Flows onward unperturbed.

It came to me as I read Ma's poems that day on my basement floor that they were a window to her soul through which I had never peered before. They did not recount the desperate struggle she and Dad waged daily to confront the Great Depression, although I saw glimpses of that in the poems she had tucked in sugar bowls in the midst of it. Instead, her poems confronted adversity with the same rigid discipline, beauty, hope, and genuine love that she always did. Born to an iron miner and a poet out in the wilderness and raised in a poor family with eight children, I had never before grasped the positive twist Ma always put on adversity until I reread, edited, and helped to publish her poems. It caused me to seek the meaning of my own life. In that search I realized that although my penmanship is bad, my artistic talents meager, and my ability to recite the names of ancient Greeks nonexistent, I have lived a wonderful, challenging life and that there is no reason to restrain my own feelings from flowing. I concluded as Ma said in another of her poems, "Meandering":

> And so, my mind, I've set you free
> To ramble where you will,
> Wandering into nooks and crannies,
> Meandering over the hill.

My meandering trip down memory lane along the River of Iron began as a search to identify the things Ma pined for and the abundance she spoke about. Growing up I had experienced the work ethic and the discipline of the rows abundantly, but not a whole lot of material abundance. Many happy moments stand out, to be sure, but let's get real. I saw up front and personal what Ma and Dad, like so many others, went through during the cataclysm known as the Great Depression. It wasn't until after they were gone that I more completely realized what they had been through. Then when I read Ma's poems I discovered that Ma and Dad had been right all along. They had always confronted reality and counseled that good steel will come through the fire. Sacrificing their dreams and themselves, they had given us an abundance of hope that survived the leanest years of the Great Depression.

Perhaps it is only when a person's life comes to an end that we look for the good in it. Much that is precious, like wisdom, can be mined from the Mountain and the rivers flowing off it. Another of Ma's poems, "As You Look at It", has this:

> Then who created the umbrageous oak
> From a tiny acorn seed?
> Or made water to flow in sparkling streams
> On which the seedlings feed?

That one brought back the morning I'd witnessed the crystal oak, and really got me reminiscing. When my life began on the Mountain of Iron, I was such a seedling. I was entirely dependent on the efforts and love of others. A whole lot of love, patience, and nurturing were expended on my behalf. My ancestors were honest people who cherished the work ethic, let there be no doubt about that. But I had a few other things going for me. Born on American soil, I entered life as a free man. Part of that freedom had been enshrined in the Northwest Ordinance, which encompassed the Mountain of Iron, and provided that schools and the means of education would forever be encouraged. Although I am a thankful beneficiary of all who helped me, I still have questions.

Before my family came on the scene, the Mountain had stood pristine while sparkling rain and snowflakes fell upon it from the heavens. It went about its business—providing a home for the water lilies, trout, and bass in its lakes and streams. Its forests exuded oxygen, burst into vivid autumn colors, and created a refuge for deer, bear, and beaver. Birds raucously called out as they soared and cavorted in its skies, and built homes near its waters and in its trees. It did all that without being looked after by humans.

Perhaps the Ojibwa were right to fear the Mountain of Iron and to turn their backs to it. Did its magnetic impulses emanate from a hidden mystical force that they and William Austin Burt's compasses felt, but knew not of? Living in homes of tree bark and animal skins, and following the teachings of medicine men, the Ojibwa survived the brutal wilderness and winters of the Marquette Iron Range for thousands of years before the Europeans came to extract iron from the mountain and then carry it away across Gitchee Gumee. The Ojibwa's instincts told them to live off the land but not despoil it.

But that lifestyle didn't satisfy the Europeans. They wanted everything the Mountain could deliver, including its furs and its forests—but most of all its ores. Fortified with their own culture and religion, they pushed the Ojibwa aside and impressed their laws, mines, and railroads upon the mountain. They brought forth a river of iron from deep within it, and changed the mountain forever. The rivers and lakes the Ojibwa fished no longer brim with trout and bass. Underground stopes I helped dig and large open pits now hollow out the Mountain of Iron. I wonder what Chief Marjijesick and his medicine men would say.

For over one hundred sixty years, half of which I have lived, ores dug from the mountain flowed into our economy. Iron extracted with brute force became the battleship graves of sailors, and was forged into the tanks and cannon that now rust away on the battlefields where the bones of soldiers decay. Its beams created high-rise havens for white-collar crime, drugs, and violence. It became rebar embedded in concrete freeways, and the vehicles that rust along them and in junkyards. Copper has become the commodity of choice stolen from abandoned buildings and public lighting. Did it have to be? Did the Ojibwa and "trembling wildlife" have just cause to fear the mountain?

In describing what the needs, purposes, and results of a person's life ought to be, others have found it useful to number them. There are the Ten Commandments and the Four Freedoms. In my sociology classes at Northern, I was exposed to Thomas's four wishes: security, new experience, recognition, and response. Law school and the practice of law confirmed that our most cherished legal rights are contained in the first ten amendments to the Constitution.

Life has taught me many things, as I have tried to show, although I have not tried to number them. Dad and Ma taught me to discipline my life—a trait that helped me at college and law school, and again while I practiced law. They also encouraged me to be wise and seek wisdom. Although on occasion I have tried to exude wisdom, unlike the Scarecrow in *The Wizard of Oz*, I can't say anyone ever imparted it to me. A few things do stand out.

The old saw that one ought not to tear down another man's house to build one of his own is one of them. Oblivious to Bitty Annala's axiom that work equals success, modern society encourages us to take shortcuts and enhance our own well-being by demeaning and damaging that of others. That happens when bogus securities or mind-altering drugs are sold to create huge profits from others' misery. But it also happens when a lawyer tears a witness apart for no reason other than to advance his career, when one politician makes a rascal of another, or when one man calls another man a nigger or a hillbilly. That, we are told, is how the system works. So be it, but there are monsters and wild beasts that await us along the path called shortcut.

In the eighty-two years of my life I have experienced much good and much evil. I lived through the Great Depression, World War II, the Holocaust, the atom bomb, the creation of the United Nations, the Korean War, the Cold War, the Vietnam War, landing a man on the moon, the assassinations of President Kennedy, his brother Robert Kennedy, and Martin Luther King Jr., the Detroit riots of 1967, the civil rights movement, Watergate, the rise and fall of the Berlin Wall, the discovery of prehuman hominids whose descendants migrated out of Africa millions of years ago and populated the earth, galaxies spinning in deep space caught by the Hubble Space Telescope, 9/11, the wars in Iraq and Afghanistan, the discovery of DNA and how to sequence the genome, the recession of 2008, global warming, and international terrorism. Lately, I've read that a man-made spacecraft recently exited the solar system, that gravity waves have been discovered, and that the Higgs boson, sometimes dubbed the "God Particle," has been discovered at the particle collider in Bern, Switzerland. I'd like to be around to learn more about those three items.

As a result of all that and our nation's efforts to achieve world stability in order to contain the atom bomb—and its efforts to maintain an educated, fully employed healthy population—our nation is now indebted to bond holders to the tune of something like seventeen trillion dollars and growing. It all happened in my lifetime, and it is a whole lot for a little kid sitting on a wood box to handle.

When I think of the travails folks lived through during my lifetime I go back to my religion certainly and to poets like Henry Wadsworth Longfellow, William Faulkner, and Rudyard Kipling. They possessed a special power to show us their vision and open our minds with a few elegant words. They put us in touch with the divine, the cosmos, and honor. Using meter and rhythm they revealed the richness of nature and the breath of the human spirit. For me it's like magic, and it began with the game Authors that we played with Ma. Consider another of her poems that I picked off my basement floor.

Lifting Chalice, holding dew
So sweet and full of grace.
I look into a blossom's heart
And see the maker's face.

Child of the Great Depression that I am, I have always been drawn to thoughts like these. This has been particularly true since my political philosophy studies under the tutelage of Dr. Richard O'Dell at Northern Michigan College. I always planned to delve more deeply into the philosophical concepts he laid before us. I recall that in one lecture Dr. O'Dell stated that the difference between a good doorknob and a bad one had been postulated by the Greek philosophers. He said that "a doorknob can never be a good doorknob unless first and foremost it is a good doorknob." Confusing at first, what came from our class discussion was knowledge that even a gold-plated doorknob won't do the work it was meant to do unless it has a good inner apparatus that reliably opens the door to which it is affixed. He encouraged the class to build a good inner apparatus for ourselves. It was the kind of stuff Ma always talked about and can be seen in her poetry.

Dr. O'Dell also taught that the balance we find in nature (e.g., a time to sow, a time to reap) ought to be fostered in government, in society, and indeed in our own lives. Yet I know from the Great Depression years, from Dad's perseverance, and from Ma's life and her poems, that there are no wizards except us and that a good inner apparatus and a balanced life are not easily achieved. None of the things I learned in my lifetime explain the Great Depression or tell me why the poverty it left behind had to be. Like the mountain feared by the Ojibwa, modern society has turned its back to it.

For me, even with the wisdom others provided, an unstated fear has always been—will the Great Depression return and separate the ones you love from the things they pine for? That thought haunted me as I assembled Ma's poems and recalled the devastation wrought by the Crash of Twenty-nine that brought the people who lived on the Mountain of Iron to their knees. Would folks have to do that one again? Call it what you will—naiveté, bravado—one of my grandiose missions as I studied economics in undergrad was to solve that problem. But in retirement I realized that during the workaday period of my life, I never gave that youthful mission much thought. The experts on television and in the newspapers made economics so horribly complicated it didn't look like anyone, let alone a hillbilly gandy dancer, would ever figure it out.

No matter what lessons the Great Depression taught, the two schools of economics that clashed in my collegiate textbooks are still with us. Keynesians claim consumer demand is the key and that downturns are caused by flagging demand and upturns by inflation of the money supply and easy credit. The federal government can put everybody back to work in Depression years if politicians enhance demand through public works projects and if they "print" money and put it in the hands of consumers. During inflation, Keynesians recommend that the government reduce the money supply by increasing interest rates and by increasing taxes to lower inflation and pay down the public debt created by a prior downturn.

While I benefited from gravel roads the WPA built on the national cuff, the trouble with Keynesian theory is that politicians don't have the backbone to pay down the debt. It keeps piling up. Too many politicos are oblivious to the harsh reality that the public debt and the interest on it can, in the end, only be paid out of taxpayer dollars. The national debt is a great big credit bubble ready to explode and a very big can to kick down the road.

Keynesian philosophy riles theorists, pundits, and politicians on the "supply side" who contend it's junk science, that the supply of goods is the key and that laissez-faire markets and private enterprise provide the solution, even though they can't tell you when or where that ever worked for very long. The supply-siders claim that huge stacks of economic data they have tabled and graphed scientifically prove that private enterprise, reduced taxes on business, and deregulation will enhance supply and prevent a depression or, if one happened, kill it off. They still insist on that today even though politicians espousing these views have cut taxes and deregulated—and recessions happen anyway.

I have never liked the Keynesian idea of giving people free money. You're supposed to work for it like I did making hay and weeding a potato field, wrapping Danish rolls, gandy dancing, scooping up muck at the Mather A, and, yes, practicing law. None of those jobs pay if you don't work. I also don't believe in killing baby pigs, leaving farm land lie fallow, and paying subsidies to farmers if they don't farm. But that doesn't mean I buy what the supply-siders are saying either. Nobody accused Herbert Hoover of overtaxing or overregulating, yet his policies preceded the Great Depression.

My foolish youthful mission had morphed into a hope that someone, maybe even a Nobel laureate, would lay bare the causes of the Great Depression, reconcile the divergent schools of economic thought into a unified economic theory, and lay down a road map to prosperity. If anyone ever did, I haven't seen it. Instead the two conflicting theories of economics soldier on. One says help the rich, the other says help the poor. To that I respond—why not help both if they need it? If a theory doesn't work, then for God's sake get rid of it. Ma put it this way in her poem "Life":

> Make each and every vicissitude
> A base for better things.

Ma and Dad lived the message in those two lines throughout the Great Depression. Angered, I began to think there on my basement floor surrounded by Ma's poems that it's time to say to hell with complicated economic theories and the puffed-up politicos and pundits who espouse them. We should pay attention to what the iron miners and gandy dancers were saying. Muck out all the slop in our textbooks and editorials like we did from the ditches draining the Mather A, or when we blasted out chunks of iron ore blocking a mill, let ideas flow again and get back to work.

I don't like to climb up on my soapbox, but why isn't anybody looking for pragmatic solutions? We'd all be better off if the experts and pundits would pipe down and do some straight thinking. Politicians stand glaring at each other across the aisles of Congress shouting "am not" and "you are too." They tie up Congress with filibusters, refuse to bring legislation to the floor, close the government down, and are willing to default on the national debt if they don't get their way. As a result, nothing gets done or—if it is—it is immediately repealed as the business cycle gyrates like a drunken gandy dancer at the Paradise Bar.

It's time to sober up. Maybe some of the ideas being bounced around have merit. How will we ever find out if we don't look at them? The ancient Greeks, whose names I have never been able to pronounce, taught that the initiation of learning comes from an admission of ignorance (i.e., if you think you already know how to do something you won't). They also counseled "moderation in everything, nothing in excess."

Why get tied up in knots over which economic theory is the elixir? They aren't. Policy doesn't have to be universal and eternal truth. If either consumers or business need help provide it. But stop and think whether programs adopted to lift the economy during a recession or depression should be kept in place during a period of inflation. Agricultural subsidies and government sponsorship of home mortgage financing are two current examples. If programs are about to drive the nation into bankruptcy, for God's sake don't filibuster—cut them back or if necessary eliminate them.

On the supply side don't demand that we cut taxes on businesses to the bone or strip out business regulations without studying which should be kept and which ones should go. It should not be a political game to buy votes. You can't get rid of *all* regulations. And you can't install shovel tracks to move stockpiles of iron ore without a section boss like Uncle Nels who studied his craft and knew what he was doing. The economy is no different. It depends on honest markets, talented people and knowledgeable referees who broker common sense, curtail fraud and inspire confidence. There's nothing wrong with making a profit—if it results from the honest efforts of blue and white collar workers and not from manipulation of the markets or irreparable damage to our environment. Maybe the Ojibwa were on to something.

Sure, some economic principles sound like pure science. Adam Smith wrote that price is determined by supply and demand. If supply goes up or if demand slackens in a free market prices fall. If demand goes up or supply falls off prices rise. These are useless truisms. They don't explain *why* supply or demand went up or down. Supply is controlled by the existence of raw materials, the availability of labor possessing the technical skills needed to create products from those raw materials—or to deliver a service— and the availability of risk capital or credit to finance the production and distribution of those products and services. No land or raw materials (i.e. iron ore) no supply. No labor (i.e. miners) no supply. No risk capital (i.e. stocks, bonds and credit) no supply. It's not science. It's business.

Adam Smith's insight says nothing about what goes wrong when the ingredients of prosperity are all present and markets crash. What is it that motivates buyers and sellers to suddenly refrain from conducting business? Is there is an element of truth in Keynesian theory? Maybe markets need a catalyst. Maybe that catalyst is confidence. Consumers need confidence that they will have a steady income if they start a family or make a purchase. Manufacturers need confidence that they can market their products at a profit if they produce them. Investors and lenders need confidence that they will earn dividends and interest and recover their principal if they invest or extend credit. What produces confidence, and how can government stimulate that? Fulminating congressmen and senators don't inspire confidence—they destroy it.

Ability to buy is the great engine that drives our economy. Ability to buy is determined by the amount of cash or credit consumers command, and not by advertising or the creation of new products. It's what consumers lacked in the Great Depression. Henry Ford proved that consumers make a difference when he increased the pay of assembly-line workers to five dollars a day so they could buy the cars they were building. World War II proved that demand can be a catalyst to prosperity when the United States Government borrowed heavily, went into the marketplace as a gigantic consumer, and purchased the munitions, personnel, and tools of war.

Prosperity comes about when the supply function and the demand function perform their roles in the marketplace. But you need an umpire to have that happen. Consumers, suppliers, and financiers are not philosopher kings. Get real. The Declaration of Independence states, "all men are created equal, that they are endowed by their Creator with certain unalienable rights, that among these are life, liberty and the pursuit of happiness." This doesn't mean, as some argue, that the right to earn one's living through private enterprise is a God-given right that may not be interfered with by government. As Dr. O'Dell taught in political philosophy, one man ought not be permitted to freely swing his arms if they are striking another man's nose. It may be great campaign rhetoric to shout that the candidate will "get government off our backs," but that ignores the words in the Declaration of Independence that follow: "that to secure these rights governments are instituted among men . . ." That clause unmistakably provides that it is the purpose of government to secure life, liberty, and the pursuit of happiness for the people who delegated to it the power to govern.

Maybe the business cycle produces a depression or a recession when supplier and consumer confidence is shattered by excessive greed—consumer, supplier, *or* financier greed—that destroys market discipline. Easy credit, expensive labor, and tax loopholes create bubbles that plug the lines of commerce with overproduction and unmarketable inventories and drive prices, profits, and wages into a downward spiral that crashes the securities industry, destroys capital formation, and cuts off the availability of credit. If monopoly, supply manipulation, price fixing, fraud, feather bedding, or government interference restricts production, then economic activity stagnates like iron ore in a jammed mill. If consumers are jobless, without funds or credit, demand falls off, inventories pile up, businesses go bust and the economy goes belly up. When that happens the poor get a whole lot poorer.

But if anyone does know what causes a recession or a depression, can you believe what they say? Our politicians demonize each other— promising to keep those rascals from getting elected and thrown out of office if they do. What I learned on the ten-acre farm, at the bakery, on the railroad, and in an iron mine was confirmed at college and in law school. Unless moderate, sensible people, rich, middle, and poor, listen to each other and come forward with practical solutions, the business cycle will keep on swinging and the river will not flow.

Economics at its core is the study of how men survive. It is what we did when we slaughtered hogs, stripped the trees off our ten-acre farm to obtain firewood and blasted out iron ore twenty-three hundred feet underground to get a paycheck. Beyond the rhetoric lies reality. The mines, cities, farms, automobiles, and roads that poor men build with their hands are more than their livelihood—they are their testament.

Sorry, Ma; sorry, Dad. I didn't intend to mount my soapbox. It's hard to tell you, but I never found out why the two of you, our family, and all our neighbors had to endure the Great Depression. I guess no one knows what causes depressions. At least I got a lifetime of lessons from you and others on ways to triumph over one.

Some may ask—"How is that done?" I've told you! "Be a good doorknob." "There's daylight in the swamp." "Pull on your boots." "Don't cry over spilled milk." "Roll up your sleeves—get busy." "Make hay while the sun shines." "Poverty is a stepping stone to happiness." "W-O-R-K = S-U-C-C-E-S-S," "Discipline," "Honesty," "Wisdom," and, when all else fails, "Give it time."

Figure 55

Ben and Elsie
Fiftieth Anniversary.
Nelson Family Photograph

Sunset at Presque Isle.
Sugarloaf Mountain is on the horizon at the extreme left.
Hogsback is off the picture to the left.
Photograph courtesy of Wendy (Olson) Cornish

POSTSCRIPT

LIKE SO MANY who migrated to America, my ancestors carved an existence from wilderness. Confronted with severe winters, extreme poverty and backbreaking labor they persevered. The courage displayed by Ole Nelson, Aletta (Pederson) Nelson, William Carne, Laura (Jenkin) Carne, Ben Nelson, and Elsie (Carne) Nelson in raising their families with humor, morality, and discipline amid the travails of the twentieth century provides a lesson for us all. They belonged to a rollicking, vibrant generation that conquered the Great Depression and lifted America to leader of the free world. They taught the value of honest work, self-sufficiency, education, and the meaning of freedom. Their efforts were not in vain—their descendants fared better.

Besides their eight children, at last count, there are today one hundred nine additional descendants of Ben and Elsie: twenty-six grandchildren, fifty-three great-grandchildren, and thirty great-great-grandchildren. Many of them earned college undergraduate and advanced degrees. One has a master's degree in psychology, one is now an English teacher working on her doctoral thesis, and another is working on an electrical engineering major. One is an academic advisor at a Big Ten university, holds three master's degrees (creative writing, history, and counseling) and earned an Ed. Sci. degree in counseling. Included among the descendants of Ben and Elsie are a chief clerk of the Upper Peninsula Power Company, a corporate tax manager for a Big Board company, a certified nutritionist, the owner of a heating / air conditioning business, a manager of a retail store, a real estate salesman, a holder of a master's degree in nursing and hospital management, homemakers, a marine biologist, an electrical engineer, a franchisee of a Wendy's restaurant, a flight attendant, an architect, a geologist, a medical doctor, two medical laboratory technicians, a lawyer, a pharmacist, a veterinarian, a computer network engineer and administrator, a computer science engineer, computer technicians, a fiction writer, a research scientist and university professor, a mechanical engineer, a mechanical drafting designer, elementary and high school teachers, a salesman for a national office supply company, several medical nurses, a bank executive and former mayor of Ishpeming, and an iron mine supervisor in charge of shipping iron pellets for Cleveland-Cliffs Iron Company.

Not bad. Ben and Elsie would be very proud of each and every one of them.

ENDNOTES

1. *Family Edition*, published by Elben LLC, a Michigan limited liability company (1997).

2. A series of pamphlets published by students and staff of the National Mine School (1983-1997).

3. *The Growth of the American Republic*, Samuel Eliot Morison and Henry Steele Commager, Oxford University Press, Volume One (1950) p. 498.

4. Some have expressed doubts that the Marquette Iron Range is in fact a mountain, but according to dictionaries I keep in my study, a mountain is an elevated area of the earth's mass having height higher than a hill. Under that definition the Marquette Iron Range is a mountain range. None of its elevations look like the Matterhorn, but its highest point, about 1,500 feet above sea level, is higher than a hill.

5. In addition to the Marquette Range other iron ranges were discovered and developed along the shores of Lake Superior, including the Menominee Range, and the Penokee-Gogebic Range (both along the Michigan-Wisconsin border), and the Vermilion and Mesabi ranges in Minnesota. *Iron Will,* Terry S. Reynolds and Virginia P. Dawson, 2011 Wayne State University Press, p. 60 *et. seq.*

6. At one point the Yoopers threatened to secede from Michigan and form their own state. Indeed, on November 9, 2013, the White House issued a map coloring all of the states in the union that had expanded their coverage of Medicaid orange, and those that did not grey. Michigan was colored orange, but horror of horrors the map entirely omitted the Upper Peninsula of Michigan. See, lead article on the front page of the *Detroit Free Press*, 11/9/2013, p. A-1. The White House later corrected the map, but the trolls never did.

7. Yoopers refer to those who live beneath the Mackinaw Bridge as "trolls".

8. See, *Geologic History of Michigan*, Prof. Paul Kiril Spiroff, Michigan College of Mining and Technology, *http://Michigan.gov/documents/deq* GIMDL-GGGHM 302331 7.pdf.

9. *Iron Will*, Terry S. Reynolds and Virginia P. Dawson, Wayne State University Press, (2011) p. 198.

10. Ibid. p. 215.

11. *Superior Heartland, A Backwoods History*, Vol. 1, Book One, p. 109, C. Fred Rydholm (1989), Published privately by C Fred Rydholm.

12. The tribal name of the Native Americans residing in what became Marquette County was "Otchipwe" which the French interpreted to be "Ojibway" and the English to be "Chippewa". But the name refers to the same people. *Superior Heartland, A Backwoods History*, Vol. 1, Book One, p. 28, C. Fred Rydholm, 1989 published privately by C. Fred Rydholm.

13. Concerning lands surveyed in the Michigan Territory for settlement by the military, the United States Surveyor General's Office located in Chillicothe, Ohio reported on November 30, 1815, that due to the "… extreme sterility and barrenness of the soil … there would not be more than one acre of a hundred, if there would be one of a thousand that would in any case admit of cultivation" (in the Upper Peninsula). See, *The Mather Mine*, Marquette County Historical Society, Marquette, Michigan (1979) p. 14.

14. *Superior Heartland, A Backwoods History*, Vol. 1, Book One, p. 103, C. Fred Rydholm (1989), Published privately by C. Fred Rydholm. It is reported in *The Mather Mine*, Marquette County Historical Society, Marquette, Michigan, p. 13 (1979), that a French Jesuit, Baron L'Houtan found the Ontonagon Boulder in 1688.

15. *Superior Heartland, A Backwoods History*, Vol. 1, Book One, p. 106, C. Fred Rydholm (1989), Published privately by C. Fred Rydholm.

16. *Superior Heartland, A Backwoods History*, Vol. 1, Book One, p. 137, C. Fred Rydholm (1989),Published privately by C Fred Rydholm.

17. If the Ojibwa ever sought to convert iron on the Marquette Range to tools or jewelry, as had been done with copper on the Keweenaw, I've uncovered no evidence of such activity, or that the Ojibwa possessed the technical skills needed to make anything from the mysterious magnetic material that exuded in great abundance from their hunting lands.

18. *Superior Heartland, A Backwoods History*, Vol. 1, Book One, p. 110, C. Fred Rydholm (1989),Published privately by C. Fred Rydholm.

19. *Superior Heartland, A Backwoods History*, Vol. 1, Book One, pp. 140–141, C. Fred Rydholm (1989) Published privately by C. Fred Rydholm.

20. *Superior Heartland, A Backwoods History*, Vol. 1, Book One, p. 128, C. Fred Rydholm (1989) Published privately by C. Fred Rydholm.

21. *Iron Will*, Terry S. Reynolds and Virginia P. Dawson, p. 15, Wayne State University Press (2011). See also *The Mather Mine*, Marquette County Historical Society, Marquette, Michigan, (1979) where on page 17 the local Ojibwa chief's name is given as "Marji Gesick." I have not been able to clear up the spelling of the chief's name.

22. It is reported in *The Mather Mine*, Marquette County Historical Society, Marquette, Michigan (1979) pp. 16–17, that after what became the Jackson Iron Company was formed in 1844 it acquired the land where the Jackson Mine was subsequently located from the United States for $2.50 an acre. Chief Marjijesick was awarded twelve shares in the new company out of 3100 shares issued. It is also reported in *The Mather Mine (p.17)* that the first post office in Marquette County was established at a forge site on the Carp River on January 12, 1847, indicating that the surge to settle Marquette County was already picking up speed.

23. The Michigan Iron Industry Museum in Negaunee, Michigan, also contains numerous exhibits and data that record the history of Iron Mining on the Marquette Iron Range.

24. *Iron Will*, Terry S. Reynolds and Virginia P. Dawson, p. 31, Wayne State University Press (2011).

25. Ibid. p.51.

26. *Iron Will*, Terry S. Reynolds and Virginia P. Dawson, Wayne State University Press, Detroit, Michigan (2011) pp. 62–63.

27. Ibid. p.63.

28. See *Geologic History of Michigan*, Prof. Kiri Spiroff, Mich. College of Mining and Technology, id. In 2012 Cleveland-Cliffs Iron Company shipped 9,865,000 long tons of pellets in 432 vessels from the loading docks in Marquette and Escanaba, Michigan.

29. Cleveland-Cliffs Iron Company Records, Cliffs Shaft Mining Museum, Ishpeming, Michigan.

30. Id.

31. *The Mining Journal*, Marquette, Michigan, June 30, 1984, p. 1B.

32. Much of the history of the Copper Country described herein was recorded in hand written notes left by my wife Judith's mother, Lois Olson, and by Judy's aunt Ethel Rowe. Sisters, Lois and Ethel were born into a family of miners and raised in Calumet and the adjoining city of Laurium in the Copper Country in the early twentieth century. There, the history of the Copper Country played out before them in real time, they breathed what is reputed to be the, "freshest, cleanest, purest and most vitalizing air on Earth", and it is where they graduated high school. They recorded numerous entertaining tales in their notes.

33. Notes of records archived in Norway list Grandma Nelson's first name as Alette, but we always knew her as Aletta (Al-let-a).

34. Bjorn and Olene married on November 11, 1871. In addition to Aletta they had five other children: Peder, Johan, Elia, Karen, and Abigail.

35. Listed with Grandpa Ole were my great-grandfather Nils Samuelsen (No. 1938) a *gaardmand* (farmer) age 60; my great-grandmother Ingeborg Samuelsen (No. 1939) a housewife age 62; and their other children, Anne Samuelsen (No. 1940) a *datter* age sixteen and Ingeborg Samuelsen (No. 1941) a datter age eleven. My great-grandmother's age may have been recorded wrong, or I copied it wrong, since if she was 62 it is not likely she would have children aged eighteen, sixteen, and eleven.

36. I was told by my sister Marian when we returned to the United States that Grandma Aletta had met Ole at his confirmation classes in Norway. She believed Grandpa Ole sent for Aletta after he arrived at New Burt.

37. None of the Nils Samuelsen family who sailed to America ever returned to Norway. Nils Samuelsen and his wife Ingeborg Samuelsen later moved to Tennessee with their two daughters Anne and Ingeborg. While there, Ingeborg, my Great-Grandmother, was lost in a winter snowstorm and perished. Her remains were not found until the snow melted in the spring. Tears would form in Dad's eyes when he spoke of her. Her daughter Anne later married, became Anne Rysta, and moved to Sioux City, Iowa. Grandpa Ole and Aletta stayed at New Burt.

38. Most people didn't wear tattoos in those years.

39. Cleveland-Cliff's records disclose that twenty-two additional iron mines had opened on the Marquette Range between 1887 and 1903 when the Carne side of my ancestors arrived there. The records show eleven were underground operations. Eight were in Ishpeming and five in Negaunee. In Ishpeming the Cleveland Lake opened in 1889 and produced 16,253,841 tons of ore from 1889 to1950, the Hartford opened in 1889 and by 1910 produced 1,950,422 tons, and the Moro opened in 1890 and by 1918 produced 1,119,854 tons. In Negaunee the Breitung Hematite opened in 1901 and by 1920 produced 1,728,976 tons, the Maas opened in 1902 and by 1950 produced 16,048,021 tons, and the Mary Charlotte opened in1903 and by 1948 produced 6,881,602 tons. In Gwinn the Austin opened in 1903 and by 1929 had produced 1,589,156 tons. The Richmond opened in Palmer in 1896 and by 1927 produced 3,604,913 tons.

40. There had been sixteen children in the Jenkin family. Three died while very young. Thirteen children appear at the Jenkin market in Grandma Carne's photograph. The only names of Grandma Carne's brothers and sisters that have been found are those of Beatrice, Margarie and Billy.

41. Grandpa Carne had sailed on the English Channel; he sported tattoos, and had been raised near Penzance—a city that had once harbored pirates. He was also one tough guy.

42. John D. Voelker is a legend in the UP. A *Detroit News Magazine* article covering him dated June 18, 1967, alluded almost incidentally to Voelker's successful campaign for election to Michigan's Supreme Court, but emphasized his life as a trout fly fisherman with color photography and described in Voelker's own words his "bout" fly casting against former heavy weight champion Jack Sharkey.

43. My sister Dort recalls, though, that Grandpa Ole may have been given the lease to the farm at New Burt by the mining company as a result of the crushing injury to his left leg.

44. The Ishpeming High School that burned in 1930 (that supplied the floors, windows and doors for our farmhouse) was featured and pictured on page 1B of the *Mining Journal* on June 30, 1984.

45. *Iron Will*, Terry S. Reynolds, and Virginia P. Dawson, 2011 Wayne State University Press pp. 139-140.

46. The history of National Mine was described in some detail by the *Detroit Free Press* in its Special Edition, "Detroit" (March 1, 1987, p. 10 et seq.) It was an eight page spread written by Thomas Bevier of the *Detroit Free Press*, captioned "Hope and Hardship in National Mine," with large, sharply focused black and white and colored photographs. Frank Moody, "The Historian of National Mine," Annie Trudell, "National Mines biggest booster," Spencer Felt and his wife Arlene and others had been interviewed and leapt off the pages of the article. Reading the article was a trip back in time. My Ma was a friend of Spencer's mother, I went to school with Spencer's sisters Pauline and Christine, I attended college at Northern Michigan College with Frank Moody and his brother James Moody, and I also worked at the Mather A when James Moody worked there. I also worked with Spencer Felt at the Corneliuson Bakery in Ishpeming. After he got his degree, Frank was employed for many years by the Red Cross. The photographs of the Moody and Felt families, Annala's store, the Post Office and a dilapidated log cabin from National Mine's "frontier past," brought back a million memories. The article explains that the village was originally named after John W. Winthrop of Boston—a promoter of one of the first mines. My Dad always called the place Winthrop, but until I read the article I didn't know why. The article explains that the name was changed when Moody's grandfather wrote to Cornwall, England to obtain workers for a new mine (presumably the National) and the letters came back addressed to "National Mine, Michigan." The *Free Press* article provides numerous details chronicling the history of National Mine. It states that the Hercules Powder Company, a dynamite factory that supplied blasting powder to all the mines on the Marquette Range, was located there. It was finally closed when the Tilden

open pit opened and new technology supplied blasting chemicals. Currently, The Tilden and the Empire, huge open pit mines that produce millions of tons of iron ore pellets annually, are operated by the Cleveland-Cliffs Iron Company immediately adjacent to the village of National Mine. It's nothing but a small village, but National Mine occupies a uniquely central place in the annals of iron mining on the Marquette Range. It's located smack in the middle of the head waters of the river of iron. Those interested in its history are encouraged to read the *Free Press* article.

47. Anyone interested in the sort of stories the kids told on the bus will find accounts chronicling some of them in booklets entitled *Red Dust*, now housed at the Marquette Regional History Center in Marquette, Michigan, although none of the stories chronicled there are as frank, and might I say ribald, as some I heard on the bus. Maxine Honkala, Sharon Richards, and Bobbie Ameen created *Red Dust* by having their students write stories of their family life as told to them by their grandparents and relatives. *Red Dust* booklets were published over a period spanning several years. My Brother Ken's wife, Loraine, sent me copies of *Red Dust* yearly as they were published.

48. I met Phillip M. Hill again at the 2013 National Mine Reunion. I had bumped into him at the University of Michigan in the 1950s when he was studying to become a pharmacist. Phil told me that William Hill, a mine inspector and relative of his, had perished in the Barnes Hecker disaster. He also cleared up a few things. He told me that his family did not refer to the location where he was raised as Finn Town, as we did. He said his family called it Finnfarm. He also reminded me that the road my family dubbed the Finn Town road had white posts dug in along its shoulders that identified it as County Road PN. He grinned at me as he explained that his family always took "PN" to mean "Poor Nelson Road."

49. In the late 1950s Dad worked at the Bunker Hill Mine in Negaunee. The Bunker Hill was old, dangerous and wet. He didn't like that one. He was nearing retirement.

50. This is the pronunciation iron miners used to describe an underground employee who worked on the company's account as opposed to the account of a contract miner.

51. The non-horseman needs to understand a few things. In nature a horse gets rid of itchy dandruff by rolling on the ground on its back. In its stall in the barn it can't do that. A curry comb is a metal device attached to a handle that has alternating rows of metal blades and metal teeth that is designed to scrape dandruff loose from a horse's hide. The brush, also hand-held, cleans away the

loosened dandruff and puts a shine on the horse's coat. Proper and repeated use of both will relieve the horse's itchy skin, and make the horseman happy to view its shiny coat.

52. To those unfamiliar with harnessing a horse, let me say that the hames are wooden strips edged in metal that fit like a set of parentheses in grooves in the horse's collar, and that hame straps are leather strips at the top and bottom of the hames that buckle together and hold the hames firmly attached to the collar. The tugs are much thicker leather straps, consisting of several plies of leather that are sewn with heavy thread, that attach to the hames on each side and trail back to the rear of the horse. Tugs are made of leather instead of chains since the latter would chafe the horse's sides and legs. Chains are affixed to the end of the tugs to allow the attachment of a whiffle tree at the rear of the horse. The whiffle tree is a crossbar made of tough wood like oak or maple with a clevis (metal fastening device) at the center that distributes a load equally to each tug. Once the configuration of a horse's harness is understood one can better understand why my Dad always claimed a horse pushed and did not pull its load.

53. The hourly wage rate for underground "company count" miners for 1937 has not been located. It is reported in *The Mather Mine*, published by the Marquette County Historical Society, 1979, Burton H. Boyum, editor, at p. 22–25, that as of December 12, 1941, "the basic wage rate was 62.5 cents per hour," and that by the end of 1945 the "Labor rate was $0.78 per hour for surface workers and $ 0.865 for underground, non-contract employees." It is assumed that the rate for underground labor in 1937 was lower than it was in 1941. By 1947, "Wages increased to $1.09 per hour for surface labor and to a minimum underground rate of $1.125 per hour. Company account miner pay was $1.175 per hour while high contract pay was $20.24 per shift compared with $16.92 the previous year." *Id.* p. 25. If the wage rate for 1937 was the same as it was reported to be in 1941 (62.5 cents an hour) and if possible over-time pay is not considered, as a "company count" underground miner Dad earned $5.00 for an eight-hour shift in 1937 ($25.00 for a forty-hour week and $1,250 a year). It isn't known how long it took Dad to become a contract miner. As you consider these labor rates remember, my Dad always paid his own way.

54. The second Louis-Schmelling fight took place on June 22, 1938, at Yankee Stadium.

55. A government pole is a sapling cut from the neighboring forest with your pocket knife that has a ball of fish line wound on the end, a sinker, and a hook.

56. My brother Fred suggests that it could have been Blackie Nault, who owned the Paradise Bar in Ishpeming in those days. My Dad used to stop there for a few

beers and to gab with his buddies from the mine. Although I don't recall how many guys named Blackie my Dad knew, trouble is I don't recall that Blackie Nault from the Paradise Bar kept draft horses. That aside it could have been him.

57. Dad's story of lifting a full grown steer may have involved the wisdom a father uses to bring his sons to manhood. I've since been told that this strongman story comes out of folklore about teenagers and young men building up their strength. Dad never explained where his stories came from.

58. There were no class A schools in the Upper Peninsula.

59. It was billed as the Regional Tournament, but since there were no Class E schools in the Lower Peninsula, it was the Class E State Championship as far as we were concerned.

60. There were no conveyor belts to carry the ore out to the shaft when I began my mining career. A year or so later I saw the first one installed at the Mather A.

61. Later, while I was employed at the Mather A, the top timber drifts under the ore body were constructed of circular steel girders that were bolted together, and spruce cribbing pieces that were inserted between the steel girders to create steel and spruce tubes under the ore body. When that was done, steel rails were placed at the base of the tube-like structure to carry the scraper.

62. *Detroit Is My Own Hometown* by Malcolm W. Bingay, The Bobs Merrill Company (1946).

Made in the USA
Lexington, KY
18 November 2014